EVENING CLASS

EVENING CLASS

MAEVE BINCHY

Delacorte Press

Published by
DELACORTE PRESS
Bantam Doubleday Dell Publishing Group, Inc.
1540 Broadway
New York, New York 10036

This work was first published in Great Britain
by Orion Books Ltd.

The trademark Delacorte Press® is registered in the U.S.
Patent and Trademark Office.

ISBN 0-385-31807-3
Book design by Julie Duquet
Manufactured in the United States of America

*To Gordon with all my love and
grazie per tutto*

EVENING CLASS

AIDAN

There was a time back in 1970 when they would love filling in a questionnaire.

Aidan might find one in a newspaper at a weekend. Are You a Thoughtful Husband? or possibly What Do You Know About Show Biz? They scored high on the answers to Are You Well Suited? and How Well Do You Treat Your Friends?

But that was long ago.

Nowadays if Nell or Aidan Dunne saw a list of questions, they didn't rush eagerly to fill them in and see how they scored. It would be too painful to answer How Often Do You Make Love? (a) More than four times a week? (b) Twice a week on average? (c) Every Saturday night? (d) Less than this? Who would want to acknowledge how very much less than this, and look up what kind of interpretation the questionnaire sages had applied to this admission?

The page would be turned nowadays if either of them saw a survey asking Are You Compatible? And there had been no row, no falling out. Aidan had not been unfaithful to Nell, and he assumed that she had not strayed either. Was it arrogant to assume this? She was an attractive-looking woman; other men would definitely find her worth a second glance, as they always had.

Aidan knew that a great many men were just smug and unobservant, and were genuinely astounded when it was proved that their wives had been having affairs. But Nell was different. Nell wouldn't meet anyone else, make love to another man. He knew her so well, he would know if this was the case. Anyway, where would she have met anyone? And if she had met someone she fancied, where would they have gone? No, it was a ludicrous idea.

Possibly everyone else felt like this. It could well be one of the things they didn't tell you about getting older. Like having aches and pains in the backs of your legs after a long walk, like not being able to hear or understand the lyrics of pop songs anymore. Maybe you just drifted apart from the person you had thought was the center of the world.

It was quite likely that every other man of forty-eight going on forty-nine felt the same. All over the world there could be men who wanted their wives to be eager and excited about everything. It wasn't only about lovemaking, it was about enthusiasm for other things as well.

It had been so long now since Nell had asked about his job, and his hopes and dreams in the school. There was a time when she had known the name of every teacher and many of the pupils, when she would talk about the large classes, and the posts of responsibility and the school excursions and plays, about Aidan's projects for the Third World.

But now she hardly knew what was happening. When the new minister for education was appointed, Nell just shrugged. I suppose she can't be worse than the last one, was her only comment. Nell knew nothing of the Transition Year except to call it a bloody luxury. Imagine giving children all that time to think and discuss and . . . find themselves . . . instead of getting down to their exams.

And Aidan didn't blame her.

He had become very dull explaining things. He could hear his own voice echoing in his ears, there was a kind of drone to it, and his daughters would raise their eyes to heaven wondering why at the ages of twenty-one and nineteen they should have to listen to any of this.

He tried not to bore them. Aidan knew it was a characteristic of teachers; they were so used to the captive audience in the classroom they could go on for far too long, approaching every subject from several sides until they were sure that the listener had grasped the drift.

He made huge efforts to key into their lives.

But Nell never had any stories or any issues to discuss about the restaurant where she worked as a cashier. "Ah, for heaven's sake, Aidan, it's a job. I sit there and I take their credit cards, or their checks or their cash, and I give them change and a receipt. And then at the end of the day I come home and at the end of the week I get my wages. And that's the way it is for ninety percent of the world. We don't have issues and dramas and power struggles; we're normal, that's all."

It was not intended to wound him or put him down, but still it was a slap in the face. It was obvious that he himself must have been going on and on about confrontations and conflicts in the staff room. And the days were gone . . . obviously long gone, when Nell was waiting eagerly to know what had happened, always rooting for him, championing his cause and declaring that his enemies were her enemies. Aidan ached for the companionship, the solidarity, and the teamwork of other times.

Perhaps when he became principal it would return.

Or was this fooling himself? Possibly the headship would still hold little interest for his wife and two daughters. His home just ticked along easily. Recently he had an odd feeling that he had died some time ago and they were all managing perfectly well. Nell went to and from the restaurant. She went to see her mother once a week; no, Aidan needn't come, she had said, it was just a nice family chat. Her mother liked to see them all regularly to know they were all right.

"And *are* you all right?" Aidan had asked anxiously.

"You're not with the Fifth Years now doing amateur philosophy," Nell had said. "I'm as all right as anyone, I suppose. Can't you leave it at that?"

But of course Aidan couldn't leave it. He told her it wasn't amateur philosophy it was Introduction to Philosophy, and it wasn't Fifth Years, it was Transition Years. He would never forget the look Nell had given him. She had begun to say something but then changed her mind. Her face was full of distant pity. She looked at him as she might have looked at a poor tramp sitting on the street, his coat tied with a rope and drinking the dregs of a ginger wine bottle.

He fared no better with his daughters.

Grania worked in the bank but had little to report from it, to her father at any rate. Sometimes he came across her talking to her friends, and she seemed much more animated. And it was the same with Brigid. The travel agency was fine, Dad, stop going on about it. Of course it's fine, and the free holiday twice a year, and the long lunch hours because three girls covered two hours.

Grania didn't want to talk about the whole system of banking and whether it was unfair to encourage people to take loans that they would find difficult to repay. She didn't invent the rule, she told him, she had an In basket on her desk and she dealt with what was in it each day. That was it. Dead simple. Brigid didn't have any views on whether the travel trade was selling tourists some kind of dream it could never deliver. "Dad, if they don't want a holiday nobody's twisting their arms, they don't have to come in and buy one."

Aidan wished he were more observant. When had all this happened . . . this growing apart? There was a time when the girls had sat all clean and shiny after their bath time in pink dressing gowns while he told them stories and Nell would look on pleased from across the room. But that was years back. There had been good times since then. When they were doing their exams, for example, Aidan remembered doing out revision sheets for them, planning how they should study to the best advantage. They had been grateful then. He remembered the celebrations when Grania got her leaving certificate and later when she was accepted in the bank. There had been a lunch on each occasion in a big hotel, the waiter had taken photographs of them all. And it had been the same with Brigid, a lunch and a picture session. They looked a perfectly happy family in those pictures. Was it all a facade?

In a way it must have been, because here he was now only a few short years later and he could not sit down with his wife and two daughters, the people he loved most in the world, and tell them his fears that he might not be made principal.

He had put in so much time in that school, worked so many extra hours, involved himself in every aspect of it, and somewhere in his bones he felt that he would be passed over.

Another man, almost precisely his own age, might well get the post. This was Tony O'Brien, a man who had never stayed on after hours to support a school team playing a home match, a man who had not involved himself in the restructuring of the curriculum, in the fund-raising for the new building project. Tony O'Brien, who smoked quite openly in the corridors of a school that was meant to be a smoke-free zone, who had his lunch in a pub, letting everyone know it was a pint and a half and a cheese sandwich. A bachelor, in no sense a family man, often seen with a girl half his age on his arm, and yet he was being suggested as a very possible successor as head of the school.

Many things had confused Aidan in the last few years, but nothing as much as this. By any standards Tony O'Brien should not be in the running at all. Aidan ran his hands through his hair, which was thinning. Tony O'Brien, of course, had a huge shock of thick brown hair falling into his eyes and resting on his collar. Surely the world hadn't gone so mad that they would take this into consideration when choosing a principal?

Lots of hair good, thinning hair bad . . . Aidan grinned. If he could laugh at some of the worst bits of the paranoia, maybe he could keep self-pity at bay. And he would have to laugh to himself. Somehow there was no one else to laugh with these days.

There was a questionnaire in one of the Sunday papers: Are You Tense? Aidan filled in the answers truthfully. He scored over 75 on the scale, which he knew was high. He wasn't, however, quite prepared for the terse and dismissive verdict. If you scored over 70, you are in fact a clenched fist. Lighten up, friend, before you explode.

They had always said that these tests were just jokes really, space fillers. That's what Aidan and Nell used to say when they emerged as less well than they had hoped from a questionnaire. But this time, of course, he was on his own. He told himself that newspapers had to think of something to take up half a page, otherwise the edition would appear with great white blanks.

But still it upset him. Aidan knew that he was jumpy, that was one thing. But a clenched fist? No wonder they might think twice about him as headmaster material.

He had written his answers on a separate sheet of paper lest anyone in the family would find and read his confessional of worries and anxieties and sleeplessness.

Sundays were the days that Aidan now found hardest to bear. In the past when they were a real family, a happy family, they had gone on picnics in the summer and taken healthy, bracing walks when the weather was cold. Aidan boasted that his family would never be like those Dublin families who didn't know anywhere except the area they lived themselves.

One Sunday he would take them on a train south and they would climb Bray Head and look into the neighboring county of Wicklow, another Sunday they would go north to the seaside villages of Rush and Lusk and Skerries, small places, each with its own character, all on the road that would eventually take them up to the Border. He had arranged day excursions to Belfast for them too, so that they would not grow up in ignorance of the other part of Ireland.

Those had been some of his happiest times, the combination of schoolteacher and father, explainer and entertainer. Daddy knew the answer to everything: where to get the bus out to Carrickfergus Castle, or the Ulster Folk Museum, and a grand place for chips before getting on the train back home.

Aidan remembered a woman on the train telling Grania and Brigid that they were lucky little girls to have a daddy who taught them so much. They had nodded solemnly to agree with her, and Nell had whispered to him that the woman had obviously fancied Aidan but she wasn't going to get her hands on him. And Aidan had felt twelve feet tall and the most important man on earth.

Now on a Sunday he felt increasingly that he was hardly noticed in his home.

They had never been people for the traditional Sunday lunch, roast beef or lamb or chicken and great dishes of potatoes and vegetables, the way so many other families were. Because of their outings and adventures, Sunday had been a casual day in their home. Aidan wished that there was some fixed point in it. He went to Mass. Nell sometimes came with him, but usually she was going on somewhere afterward to meet one of her sisters or a friend from work. And, of course, nowadays the shops were open on Sundays, so there were plenty of places to go.

The girls never went to Mass. It was useless to talk to them. He had given up when they were seventeen. They didn't get up until lunchtime and then they made sandwiches, looked at whatever they had videotaped during the week, lounged around in dressing gowns, washed their hair, their clothes, spoke on the phone to friends, asked other friends in for coffee.

They behaved as if they lived in a flat together with their mother as a pleasant, eccentric landlady who had to be humored. Grania and Brigid contributed a very small amount of money each for bed and board, and handed it over with a bad grace, as if they were being bled dry. To his knowledge they contributed nothing else to the household budget. Not a tin of biscuits, a tub of ice cream, or a carton of fabric softener ever came from their purses, but they were quick to grizzle if these things weren't readily available.

Aidan wondered how Tony O'Brien spent his Sundays.

He knew that Tony certainly didn't go to Mass, he had made that clear to the pupils when they questioned him: "Sir, sir, do you go to Mass on Sundays?"

"Sometimes I do, when I feel in the mood for talking to God," Tony O'Brien had said.

Aidan knew this. It had been reported gleefully by the boys and girls, who used it as ammunition against those who said they had to go every Sunday under pain of mortal sin.

He had been very clever, too clever, Aidan thought. He didn't deny the existence of God, instead he had made out that he was a friend of God's and friends only drop in to have a chat when they are in good form. It made Tony O'Brien have the inside track somehow while Aidan Dunne was left on the outside, no friend of the Almighty, just a time server. It was one of the many annoying and unfair things about it all.

On a Sunday Tony O'Brien probably got up late . . . he lived in what they called a town house nowadays, which was the equivalent of a flat. Just one big room and kitchen downstairs, and one big bedroom and bathroom upstairs. The door opened straight onto the street. He had been observed leaving in the morning accompanied by young women.

There was a time when that would have ended his career let alone his chances of promotion . . . back in the 1960s teachers had been sacked for having relationships outside marriage. Not, of course, that this was right. In fact, they had all protested very strongly at the time. But still, a man who had never committed to any woman, to parade a succession of them through his town house, and still be considered headmaster material, a role model for the students . . . that wasn't right either.

What would Tony O'Brien be doing now, at two-thirty on a wet Sunday? Maybe around to lunch at one of the other teachers' houses. Aidan had never been able to ask him since they literally didn't *have* lunch, and Nell would reasonably have inquired why he should impose on them a man he had been denouncing for five years. He might still be entertaining a lady from last night. Tony O'Brien said he owed a great debt of gratitude to the people of China since there was an excellent take-away only three doors away . . . lemon chicken, sesame toast, and chili prawns were always great with a bottle of Australian Chardonnay and the Sunday papers. Imagine, at his age, a man who could be a grandfather, entertaining girls and buying Chinese food on a Sunday.

But then again, why not?

Aidan Dunne was a fair man. He had to admit that people had a choice in such matters. Tony O'Brien didn't drag these women back to his town house by their hair. There was no law that said he should be married and bring up two distant daughters as Aidan had done. And in a way it was to the man's credit that he wasn't a hypocrite, he didn't try to disguise his lifestyle.

It was just that things had changed so very much. Someone had moved the goalposts about what was acceptable and what was not, and they hadn't consulted Aidan first.

And how would Tony spend the rest of the day?

Surely they wouldn't go back to bed again for the afternoon? Maybe he would go for a walk or the girl would go home and Tony would play music; he often spoke of his CDs. When he had won £350 on the match four of the Lotto, he had hired a carpenter who was working on the school extension, and paid him the money straight out to make a rack that would hold five hundred CDs. Everyone had been impressed. Aidan had been jealous. Where would you get the money to buy that many CDs? He knew for a fact that Tony O'Brien bought about three a week. When would you get the time to listen to them? And then Tony would stroll down to the pub and meet a few friends, or go to a foreign-language movie with subtitles, or to a jazz club.

Maybe it was all this moving around that made him more interesting and gave him the edge on everyone else. Certainly on Aidan. Aidan's Sundays would be nothing that would interest anyone.

When he came back from late Mass around one o'clock and asked would anyone like a bacon-and-egg, there was a chorus of disgust from his daughters: "God no, Daddy!" or "Daddy, please don't even mention something like that, and could you keep the kitchen door closed if you're going to have one?" If Nell were at home, she might raise her eyes from a novel and ask, Why? Her tone was never hostile only bewildered as if it were the most unlikely suggestion that had ever been made. Left to herself Nell might make a salad sandwich at three.

Aidan thought back wistfully to his mother's table, where the chat of the week took place and no one was excused without a very good reason. Of course, dismantling this had been all his own doing. Making them into free spirits who would discover the length and breadth of County Dublin and even the neighboring counties on their one full day off. How could he have known it would lead to his being displaced and restless, wandering from the kitchen where everyone heated up their own food in a microwave, to the sitting room where there was some program that he didn't want to see on television, to the bedroom where it was so long since he had made love with his wife, he could barely endure looking at it until it was time to go to sleep.

There was, of course, the dining room. The room with the heavy dark furniture that they had hardly used since they bought the house. Even if they had been people who entertained, it was too small and poky. Once or twice recently Nell had suggested casually that Aidan should make it into a study for himself. But he had resisted. He felt that if he turned it into a copy of his room at the school, he might somehow lose his identity as head of this house, as father, provider, and man who once believed that this was the center of the world.

He also feared that if he made himself too much at home there, then the next step would be that he should sleep there too. After all, there was a downstairs cloakroom. It would be perfectly feasible to leave the three women to roam the upstairs area.

He must never do that, he must fight to keep his place in the family as he was fighting to keep his presence in the minds of the Board of Management, the men and women who would choose the next principal of Mountainview College.

His mother had never understood why the school wasn't called Saint something college. That's what all schools were called. It was hard to explain to her that things were different now, a changed setup, but he kept reassuring her that there were both a priest and a nun on the Board of Management. They didn't make all the decisions but were there to give a voice to the role the religious had played in Irish education over the years.

Aidan's mother had sniffed. Things had come to a strange state when priests and nuns were meant to be pleased that they had a place on the board instead of running it the way God intended. In vain Aidan had tried to explain about the fall in vocations. Even secondary schools ostensibly run by religious orders had in the nineties only a very few religious in teaching positions. The numbers just weren't there.

Nell had heard him arguing the situation with his mother once and had suggested that he save his breath. "Tell her they still run it, Aidan. It makes for an easier life. And of course in a way they do. People are afraid of them." It irritated him greatly when Nell spoke like this. Nell had no reason to fear the power of the Catholic Church. She had attended its services for as long as it had suited her, had abandoned confession and any of the Pope's teaching on contraception at an early stage. Why should she pretend that it had been a burden that lay heavily on her? But he didn't fight her on this. He was calm and accepting as in so many things. She had no time for his mother; no hostility, but no interest in her at all.

Sometimes his mother wondered when she would get invited for dinner and Aidan had to say that the way things were they were in a state of flux, but once they got organized . . .

He had been saying this for over two decades, and as an excuse it had worn thin. And it wasn't fair to fault Nell over this. It wasn't as if she was constantly inviting her own mother around or anything. His mother had been asked to any family celebration in hotels, of course. But it wasn't the same. And it had been so long since there was anything to celebrate. Except, of course, the hope that he would be made principal.

"DID YOU HAVE a good weekend?" Tony O'Brien asked him in the staff room.

Aidan looked at him surprised. It was so long since anyone had inquired. "Quiet, you know," Aidan said.

"Oh well, lucky you. I was at a party last night and I'm suffering after it. Still, only three and a half hours till the good old rehydrating lunchtime pint," Tony groaned.

"Aren't you marvelous, the stamina I mean." Aidan hoped the bitterness and criticism were not too obvious in his voice.

"Not at all, I'm far too long in the tooth for this, but I don't have the consolations of wife and family like all the rest of you do." Tony's smile was warm. If you didn't know him and his lifestyle, you'd have believed that he was genuinely wistful, Aidan thought to himself.

They walked together along the corridors of Mountainview College, the place his mother would like to have been called Saint Kevin's or, even more particularly, Saint Anthony's. Anthony was the saint who found lost things, and his mother had increasing calls on him as she got older. He found her glasses a dozen times a day. The least that people could do was thank him by naming the local school after him. Still, when her son was principal . . . she lived in hope.

The children ran past them, some of them chorusing "good morning," others looking sullenly away. Aidan Dunne knew them all, and their parents. And remembered many of their elder brothers and sisters. Tony O'Brien knew hardly any of them. It was so unfair.

"I met someone who knew you last night," Tony O'Brien said suddenly.

"At a party? I doubt that." Aidan smiled.

"No, definitely she did. When I told her I taught here she asked did I know you."

"And who was she?" Aidan was interested in spite of himself.

"I never got her name. Nice girl."

"An ex-pupil possibly?"

"No, then she'd have known me."

"A mystery indeed," Aidan said, and watched as Tony O'Brien went into Fifth Year.

The silence that fell immediately was beyond explanation. Why did they respect him so much, fear to be caught talking, behaving badly?

Tony O'Brien didn't remember their names, for heaven's sake. He barely marked their work, he lost not an hour's sleep over their examination results. Basically he didn't care about them very much. And yet they sought his approval. Aidan couldn't understand it. In sixteen-year-old boys and girls.

You always heard that women were meant to like men who treated them hard. He felt a flicker of relief that Nell had never crossed Tony O'Brien's path. Then it was followed by another flicker, a sense of recognition that somehow Nell had left him long ago.

Aidan Dunne went into the Fourth Years and stood at the door for three minutes until they gradually came to a sort of silence for him.

He thought that Mr. Walsh, the elderly principal, may have passed by behind him in the corridor. But he may have imagined it. You always imagined that the principal was passing by when your class was in disorder. It was something every single teacher he ever met admitted to. Aidan knew that it was a trivial worry. The principal admired him far too much to care if Fourth Years were a bit noisier than usual. Aidan was the most responsible teacher in Mountainview. Everyone knew that.

⌖

THAT WAS THE afternoon that Mr. Walsh called him into the principal's office. He was a man whose retirement could not come quick enough. Today for the first time there was no small talk.

"You and I feel the same about a lot of things, Aidan."

"I hope so, Mr. Walsh."

"Yes, we look at the world from the same viewpoint. But it's not enough."

"I don't know exactly what you mean." And Aidan spoke only the truth. Was this a philosophical discussion? Was it a warning? A reprimand?

"It's the system, you see. The way they run things. The principal doesn't have a vote. Sits there like a bloody eunuch, that's what it amounts to."

"A vote?" Aidan thought he knew where this was going, but decided to pretend not to.

It had been a wrong calculation. It only annoyed the Principal. "Come on, man, you know what I'm talking about. The job, the job, man."

"Well, yes." Aidan now felt foolish.

"I'm a nonvoting member of the Board of Management. I don't have a say. If I did you'd be in this job in September. I'd give you a few bits of advice about taking no nonsense from those louts in Fourth Year. But I still think you're the man with the values, and the sense of what's right for a school."

"Thank you, Mr. Walsh, that's very good to know."

"Man, will you listen to me before you mouth these things . . . there's nothing to thank me for. I can't *do* anything for you, that's what I'm trying to tell you, Aidan." The elder man looked at him despairingly, as if Aidan were some very slow-learning child in First Year.

The look was not unlike the way Nell looked at him sometimes, Aidan realized with a great feeling of sadness. He had been teaching other people's children since he was twenty-two years of age, over twenty-six years now, yet he did not know how to respond to a man who was trying hard to help him; he had only managed to annoy him.

The Principal was looking at him intently. For all that Aidan knew, Mr. Walsh might be able to read his thoughts, recognize the realization that had just sunk into Aidan's brain. "Come on now, pull yourself together. Don't look so stricken. I might be wrong, I could have it all wrong. I'm an old horse going out to grass, and I suppose I just wanted to cover myself in case it didn't go in your favor."

Aidan could see that the Principal deeply regretted having spoken at all. "No, no. I greatly appreciate it, I mean you are very good to tell me where you stand in all this . . . I mean . . ." Aidan's voice trickled away.

"It wouldn't be the end of the world, you know . . . suppose you didn't get it."

"No no, absolutely not."

"I mean, you're a family man, many compensations. Lots of life going on at home, not wedded to this place like I was for so long." Mr. Walsh had been a widower for many years, his only son visited him but rarely.

"Utterly right, just as you say," Aidan said.

"But?" The older man looked kind, approachable.

Aidan spoke slowly. "You're right, it's not the end of the world, but I suppose I thought . . . hoped that it might be a new beginning, liven everything up in my own life. I wouldn't mind the extra hours, I never did. I spend a lot of hours here already. In a way I am a bit like you, you know, wedded to Mountainview."

"I know you are." Mr. Walsh was gentle.

"I never found any of it a chore. I liked my classes and particularly the Transition Year when you can bring them out of themselves a bit, get to know them, let them think. And I even like the parent–teacher evenings which everyone else hates, because I can remember all the kids and . . . I suppose I like it all except for the politics of it, the sort of jostling-for-position bit." Aidan stopped suddenly. He was afraid there would be a break in his voice, and also he realized that *his* jostling hadn't worked.

Mr. Walsh was silent.

Outside the room were the noises of a school at four-thirty in the afternoon. In the distance the sounds of bicycle bells shrilling, doors banging, voices shouting as they ran for the buses in each direction. Soon the sound of the cleaners with their buckets and mops, and the hum of the electric polisher, would be heard. It was so familiar, so safe. And until this moment Aidan had thought that there was a very sporting chance that this would be his.

"I suppose it's Tony O'Brien," he said in a defeated tone.

"He seems to be the one they want. Nothing definite yet, not till next week, but that's where their thinking lies."

"I wonder why." Aidan felt almost dizzy with jealousy and confusion.

"Oh search me, Aidan. The man's not even a practicing Catholic. He has the morals of a tomcat. He doesn't love the place, care about it like we do, but they think he's the man for the times that are in it. Tough ways of dealing with tough problems."

"Like beating an eighteen-year-old boy nearly senseless," Aidan said.

"Well, they all think that the boy was a drug dealer, and he certainly didn't come anywhere near the school again."

"You can't run a place like that," Aidan said.

"You wouldn't and I wouldn't but our day is over."

"You're sixty-five, with respect, Mr. Walsh. I am only forty-eight, I didn't think my day was over."

"And it needn't be, Aidan. That's what I'm telling you. You've got a lovely wife and daughters, a life out there. You should build on all that. Don't let Mountainview become like a mistress to you."

"You're very kind and I appreciate what you say. No, I'm not just mouthing words. Truly I do appreciate being warned in advance, makes me look less foolish." And he left the room with a very straight back.

∽

AT HOME HE found Nell in her black dress and yellow scarf, the uniform she wore for work in the restaurant.

"But you don't work Monday night," he cried in dismay.

"They were shorthanded, and I thought why not, there's nothing on television," she said. Then possibly she saw his face. "There's a nice bit of steak in the fridge," she said. "And some of Saturday's potatoes . . . they'd be grand fried up with an onion. Right?"

"Right," he said. He wouldn't have told her anyway. Maybe it was better that Nell was going out. "Are the girls home?" he asked.

"Grania's taken possession of the bathroom. Heavy date tonight, apparently."

"Anyone we know?" He didn't know why he said it. He could see her irritation.

"How would it be anyone we know?"

"Remember when they were toddlers and we knew all their friends?" Aidan said.

"Yes, and remember too when they kept us awake all night roaring and bawling. I'll be off now."

"Fine, take care." His voice was flat.

"Are you all right, Aidan?"

"Would it matter all that much if I were or I weren't?"

"What kind of an answer is that? There's very little point in asking you a civil question if this is all the response I get."

"I mean it. Does it matter?"

"Not if you're going to put on this self-pitying thing. We're all tired, Aidan, life's hard for everyone. Why do you think you're the only one with problems?"

"What problems do you have? You never tell me."

"And as sure as hell I'm not going to tell you now with three minutes before the bus."

She was gone.

He made a cup of instant coffee and sat down at the kitchen table. Brigid came in. She was dark-haired, freckled like he was but fortunately less square. Her elder sister had Nell's blond good looks.

"Daddy, it's not fair, she's been in the bathroom for nearly an hour. She was home at five-thirty and she went in at six and now it's nearly seven. Daddy, tell her to get out and let me in."

"No," he said quietly.

"What do you mean no?" Brigid was startled.

What would he usually have said? Something bland, trying to keep the peace, reminding her there was a shower in the downstairs cloakroom. But tonight he hadn't the energy to placate them. Let them fight, he would make no effort to stop them.

"You're grown-up women, sort out the bathroom between you," he said, and walked out with his coffee into the dining room, closing the door behind him.

He sat still for a while and looked around him. It seemed to signify all that was wrong with the life they lived. There were no happy family meals around this big bleak table. Friends and extended family never drew up those dark chairs to talk animatedly.

When Grania and Brigid brought friends home, they took them up to their bedrooms or giggled with Nell in the kitchen. Aidan was left in the sitting room looking at television programs that he didn't want to see. Wouldn't it be better if he had his own little place, somewhere he could feel at peace?

He had seen a desk that he would love in a secondhand shop, one of those marvelous desks with a flap that came down and you sat and wrote on it as people were meant to do. And he would have fresh flowers in the room because he liked their beauty and he didn't mind about changing the water every day, which Nell said was a bore.

And there was a nice light that came in the window here during the daytime, a soft light that they never saw. Maybe he could get a window-seat or sofa and put it there, and get big drapey curtains. And he could sit and read, and invite friends in, well, whoever there was, because he knew now there would be no life for him from the family anymore. He would have to realize this and stop hoping that things would change.

He could have a wall with books on it, and maybe tapes until he got a CD player. Or maybe he would never get a CD player, he didn't have to try to compete with Tony O'Brien anymore. He could put up pictures on the wall, frescoes from Florence, or those heads, those graceful necks and heads of Leonardo da Vinci. And he could play arias to himself, and read articles in magazines about the great operas. Mr. Walsh thought he had a life. It was time for him to get this life. His other life was over. He would not be married to Mountainview from now on. He sat warming his hands on the coffee cup. This room would need more heating, but that could be seen to. And it would need some lamps, the harsh center light gave it no shadows, no mystery.

There was a knock on the door. His blond daughter, Grania, stood there, dressed for her date. "Are you all right, Daddy?" she asked. "Brigid said you were a bit odd, I was wondering if you were sick."

"No, I'm fine," he said. But his voice seemed to come from far away. If it seemed far to him it must be very far to Grania; he forced a smile. "Are you going somewhere nice?" he asked.

She was relieved to see him more himself. "I don't know. I met a gorgeous fellow, but listen I'll tell you about it sometime." Her face was soft, kinder than it had been for a long while.

"Tell me now," he said.

She shuffled. "No, I can't yet, I have to see how we get on. If there's anything to tell, you'll be the first to know."

He felt unbearably sad. This girl whose hand he had held for so long, who used to laugh at his jokes and think he knew everything, and she could hardly wait to get away. "That's fine," he said.

"Don't sit in here, Daddy. It's cold and lonely."

He wanted to say it was cold and lonely everywhere, but he didn't. "Enjoy your night," he said.

❧

HE CAME BACK and sat by the television.

"What are you watching tonight?" he asked Brigid.

"What would you like, Daddy?" she countered.

He must have taken this blow much worse than he believed, his naked disappointment and sense of injustice had to be showing in his face if both his daughters . . .

He looked at his younger child, her freckled face and big brown eyes so dear and loved and familiar since she was a baby in the pram. She was normally so impatient with him, tonight she looked at him as if he were someone on a stretcher in a hospital corridor, with that wave of sympathy that washes over you for a complete stranger going through a very bad time.

They sat beside each other until eleven-thirty looking at television programs that neither of them liked, but both with an air of pleasure that they were pleasing the other.

Aidan was in bed when Nell came home at one o'clock. The light was out but he was not asleep. He heard the taxi pulling up outside the door; they paid for a cab home when she was on the late shift.

She came into the room quietly. He could smell toothpaste and talcum powder, so she had washed in the bathroom rather than disturb him by using the handbasin in their bedroom. She had a bedside light that pointed downward at whatever book she was reading and didn't shine in his eyes, so often he had lain there listening as she turned the pages. No words between them would ever be as interesting as the paperbacks she and her friends and sisters read, so nowadays he didn't offer them.

Even tonight, when his heart was like lead and he wanted to hold her in his arms and cry into her soft clean skin and tell her about Tony O'Brien, who should not be allowed to do dinner duty but who was going to get the headship because he was more upfront whatever that might mean. He would like to have told her that he was sorry she had to go in and sit in a cash desk watching rich people eat and get drunk and pay their bills because it was better than anything else a Monday night might offer a married couple with two grown daughters. But he lay there and heard the faraway town hall clock strike the hours.

At two o'clock Nell put down her book with a little sigh and went to sleep, as far from him on her side of the bed as if she were sleeping in the next room. When the town hall said it was four o'clock, Aidan realized that Grania would only have three hours sleep before she went to work.

But there was nothing he could do or say. It was clearly understood that the girls lived their own lives without interrogation. He had not liked to think about it but had accepted that they had been to the Family Planning Association. They came home at the times that suited them and if they did *not* come home then they called at eight o'clock during breakfast to say they were all right . . . that they had stayed over with a girlfriend. This was the polite fiction that covered the Lord knew what. But as Nell said, it was often the actual truth, and she much preferred Grania and Brigid staying in some other girl's flat rather than risk being driven home by a drunk or not getting a taxi in the small hours of the morning.

Still, Aidan was relieved when he heard the hall door click and the light footsteps running up the stairs. At her age she could survive on three hours sleep. And it would be three hours more than he would have.

His mind was racing with foolish plans. He could resign from the school as a protest. Surely he could get work in a private college, sixth-year colleges, for example, where they did intensive work. Aidan as a Latin teacher would be useful there, there were so many careers where students still needed Latin. He could appeal to the Board of Management, list the ways in which he had helped the school, the hours he had put in to see that it got its rightful place in the community, his liaising with third-level education so that they would come and give the children talks and pointers about the future, his environmental studies backed up by the wildlife garden.

Without appearing to do so, he could let it be known that Tony O'Brien was a destructive element, that the very fact of using violence against an ex-pupil on the school premises sent the worst possible signal to those who were meant to follow his leadership. Or could he write an anonymous letter to the religious members of the board, to the pleasant open-faced priest and the rather serious nun, who might have no idea of Tony O'Brien's loose moral code? Or could he get some of the parents to set up an action group? There were many, many things he could do.

Or else he would accept Mr. Walsh's view of him and become a man with a life outside the school, do up the dining room, make it his last-ditch stand against all the disappointments that life had thrown at him. His head felt as if someone had attached a lead weight to it during the night, but since he hadn't closed his eyes he knew that this could not have happened.

He shaved very carefully; he would not appear at school with little bits of Elastoplast on his face. He looked around his bathroom as if he had never seen it before. On every inch of available walls were prints of Venice, big shiny reproductions of Turners that he had bought when he went to the Tate Gallery. When the children were young, they used to talk of going to the Venice Room not the bathroom; now they probably didn't see them at all, the prints were the wallpaper they almost obscured.

He touched them and wondered would he ever go there again. He had been there twice as a young man, and then they had spent their honeymoon in Italy when he had shown Nell his Venice, his Rome, his Florence, his Siena. It had been a wonderful time, but they had never gone back. When the children were young, there hadn't been the money or the time, and then lately . . . well . . . who would have come with him? And it would have been a statement to have gone alone. Still, in the future there might have to be statements, and surely his soul was not so dead that it would not respond to the beauty of Italy?

Somewhere along the line they had all agreed not to talk at breakfast. And as a ceremony somehow it worked well for them. The coffee percolator was ready at eight, and the radio news switched on. A brightly colored Italian dish of grapefruit was on the table. Everyone helped themselves and prepared their own. A basket of bread was there, and an electric toaster sat on a tray with a picture of the Trevi Fountain on it. It had been a gift from Nell on his fortieth birthday. By twenty past eight Aidan and the girls had gone, all leaving their mug and plates in the dishwasher to minimize the clearing up.

He didn't give his wife a bad life, Aidan thought to himself. He had lived up to the promises he had made. It wasn't an elegant house, but it had radiators and appliances and he paid for the windows to be cleaned three times a year, the carpet to be steamed every two years, and the house painted on the outside every three years.

Stop thinking in this ridiculous petty clerk way, Aidan warned himself, and forcing a smile on his face began his exit.

"Nice evening last night, Grania?" he asked.

"Yeah, okay." There was no sign of the hesitant confidences of last night. No wondering about whether people were sincere or not.

"Good, good." He nodded. "Was it busy in the restaurant?" he asked Nell.

"Fair for a Monday night, you know, nothing spectacular," she said. She spoke perfectly pleasantly but as if to a stranger she had met on a bus.

Aidan took up his briefcase and left for school. His mistress, Mountainview College. What a fanciful idea. She certainly didn't have the allures of a lover to him this morning.

He stood for a moment at the gates of the school yard, scene of the disgraceful and brutal fight between Tony O'Brien and that boy, whose ribs were broken and who needed stitches over his eye and in his lower lip. The yard was untidy with litter blowing in the early morning breezes. The bicycle shed needed to be painted, the bikes were not properly stacked. Outside the gates the bus stop was open and exposed to the winds. If Bus Eireann would not provide a proper bus shelter for the children who waited there after school, then the Vocational Education Committee should do so, and if they refused, a parents' committee would raise the funds. These were the kinds of things Aidan Dunne had intended to do when he was principal. Things that would never be done now.

He nodded gruffly to the children who saluted him, instead of addressing them all by name, which was his usual way, and he walked into the staff room to find no one there except Tony O'Brien mixing a headache seltzer in a glass.

"I'm getting too old for these nights," he confided to Aidan.

Aidan longed to ask him why he didn't just cut them out, but that would be counterproductive. He must make no false stupid moves, in fact no moves at all until he had worked out what his plan was to be. He must continue in his bland, good-natured way.

"I suppose all work and no play . . ." he began.

But Tony O'Brien was in no mood to hear platitudes. "I think forty-five is a sort of watershed. It's half of ninety after all, it's telling you something. Not that some of us listen." He drained the glass and smacked his lips.

"Was it worth it, I mean the late night?"

"Who knows if it's ever worth it, Aidan. I met a nice little girl, but what's the good of that when you have to face the Fourth Years." He shook his head like a dog coming out of the sea trying to get rid of the water. And this man was going to run Mountainview College for the

next twenty years while poor old Mr. Dunne was expected to sit by and
let it happen. Tony O'Brien gave him a heavy clap on the shoulder.
"Still, *ave atque vale* as you Latinists say. I have to be getting on, only
four hours and three minutes before I stand with that healing pint in my
hand."

Aidan would not have thought that Tony O'Brien would know the
Latin words for hallo and good-bye. He himself had never used any
Latin phrases in the staff room, aware that many of his colleagues might
not have studied it and fearing to show off in front of them. It just
showed you must never underestimate the enemy.

The day passed as days always pass, whether you have a hangover
like Tony O'Brien, or a heavy heart like Aidan Dunne, and the next
passed, and the next. Aidan still had settled on no definite plan of action.
He could never find the right moment to tell them at home that his hopes
of being principal had been misplaced. In fact, he thought it would be
easier to say nothing until the decision was announced, let it appear a
surprise to everyone.

And he had not forgotten his plans to make himself a room. He sold
the dining table and chairs and bought the little desk. When his wife
worked in Quentin's restaurant and his daughters went out on their
dates, he sat and planned it for himself. Gradually he assembled little
bits of his dream: secondhand picture frames, a low table for near the
window, a big cheap sofa that fitted the space exactly. And one day he
would get loose covers, something in gold or yellow, a sunny color, and
he would get a square of carpet that would be a splash of some other
color, orange, purple, something with life and vigor.

They weren't very interested at home, so he didn't tell them his plans.
In a way he felt that his wife and daughters thought it was yet another
harmless little interest for him, like the projects in Transition Year and
his long struggle to get a few meters of wildlife garden up and running in
Mountainview.

❧

"ANY WORD OF the big job above in the school?" Nell asked unexpectedly one evening when the four of them were seated around the kitchen
table.

He felt his heart lurch at the lie. "Not a whisper. But they'll be voting next week, that's for sure." He seemed calm and unruffled.

"You're bound to get it. Old Walsh loves the ground you walk on," Nell said.

"He doesn't have a vote, as it happens, so that's no use to me." Aidan gave a nervous little laugh.

"Surely you'll get it, Daddy?" Brigid said.

"You never know, people want different things in principals. I'm sort of slow and steady, but that mightn't be what's needed these days." He spread out his hands in a gesture to show that it was all beyond him but wouldn't matter very much either way.

"But who would they have if they didn't have you?" Grania wanted to know.

"Wouldn't I be doing the horoscope column if I knew that? An outsider maybe, someone inside that we hadn't reckoned on . . ." He sounded good-natured and full of fair play. The job would go to the best man or woman. It was as simple as that.

"But you don't think they'll pass you over?" Nell said.

There was something that he hated in her tone. It was a kind of disbelief that he could possibly let this one slip. It was the phrase "passed over," so dismissive, so hurtful. But she didn't know, she couldn't guess, that it had already happened.

Aidan willed his smile to look confident. "Passed over? Me? Never!" he cried.

"That's more like it, Daddy," said Grania, before going upstairs to spend further time in the bathroom, where she possibly never saw any more the beautiful images of Venice on the wall, only her face in the mirror and her anxieties that it should look good for whatever outing was planned tonight.

It was their sixth date. Grania knew now that he definitely wasn't married. She had asked him enough questions to have tripped him up. Every night so far he had wanted her to come back to his place for coffee. Every night so far she had said no. But tonight could be different. She really liked him. He knew so much about things, and he was far more interesting than people of her own age. He wasn't one of those middle-aged ravers who pretended they were twenty years younger.

There was only one problem. Tony worked at Dad's school. She had asked him on the very first time she met him whether he knew an Aidan Dunne, but hadn't said he was her father. It seemed an ageist sort of thing to say, putting herself in a different generation. And there were loads of Dunnes around the place, it wasn't as if Tony would make the connection. There wasn't any point in mentioning it to Dad, not yet anyway, not until it developed into anything, if it did. And if it were the real thing, then everything else like him working in the same place as Dad would fall into place, and Grania made a silly face at herself in the mirror and thought that maybe Tony would have to be even nicer than ever to her if she was going to be the principal's daughter.

Tony sat in the bar and dragged deep on his cigarette. This was one thing he was going to have to cut down on when he was principal. There really couldn't be any more smoking on the premises. And probably fewer pints at lunchtime. It hadn't been actually spelled out, but it had been hinted at. Heavily. But that was it. Not a huge price to pay for a good job. And they weren't going to ask about his social life. It might still be Holy Catholic Ireland, but it was the 1990s after all.

And by extraordinary timing he had just met a girl who really did hold his attention, and might well be around for more than a few weeks duration. A bright, lively girl called Grania, worked in the bank. Sharp as anything, but not at all hard or tough. She was warm and generous in her outlook. They didn't come in that kind of package often. She was twenty-one, which was, of course, a problem. Less than half his age, but she wouldn't always be that. When he was sixty she'd be thirty-five, which was half of seventy when you came to think of it. She'd be catching up all the time.

She hadn't come back to the town house with him, but she had been very frank. It wasn't because she was afraid of sex, it was just that she wasn't ready for it with him yet, that was all, and if they were to get along together, then they must respect each other and not one of them force the other. He had agreed with her, that seemed perfectly fair. And for once it did. Normally he would have regarded such a response as a challenge, but not with Grania. He was quite ready to wait. And she had assured him that she wasn't going to play games.

He saw her come into the bar and he felt lighter and happier than he had for a long time. He wasn't going to play games either. "You look lovely," he said. "Thank you for dressing up for me, I appreciate it."

"You're worth it," she said simply.

They drank together, like people who had always known each other, interrupting, laughing, eager to hear what the other would say.

"There are lots of things we could do this evening . . ." Tony O'Brien said. "There's a New Orleans evening, you know, Creole food and jazz in one of the hotels, or there was this movie we were talking about last night . . . or I could cook for you at home. Show you what a great chef I am."

Grania laughed. "Am I to believe that you'll be making me wontons and Peking duck? You see, I remember that you said you had a neighboring Chinese restaurant."

"No, if you come home with me I'll cook for you myself. To show you how much it means to me. I won't just get menu A or menu B, good and all as they may be." Tony O'Brien had not spoken so directly for a long time.

"I'd love to come home with you, Tony," Grania said very simply, without a hint of playing games.

༄

AIDAN SLEPT IN fits and starts. And then near dawn he felt wide awake and clearheaded. All he had was the doddering word of a retiring principal, a man fussed and confused by the way the world was going. The vote had not been taken, there was nothing to be depressed about, no excuses to make, action to take, career to abandon. Today would be a much, much better day now that he was clear about all this.

He would speak to Mr. Walsh, the present principal, and ask him briefly and directly if his remarks of some days ago had any substance and intent, or if they were mere speculation. After all, as a nonvoting member he might also have been a nonlistening member to their deliberations. He would be brief, Aidan told himself. That was his weakness, a tendency to go on at too great a length. But yet he would be crystal clear. What was it that the poet Horace said? Horace had a word for every occasion. *Brevis esse laboro / Obscurus fio.* Yes, that was it, the more I struggle to be brief, the more unintelligible I become. In the kitchen Brigid and Nell exchanged glances and shrugs when they heard him whistling. He wasn't a very good whistler, but nobody could remember when he had last even attempted it.

Just after eight o'clock the phone rang.

"Three guesses," Brigid said, reaching for more toast.

"She's very reliable, you both are," Nell said, and went to answer it.

Aidan wondered was it very reliable for one of his daughters to spend the night with a man who had been described by the other as a heavy date. About whom only a week ago she had raised tentative worries, whether he was reliable . . . sincere. Aidan didn't voice these wonderings. He watched Nell at the phone.

"Sure, fine, good. Do you have proper clothes to go into the bank in or will you come back here? Oh, you brought a sweater, how lucky. Righto, love, see you this evening."

"And how did she seem?" Aidan asked.

"Now, Aidan, don't start taking attitudes. We've always agreed that it's much wiser that Grania should stay with Fiona in town instead of getting a dodgy lift home."

He nodded. None of them thought for a moment that Grania was staying with Fiona.

"NO PROBLEMS, THEN?" Tony asked.

"No, I told you . . . they treat me as a grown-up."

"And so do I in a different way." He reached out for her as she sat on the edge of the bed.

"No, Tony, I can't possibly. We have to go to work. I have to get to the bank, you have to go to Mountainview."

He was pleased that she remembered the name of the place he worked. "No, they won't mind, they're very lax there, let the teachers do what they like most of the time."

She laughed at him. "No that's not true, not even a little bit true. Get up and have a shower, I'll put on some coffee. Where's the machine?"

"It's only instant, I'm afraid."

"Oh that's not classy enough for me at all I'm afraid, Mr. O'Brien," she said, shaking her head at him in mock disapproval. "Things will have to improve round here if I am to visit again."

"I was hoping you'd pay a visit this evening," he said.

Their eyes met. There was no guile.

"Yes, if you have real coffee," she said.

"Consider it done," he said.

Grania had toast, Tony had two cigarettes.

"You really should cut down on those," she said. "I could hear you wheeze all night."

"That was passion," he said.

"No, it was cigarettes." She was firm.

Perhaps, perhaps for this lively, bright young woman he might, he just might, be able to cut them out. It was bad enough to be so much older than her, he didn't want to be so much wheezier as well. "I might change you know," he said seriously. "There are going to be a lot of changes in my life at work for one thing, but more important, now that I've met you I think I might have the strength to cut out a lot of the rubbishy bits."

"Believe me, I'll help you," Grania said, reaching for his hand across the table. "And you must help me too. Help me to keep my mind alert and busy. I've stopped reading since I left school. I want to read again."

"I think we should both take the day off to cement this promise," he said, only half joking.

"Hey, you won't even be thinking about suggesting that next term." She laughed.

"Why next term?" How could she have known of his promotion? Nobody knew except the board, who had offered him the job. It was to be kept totally secret until it was announced.

She had not meant to tell him yet about her father's being on the staff, but somehow with all they had shared it seemed pointless to keep it secret any longer. It would have to come out sometime, and anyway, she was so proud of Dad's new post. "Well, you'll want to keep well in with my father, he's going to be the principal of Mountainview."

"Your father's going to be *what*?"

"Principal. It's a secret until next week but I think everyone expected it."

"What's your father's name?"

"Dunne like mine. He's the Latin teacher, Aidan Dunne. Remember I asked you did you know him the first time we met."

"You didn't say he was your father."

"No, well it was a crowded place and I didn't want to be making myself sound too babyish. And later it didn't matter."

"Oh my God," said Tony O'Brien. He didn't look at all pleased.

Grania bit her lip and regretted that she had ever mentioned it. "Please don't say to him that you know, please."

"He told you this? That he was going to be principal?" Tony O'Brien's face was hardly able to register the shock. "When? When did he tell you this? Was it a long time ago?"

"He's been talking about it for ages, but he told us last night."

"Last night? No, you must be mistaken, you must have misunderstood."

"Of course I didn't misunderstand, we were just talking about it before I came out to meet you."

"And did you tell him that you were meeting me?" He looked almost wild.

"No. Tony, what is it?"

He held both her hands in his and spoke very slowly and carefully. "This is the most important thing I have ever said in my whole life. In my whole long life, Grania. You must never, never tell your father what you told me now. Never."

She laughed nervously and tried to draw her hands away. "Oh come on, you're behaving like someone in a melodrama."

"It's a bit like that, honestly."

"I'm never to tell my father I met you, know you, like you . . . what kind of relationship is that?" Her eyes blazed at him across the breakfast table.

"No, of course we'll tell him. But later, not a lot later, but there's something else I have to tell him first."

"Tell me?" she asked.

"I can't. If there's any dignity to be left anywhere in this whole world it depends on your trusting me this minute and believing I want the best, the very, very best for you."

"How can I believe anything if you won't tell me what all the mystery is about?"

"It's about faith and trust."

"It's about keeping me in the dark, that's what it is and I hate it."

"What have you to lose by trusting me, Grania? Listen, two weeks ago we hadn't even met, now we think we love each other. Can't you give it just a day or two till I sort something out." He was standing up and putting on his jacket. For a man who had said Mountainview College was a lax place where it didn't matter what time you rolled in, Tony O'Brien seemed in a very great hurry.

❧

AIDAN DUNNE WAS in the staff room. He looked slightly excited, feverish even. His eyes were unnaturally bright. Was it possible that he could be suffering from some kind of delusion? Or did he suspect that his beloved daughter had been seduced by a man as old as himself but ten times as unreliable?

"Aidan, I want to talk to you very, very urgently," Tony O'Brien said in an undertone.

"After school hours possibly, Tony . . ."

"This very minute. Come on, we'll go to the library."

"Tony, the bell will go in five minutes."

"To hell with the bell." Tony half pulled, half dragged him out of the staff room.

In the library two studious girls from Sixth Year looked up, startled.

"Out," Tony O'Brien said in a voice that wasn't going to be argued with.

One of them tried to protest. "But we're *studying* here, we were looking up—"

"Did you hear me?"

This time she got the message and they were gone.

"That's no way to treat children, we're meant to encourage them, lead them *into* the library, for heaven's sake, not throw them out of it like some bouncer in these nightclubs you go to. What example is that for them to follow?"

"We're not here to be some example to them, we're here to teach them. To put some information into their heads. It's as simple as that."

Aidan looked at him aghast, and then he spoke. "I'll thank you not to give me the benefit of your half-baked hungover philosophies at this time in the morning or any time. Let me back to my classes this minute."

"Aidan." Tony O'Brien's voice had changed. "Aidan, listen to me. I'm going to be the principal. They were going to announce it next week, but I think it's better if I make them do it today."

"What, what . . . why do you want to do that?" Aidan felt he had had a blow in the stomach. This was too soon, he wasn't ready for it. There was no proof. Nothing was fixed yet.

"So that all this nonsense in your head can be knocked out if it, so that you don't go round believing that it's you who's getting the job . . . upsetting yourself, upsetting other people . . . that's why."

Aidan looked at Tony O'Brien. "Why are you doing this to me, Tony, why? Suppose they do give you the job, is your first response to drag me in here and start rubbing my nose in it, the fact that you . . . you who don't give a tuppenny damn about Mountainview are going to get the job? Have you no dignity at all? Can't you even wait until the board offer you the job before you start gloating? Are you so bloody confident, so eager . . . ?"

"Aidan, you can't have gone on believing that it was going to be you. Did that old blatherer Walsh not tell you? They all thought he would mark your card about it, he actually said that he *had* told you."

"He said it was likely that you might get it, and I might add that he said he would be very sorry indeed if you did."

A child put his head around the library door and stared with amazement at the two red-faced teachers confronting each other across a table.

Tony O'Brien let a roar that nearly lifted the child up in the air. "Get the hell out of here you interfering young pup, and back to your classroom."

White-faced, the boy looked at Aidan Dunne for confirmation.

"That's the boy, Declan. Tell the class to open their Virgil, I'll be along shortly." The door closed.

"You know all their names," Tony O'Brien said wonderingly.

"You hardly know *any* of them," Aidan Dunne said flatly.

"Being principal doesn't have anything to do with being a Dale Carnegie figure, a Mister Nice Guy, you know."

"Evidently not," Aidan agreed. They were much calmer now, the heat and fury had gone from both of them.

"I'm going to need you, Aidan, to help me, if we're going to keep this place afloat at all."

But Aidan was stiff, rigid with his disappointment and humiliation. "No, it's too much to ask. I may be easygoing but I can't do this. I couldn't stay on here. Not now."

"But what will you do, in the name of God?"

"I'm not completely washed up you know, there *are* places that would be glad of me, even though this one doesn't seem to be."

"They rely on you here, you great fool. You're the cornerstone of Mountainview, you know that."

"Not cornerstone enough to want me as principal."

"Do I have to spell it out for you. The job of principal is changing. They don't want a wise preacher up in that office . . . they need someone with a loud voice who's not afraid to argue with the VEC, with the Department of Education, to get the guards in here if there's vandalism or drugs, to deal with the parents if they start bleating . . ."

"I couldn't work under you, Tony, I don't respect you as a teacher."

"You don't have to respect me as a teacher."

"Yes I would. You see, I couldn't go along with the things that you would want or the things you'd ignore."

"Give me one example, one, now this minute. What did you think of as you were coming in the school gate . . . what one thing would *you* do as principal?"

"I'd get the place painted, it's dirty, shabby . . ."

"Okay, snap. That's what I'd do too."

"Oh you just say that."

"No, Aidan, I don't bloody say that, but even better I know how I'm going to do it. You wouldn't know where to start. I'm going to get a young fellow I know in the evening paper to come up here with a photographer and do an article called 'Magnificent Mountainview,' showing the peeling paint, the rusty railings, the sign with the letters missing."

"You'd never humiliate the place like that?"

"It wouldn't be humiliation. The day after the article appears I'll have the board agree to a huge refurbishing job. We can announce details of it, say it was all on line and that local sponsors are going to take part . . . list who is going to do what . . . you know, garden centers, paint shops, that wrought-iron place for the school sign . . . I've a list as long as my arm."

Aidan looked down at his hands. He knew that he himself could not have set up something like this, a plan that was sure to work. This time next year Mountainview would have a face-lift, one that he would never have been able to organize. It left him more bereft than ever. "I couldn't stay, Tony. I'd feel so humbled, passed over."

"But no one here thought you were going to get it."

"I thought it." He said it simply.

"Well then, the humiliation that you speak of is only in your mind."

"And my family, of course . . . they think it is in the bag for me . . . they're waiting to celebrate."

There was a lump in Tony O'Brien's throat. He knew this was true. This man's glowing daughter was so proud of her father's new post. But there was no time for sentiment, only action.

"Then give them something to celebrate."

"Like what, for example?"

"Suppose there was no race to be principal. Suppose you could have some position in the school, bring in something new . . . set up something . . . what would you like to do?"

"Look, I know you mean well, Tony, and I'm grateful to you for it, but I'm not into let's pretend at the moment."

"I'm the principal, can't you get that into your head? I can do what I like, there's no let's pretend about it. I want you on my side. I want you to be enthusiastic, not a Moaning Minnie. Tell me what you'd do, for God's sake, man . . . if you were given the go-ahead."

"Well, you wouldn't wear it because it's not got much to do with the school, but I think we should have evening classes."

"What?"

"There, I knew you wouldn't want it."

"I didn't say I didn't want it. What kind of evening classes?"

The two men talked on in the library, and oddly, their classrooms were curiously quiet. Normally the noise level of any room left without a teacher could reach a very high decibel level indeed. But the two studious girls who had been thrown out of the library by Mr. O'Brien had scuttled to their classroom with news of their eviction and of Mr. O'Brien's face. It was agreed that the geography teacher was on the warpath and it was probably better to keep things fairly low until he arrived. They had all seen him in a temper at some stage, and it wasn't something you'd want to bring on yourselves.

Declan, who had been instructed to tell his class to get out their Virgil, spoke in low tones. "I think they were arm-wrestling," he said. "They were purple in the face, both of them, and Mr. Dunne spoke as if there was a knife held in his back."

They looked at him, round-faced. Declan was not a boy with much imagination, it must be true. They got out their Virgils obediently. They didn't study them or translate them or anything, that had not been part of the instructions, but every child in the class had an open copy of the *Aeneid* Book IV ready, and they looked at the door fearfully in case Mr. Dunne should come staggering in with blood coming down his shoulder blades.

The announcement was made that afternoon. It was in two parts.

A pilot scheme for adult education classes would begin in September under the supervision of Mr. Aidan Dunne. The present principal, Mr. John Walsh, having reached retirement age, would now stand down and his post would be filled by Mr. Anthony O'Brien.

⤜⤜

IN THE STAFF room there seemed to be as many congratulations for Aidan as for Tony. Two bottles of sparkling wine were opened, and people's health was drunk from mugs.

Imagine, evening classes. The subject had been brought up before but always to be knocked down. It was the wrong area, too much competition from other adult education centers, trouble heating the school, the business of keeping on the caretaker after hours, the whole notion of classes being self-funding. How had it happened now?

"Apparently Aidan persuaded them," Tony O'Brien said, pouring more fizzy drink into the school mugs.

It was time to go home.

"I don't know what to say," Aidan said to his new principal.

"We made a deal. You got what you wanted, you are to go straight home to your wife and family and present it as that. Because this *is* what you want. You don't want all the shit of fighting with people morning, noon, and night, which is what being the principal is about. Just remember that, present it to them as it is."

"Can I ask you something, Tony? Why does it matter to you one way or the other how I present things to my family?"

"Simple. I need you, I told you that. But I need you as a happy, successful man. If you present yourself in this old self-pitying I-was-passed-over role, then you'll begin to believe it all over again."

"That makes sense."

"And they'll be pleased for you that you have got what you really wanted all along."

As Aidan walked out the school gate he paused for a moment and felt its peeling paint and looked at the rusting locks. Tony was right, he wouldn't have known where to begin on a project like this. Then he looked at the annex where he and Tony had decided the evening classes should be held. It had its own entrance, they wouldn't have to trek through the whole school. It had cloakrooms and two big classrooms. It would be ideal.

Tony was an odd guy, there were no two ways about it. He had even suggested to him that he come home and meet the family, but Tony had said not yet. Wait until September when the new term began, he had insisted.

Who knew what would have happened by September.

Those were his words. As odd as two left shoes, but quite possibly the best thing that could happen to Mountainview.

INSIDE THE BUILDING Tony O'Brien inhaled deeply. He would smoke in his own office from now on, but never outside it.

He watched Aidan Dunne hold the gate and even stroke it lovingly. He was a good teacher and a good man. He was worth the sacrifice about the evening classes. All the bloody work that lay ahead, the fights with this committee and that board, and the lying promises that the classes would be self-financing when everyone knew there wasn't a chance that they would be.

He sighed deeply and hoped that Aidan would handle it right at home. Otherwise, his own future with Grania Dunne, the first girl to whom he could even consider a real commitment, would be a very rocky future indeed.

❧

"I HAVE VERY good news," Aidan said at supper.

He told them about the evening classes, the pilot scheme, the annex, the funds at his disposal, and how he would have Italian language and culture.

His enthusiasm was catching. They asked him questions. Would he have walls to put up pictures, posters, maps? Would these things remain up all week? What kinds of experts should he invite to lecture? Would there be Italian cookery? And arias from operas as well?

"Won't you find this a lot of extra work as well as being principal?" Nell asked.

"Oh no, I'm doing it instead of being principal," he explained eagerly, and he looked at their faces. Nobody missed a beat, it seemed to them a perfectly reasonable alternative. And oddly it began more and more to seem that way to him too. Maybe that crazy old Tony O'Brien was more intelligent than people gave him credit for. They talked on like a real family. What numbers would they need? Should it be more conversational Italian suitable for holidays? Or something more ambitious? The dishes were pushed aside on the table as Aidan made notes.

Later, much later it seemed, Brigid asked: "Who will become principal now if you're not going to do it?"

"Oh a man called Tony O'Brien, the geography teacher, a good fellow. He'll do all right for Mountainview."

"I knew it wouldn't be a woman," Nell said, sniffing.

"Now there *were* two women I believe in the running, but they gave it to the right person," Aidan said. He poured them another glass of wine from the bottle he had bought to celebrate his good news. Soon he would move into his room; he was going to measure it tonight for the shelves. One of the teachers at school did carpentry in his spare time, he would build the bookshelves and little racks for Italian plates.

They didn't notice Grania getting up quietly and leaving the room.

❧

HE SAT IN the sitting room and waited. She would have to come, just to tell him how much she hated him. That if nothing else. The doorbell rang and she stood there, eyes red from weeping.

"I bought a coffee machine," he said. "And some fine ground Colombian blend. Was that right?"

She walked into the room. Young but not confident, not anymore. "You are such a bastard, such a terrible deceitful bastard."

"No, I'm not." His voice was very quiet. "I am an honorable man. You must believe me."

"Why should I believe the daylight from you? You were laughing all the time at me, laughing at my father, even at the notion of a coffee percolator. Well, laugh as much as you like. I came to tell you that you are the lowest of the low, and I hope you are the worst I meet. I hope I have a very long life and that I meet hundreds and hundreds of people and that this is the very worst that will ever happen to me, to trust someone who doesn't give a damn about people's feelings. If there *is* a God then please, please God let this be the very lowest I ever meet." Her hurt was so great, he didn't even dare to stretch out a hand to her.

"This morning I didn't know you were Aidan Dunne's daughter. This morning I didn't know that Aidan thought he was getting the headship," he began.

"You *could* have told me, you *could* have told me," she cried.

Suddenly he was very tired. It had been a long day. He spoke quietly. "No I could *not* have told you. I could not have said, 'Your father's got it wrong, actually it's yours truly who is getting the job.' If there was loyalty involved, mine was to him, my duty was to make sure he didn't make a fool of himself, didn't set himself up for disappointment, and that he got what was rightfully his . . . a new position of power and authority."

"Oh I see." Her voice was scornful. "Give him the evening classes, a little pat on the head."

Tony O'Brien's voice was cold. "Well, of course, if that's the way you see it I can't hope to change your mind. If you don't see it for what it is, a breakthrough, a challenge, possibly the beginning of something that will change people's lives, most of all your father's life, then I'm sorry. Sorry and surprised. I thought you would have been more understanding."

"I'm not in your classroom, Mr. O'Brien, sir. I'm not fooled by this shaking-your-head-more-in-sorrow-than-in-anger bit. You made a fool of my father and me."

"How did I do that?"

"He doesn't know that you slept with his daughter, heard of his hopes and ran in and took his job. That's how."

"And have you told him all these things to make him feel better?"

"You know I haven't. But the sleeping-with-his-daughter bit isn't important. If ever there was a one-night stand that was it."

"I hope you'll change your mind, Grania. I am very *very* fond of you, and attracted to you."

"Yeah."

"No, not 'Yeah.' It's true what I say. Odd as it may seem to you it's not your age and your looks that appeal to me. I have had many young attractive girlfriends and should I want company I feel sure I could find more. But you are different. If you walk out on me I'll have lost something very important. You can believe it or not as you will, but very truthfully that's what I feel."

This time she was silent. They looked at each other for a while. Then he spoke. "Your father asked me to come and meet the family but I said we should wait until September. I said to him that September was a long way away and who knows what could have happened by then." She shrugged. "I wasn't thinking of myself, actually, I was thinking of you. Either you'll still be full of scorn and anger about me, and you can be out the day I call. Or maybe we will love each other fully and truly and know that all that happened here today was just some spectacularly bad timing."

She said nothing.

"So September it is," he said.

"Right." She turned to go.

"I'll leave it to you to contact me, Grania. I'll be here, I'd love to see you again. We don't have to be lovers if you don't want to be. If you were a one-night stand I'd be happy to see you go. If I didn't feel the way I do I'd think that maybe it was all too complicated and it would be for the best that we end it now. But I'll be here, hoping you come back."

Her face was still hard and upset. "Ringing first, of course, to make sure you haven't company as you put it," she said.

"I won't have company until you come back," he said.

She held out her hand. "I don't think I'll be back," she said.

"No, well, let's agree never say never." His grin was good-natured. He stood at the doorway as she walked down the road, her hands in the pockets of her jacket, her head down. She was lonely and lost. He wanted to run and swoop her back to him, but it was too soon.

And yet he had done what he had to do. There could have been no future for them at all if he had sat down behind Aidan's back and told the man's daughter what he didn't know himself. He wondered what a betting man would give as odds about her ever coming back to him. Fifty-fifty he decided.

Which were much more hopeful odds than anyone would get on whether the evening classes would succeed. That was a bet that no sane person would take. They were doomed before they even began.

SIGNORA

For years, yes years, when Nora O'Donoghue lived in Sicily, she had received no letter at all from home.

She used to look hopefully at *il postino* as he came up the little street under the hot blue sky. But there was never a letter from Ireland, even though she wrote regularly on the first of every month to tell them how she was getting on. She had bought carbon paper; it was another thing hard to describe and translate in the shop where they sold writing paper and pencils and envelopes. But Nora needed to know what she had told them already, so that she would not contradict herself when she wrote. Since the whole life she described was a lie, she might as well make it the same lie. They would never reply, but they would read the letters. They would pass them from one to the other with heavy sighs, raised eyebrows, and deep shakes of the head. Poor stupid, headstrong Nora who couldn't see what a fool she had made of herself, wouldn't cut her losses and come back home.

"There was no reasoning with her," her mother would say.

"The girl was beyond help and showed no remorse" would be her father's view. He was a very religious man, and in his eyes the sin of having loved Mario outside marriage was greater far than having followed him out to the remote village of Annunziata even when he had said he wouldn't marry her.

If she had known that they wouldn't get in touch at all, she would have pretended that she and Mario *were* married. At least her old father would have slept easier in his bed and not feared so much the thought of meeting God and explaining the mortal sin of his daughter's adultery.

But then she would not have been able to do that because Mario had insisted on being upfront with them.

"I would love to marry your daughter," he had said, with his big dark eyes looking from her father to her mother backward and forward. "But sadly, sadly it is not possible. My family want me very much to marry Gabriella and her family also want the marriage. We are Sicilians; we can't disobey what our families want. I'm sure it is very much the same in Ireland." He had pleaded for an understanding, a tolerance and almost a pat on the head.

He had lived with their daughter for two years in London. They had come over to confront him. He had been in his own mind admirably truthful and fair. What more could they want of him?

Well, they wanted him gone from her life, for one thing.

They wanted Nora to come back to Ireland and hope and pray that no one would ever know of this unfortunate episode in her life, or her marriage chances, which were already slim would be further lessened.

She tried to make allowances for them. It was 1969, but then they did live in a one-horse town; they even thought coming up to Dublin was an ordeal. What had they made of their visit to London to see their daughter living in sin, and then accept the news that she would follow this man to Sicily?

The answer was they had gone into complete shock and did not reply to her letters.

She could forgive them. Yes, part of her really did forgive them, but she could never forgive her two sisters and two brothers. They were young; they must have understood love, though to look at the people they had married you might wonder. But they had all grown up together, struggled to get out of the lonely, remote little town where they lived. They had shared the anxiety of their mother's hysterectomy, their father's fall on the ice that had left him frail. They had always consulted each other about the future, about what would happen if either Mam or Dad were left alone. Neither could manage. They had all agreed that the little farm would be sold and the money used to keep whoever it was that was left alive in a flat in Dublin somewhere adjacent to them all.

Nora realized that her having decamped to Sicily didn't suit that long-term plan at all. It reduced the help force by more than twenty percent. Since Nora wasn't married the others would have assumed that she might take sole charge of a parent. She had reduced the help force by one hundred percent. Possibly that was why she never heard from them. She assumed that they would write and tell her if either Mam or Dad was very ill, or even had died.

But then sometimes she didn't know if they would do that. She seemed so remote to them, as if she herself had died already. So she relied on a friend, a good, kind friend called Brenda, who had worked with her in the hotel business. Brenda called from time to time to visit the O'Donoghues. It was not difficult for Brenda to shake her head with them over the foolishness of their daughter Nora. Brenda had spent days and nights trying to persuade, cajole, warn, and threaten Nora about how unwise was her plan to follow Mario to his village of Annunziata and face the collective rage of two families.

Brenda would be welcome in that house because nobody knew she kept in touch and told the emigrant what was happening back home. So it was through Brenda that Nora learned of new nieces and nephews, of the outbuilding on the farmhouse, of the sale of three acres, and the small trailer that was now attached to the back of the family car. Brenda wrote and told her how they watched television a lot, and had been given a microwave oven for Christmas by their children. Well, by the children they acknowledged.

Brenda did try to make them write. She had said she was sure Nora would love to hear from them; it must be lonely for her out there. But they had laughed and said: "Oh, no, it wasn't at all lonely for Lady Nora, who was having a fine time in Annunziata, living the life of Riley with the whole place probably gossiping about her and ruining the repu-tation of all Irishwomen in front of these people."

Brenda was married to a man that they had both laughed at years back, a man called Pillow Case, for some reason they had all forgotten. They had no children and they both worked in a restaurant now. Patrick, as she now called Pillow Case, was the chef and Brenda was the manageress. The owner lived mainly abroad and was content to leave it to them. She wrote that it was as good as having your own place without the financial worries. She seemed content, but then perhaps she wasn't telling the truth either.

Nora certainly never told Brenda about how it had turned out; the years of living in a place smaller than the village she had come from in Ireland and loving the man who lived across the little piazza, a man who could come to visit her only with huge subterfuge, and as the years went on he made less and less effort to try to find the opportunities.

Nora wrote about the beautiful village of Annunziata and its white buildings where everyone had little black wrought-iron balconies and filled them with pots of geraniums or busy lizzies, but not just one or two pots like at home, whole clusters of them. And how there was a gate outside the village where you could stand and look down on the valley. And the church had some lovely ceramics that visitors were coming to visit more and more.

Mario and Gabriella ran the local hotel and they did lunches now for visitors and it was very successful. Everyone in Annunziata was pleased because it meant that other people, like wonderful Signora Leone who sold postcards and little pictures of the church, and Nora's great friends Paolo and Gianna, who made little pottery dishes and jugs with Annunziata written on them, made some money. And people sold oranges and flowers from baskets. And even she, Nora, benefited from the tourists since as well as making her lace-trimmed handkerchiefs and table runners for sale, she also gave little guided tours for English-speaking visitors. She took them round the church and told of its history, and pointed out the places in the valley where there had been battles and possibly Roman settlements and certainly centuries of adventure.

She never found it necessary to tell Brenda about Mario and Gabriella's children, five of them in all, with big dark eyes looking at her suspiciously with sullen downcast glances from across the piazza. Too young to know who she was and why she was hated and feared, too knowing to think she was just another neighbor and friend.

Since Brenda and Pillow Case didn't have any children of their own, they wouldn't be interested in these handsome, unsmiling Sicilian children who looked across from the steps of their family hotel at the little room where Signora sat sewing and surveying all that passed by.

That's what they called her in Annunziata, just Signora. She had said she was a widow when she arrived. It was so like her own name Nora anyway, she felt she had been meant to be called that always.

And even had there been anyone who truly loved her and cared about her life, how hard it would have been to try to explain what her life was like in this village. A place she would have scorned if it were back in Ireland, no cinema, no dance hall, no supermarket, the local bus irregular and the journeys when it did arrive positively endless.

But here she loved every stone of the place because it was where Mario lived and worked and sang in his hotel, and eventually raised his sons and daughters, and smiled up at her as she sat sewing in her window. She would nod at him graciously, not noticing as the years went by. And the passionate years in London that ended in 1969 were long forgotten by everyone except Mario and Signora.

Of course, Mario must have remembered them with love and longing and regret as she did, otherwise why would he have stolen into her bed some nights using the key that she had made for him. Creeping across the dark square when his wife was asleep. She knew never to expect him on a night there was a moon. Too many other eyes might have seen a figure crossing the piazza and known that Mario was wandering from the wife to the foreign woman, the strange foreign woman with the big wild eyes and long red hair.

Occasionally Signora asked herself was there any possibility that she *could* be mad, which was what her family at home thought and was almost certainly the view of the citizens of Annunziata.

❧

OTHER WOMEN WOULD surely have let him go, cried over the loss of his love and got on with their lives. She had only been twenty-four back in 1969 and she lived through her thirties, sewing and smiling and speaking Italian, but never in public to the man she loved. All that time in London when he had begged her to learn his language, telling her how beautiful it was, she had learned hardly a word, telling him that he was the one who must learn English so they could open a twelve-bedroom hotel in

Ireland and make their fortune. And all the time Mario had laughed and told her that she was his redheaded *principessa,* the loveliest girl in the world.

Signora had some memories that she did not run past herself in the little picture show of memories that she played in her mind.

She didn't think of the white-hot anger of Mario when she followed him to Annunziata and got off the bus that day, recognizing his father's little hotel immediately from the description. His face had hardened in a way that frightened her to think about. He had pointed to a van that was parked outside and motioned her to get in. He had driven very fast, taking corners at a terrible speed, and then turned suddenly off that road into a secluded olive grove where no one could see them. She reached for him, yearning as she had been yearning since she had set out on her journey.

But he pushed her away from him and pointed to the valley down below.

"See those vines, those belong to Gabriella's father, see the ones there, they belong to my father. It has always been known that we will marry. You have no right to come here like this and make things bad for me."

"I have every right. I love you, you love me." It had been so simple.

His face was working with the emotion of bewilderment. "You cannot say that I have not been honest, I *told* you this, I *told* your parents. I never pretended that I was not involved with and promised to Gabriella."

"Not in bed you didn't, you spoke of no Gabriella then," she had pleaded.

"Nobody speaks of another woman in bed, Nora. Be reasonable, go away, go home, go back to Ireland."

"I can't go home," Nora had said simply. "I have to be where you are. It's just the way things are. I will stay here forever."

And that was the way it was.

The years passed and by sheer grit Signora became a part of the life of Annunziata. Not really accepted, because nobody knew exactly why she was there and her explanation that she loved Italy was not considered enough. She lived in two rooms in a house on the square. Her rent was low because she kept an eye on the elderly couple who owned the house, brought them steaming cups of *caffè latte* in the morning, and did their shopping for them.

But she was no trouble. She didn't sleep with the menfolk or drink in the bars. She taught English in the little school every Friday morning. She sewed little fancies and took them every few months to a big town to sell them.

❧

SHE LEARNED ITALIAN from a little book and it became tattered as she went over and over the phrases, asking herself questions and answering them, her soft Irish voice eventually mastering the Italian sounds.

She sat in her room and watched the wedding of Mario and Gabriella, sewing all the time and letting no tear fall on the linen that she was embroidering. The fact that he looked up at her as the bells rang from the little campanile of the church in the square was enough. He was walking with his brothers and Gabriella's brothers to be married because it was their way. A tradition that involved families marrying each other to keep the land. It had nothing to do with his love for her or hers for him. That couldn't be affected by something like this.

And she watched from this window as his children were carried to the church to be christened. Families needed sons in this part of the world. It didn't hurt her. She knew that if he could have it another way then she would have been his *principessa irlandese* for all to see.

Signora realized that many of the men in Annunziata knew there was something between Mario and herself. But it didn't worry them, it made Mario more of a man than ever in their eyes. She always believed that the women knew nothing of their love. She never thought it odd that they didn't invite her to join them when they went to market together, or to gather the grapes that were not used for wine, or to pick the wild flowers for the festival. They were happy when she made beautiful clothes to deck the statue of Our Lady.

They smiled at her over the years as she stumbled through and then mastered their language. They had stopped asking her when she was going home, back to her island. It was as if they had been watching her and she had passed some test. She wasn't upsetting anyone, she could stay.

❧

AND AFTER TWELVE years she started hearing from her sisters. Inconse-
quential letters from Rita and Helen. Nothing that referred to anything
that *she* had written herself. No mention that they had heard from her
on birthdays and at Christmas and read all the letters she had written to
their parents. Instead they wrote about their marriages and their children
and how times were hard and everything was expensive and time was
short, and everything was pressure these days.

At first Signora was delighted to hear from them. She had long
wanted something that brought her two worlds together. The letters
from Brenda went a little way along the road but didn't connect with her
past, with her family life. She replied eagerly, asking questions about the
family and how her parents were, and had they become at all reconciled
to the Situation. Since this drew no response, Signora wrote different
kinds of questions seeking their views on subjects from the IRA hunger
strikers, to Ronald Reagan being elected president of America, and the
engagement of Prince Charles and Lady Di. None of these were ever
answered, and no matter how much she told them about Annunziata,
they never commented on it at all.

Brenda's note said she wasn't at all surprised by the arrival of letters
from Rita and Helen.

"Any day now you'll be hearing from the brothers as well," she
wrote. "The hard truth is that your father is very frail. He may have to
go into hospital on a permanent basis, and then what will become of
your mother? Nora, I tell you this harshly, because it is harsh and sad
news. And you know well that I think you were foolish to go to that
godforsaken spot on a mountain and watch the man who said he loved
you flaunt his family in front of you . . . but still by God I don't think
you should come home to be a minder to your mother who wouldn't
give you the time of day or even reply to your letters."

Signora read this letter sadly. Surely Brenda must be mistaken. And
surely she had read the situation all wrong. Rita and Helen were writing
because they wanted to keep in touch. Then came the letter saying that
Dad was going to hospital and wondering when Nora would come home
and take things over.

It was springtime and Annunziata had never looked more beautiful. But Signora looked pale and sad. Even the people who did not trust her were concerned. The Leone family who sold the postcards and little drawings called to see her. Would she like a little soup, *brodetto,* it was a broth with beaten egg and lemon juice? She thanked them, but her face was wan and her tone was flat. They worried about her.

Across the piazza in the hotel, the word reached dark, handsome Mario and Gabriella, his solid, dutiful wife, that Signora was not well. Perhaps someone should send for the *dottore.*

Gabriella's brothers frowned. When a woman had a mystery frailty in Annunziata, it often meant one thing: that she was pregnant.

The same thought had crossed Mario's mind. But he met their glances levelly. "Can't be that, she's nearly forty," he said.

Still, they waited for the doctor, hoping he would let fall some information over a glass of sambucca, which was his little weakness.

"It's all in the head," the doctor said confidentially. "Strange woman, nothing physical wrong with her, just a great sadness."

"Why does she not go home to where she comes from then?" asked the eldest brother of Gabriella. He was the head of the family since his father had died. He had heard the odd, troublesome rumor about his brother-in-law and Signora. But he knew it couldn't possibly be true. The man could not be so stupid as to do something like that right on his doorstep.

The people of the village watched as Signora's shoulders drooped, and not even the Leone family were able to throw any light on it. Poor Signora. She just sat there, her eyes far away.

One night when his family slept, Mario crept in and up the stairs to her bed.

"What has happened? Everyone says that you have an illness and that you are losing your mind," he said as he put his arms around her and pulled up the quilt that she had embroidered with the names of Italian cities: Firenze, Napoli, Milano, Venezia, Genova. All in different colors and with little flowers around them. It was a labor of love, she told Mario. When she did the stitching, she thought how lucky she was to have come to this land and to live near the man she loved; not everyone was as lucky as she was.

That night she didn't sound like one of the luckiest women in the world. She sighed heavily and lay like lead on the bed instead of turning to welcome Mario joyfully. She said nothing at all.

"Signora." He called her that too, like everyone else. It would have marked him out if he had uttered her real name. "Dear, dear Signora, many, many times I have told you to go away from here, that there is no life for you in Annunziata. But you insist that you stay and it is your decision. People here have begun to know and like you. They tell me you had the doctor. I don't want you to be sad, tell me what has happened."

"You know what has happened." Her voice was very dead.

"No what is it?"

"You asked the doctor. I saw him go into the hotel after he left me. He told you I am sick in the mind, that's all."

"But why? Why now? You have been here so long when you couldn't speak Italian, when you knew nobody? That was the time to be sick in the mind, not now when you have been ten years as a part of this town."

"Over eleven years, Mario. Nearly twelve."

"Yes, well, whatever."

"I am sad because I thought my family missed me and loved me, and now I realize that they just want me to be a nursemaid to my old mother." She never turned to look at him. She lay cold and dead without response to his touches.

"You don't want to be with me, happy like it always is and so good?" He was very surprised.

"No, Mario, not now. Thank you very, very much but not tonight."

He got out of bed and came around to look at her. He lit the candle in the pottery holder, her room did not run to a bedside light. She lay there white-faced, her long red hair on the pillow, under the absurd coverlet with all the cities' names on it. He was at a loss for words. "Soon you must do the places of Sicily," he said. "Catania, Palermo, Cefalù, Agrigento . . ."

She sighed again.

He left troubled. But the hills around Annunziata covered each day with new flowers had healing powers, and Signora walked among them until the color came back to her face.

The Leone family sometimes packed her a little basket with bread and cheese and olives, and Gabriella, the stony-faced wife of Mario, gave her a bottle of marsala, saying that some people drank it as a tonic. The

Leone family invited her to lunch on a Sunday and cooked pasta Norma, with aubergines and tomatoes.

"Do you know why it's called pasta Norma, Signora?"

"No, Signora Leone. I'm afraid I don't."

"Because it's so good it is reaching the same height of perfection as the opera *Norma* by Bellini."

"Who was, of course, Sicilian," Signora finished proudly.

They patted her hand. She knew so much about their country, their village. Who could fail to be delighted with her?

Paolo and Gianna, who had the little pottery shop, made her a special jug. They had written *Signora d'Irlanda* on it. And they put a little piece of gauze over it with beads at the edge. It was to keep her water fresh at night. No flies could get in, or dust in the hot summers. People came in and did little jobs for the old couple whose house she lived in, so that Signora would not have to worry about earning her rent. And, bathed in all this friendship and indeed love, she became well and strong again. And she knew she was loved here even if she wasn't loved back home in Dublin, where the letters were written with greater frequency wanting to know her plans.

She wrote back almost dreamily of life in Annunziata, and how she was so needed here, the old people upstairs who relied on her. The Leone family who fought so often and so volubly, she had to go to lunch there every Sunday to make sure they didn't kill each other. She wrote about Mario's hotel and how much it depended on tourism, so everyone in the village had to pull together to get the visitors to come. Her own job was to guide tourists around, and she had found a lovely place to take them on a little escorted walk, to a kind of ledge that looked down over the valleys and up at the mountain.

She had suggested that Mario's younger brother open a little cafe there. It was called Vista del Monte, mountain view . . . but didn't it sound so much more wonderful in Italian?

She expressed sympathy for her father, who now spent much of his time in hospital. How right it had been for them to sell the farm and move to Dublin. And for Mother, now struggling, they told her, to manage in a flat in Dublin. So often they had explained that the flat had an extra bedroom, and so often she ignored the information, only inquiring after her parents' health and wondering vaguely about the postal services, saying that she had written so regularly since 1969 and now here they were in the eighties and yet her parents had never been able to reply to a letter. Surely the only explanation was that all the letters must have gone astray.

Brenda wrote a letter of high approval.

"Good girl yourself. You have them totally confused. I'd say you'll have a letter from your mother within the month. But stick to your guns. Don't come home for her. She wouldn't write unless she had to."

The letter came and Signora's heart turned over at her mother's familiar writing. Yes, familiar even after all these years. She knew every word had been dictated by Helen and Rita.

It skated over twelve years of silence, of obstinate refusal to reply to the beseechings of her lonely daughter overseas. It blamed most of it on "your father's very doctrinaire attitudes to morality." Signora smiled wanly to herself at the phrase. If she were to look at a writing pad for a hundred years, her mother would not have come up with such an expression.

In the last paragraph the letter said: "Please come home, Nora. Come home and live with us. We will not interfere with your life but we need you, otherwise we would not ask."

And otherwise they would not have written, Signora thought to herself. She was surprised that she did not feel more bitter, but that had all passed now. She had been through it when Brenda had written saying how they didn't care about her as a person, only as someone who would look after elderly and unbending parents.

Here in her peaceful life she could afford to feel sorry for them. Compared to what she had in life, her own family had nothing at all. She wrote gently and explained that she could not come. If they had read her letters, they would realize how much she was needed here now. And that, of course, if they had let her know in the past that they wanted her as part of their life, then she would have made plans not to get so involved in the life of this beautiful, peaceful place. But, of course, how could she have known that they would call on her? They had never been in touch, and she was sure they would understand.

AND THE YEARS went on.

Signora's hair got streaks of gray in the red. But unlike the dark women who surrounded her it didn't seem to age her. Her hair just looked bleached by the sun. Gabriella looked matronly now. She sat at the desk of the hotel, her face heavier and rounder, her eyes much more beady than when they had flashed with jealousy across the piazza. Her sons were tall and difficult, no longer the little dark-eyed angels who did whatever they were asked to do.

Probably Mario had got older too, but Signora didn't see it. He came to her room . . . less frequently . . . and often just to lie there with his arm around her.

The quilt had hardly any space on it now for more cities. Signora had put in smaller places that appealed to her.

"You should not put Giardini-Naxos there among the big places, it's only a tiny place," Mario complained.

"No, I don't agree. When I went to Taormina I went out there on the bus, it was a lovely place . . . its own atmosphere, its own character, a lot of tourism. No, no, it deserves a place." And sometimes Mario would sigh heavily as if he had too many problems. He told her his worries. His second boy was wild. He was going to New York, aged only twenty. He was too young, he would get in with all the wrong people. No good would come of it.

"He's in with all the wrong people here," Signora said soothingly. "Possibly in New York he will be more timid, less assured. Let him go with your blessing because he'll go anyway."

"You are very, very wise, Signora," he said, and lay with his head tucked companionably on her shoulder.

She didn't close her eyes, she looked at the dark ceiling and thought of the times in this room when he had told her she was foolish, the most foolish, stupid woman in the world, to have followed him here. Here where there was no future for her. And the years had turned it all into wisdom. How strange the world was.

And then the daughter of Mario and Gabriella became pregnant. The boy was not at all the kind of husband they would have wanted for her, a boy from the countryside who washed pots in the kitchen of the hotel in the piazza. Mario came and cried in her room about this, his daughter, a child, a little child herself. The disgrace, the shame.

It was 1994, she told him. Even in Ireland it was no longer a disgrace and a shame. It was the way life went on. You coped with it. Perhaps the boy could come and work in Vista del Monte, expand it a little, then he would be seen to have his own place.

That was her fiftieth birthday, but Signora didn't tell Mario, she didn't tell anyone. She had embroidered herself a little cushion cover with *Buon' Compleanno,* Happy Birthday, on it. She fingered it when Mario had gone, his tears for his defiled daughter dried. "I wonder am I really mad as I feared all those years ago."

She watched from her window as the young Maria was married to the boy who worked in the kitchen, just as she had watched Mario and Gabriella go to the church. The bells of the campanile were still the same, ringing over the mountain the way bells should ring.

Imagine being in her fifties. She didn't feel a day older than she had when she came here. She didn't have a single regret. Were there many people in this or any other place who could say the same?

And, of course, she had been right in her predictions. Maria was married to the man who was not worthy of her and her family, but the loss was made up by the boy's having to work night and day in Vista del Monte. If people might have gossiped about it, it was only for a few days.

And their second son, the boy who was wild, went to New York, and the news was that he was as good as gold. He was working in his cousin's trattoria and saving money every week for the day when he would buy his own place back home on the island of Sicily.

SIGNORA ALWAYS SLEPT with her window on the square slightly open, so she was one of the first to hear the news when the brothers of Gabriella, thickset men, middle-aged now, came running from their cars. First she heard them wake the *dottore* in his house. Signora stood in the shadows of her shutter and watched. There had been an accident, that much was obvious.

She peered to see what had happened. Please God may it not be one of their children. They had already had too many problems with that family.

And then she saw the solid figure of Gabriella on the doorstep, in her nightdress, with a shawl around her shoulders. Her hands were to her face and the sky was rent apart by her cries.

"*Mario, Mario . . .*"

The sound went up into the mountains around Annunziata and down into the valleys.

And the sound went into Signora's bedroom, and chilled her heart as she watched them lift the body out of the car.

She didn't know how long she stood there, like stone. But soon, as the square filled up in the moonlight with his family and neighbors and friends, she found herself among them, the tears flowing unchecked. She saw his face with the bloodstains and the bruising. He had been driving home from a village not far away. He had missed a corner. The car had turned over many times.

She knew she must touch his face. Nothing would ever settle down in the world unless she touched him, kissed him even as his sisters and children and wife were doing. She moved toward him, unaware of anyone looking at her, forgetful entirely of the years of secrecy and covering up.

When she was quite near him, she felt hands reaching out to her and keen bodies in the crowd pulled her back. Signora Leone, her friends the pottery makers Paolo and Gianna, and, strange as it seemed even afterward, two of the brothers of Gabriella. They just moved her away, back from where the eyes of Annunziata would see her naked grief and the memories of the village would store yet one more amazing happening, the night when the *Signora irlandese* broke down and admitted in public her love for the man who ran the hotel.

She was in houses that night where she had never been before, and people gave her strong brandy to drink and someone stroked her hand. Outside the walls of these houses she could hear the wailing and the prayers, and sometimes she stood to go and stand at her rightful place by his body, but always gentle hands held her back.

On the day of his funeral, pale and calm she sat at her window, her head bowed as they carried his coffin out from the hotel and across the square to the church with the frescoes and ceramics. The bell was one lonely, mournful sound. Nobody looked up at her window. Nobody saw the tears fall down her face and splash onto the embroidery that lay in her lap.

And after that they all assumed that she should now be leaving, that it was time for her to go home.

Little by little she realized it. Signora Leone would say: "Before you go back you must come once with me to the great passion procession in my hometown Trapani . . . you will be able to tell the people back in Ireland about it all."

And Paolo and Gianna gave her a big plate they had made specially for her return. "You can put on it all the fruits that are grown in Ireland and the plate will remind you of your time in Annunziata." They seemed to think that this is what she would do.

But Signora had no home to go to, she didn't want to move. She was in her fifties, she had lived here since before she was thirty. This is where she would die. One day the churchbell here would ring for her funeral, too, she had money to pay for it all ready in a little carved wooden box.

So she took no notice of the hints that were getting heavier, and the advice that was trembling on lips waiting to be given.

Not until Gabriella came to see her.

Gabriella crossed the square in her dark mourning clothes. Her face looked old, as if it was set in lines of grief and sorrow. She had never come to Signora's rooms before. She knocked on the door as if she had been expected. Signora fussed to make her guest welcome, offering her a little fruit juice and water, a biscuit from the tin. Then she sat and waited.

Gabriella walked around the two small rooms. She fingered the coverlet on the bed with all its intricately woven place names.

"It's exquisite, Signora," she said.

"You are too kind, Signora Gabriella."

Then there was a long silence.

"Will you go back soon to your country?" Gabriella asked eventually.

"There is nobody for me to go back to," Signora said simply.

"But there is nobody here, nobody that you should want to stay for. Not now." Gabriella was equally direct.

Signora nodded as if to agree. "But in Ireland, Signora Gabriella, there is nobody at all. I came here when I was a young girl, now I am a woman, middle-aged, about to approach the beginning of old age. I thought I would stay here." Their eyes met.

"You do not have friends here, not a real life, Signora."

"I have more than I have in Ireland."

"You could pick up a life again in Ireland. Your friends there, your family, would be happy to see you return."

"Do you want me to go away from here, Signora Gabriella?" The question was very straight. She just wanted to know.

"He always said you would go if he were to die. He said you would go back to your people and leave me here with my people to mourn my husband."

Signora looked at her in amazement. Mario had made this promise on her behalf, without any guarantee. "Did he say that I had agreed to do this?"

"He said it was what would happen. And that if I, Gabriella, were to die, he told me that he would not marry you, because it would cause a scandal and my name would be lessened. They would think that always he had wanted to marry you."

"And did this please you?"

"No, these things didn't please me, Signora. I didn't want to think of Mario dead, or of my being dead. We are young people. But I suppose it gave me the dignity that I need. I didn't need to fear you. You would not stay on here against the tradition of the place and share in the mourning for the man who was gone."

The sounds of the square went on outside, meat deliveries to the hotel, a van of clay supplies being carried into the pottery shop, children coming home from school laughing and calling to each other. Dogs barking, and somewhere birds singing too. Mario had told her about dignity and tradition and how important they were to him and his family.

It was as if he were speaking to her now from the grave. He was sending her a message, asking her to go home.

She spoke very slowly. "I think at the end of the month, Signora Gabriella. That is when I will go back to Ireland."

The other woman's eyes were full with gratitude and relief. She reached out both her hands and took Signora's. "I am sure you will be much happier, much more at peace," she said.

"Yes, yes," Signora said slowly, letting the words hang there in the warm afternoon air.

"*Sì sì . . . veramente.*"

❧

SHE ONLY BARELY had the money for the fare. Somehow her friends knew this.

Signora Leone came and pressed the bundles of lire into her hand. "Please, Signora. Please. It's thanks to you I have such a good living, please take it."

It was the same with Paoulo and Gianna. Their pottery business would not have got started if it had not been for Signora. "Regard it as a tiny commission."

And the old couple who owned the room where she had lived most of her adult life. They said she had improved the property so well, she deserved some compensation.

On the day that the bus came to take her with her belongings to the town with the airport, Gabriella came out on her steps. She didn't speak and neither did Signora, but they bowed to each other. Their faces were grave and respectful. Some of those who watched the little scene knew what was being said. They knew that one woman was thanking the other with all her heart in a way that could never be put into words, and wishing her good fortune in whatever lay ahead.

❧

IT WAS LOUD and crowded in the city, and the airport was full of noise and bustle, not the happy, easy bustle of Annunziata but people rushing without meeting each other's gaze. It would be like this in Dublin, too, when she got back there, but Signora decided not to think about it.

She had made no plans, she would just do what seemed the right thing to do when she got there. No point in wasting her journey planning what could not be planned. She had told no one that she was coming. Not her family, not even Brenda. She would find a room and look after herself as she had always done, and then she would work out what to do next.

On the plane she began talking to a boy. He was about ten, the age of Mario and Gabriella's youngest son, Enrico. Automatically she spoke to him in Italian but he looked away confused.

Signora looked out the window. She would never know what would happen to Enrico, or his brother in New York, or his sister married to the kitchen help and up in Vista del Monte. She would not know who came to live in her room. And whoever it was would never know of her long years there, and why she had spent them.

It was like swimming out to sea and not knowing what would happen where you had left and what was going to happen where you would arrive.

She changed planes in London. She had no wish to spend any time there. Not to visit the old haunts where she had lived with Mario in a different life. Not to look up people long forgotten, and places only barely remembered. No, she would go on to Dublin. To whatever lay ahead.

IT HAD ALL changed so much. The place was much, much bigger than she remembered. There were flights arriving from all over the world. When she had left, most of the big international flights had gone in and out of Shannon Airport. She hadn't known that things would be so different. Like the road in from the airport. When she had left, the bus had wound its way out through housing estates, now it came in on a motorway with flowers planted on each side. Heavens, how Ireland was keeping up with the times!

An American woman on the bus asked her where she was staying.

"I'm not absolutely sure," Signora explained. "I'll find somewhere."

"Are you a native or a visitor?"

"I came from here a long time ago," Signora said.

"Same as me . . . looking for ancestors." The American woman was pleased. She was giving a week to find her roots, she thought that should be long enough.

"Oh definitely," Signora said, realizing how hard it was to find instantly the right response in English. She had been about to say *certo*.

How affected it would sound breaking into Italian, they would think she was showing off. She must watch for it.

Signora got out of her bus and walked up the quays beside the Liffey to O'Connell Bridge. All around her there were young people, tall, confident, laughing, in groups. She remembered reading somewhere about this youthful population, half the country under the age of twenty-four, was it?

She hadn't expected to see such proof of it. And they were dressed brightly too. Before she had gone to England to work, Dublin had been a gray and drab place. A lot of the buildings had been cleaned, there were smart cars, expensive cars in the busy traffic lanes. She remembered more bicycles and secondhand cars. The shops were bright and opened up. Her eye caught the magazines, girls with big bosoms, surely these had been banned when she was last here or was she living in some kind of cloud-cuckoo-land?

For some reason she kept walking down the Liffey after O'Connell Bridge. It was almost as if she were following the crowd, and there she found Temple Bar. It was like the Left Bank in Paris, when once she had gone there so many years ago with Mario for a long weekend. Cobbled streets, outdoor cafes, each place full of young people calling to each other and waving at those they knew.

Nobody had told her Dublin was like this. But then would Brenda, married to Pillow Case and working in a much more settled kind of place, have even visited these streets?

Her sisters and their hard-up husbands, her two brothers and their inert wives . . . they were not people who'd have discovered Temple Bar. If they knew of it, then it would be surely only to shake their heads.

Signora thought it was wonderful. It was a whole new world, she couldn't get enough of it. Eventually she sat down to have a coffee.

A girl of about eighteen with long red hair, like her own many years ago, served her coffee. She thought Signora was a foreigner.

"What country are you from?" she asked in slow English, mouthing the words.

"Sicilia, in Italia," Signora said.

"Beautiful country but I tell you I'm not going there again until I can speak the language though."

"And why is that?"

"Well, I'd want to know what the fellows are saying, I mean you wouldn't know what you were letting yourself in for if you didn't know what they were saying."

"I didn't speak any Italian when I went there, and I sure didn't know what I was letting myself in for," Signora said. "But you know it worked out all right . . . no, more than all right. It was wonderful."

"How long did you stay for?"

"A long time. Twenty-six years." Her voice sounded wondering.

The girl, who wasn't born when she had set out on this adventure, looked at her in amazement. "You stayed all that time, you must have loved it."

"Oh, I did, I did."

"And when did you come back?"

"Today," Signora said.

She sighed heavily and wondered had she imagined that the girl looked at her slightly differently, as if she had somehow revealed herself to be a little strange. Signora knew she must watch that she didn't let people think that. No letting Italian phrases fall, no sighing, no saying strange, disconnected things.

The girl was about to move away.

"Excuse me, this seems a very nice part of Dublin. Is this the kind of place I could rent a room, do you think?" Now the girl knew she was odd. Perhaps people didn't call them rooms anymore. Should she have said apartment? flat? place to stay? "Just somewhere simple," Signora said.

She listened glumly as she learned that this was one of the most fashionable parts of town; everyone wanted to live here. There were penthouse apartments, pop stars had bought hotels, business people had invested in town houses. The place was coming down with restaurants. It was the last word now.

"I see." Signora did see something, she saw she had a lot to learn about the city she had returned to. "And please could you tell me where *would* be a place that would be good value to stay, somewhere that hadn't become the last word?"

The girl shook her head of long, dark red hair. It was hard to know. She seemed to be trying to work out whether Signora had any money at all, whether she would have to work for her keep, how long she would perch in wherever she landed.

Signora decided to help her. "I have enough money for bed and breakfast for a week, but then I'll have to find a cheap place and maybe somewhere I could do some jobs . . . maybe mind children."

The girl was doubtful. "They usually want young ones to mind kids," she said.

"Or maybe over a restaurant and work in it?"

"No, I wouldn't get your hopes up over that honestly . . . we all want those kinds of places. They're very hard to get."

She was nice, the girl. Her face was pitying, of course, but Signora would have to get used to a lot of that in what lay ahead. She decided to be brisk to hide her messiness, anything to make her acceptable and not to appear like a doddery old bag lady.

"Is that your name there on your apron? Suzi?"

"Yes. I'm afraid my mother was a Suzi Quatro fan." She saw the blank look. "The singer, you know? She was big years ago, maybe not in Italy."

"I'm sure she was, it's just that I wasn't listening then. Now, Suzi, I can't take up your day with all my problems, but if you could give me just half a minute I'd love you to tell me what area would be a nice cheap one where I should start looking."

Suzi listed off the names of places that used to be small areas, suburbs if not exactly villages, well outside the city when Signora was young, but now apparently they were big, sprawling working-class estates. Half the people there would take someone in to rent a room if their kids had left home maybe. As long as it was cash. It wouldn't be wise to mention that she herself was badly off. Be fairly secretive about things, they liked that.

"You're very good to me, Suzi. How do you know all about things like this at your age?"

"Well, that's where I grew up, I know the scene."

Signora knew she must not tire the patience of this nice child. She reached for her purse to get out the money for the coffee.

"Thank you very much for your help . . . I do appreciate it. And if I do get settled I'll come in and give you a little gift."

She saw Suzi pause and bite her lip as if to decide something.

"What's your name?" Suzi asked.

"Now I know this sounds funny but my name is Signora. It's not that I'm trying to be formal, but that's what they called me and what I like to be called."

"Are you serious about not minding what kind of a place it is?"

"Absolutely serious." Her face was honest. It was quite clear that Signora couldn't understand people who cared about their possessions.

"Listen. I don't get on with my family myself, so I don't live at home anymore. And only a couple of weeks ago they were talking about trying to get someone to take my room. It's empty, and they could well do with a few pounds a week, it would have to be cash you know and you'd have to say you were a friend in case anyone asked . . . because of income tax."

"Do you think I could?" Signora's eyes were shining.

"Listen, now." Suzi was anxious there should be no misunderstandings. "We're talking about a very ordinary house in an estate of houses that look the same, some a bit better, some a bit worse . . . it wouldn't be gracious or anything. They have the telly on all the time, they shout to each other over it and of course my brother's there, Jerry. He's fourteen and awful."

"I just need a place to stay. I'm sure it would be lovely."

Suzi wrote down the address and told her which bus to take. "Why don't you go down their road and ask a few people who I know definitely won't be able to have you and then go by chance as it were to my house and ask. Mention the money first and say it won't be for long. They'd like you because you're a bit older like, respectable is what they'll say. They'll take you, but don't say you came from me."

Signora gave her a long look. "Did they not like your boyfriend?"

"Boyfriends," Suzi corrected her. "My father says I'm a slut, but please don't try to deny it when he tells you because it will show you've met me." Suzi's face looked hard.

Signora wondered had her own face been hard like that when she set out for Sicily all those years ago.

⁓

SHE TOOK THE bus and wondered at how the city she had once lived in had grown and spread so wide. In the evening light children played in the streets among the traffic, and then they went farther afield, in where there were small gardens and children cycled round in circles, leaning on gates and running in and out of each other's gardens.

Signora called at the houses that Suzi had suggested. Dublin men and women told her that their houses were full and they needed all the space they had.

"Can you suggest anyone?" she asked.

"Try the Sullivans," someone suggested.

Now she had her reason. She knocked on the door. Would this be her new home? Was this the roof she would lie under and hope to ease the pain of losing her life in Annunziata? Not only the man she loved but her whole life, her future, her burial with the bells ringing for her. Everything. She must not try to like it in case they said no.

Jerry opened the door, his mouth was full. He had red hair and freckles and he had a sandwich in his hand.

"Yeah?" he said.

"Could I speak to your mother or your father please?"

"What about?" Jerry asked.

This was a household where he had obviously welcomed in people who should not have been welcomed in the past.

"I was wondering if I could rent a room," Signora began. She knew that inside they had turned down the television to hear what was happening on the doorstep.

"A room *here*?" Jerry was so utterly disbelieving that Signora thought maybe he was right, it did seem a foolish notion. But then her life had been based on a series of foolish notions. Why stop now?

"So perhaps I could talk to them?"

The boy's father came to the door. A big man with tufts of hair on each side of his head, looking like handles that he could be lifted by. He was about Signora's age, she supposed, but red-faced and as if the years had taken their toll. He was wiping his hands down the sides of his trousers, as if about to shake hands.

"Can I help you?" he said suspiciously.

Signora explained that she had been looking for a place in the area, and that the Quinns in number 22 had sent her over here in case they might have a spare room. She sort of implied that she had known the Quinns; it gave her an introduction.

"Peggy, will you come out here?" he called. And a woman with tired, dark shadows under her eyes and straight hair pushed behind her ears came out smoking and coughing at the same time.

"What is it?" she asked unwelcomingly.

It was not very promising, but Signora told her tale again.

"And what has you looking for a room up in this area?"

"I have been away from Ireland for a long time, I don't know many places now but I do need somewhere to live. I had no idea that things had become so expensive and . . . well . . . I came out this way because you can see the mountains from here," she said.

For some reason this seemed to please them. Maybe it was because it was so without guile.

"We never had boarders," the woman said.

"I would be no trouble, I would sit in my room."

"You wouldn't want to eat with us?" The man indicated a table with a plate of very thick, unappetizing sandwiches, butter still in its foil paper, and the milk still in the bottle.

"No, no thank you so much. Suppose I were to buy an electric kettle, I eat mainly salads, and I suppose I could have an electric ring thing. You know, to heat up soups?"

"You haven't even seen the room," the woman said.

"Can you show it to me?" Her voice was gentle but authoritative.

Together they all walked up the stairs, watched by Jerry from below.

It was a small room with a handbasin. An empty wardrobe and an empty bookcase, no pictures on the walls. Not much memory of the years that the beautiful, vibrant Suzi with her long dark red hair and her flashing eyes had spent in this room.

Outside the window it was getting dark. The room was at the back of the house. It looked out over wasteland that would soon be more houses, but at the moment there was nothing between her and the mountain.

"It's good to have a beautiful view like this," Signora said. "I have been living in Italy, they would call this Vista del Monte, mountain view."

"That's the name of the school the young lad goes to, Mountainview," said the big man.

Signora smiled at him. "If you'll have me, Mrs. Sullivan, Mr. Sullivan
. . . I think I've come to a lovely place," she said.

She saw them exchange glances, wondering was she cracked in the
head, were they wise to let her into the house.

They showed her the bathroom. They would tidy it up a bit, they said,
and give her a rack for her towel.

∽

THEY SAT DOWNSTAIRS and talked, and it was as if her very gentleness
seemed to impose more manners on them. The man cleared the food
away from the table, the woman put out her cigarette and turned off the
television. The boy sat in the far corner watching with interest.

They explained that there was a couple across the road who made a
living out of informing the tax offices on other people's business, and if
she did come, she would have to be a relation so that the busybodies
couldn't report there was a paying guest contributing to the household
expenses.

"A cousin maybe." Signora seemed excited at the thought of the subterfuge.

She told them she had lived long years in Italy, and having seen several pictures of the Pope and the Sacred Heart on the walls, she added
that her Italian husband had died there recently and she had come home
to Ireland to make her life here.

"And have you no family here?"

"I do have some relations. I will look them up in time," said Signora,
who had a mother, a father, two sisters, and two brothers living in this
city.

They told her that times were hard and that Jimmy worked as a
driver, freelance sort of. Hackney cabs, vans, whatever was going, and
that Peggy worked in the supermarket at the checkout.

And then the conversation came back to the room upstairs.

"The room belonged to someone else in the family?" Signora inquired
politely.

They told her of a daughter who preferred to live nearer the city. Then
they talked of money, and she showed them her wallet. She had five
weeks rent. Would they like a month in advance? she wondered.

They looked at each other, the Sullivans, faces anxious. They were suspicious of unworldly people like this who showed you their entire wallet.

"Is that all you have in the world?"

"It's all I have now but I will have more when I get some work." Signora seemed unruffled by the thought of it. They were still uneasy. "Perhaps I could step outside while you talk it over," she said, and went out to the back garden, where she looked at the distant, faraway mountains that some people called hills. They weren't rugged and sharp and blue like her mountains were back in Sicily.

People would be going about their business there in Annunziata. Would any of them wonder about Signora and where she was going to lay her head tonight?

THE SULLIVANS CAME to the door, their decision made.

"I suppose, being a bit short and everything, you'll want to stay immediately, if you are going to be here that is?" said Jimmy Sullivan.

"Oh, tonight would be great," Signora said.

"Well, you can come for a week and if you like us and we like you we can talk about it being for a bit longer," Peggy said.

Signora's eyes lit up. *"Grazie, grazie,"* she said before she could help herself. "I lived there so long, you see," she said apologetically.

They didn't mind, she was obviously a harmless eccentric.

"Come on up and help me make the bed," Peggy said.

Young Jerry's eyes followed them wordlessly.

"I'll be no trouble, Jerry," Signora said.

"How did you know I was called Jerry?" he asked.

Surely his parents must have spoken to him. This was a slipup, but Signora was used to covering her tracks. "Because it's your name," she said simply.

And it seemed to satisfy him.

Peggy got out sheets and blankets. "Suzi had one of those candlewick bedspreads but she took it with her when she went," Peggy said.

"Do you miss her?"

"She comes round once a week, but usually when her father's out.

They never saw eye to eye, not since she was about ten years of age. It's a pity but that's the way it is. Better for her to live on her own rather than all the barneys they had here."

Signora unpacked the coverlet with all the Italian place names embroidered on it. She had wrapped it in tissue paper and had used it to keep her jug safe. She had brought few possessions with her, she was happy to unpack them so that Peggy Sullivan could see how blameless and innocent was her lifestyle.

Peggy's eyes were round with amazement.

"Where on earth did you get that, it's beautiful." She gaped.

"I made it myself over the years, adding names here and there. Look there's Rome, and that's Annunziata, the place I lived."

Peggy's eyes had tears in them. "And you and he lay under this . . . how sad that he died."

"Yes, yes it was."

"Was he sick for a long time?"

"No, killed in an accident."

"Do you have a picture of him, to put up here maybe?" Peggy patted the top of the chest of drawers.

"No, I have no pictures of Mario, only in my heart and mind."

The words hung there between them.

Peggy Sullivan decided to talk of something else. "I tell you if you can do sewing like that it won't be long till you get a job. Anyone would take you on."

"I never thought of earning my living by sewing." Signora's face was far away.

"Well, what were you going to take up?"

"Teaching maybe, being a guide. I used to sell little embroidered things, fine-detailed work for tourists in Sicily. But I didn't think they'd want them here."

"You could do shamrocks and harps, I suppose," Peggy said. But neither of them liked the thought of it very much. They finished the room. Signora hung up her few garments and seemed well pleased with it all.

"Thank you for giving me a new home so quickly. I was just saying to your son I'll be no trouble."

"Don't mind him, he's trouble enough for us all, bone-idle lazy. He has our hearts broken. At least Suzi's bright, that fellow will end in the gutter."

"I'm sure it's just a phase." Signora had talked like this to Mario about his sons, soothing, optimistic. It was what parents wanted to hear.

"It's a long phase if that's what it is. Listen, will you come down and have a drink with us before you go to bed?"

"No, thank you. I'll start as I mean to go on. I'm tired now. I'll sleep."

"But you don't even have a kettle to make yourself a cup of tea."

"Thank you, truly I am fine."

Peggy left her and went downstairs. Jimmy had a sports program on television. "Turn it down a bit, Jimmy. The woman's tired, she's been traveling all day."

"God Almighty, is it going to be like when those two were babies, shush this and shush that?"

"No it's not, and you're as anxious for her money as I am."

"She's as odd as two left shoes. Did you get anything out of her at all?"

"She says she was married and her husband was killed in an accident. That's what she says."

"And you don't believe her, obviously?"

"Well, she has no picture of him. She doesn't *look* married. And she's got this thing on the bed. It's like a priest's vestment, a quilt. You'd never have time to do that if you were married."

"You read too many books and see too many films, that's your trouble."

"She is a bit mad though, Jimmy, not the full shilling."

"She's hardly an ax murderer, is she?"

"No, but she might have been a nun, she has that sort of still way about her. I'd say that's what she was. Is, even. You never know these days."

"It could be." Jimmy was thoughtful. "Well, in case she *is* a nun don't be too free with telling her all that Suzi gets up to. She'd be out of here in a flash if she knew how that young rossie that we reared carries on."

SIGNORA STOOD AT her window and looked across the waste ground at the mountains.

Could this place ever be her home?

Would she give in when she saw a mother and father more frail and dependent than when she had left? Would she forgive their slights and their coldness, the lack of response once they knew she was not going to run home obediently and do the single daughter's duty for them?

Or would she stay in this small shabby house with noisy people banging around downstairs, a sullen boy, a disaffected daughter? Signora knew she *would* be kind to this family, the Sullivans, whom she had never met before this day.

She would try to bring about a reconciliation between Suzi and her father. She would find some way to interest the sullen child in his work. In time she would hem the curtains, she would mend the frayed cushions in the sitting room, and put ribbon on the edges of the towels in the bathroom. But she would do it slowly. Her years in Annunziata had taught her patience.

She would not go tomorrow and look at her mother's house or visit the home where her father lived.

She would, however, go to see Brenda and Pillow Case and she would remember to refer to him as Patrick. They would be even more pleased to see her once they realized she had found herself accommodation and was about to look for work. Maybe they might even have something in their restaurant. She could wash up and prepare vegetables in the kitchen, like the boy who had married Mario's daughter.

Signora washed and undressed. She put on the white nightdress with the little rosebuds she had embroidered around the neckline. Mario had said he loved it; she remembered his hands stroking the rosebuds before he would stroke her.

Mario, asleep now in a graveyard that looked out over the valleys and mountains. He had known her well in the end, known she would follow his advice after his death even though she had not done so in his lifetime. Still, all in all he was probably glad she had stayed, glad she had come and lived in his village for twenty-six years, and he would be glad to know that she had left as he wanted her to do, to give his widow dignity and respect.

She had made him happy so often under this very quilt and wearing this very nightdress. She had made him happy by listening to his worries, stroking his head, and giving him gentle thoughts and suggestions. She listened to the strange unfamiliar dogs barking and the children shouting to each other.

Soon she would sleep and tomorrow her new life would start.

BRENDA ALWAYS WALKED through the dining room of Quentin's at midday. It was a routine. In a nearby church the Angelus rang over a Dublin that rarely paused to acknowledge it by saying prayers these days, as people had done when Brenda was a young girl. She wore a plain-colored dress always with a crisp clean white collar. Her makeup was freshly applied, and she checked each table carefully. The waiters knew they might as well get it right in the beginning because Brenda had such high standards. Mr. Quentin, who lived abroad, always said that his name was good in Dublin entirely due to Brenda and Patrick, and Brenda wanted to keep it that way.

Most of the staff had been there for a while; they knew each other's ways and worked well as a team. There were regular customers, who all liked to be addressed by name, and Brenda had stressed how important it was to remember small details about the customers. Had they enjoyed their holiday? Were they writing a new book? Glad to see their photograph in the *Irish Times*, nice to hear their horse won at the Curragh.

Although her husband, Patrick, thought that they came for the food, Brenda knew that their clientele came to be welcomed, and to be made much of as well. She had spent too many years being nice to people who were nobodies, watching them turn into somebodies and always remembering the flattering reception they got in Quentin's. This was the basis of the regular lunch trade, even when economic times were meant to be hard and belts were reported to be in need of tightening.

Brenda adjusted the flowers on a table by the window and heard the door opening. Nobody came to lunch at this time. Dubliners were late lunch-eaters anyway, and Quentin's never saw anyone until well after twelve-thirty.

The woman came in hesitantly. She was about fifty or maybe more, long hair streaked in gray but with the remains of red in it, and it was tied back loosely with a colored scarf. She wore a long brown skirt almost to her ankles and an old-fashioned jacket, like people wore way back in the seventies. She was neither shabby nor smart, she was just totally different. She was about to approach Nell Dunne, already seated in her place at the cash desk, when Brenda realized who she was.

"Nora O'Donoghue!" she called out excitedly. It had been a lifetime since she had seen her friend. The young waiters and Mrs. Dunne at the desk looked surprised to see Brenda, the impeccable Brenda Brennan, running across to embrace this unlikely-looking woman. "My God, you actually left that place, you actually got on a plane and came home."

"I came back, yes," Signora said.

Suddenly Brenda looked worried. "It's not . . . I mean your father didn't die or anything?"

"No, not that I know of."

"So you haven't gone back to them?"

"Oh no. No, not at all."

"Great, I knew you wouldn't give in. And tell me, how's the love of your life?"

And then Signora's face changed. All the color and life seemed to go out of it. "He's dead, Brenda. Mario died. He was killed on the road, on a corner. He's in a churchyard in Annunziata now."

Even saying it had drained her; she looked as if she were about to faint. In forty minutes the place would fill up. Brenda Brennan had to be out there, the face of Quentin's, not crying with a friend over a lost love. She thought quickly. There was one booth that she usually reserved for lovers, or people having discreet lunches. She would take it for Nora. She led her friend to the table, and called for a large brandy and a glass of iced water. One of them would surely help.

With a practiced eye and hand she changed the reservation list, and asked Nell Dunne to photocopy the new version.

Nell was almost too interested in events. "Is there anything at all we can do to help . . . the situation, Ms. Brennan?"

"Yes, thank you, Nell. Photocopy the new seating plan, make sure the waiters have it and that there's a copy in the kitchen. Thank you." She was brisk and barely courteous. Sometimes Nell Dunne annoyed her, although she never knew quite why.

And then Brenda Brennan, who was known as the Ice Maiden by staff and customer alike, went into the booth and cried tears with her friend over the death of this man Mario whose wife had crossed the square to tell Nora to go home to where she belonged.

It was a nightmare and yet it was a love story. Brenda wondered wistfully for a while what it must have been like to have loved like this, so wildly and without care for the consequences, without planning for the future.

The guests wouldn't see Signora in her booth any more than they ever saw the government minister and his lady friend who often dined there, or the head-hunters lunching a likely candidate from another company. It was safe to leave her there alone.

Brenda dried her eyes, touched up her makeup, straightened her collar, and went to work. Signora, peering around from time to time, saw with amazement her friend Brenda escorting wealthy, confident people to tables, asking them about their families, their business deals . . . And the prices on the menu! It would have kept a family for a whole week in Annunziata. *Where* did these people get the money?

"Chef has some very fresh brill today which he recommends highly, and there's a medley of wild mushrooms . . . but I'll leave it with you and Charles will come and take your order when you're ready."

How had Brenda learned to talk like this, to refer to Pillow Case as Chef in some kind of awe, to hold herself so straight? To be *so* confident? While Signora had lived striving to be deferential, to find a background to live in, other people had been putting themselves forward. This is what she would have to learn in her new life. If she was to survive.

Signora blew her nose and straightened herself up. She didn't hunch over the table anymore, looking at the menu with frightened eyes. Instead she ordered a tomato salad followed by beef. It had been *so* long since she had eaten meat. Her budget hadn't run to it, and probably would not ever run to it again. She closed her eyes feeling almost faint at the prices on the menu, but Brenda had insisted. Have what she liked, this was her welcome-home lunch. Without her asking for it a bottle of Chianti appeared. Signora steeled herself not to look it up on the price list. It was a gift and she would accept it as such.

Once she began to eat, she realized just how hungry she was. She'd had hardly anything to eat on the plane, she was too excited, nervous rather. And then last night at the Sullivans' she had not eaten. The tomato salad was delicious. Fresh basil sprinkled over the plate. When had they heard about things like this in Ireland? The beef was served rare, the vegetables crisp and firm, not soft and swimming in water the way she had thought all vegetables used to be before she learned how to cook them properly.

When she had finished, she felt much stronger.

"It's all right, I won't cry again," she said when the lunchtime crowd had left and Brenda slid in opposite her.

"You're not to go back to your mother, Nora. I don't want to come between families, but really and truly she was never a mother to you when you needed it, why should you be a daughter to her now when she needs it."

"No, no I don't feel any sense of duty about it at all."

"Thank God, for that," Brenda said, relieved.

"But I will need to work, to earn a living, to pay my way. Do you need anyone here to peel potatoes, clean up or anything?"

Gently Brenda told her friend that it wouldn't work out, and they had youngsters, trainees. They had been themselves trainees all those years ago. Before . . . well, before everything changed.

"Anyway, Nora, you're too old to do that, you're too well trained. You can do all kinds of things, work in an office, teach Italian maybe."

"No, I'm too old, that's the problem. I never used a typewriter, let alone a computer. I don't have any qualifications to teach."

"You'd better sign on to get some money, anyway." Brenda was always practical.

"Sign on?"

"For the dole, for unemployment benefit."

"I can't do that, I'm not entitled."

"Yes, you are. You're Irish, aren't you?"

"But I lived away for so long, I contributed nothing to the country." She was adamant.

Brenda looked worried. "You can't start being like Mother Teresa here, you know. This is the real world, you have to look to yourself and take what's being offered."

"Brenda, don't worry about me, I'm a survivor. Look what I survived for a quarter of a century. Most people would not have done that. I found a place to live within hours of coming back to Dublin. I'll find a job too."

Signora was brought into the kitchen to meet Pillow Case, whom she managed to call Patrick with difficulty. He was courteous and grave as he welcomed her back and sympathized formally on the death of her husband. Did he think Mario really had been her husband or was it just for appearances in front of these young people who watched him with reverence?

Signora thanked them for the delicious meal and said she would return to eat there again under her own steam.

"We are going to have an Italian season of cooking soon. Perhaps you would translate the menus for us?" Patrick suggested.

"Oh I'd be delighted." Signora's face lit up. This would go some way toward paying for a meal that would have cost more than she could hope to earn in two weeks.

"It would be all done officially, for a fee and everything," Patrick insisted. How had the Brennans become so smooth and sophisticated? Offering her money without being seen to give her a handout.

Signora's will strengthened even further. "Well, we'll discuss that when the time comes. I won't delay you and I'll be in touch next week to tell you my progress." She left swiftly without protracted good-byes. That was something she had learned over the years in her village. People liked you more if you didn't stay on interminably, if they realized that a conversation was going to have an end.

She bought tea bags and biscuits, and as a luxury a cake of nice soap.

She asked several restaurants for kitchen work and was politely refused everywhere. She tried a supermarket for shelf stacking and newsagents for a job as an assistant or someone to open the piles of papers and magazines for them. She felt that they looked at her puzzled. Sometimes they asked her why she wasn't going through the job centre, and she looked at them with vague eyes that confirmed their view that she might be a bit simple.

But she did not give in. Until five o'clock she sought work. Then she took a bus to where her mother lived. The flats were in their own grounds, raised flower beds with little bushes and ground cover provided the landscaping as it was called. A lot of the doors had ramps as well as steps. This was a development, purpose built for the needs of the elderly.

With mature trees and bushes around it and built in red brick, it looked solid and safe, something that would appeal to those who had sold their family homes to end their days here.

Signora sat quietly hidden by a large tree. She held her paper bag of possessions on her lap and watched the doorway of number 23 for what must have been a long time. She was so used to being still, she never noticed time pass. She never wore a watch, so time and its passing were not important to her. She would watch until she saw her mother, if not today then another day, and once she saw her then she would know what to do. She could make no decision until she had seen her mother's face. Perhaps pity would be uppermost in her heart, or love from the old days, or forgiveness. Perhaps she might see her mother only as another stranger and one who had spurned love and friendship in the past.

Signora trusted feelings. She knew she would know.

Nobody went in or out of number 23 that evening. At ten o'clock Signora gave up her post and took a bus back to the Sullivans'. She let herself in quietly and went upstairs, calling good night into the room where the television blared. The boy, Jerry, sat with them watching. No wonder the child didn't pay much attention at school if he was up till all hours watching westerns.

They had found her an electric ring and an old kettle. She made herself tea and looked out at the mountains.

Already in thirty-six hours there was a little veil in her mind over the memory of Annunziata and the walk out to Vista del Monte. She wondered would Gabriella ever be sorry that she had sent Signora away. Would Paolo and Gianna miss her? Would Signora Leone wonder how her friend the Irishwoman was faring far across the sea? Then she washed with the nice soap that smelled of sandalwood, and slept. She didn't hear the sound of the gunfights in the saloons or the flight of the covered wagons. She slept long and deeply.

When she got up, the house was empty. Peggy gone to her supermarket, Jimmy out on a driving job, and Jerry putting in the day at his school. She set out on her journey. This time she would target her mother's home for a morning stakeout. She would look for jobs later on. Again she sat behind her familiar tree, and this time she didn't have long to wait. A small car drew up outside number 23 and a matronly woman, thickset with very tightly permed red hair, got out. With a gasp she realized this was her younger sister, Rita. She looked so settled in her ways, so middle-aged even though she must only be forty-six. She had been a girl when Signora left, and of course there had been no photograph, any more than there had been warm family letters in the meantime. She must remember that. They only wrote when they needed her, when the comfort of their own lives seemed bigger than the effort of getting in touch with the madwoman who had disgraced herself by fleeing to Sicily to follow a married man.

Rita looked stiff and tense.

She reminded Signora of Gabriella's mother, a small, angry woman whose eyes darted around her seeing faults everywhere but not being able to define them. She was meant to suffer with her nerves, they said. Could this really be Rita, her little sister, this woman with shoulders hunched, with feet squashed into shoes that were too tight, taking a dozen short fussy steps when four would have done? Signora watched aghast from behind her tree. The door of the car was open, she must be going in to collect Mother. She braced herself for the shock. If Rita looked old, what must Mother be like now?

She thought of the old people in Annunziata. Small, bent often over sticks, sitting out in the square watching people go by, always smiling, often touching her skirt and looking at the embroidery . . . *"Bella bellissima,"* they would say.

Her mother would not be like that. Her mother was a well-preserved seventy-seven. She wore a brown dress and brown cardigan over it. Her hair was pulled back as it had always been into that unfashionable bun Mario had commented on all those years ago. "Your mother would be handsome if she let her hair be more free."

Imagine, her mother then must have been only a little older than she was now. So hard, so set in her ways, so willing to go along with the religious line although she did not feel it in her heart. If her mother had just stood up for her, things would have been different. For years Signora could have had a lifeline to home, and she might well have come back and looked after them even in the country, the small farm that they hated leaving.

But now? They were only yards away from her . . . she could have called out and they would have heard.

She saw Rita's body stiffen still further in irritation and resentment as their mother scolded. "All right, all *right*. I'm getting in, no need to rush me. You'll be old one day yourself, you know." There was no pleasure at seeing each other, no gratitude for the lift to the hospital, no shared solidarity or sympathy about going to see an old man who could no longer live at home.

This must be Rita's day, the next one would be Helen's, and the sisters-in-law must do a small amount of the joyless transporting and minding. No wonder they wanted the madwoman back from Italy. The car drove off with the two stern figures upright in it, not talking to each other, animatedly or at all. How had she learned to love so much, Signora wondered, coming as she did from such a loveless family. It had indeed made up her mind for her. Signora walked out of the neatly landscaped gardens, her head held high. It was clear to her now. She would have no regret, no residual guilt.

❧

THE AFTERNOON WAS as dispiriting as the previous one in terms of job hunting but she refused to let it get her down. When her journeying brought her toward the River Liffey again, she sought out the coffee shop where Suzi worked. The girl looked up, pleased.

"You actually went there! My mam told me they had got a lodger out of a clear blue sky."

"It's very nice, I wanted to thank you."

"No it's not very nice but it'll tide you over."

"I can see the mountains from your bedroom."

"Yeah, and about twenty tons of waste earth waiting for more little boxes to be built on it."

"It's just what I need, thank you again."

"They think you might be a nun, are you?"

"No, no. Far from a nun I'm afraid."

"Mam says you say your husband died."

"In a sort of a way that's true."

"He sort of died . . . is that what you mean?"

Signora looked very calm; it was easy to see why people might mistake her for a nun. "No, I meant that in a sort of a way he was my husband, but I didn't see any need to explain all that to your mother and father."

"No need at all, much wiser not to," Suzi said, and poured her a cup of coffee. "On the house," she whispered.

Signora smiled to herself, thinking that if she played her cards right she might be able to eat for nothing all around Dublin. "I had a free lunch in Quentin's; I am doing well," she confided to Suzi.

"That's where I'd love to work," Suzi said. "I'd dress up in black trousers just like the waiters. I'd be the only woman apart from Ms. Brennan."

"You know of Ms. Brennan?"

"She's a legend," said Suzi. "I want to work with her for about three years, learn everything there is to know, then open my own place."

Signora gave a sigh of envy. How great to think this was possible, rather than a further series of refusals as a washer-up. "Tell me why can't I get a job, just an ordinary job cleaning, tidying up, anything. What's wrong with me? Is it just that I'm too old?"

Suzi bit her lip. "I think it's that you look a bit too good for the jobs you're looking for. Like, you look a bit too smart for staying in my parents' house, it makes people uneasy. They might think that it's a bit odd. And they're afraid of odd people."

"So what should I do, do you think?"

"Maybe you should aim for something a bit higher up, like a receptionist or maybe . . . my mam says you've an embroidered bedspread that would take the sight out of your eyes. Maybe you could take that to a shop and show them. You know, the right kind of shop."

"I wouldn't have the confidence."

"If you lived with a fellow out in Italy at your age, a fellow that wasn't your husband, you've all the confidence that it needs," said Suzi.

And they made a list of the designers and fashion shops where really top-market embroidery might find a home. As she watched Suzi sucking the pencil to think of more places to write down, Signora felt a huge fantasy flood over her. Maybe some day she might bring this lovely girl back with her to Annunziata, say that she was her niece, they had the same red hair. She could show the people there she had a life in Ireland and let the Irish know she was a person of importance in Italy. But it was only a dream, and there was Suzi talking about her hair.

"I have this friend who works in a real posh place cutting hair and they need guinea pigs on training nights. Why don't you go down there? You'll get a great styling for only two pounds. It costs you twenty . . . thirty times that if you went for real."

Could people really pay sixty pounds to have their hair cut? The world had gone mad. Mario had always loved her long hair. Mario was dead. He had sent her a message telling her go back to Ireland, he would expect her to cut her hair if it was necessary to do so. "Where is this place?" Signora asked, and took down the address.

❧

"JIMMY, SHE'S CUT her hair," whispered Peggy Sullivan.

Jimmy was listening to an in-depth interview with a soccer manager. "Yeah, great," he said.

"No honestly, she's not what she pretends, I saw her coming in. You wouldn't know her, she looks twenty years younger."

"Good, good." Jimmy raised the volume a bit, but Peggy took the control and turned it down.

"Have some respect. We're taking the woman's money, we don't have to deafen her as well."

"All right, but hush talking."

Peggy sat brooding. This Signora, as she called herself, was very odd altogether. No one could be as simple as she was and survive. No one with that little money could get a haircut that must have cost a fortune. Peggy hated mysteries and this was a very deep mystery indeed.

❧

"YOU'LL HAVE TO forgive me if I take my bedspread with me today. I didn't want you to think I was taking away all the furnishings or anything," Signora explained to them at their breakfast next morning. "You see, I think people are a bit confused by me. I have to show them that I can do *some* kind of work. I got my hair cut in a place that needed people to experiment on. Do you think it makes me look more ordinary?"

"It's very nice indeed, Signora," said Jimmy Sullivan.

"It looks most expensive, certainly." Peggy approved.

"Is it dyed?" asked Jerry with interest.

"No, it's got henna in it, but they said it was an unusual color already, like a wild animal," Signora said, not at all offended by Jerry's question or the verdict of the young hairdressers.

❧

IT WAS PLEASING that everyone liked her work so much and admired the intricate stitching and the imaginative mingling of place names with flowers. But there were no jobs. They said they would keep her name on file and were surprised by the address, as if they thought she would live somewhere more elegant. It was a day of refusals like other days, but somehow they seemed to be given with more respect and less bewilderment. Dress designers, boutiques and two theater companies looked at her handwork with genuine interest. Suzi had been right that she should aim high.

Could she dare try to be a guide or a teacher as she had done so confidently for half her adult life in a Sicilian village?

❧

SHE GOT INTO the habit of talking to Jerry in the evenings.

He would come and knock on her door. "Are you busy, Mrs. Signora?"

"No, come in, Jerry. It's nice to have company."

"You could always come downstairs, you know. They wouldn't mind."

"No, no. I rented a room from your parents, I want them to like having me here in the house, not living on top of them."

"What are you doing, Mrs. Signora?"

"I'm making little baby dresses for a boutique. They told me they would take four. They have to be good because I spent some of my savings on the material, so I can't afford for them not to take them."

"Are you poor, Mrs. Signora?"

"Not really, but I don't have much money." It seemed quite a natural, reasonable answer. It satisfied Jerry totally. "Why don't you bring your homework up here, Jerry?" she suggested. "Then you could be company for me and I could give you a hand if you needed it."

◇

THEY SAT TOGETHER all through the month of May, chatting easily. Jerry advised her to make five baby dresses and pretend she thought they'd ordered five. It had been great advice, they took all five and wanted more.

Signora showed huge interest in Jerry's homework. "Read me that poem again, let's see what does it mean?"

"It's only an old poem, Mrs. Signora."

"I know, but it must mean *something*. Let's think." Together they would recite: " 'Nine bean-rows will I have there.' I wonder why he wanted nine."

"He was only an old poet, Mrs. Signora. I don't suppose he knew what he wanted."

" 'And live alone in the bee-loud glade.' Imagine that, Jerry. He only wanted to hear the sound of the bees around him, he didn't want the noise of the city."

"He was old, of course," Jerry explained.

"Who was?"

"Yeats, you know, who wrote the poem."

◇

LITTLE BY LITTLE she made him interested in everything.

She pretended her own memory was bad. As she sewed she asked him to say it to her over and over. So Jerry Sullivan learned his poetry, wrote his essays, attempted his maths. The only thing he was remotely interested in was geography. It had to do with a teacher, Mr. O'Brien. He was a great fellow apparently. Mr. O'Brien used to teach about river beds and soil strata and erosion and a rake of things, but he always expected you to know it. The other teachers didn't expect you to, that was the difference.

"He's going to be the head, you know, next year," Jerry explained.

"Oh. And are people in Mountainview school pleased about that?"

"Yeah, I think so. Old Walsh was a terrible bollocks."

She looked at him vaguely, as if she didn't understand the word. It worked every time.

"Mr. Walsh, the old fellow who's head at the moment, he's not good at all."

"Ah I see."

Jerry's language had improved beyond all recognition, Suzi reported to Signora. And what was more, some teacher at school had said that his work had taken a turn for the better as well. "It's they should be paying you," Suzi said. "You're like a private governess. Isn't it a pity you couldn't get a job teaching."

"Your mother's asking me to tea on Thursday so that I can meet you," Signora said. "I think Jerry's teacher is calling then too. She probably wanted a bit of support."

"He's a real lady's man, Tony O'Brien is. I've heard a tale or two about him, you'd want to watch yourself there, Signora. With your smart new hairdo and all he could have his way with you."

"I'm not ever going to be interested in a man again." She spoke simply.

"Oh, I said that after the second-last fellow, but suddenly the interest came back."

❦

THE TEA PARTY began awkwardly.

Peggy Sullivan was not a natural hostess, so Signora took over the conversation, gently, almost dreamily talking about all the changes in Ireland she noticed and most of them were for the better. "The schools are all so bright and cheerful nowadays, and Jerry tells me of the great projects you do in geography class. We had nothing like that when I was at school."

And after that everything thawed. Peggy Sullivan had seen the visit of the schoolteacher as a possible list of complaints against her son. She hadn't hoped that her daughter and Signora would get on so well. Or that Jerry would actually tell Mr. O'Brien that he was doing a project on place names, trying to find out why all the streets around here were called what they were. Jimmy came home in the middle of it all, and

Signora explained that Jerry was lucky to have a father who knew the city so well, he was better than any map.

They talked like a normal family. More polite than many Tony O'Brien had visited. He had always thought young Jerry Sullivan was part of the group for whom there was no hope. But this odd, unsettling woman who seemed to have taken over the household obviously had a good effect on the kid too.

"You must have loved Italy to stay there so long."

"I did, very, very much."

"I've never been there myself, but a colleague of mine above in the school, Aidan Dunne, now he'd live, sleep, and breathe Italy to you if you let him."

"Mr. Dunne, he teaches Latin," Jerry said in a glum voice.

"Latin? You could learn Latin, Jerry." Signora's eyes lit up.

"Oh it's only for brainy people, ones going on to university to be lawyers and doctors and things."

"No, it's not." Signora and Tony O'Brien spoke at the same time.

"Please . . ." He motioned her to speak.

"Well, I wish I had learned Latin because it's sort of the root of all other languages, like French and Italian and Spanish. If you know the Latin word you know where everything comes from." She spoke enthusiastically.

Tony O'Brien said: "God you really should meet Aidan Dunne, that's what he's been saying for years. I like kids to learn it because it's logical. Like doing a crossword, trains them to think and there's no problem with an accent."

When the teacher had gone, they all talked together eagerly. Signora knew that Suzi would come home a little more regularly now, and wouldn't have to avoid her father. Somehow fences had been mended.

❧

SIGNORA MET BRENDA for a walk in Stephen's Green. Brenda brought stale bread for the ducks and they fed them together, peaceable in the sunshine.

"I go to see your mother every month, will I tell her you're home?" Brenda asked.

"What do you think?"

"I think no, but then that's just because I'm still afraid you'll go and live with her."

"You don't know me at all. I am as hard as hell. Do you like her as a person? Truthfully now?"

"No, not very much. I went to please you in the beginning and then I got sucked into it because she seems so miserable, complaining about Rita and Helen and the awful daughters-in-law as she calls them."

"I'll go and see her. I won't have you trying to cover over for me."

"Don't go, you'll give in."

"Believe me, that will not happen."

SHE CALLED ON her mother that afternoon. Just went and rang on the bell of number 23.

Her mother looked at her confused. "Yes?" she said.

"I'm Nora, Mother. I've come to visit you."

No smile, no arms outstretched, no welcome. Just hostility in the small brown eyes that looked back at her. They stood almost frozen in the doorway. Her mother had not moved back to let her enter, and Nora would not ask could she come in.

But she did speak again. "I came to see how you are and to ask whether Daddy would like me to go and see him in the home or not. I want to do what's best for everyone."

Her mothers lip curled. "When did you ever want to do what was best for anyone except yourself?" she said. Signora stood calm in the doorway. It was at times like this that her habit of stillness came into its own. Eventually her mother moved back into the apartment. "Come in as you're here," she said ungraciously.

Signora recognized a few, but not many, pieces from her home. There was a cabinet, where the good china and the few small bits of silver were kept. You could hardly see into it years ago, any more than you could see now. There were no pictures on the wall, or books on the bookshelf. A big television set dominated the room, a bottle with orange squash stood on a tin tray on the dining table. There were no flowers, no sign at all of any enjoyment of life. Her mother did not offer her a seat, so

Signora sat at the dining table. She wondered had it known many meals served on it, but then she was not in a position to criticize. For twenty-six years she had lived in rooms where nobody was entertained to a dinner. Maybe it ran in the family.

"I suppose you'll want to smoke all over the place."

"No, Mother. I never smoked."

"How would I know what you do or don't do?"

"Indeed, Mother, how would you?" Her voice was calm, not challenging.

"And are you home on a holiday or what?"

In the level voice that was driving her mother mad, Signora explained that she had come home to live, that she had found a room and some small sewing jobs. She hoped to get further work to keep herself. She ignored her mother's scornful sniff at the area where she was living. She paused then and waited politely for some reaction.

"And did he throw you out in the end, Mario or whatever his name is?"

"You know his name was Mario, Mother. You met him. And no he didn't throw me out. If he were alive I would still be there. He was killed very tragically, Mother, I know you'll be sorry to hear, in an accident on a mountain road. So then I decided to come home and live in Ireland." Again she waited.

"I suppose they didn't want you there in that place once he wasn't there to protect you, is that what happened?"

"No, you're wrong. They wanted what was best for me, all of them."

Her mother snorted again. The silence hung between them.

Her mother couldn't take it. "So you're going to live with these people up in that tough estate, full of the unemployed and criminals, rather than with your own flesh and blood. Is this what we are to expect?"

"It's very kind of you to offer me a home, Mother, but we have been strangers for too long. I have developed my little ways and I am sure you have yours. You didn't want to know about my life, so I would only bore you talking about it, you made that clear. But perhaps I can come and see you every now and then, and tell me if Father would like me to visit or not."

"Oh, you can take your talk of visits with you when you go. None of us want you and that is a fact."

"I would hate to think that. I tried to keep in touch with everyone. I wrote letter after letter. I know nothing about my six nieces and five nephews. I would love to get to know them now that I am home."

"Well, none of them want anything to do with you, I can tell you that, half cracked as you were thinking you can come back here and take up as if nothing has happened. You could have turned out a somebody. Look at that friend of yours, Brenda, a nice groomed person, married and a good job and all. *She's* the kind of girl any woman would like as a daughter."

"And of course you have Helen and Rita," Signora added. There was a half snort this time, showing that they had been less than totally satisfactory. "Anyway, Mother, now that I'm back perhaps I could take you out somewhere for a meal sometimes, or we could go into town for afternoon tea. And I'll inquire at the home whether Father would like a visit or not."

There was a silence. It was all too much for her mother to take in. She had not given her address, just the area. Her sisters could not come and track her down. She felt no qualms. This was not a woman who had loved her or thought of her welfare, not at any time during the long years she had pleaded for friendship and contact.

She stood up to leave.

"Oh, you're very high and mighty. But you're a middle-aged woman, don't think any man in Dublin will have you after all you've been through. I know there's divorce and all now for all it broke your father's heart, but still you wouldn't find many men in Ireland willing to take on a fifty-year-old woman like yourself, another man's leavings."

"No indeed, Mother, so it's just as well I don't have any plans in that direction. I'll write you a little note and come and see you in a few weeks time."

"Weeks?" her mother said.

"Yes indeed, and maybe I'll bring along a cake or a cherry log from Bewleys with me and we could have tea. But we'll see. And give my warmest wishes to Helen and Rita, and tell them I'll write to them too."

She was gone before her mother could realize it. She knew she would be on the phone to one of her daughters within minutes. Nothing as dramatic as this had happened in years.

SHE FELT NO sadness. That was all over long ago. She felt no guilt. Her only responsibility now was to keep herself sane and strong and self-employed. She must not learn to be dependent on the Sullivan family, no matter how attracted she felt to their handsome daughter and protective of their surly son. She must not be a burden to Brenda and Patrick, who were obviously the success story of their generation in Dublin, and she could not rely on the boutiques that would give her no guarantees that they could sell her intricate embroidery.

She must get a teaching job of some sort. It didn't matter that she had no real qualifications, at least she knew how to teach Italian to beginners. Had she not taught herself? Perhaps this man up in Jerry's school, the one that Tony O'Brien said was a lover of Italy . . . He might know some group, some little organization that could do with Italian lessons. It didn't matter if it wasn't well paid, she would love to be speaking that beautiful language again . . . letting it roll around her tongue.

What was his name? Mr. Dunne? That was it. Mr. Aidan Dunne. Nothing could be lost by asking, and if he loved Italian, he would be on her side already.

She took the bus to the school. What a different place to her own Vista del Monte, where the summer flowers would be cascading down the hills already. This was a concrete yard, a shambles of a bicycle shed, litter everywhere, and the whole building needed badly to be painted. Why couldn't they have had some greenery growing over the walls?

Signora knew that a community school or college or whatever it was did not have any funds or legacies or donations to make the place more stylish. But really, was it any wonder that children like Jerry Sullivan didn't feel any great sense of pride in their school?

"He'd be in the staff room," a group said when she asked for Mr. Dunne, the Latin teacher.

She knocked on the door and a man came to answer it. He had thinning brown hair and anxious eyes. He was in his shirtsleeves, but she could see his jacket hanging on a chair behind him. It was lunch hour and all the other teachers were obviously out, but Mr. Dunne seemed to be guarding the fort. Somehow she had thought he would be an old man. Something to do with teaching Latin possibly. But he looked only around her own age or younger. Still, by today's standards that *was* old, much nearer to retirement than starting out.

"I've come to talk to you about Italian, Mr. Dunne," she said.

"Do you know I *knew* some day someone would knock at the door and say that to me," Aidan Dunne said.

They smiled at each other, and it was quite clear that they were going to be friends. They sat in the big, untidy staff room that looked out on the mountains, and they talked as if they had known each other always. Aidan Dunne explained about the evening class that was his heart's desire, but said he had got terrible news that very morning. The funding had not been passed by the authorities. They would never now be able to afford a qualified teacher. The new principal-elect had promised a small sum from his own funds, but that would go to do up the classrooms and get the place ready. Aidan Dunne said that his heart had been low in case the whole project might have to be scrapped, but now he felt a glimmer of hope again.

Signora told how she had lived so long in the Sicilian hills and that she could teach not just the language but perhaps something of the culture as well. Could there be a class on Italian artists and sculptors and frescoes, for example, that would be three topics, and then there could be Italian music, and opera and religious music. And then there could be wines and food, you know the fruits and vegetables and the *frutti del mare,* and really there was so much as well as the conversation and the holiday phrases, so much to add to the grammar and the learning of the language itself.

Her eyes were bright, she looked a younger woman than the tall person with anxious eyes who had stood at the door. Aidan heard the swelling sounds of children's voices in the corridor. It meant that the lunch hour was nearly over. The other teachers would be in soon, the magic would end.

She seemed to understand this without his saying it. "I'm staying too long, you have work to do. But do you think we might talk of it again?"

"We get out at four o'clock. Now I sound like the children," Aidan said.

She smiled at him. "That's what must be wonderful about working in a school, you are always young and think like the children."

"I wish it were always like that," Aidan said.

"When I taught English in Annunziata I used to look at their faces and I might think . . . they don't know something but when I have finished they will know it. It was a good feeling."

He was admiring her openly now, this man struggling into his jacket to go back to the classroom. It had been a long time since Signora had felt herself admired. In Annunziata they respected her in some strange way. And, of course, Mario had loved her, there was no question of that. He had loved her with all his heart. But he had never admired her. He had come to her in the dark. He had held her body to him and he had told her his worries, but there had never been a look of admiration in his eyes.

Signora liked it, as she liked this good man struggling to share his own love of another land with the people hereabouts. His fear was that they didn't have enough money for leisure-time education themselves to make such a study worthwhile.

"Will I wait outside the school for you?" she asked. "We could talk more then after four o'clock."

"I wouldn't want to keep you," he began.

"I have nothing else to do." She had no disguises.

"Would you care to sit in our library?" he asked.

"Very much."

He walked her along the corridor as crowds of children shoved past them. There were always strangers in a big school like this, a new face wasn't interesting enough to make them look twice. Except, of course, for young Jerry Sullivan, who did a double take.

"Jesus, Signora . . ." he said in amazement.

"Hallo, Jerry," she said pleasantly, as if she were here in this school the whole time.

She sat in the library reading through what they had in their Italian section, mainly secondhand books obviously bought with his own money by Aidan Dunne. He was such a kind man, an enthusiast, perhaps he could help her. And she could help him. For the first time since she had come back to Ireland, Signora felt relaxed, not just holding on by her fingernails. She stretched and yawned in the summer sunshine.

Even though she was going to teach Italian, she felt sure of it, she didn't think of Italy. She thought of Dublin, she wondered where they would find the people to attend the class. She and Mr. Dunne. She and Aidan. She pulled herself together a little. She must not be fanciful. That had been her undoing, people said. She was full of mad notions and didn't see reality.

Two hours had passed and Aidan Dunne stood at the door of the big room. He was smiling all over his face. "I don't have a car," he said. "I don't suppose you do?"

"I've barely my bus fare," Signora said.

BILL

Life would have been much easier, Bill Burke thought, if only he could have been in love with Grania Dunne.

She was about his own age. She came from a normal kind of home, her father was a teacher up in Mountainview school, her mother worked in the cash desk of Quentin's restaurant. She was good-looking and easy to talk to.

They used to grumble together about the bank sometimes, and wonder how it was that greedy, selfish people always got on well. Grania used to ask about his sister, and give him books for her. And perhaps Grania might have loved him, too, if things only had been different.

It was easy to talk about love to a good friend who understood. Bill understood when Grania told him about this very old man she just couldn't get out of her mind even though she had tried and tried. He was as old as her own father, and smoked and wheezed and would probably be dead in a couple of years the way he went on, but she had never met anyone who attracted her so much.

She couldn't possibly get together with him because he had lied to her and not told her that he was going to be principal of the school when he knew all along. And Grania's father would have a stroke and drop dead if he knew that she had been seeing this Tony O'Brien and even slept with him. Once.

She had tried going out with other people, but it just hadn't worked. She kept thinking about him and the way the lines came out from the sides of his eyes when he smiled. It was so unfair. What part of the human mind or body was so inefficient that it could make you think you loved someone so wildly unsuitable.

Bill agreed in the most heartfelt way possible. He, too, was a victim of this unsuitable streak. He loved Lizzie Duffy, the most improbable person in the world. Lizzie was a beautiful, troublesome bad debt, who had broken every rule and was still somehow allowed more credit than any customer in this or any branch.

Lizzie loved Bill too. Or *said* she did, or *thought* she did. She said she had never met anyone so serious and owlish and honorable and silly in her whole life. And, indeed, compared to Lizzie's other friends, he was all of these things. Most of them just laughed at nothing and had very little interest in getting or keeping jobs, but a huge interest in travel and having fun. It was idiotic loving Lizzie.

But Bill and Grania told each other seriously over coffee that if life was all about loving suitable people, then it would be both very easy and very dull.

Lizzie never asked about Bill's big sister, Olive. She had met her, of course, once when she came to visit. Olive was slow, that was all, just slow. She didn't have any disease or illness that had a name. She was twenty-five and she behaved as if she were eight. A very nice eager eight.

Once you knew this there was no problem with Olive. She would tell you stories from books like any eight-year-old, she would be enthusiastic about things she had seen on television. Sometimes she was loud and awkward, and because Olive was big she knocked things over. But there were never any scenes or moods with Olive, she was interested in everything and everyone and thought that there was nobody on earth like her family. "My mother makes the best cakes in the world," she would tell people, and Bill's mother, who had never done more than decorate a bought sponge cake, would smile proudly. "My father runs the big supermarket," Olive said, and her father, who worked at the bacon counter there, smiled indulgently.

"My brother Bill's a bank manager" was the one that got a wry smile from Bill, and indeed Grania, when he told her. "That'll be the day," he said.

"You don't want it, it will only show you've given in, compromised," Grania said encouragingly.

Lizzie shared Olive's view. "You must rise high in banking," she said to Bill often. "I can only marry a successful man, and when we are twenty-five and get married you'll have to be well on your way to the top."

Even though it was said with Lizzie's wonderful sparkling laugh showing all her tiny white teeth, and a toss of the legendary blond curls, Bill knew that Lizzie meant it. She said she could never marry a failure; it would be so cruel, because she would just drag them both down. But she would seriously consider marrying Bill in two years time when they were both a quarter of a century old, because she would be getting past her sell-by date then and it would be time to settle down.

Lizzie had been refused a loan because she had not repaid the first one, her Visa card had been withdrawn and Bill had seen letters go out to her saying: "Unless you lodge by five o'clock tomorrow the bank will have no option . . ." But somehow the bank always found an option. Lizzie would arrive tearful on some occasions, brimming with confidence and a new job on others. She never went under. And always she was entirely unrepentant.

"Oh for heaven's sake, Bill, banks don't have a heart or a soul. They only want to make money and not to risk losing money. They are the enemy."

"They're not my enemy," Bill said. "They're my employers."

"Lizzie don't," he would say despairingly as she would order another bottle of wine. Because he knew that she didn't have the money to pay for it, he would have to, and it was becoming increasingly difficult. He wanted to contribute at home; his salary was so much better than his father's wages, and they had sacrificed a lot to give him the kind of start he had got. But with Lizzie it was impossible to save. Bill had wanted to buy a new jacket, but it was out of the question. He wished Lizzie would stop talking about a holiday, there literally wasn't the money for one.

And how was he meant to put aside the money to be wealthy at the age of twenty-five so that he and Lizzie could get married?

Bill was hoping it would be a warm summer. Lizzie might just about tolerate staying in Ireland if the sun shone. But if it was overcast and all her friends were talking about this Greek island, that Greek island, and how cheap it was to live in Turkey for a month, then she would become very restless indeed. Bill could not get a loan from the bank he worked in. It was a diamond-hard rule. But of course it was always possible elsewhere. Possible and highly undesirable. He wondered if he was a mean man. He thought not, but then who really knew what they were like themselves.

"I suppose we are only what other people think we are," he said to Grania at coffee.

"I don't think so, that would mean we might be acting the whole time," she said.

"Do I look like an owl?" he asked.

"Of course not." Grania sighed. She had been through this before.

"It's not even as if I wore glasses," Bill complained. "I suppose I have a round face and sort of straight hair."

"Owls don't have hair at all, they have feathers," Grania said.

This only served to confuse Bill further. "Then what makes them think I'm like one?" he said.

There was a lecture that evening at the bank on opportunities. Grania and Bill sat together. They heard of courses and schemes, and how the bank wanted the staff to specialize in different areas, and how the world was open to bright young men and women with a command of languages and different skills and training. The salary working abroad would, of course, be greater since it would include an overseas allowance. The opportunities would present themselves in a year and interested staff were advised to prepare themselves well in advance since the competition would be keen.

"Are you going to apply for any course?" Bill asked.

Grania looked troubled. "There are ways I want to, because it might get me out of here, get me away from chances of seeing Tony O'Brien. But then I don't want to be thinking about him in some other part of the world. What's the point of that? I might as well be miserable here where I know what he's up to than in some far-off place where I don't."

"And he wants you back?" Bill had heard the story many times.

"Yes, he sends me a postcard every week to the bank. Look, here's this week's one." Grania took out a picture of a coffee plantation. On the back were three words: *Still waiting, Tony.*

"He doesn't *say* very much," Bill complained.

"No, but it's a kind of series," Grania explained. "There was one that said 'Still brewing,' and another that said 'Still hoping.' It's a message that he's leaving it all up to me."

"Is it a code?" Bill was bewildered.

"It's a reference to the fact that I said I wouldn't go back to him unless he bought a proper coffee percolator."

"And he did?"

"Yes, of course he did, Bill. But that wasn't the point."

"Women are very complicated." Bill sighed.

"No they're not. They're perfectly ordinary and straightforward. Not necessarily little Miss Retail Therapy that you've got yourself involved with, but most of us are."

Grania thought that Lizzie was hopeless. Bill thought that Grania should go back to this old man and have coffee and bed and whatever else he was sending messages about, because she sure as hell wasn't enjoying life without him.

The lecture had started Bill thinking. Suppose he were to get a posting abroad. Suppose he actually *did* succeed in being chosen as one of the experimental task force going to a European capital as part of the expansion process. Imagine the difference it would make. He would be earning real money for the first time in his life. He would have freedom. He need not spend the evenings at home playing with Olive and telling his parents choice bits of the day that would show him in a successful light.

Lizzie might come and live with him in Paris or Rome or Madrid, they could have a little flat, and sleep together every night rather than his just going to her place and then coming home again afterward . . . a habit that Lizzie found screamingly funny and quite suitable since she didn't get up until just before noon and it was nice not to be wakened by someone leaving to go to something as extraordinary as the bank.

He began to look at brochures about intensive language courses. They were very expensive. The language laboratory ones were out of the question. He didn't have time or energy for them either. A day in the bank took it out of him, he felt tired in the evening and not able to concentrate. And since the whole point was to make enough money to build a life for Lizzie, he must not risk losing her by absenting himself from her and her crowd of friends.

Not for the first time he wished that he loved a different kind of person. But it was like measles, wasn't it. Once you got love, it was there. You had to wait to get cured of it or it worked itself out someday. As usual he consulted his friend Grania, and for once she had something specific to offer, rather than what he felt was a vague threat that he was on a helter-skelter to hell by loving Lizzie.

"My father is starting an evening class in Italian up in his school," she said. "It begins in September and they're looking far and wide for pupils."

"Would it be any good?"

"I don't know. I'm meant to be drumming up a bit of business for it." Grania was always so honest. It was one of the many things he liked about her. She wouldn't pretend. "At least it's cheap," she said. "They've put as much money as they can into it and unless he gets thirty pupils the class will fall on its face. I couldn't bear that for my father."

"Are you signing up then?"

"No, he said that would be humiliating for him. If his whole family had to join, it would look pathetic."

"I suppose it would. But would it be any help at all in banking? Do you think it would have the terms and the technical kinds of phrases?"

"I doubt that, but they'd have hallo and good-bye and how's your father. And I suppose if you were out in Italy you'd have to be able to say all that to people like we do here."

"Yes." Bill was doubtful.

"Jesus, Bill, what technical phrases do you and I use here every day, except debit and credit, I bet she'd teach you those."

"Who?"

"The one he's hired. A real Italian, he calls her Signora. He says she's great altogether."

"And when does the class start?"

"September fifth, if they have the numbers."

"And do you have to pay the whole year in advance?"

"Only the term. I'll get you a leaflet. If you were going to do it then you might as well do it there, Bill. You'd be keeping my poor old father sane."

"And will I see Tony, the one who writes all these long, passionate letters?" Bill asked.

"God, don't mention Tony, you're only told this in great secrecy." Grania sounded worried.

He patted her hand. "I'm only having a bit of fun with you, of course I know it's a secret. But I'll have a look at him if I see him, and tell you what I think."

"I hope you'll like him." Grania looked suddenly very young and vulnerable.

"I'm sure he's so fabulous that I'll be sending you postcards about him myself," said Bill with his smile of encouragement that Grania was relying on so much in a world that knew nothing of Tony O'Brien.

∼

BILL TOLD HIS parents that night that he was going to learn Italian.

Olive was very excited. "Bill's going to Italy. Bill's going to Italy to run a bank," she told the next-door neighbors.

They were used to Olive. "That's great," they said indulgently. "Will you miss him?"

"When he goes there he'll bring us all over to Italy to stay with him," Olive said confidently.

From his bedroom Bill heard, and his heart felt heavy. His mother had thought learning Italian was a great idea. It was a beautiful language. She loved to hear the Pope speak it, and she loved the song "O Sole Mio." His father had said that it was great to see a boy bettering himself all the time, and he had always known that those extra grinds for the leaving certificate had been an investment. His mother asked casually whether Lizzie would go to the Italian classes.

Bill had never thought of Lizzie as being disciplined or organized enough to spend two sessions of two hours each learning something. Surely she would prefer to be out with her friends laughing and drinking very expensive multicolored cocktails. "She hasn't decided yet," he said firmly. He knew how much they disapproved of Lizzie. Her one visit had not been a success. Her skirt too short, her neckline too low, her laughter too wide and nonspecific, and her grasp of their life so minimal.

But he had been resolute. Lizzie was the girl he loved. She was the woman he would marry in two years time when he was twenty-five. He would hear no disparaging word about Lizzie in his home, and they respected him for this. Sometimes Bill wondered about his wedding day. His parents would be so excited. His mother would talk for ages about the hat she was going to buy and perhaps buy several before settling on the right one. There would be a lot of discussion, too, about an outfit for Olive, something that would be discreet and yet smart. His father would discuss the timing of the wedding, hoping that it was convenient for the supermarket. He had worked in this store since he was a boy, watching it change character all the time, never realizing his own worth and always fearing that change of manager might mean his walking papers. Sometimes Bill wanted to shake him and tell him that he was worth more than the rest of the employees combined, and that everyone would realize this. But his father, in his fifties, without any of the qualifications and skills of young men, would never have believed him. He would remain fearful of the supermarket and grateful to it for the rest of his days.

Lizzie's family on her side of the church was always fairly vague in Bill's dream of a wedding day. She talked of her mother who lived in West Cork because she preferred it there, and her father who lived in Galway because that's where his pals were. She had a sister in the States and a brother who was working in a ski resort and hadn't come home for ages. Bill couldn't quite imagine them all gathering together.

He told Lizzie about the class. "Would you like to learn too?" he asked hopefully.

"Whatever for?" Lizzie's infectious laughter had him laughing, too, although he didn't know why.

"Well, so that you could speak a bit of it if we went there, you know."

"But don't they speak English?"

"Some of them, but wouldn't it be great to speak to them in their own language."

"And we'd learn to do that up in a ropy old school like Mountainview?"

"It's meant to be quite a good school, they say." He felt stung with loyalty to Grania and her father.

"It may be, but look at the place it's in. You'd need a flak jacket to get through those housing estates."

"It's a deprived area certainly," Bill said. "But they're just poor, that's all."

"Poor," cried Lizzie. "We're all poor, for heaven's sake, but we don't go on like they do up there."

Bill wondered, as he so often did, about Lizzie's values. How could she compare herself with the families who lived on welfare and social security? the many households where there had never been a job? Still, it was part of her innocence. You didn't love people to change them. He had known that for a long time.

"Well, I'm going to do it anyway," he said. "There's a bus stop right outside the school and the lessons are on Tuesdays and Thursdays."

Lizzie turned over the little leaflet. "I would do it to support you, Bill, but honestly I just don't have the money." Her eyes were enormous. It would be wonderful to have her sitting beside him mouthing the words, learning the language.

"I'll pay for your course," Bill Burke said. Now he would definitely have to go to another bank and get a loan.

They were nice in the other bank and sympathetic. They had to do the same themselves, they all had to borrow elsewhere. There was no problem about setting it up.

"You can get more than that," the helpful young bank official said, just as Bill would have said himself.

"I know but the bit about paying it back . . . I seem to have so many calls each month."

"Tell me about it," said the boy. "And the price of clothes is disgraceful. Anything you'd want to be seen in costs an arm and a leg."

Bill thought of the jacket, and he thought of his parents and Olive. He'd love to give them some little end-of-summer treat. He got a loan exactly twice what he had gone into the bank intending to borrow.

GRANIA TOLD BILL that her father was absolutely delighted about her recruiting two new members for the class. There were twenty-two already. Things were looking good and still a week to go. They had decided that even if they didn't make the full thirty they would have the first term's lessons anyway so as not to disappoint those who had enrolled, and to avoid embarrassing themselves at the very outset.

"Once it gets going there might be word of mouth," Bill said.

"They say there's usually a great falloff after lesson three," Grania said. "But let's not be downhearted. I'm going to work on my friend Fiona tonight."

"Fiona who works in the hospital?" Bill had a feeling that Grania was matchmaking for him here. She always mentioned Fiona in approving terms, just after something Lizzie had done turned out to have been particularly silly or difficult.

"Yeah, you know about Fiona, I'm always talking about her. Great friend of mine and Brigid's. We can always say we're staying with her when we're not, if you know what I mean."

"I know what you mean, but do your parents?" Bill asked.

"They don't think about it, that's what parents do. They put these things to the back of their minds."

"Is Fiona asked to cover for you often?"

"Not for me since . . . well since that night with Tony ages ago. You see, it was the very next day I discovered about him being such a rat and taking my father's job. Did I tell you?"

She had, many times, but Bill was very kind. "I think you said that the timing was bad."

"It couldn't have been worse," Grania raged. "If I had known earlier I wouldn't have given him the time of day, and if it were later then I might have been so committed to him that there was no turning back." She fumed at the unfairness of it all.

"Suppose you did decide to go back to him, would that finish your father off entirely?"

Grania looked at him sharply. Bill must be psychic to know that she had tossed and turned all last night thinking that she might approach Tony O'Brien again. He had left the ball so firmly in her court, and he had sent encouraging messages in the form of postcards. In a way it was discourteous not to respond to him in some manner. But she had thought of the damage it would do to her father. He had been so sure that the post of principal was his; he *must* have felt it more keenly than he had shown. "You know, I *was* thinking about that," Grania said slowly. "And I worked out that I might wait a bit, you know, until things are better in my dad's life. Then he might be able to face up to something like that."

"Does he talk about things with your mother, do you think?"

Grania shook her head. "They hardly talk at all. My mother's only interested in the restaurant and going to see her sisters. Dad spends most of his time doing up a sort of study for himself. He's very lonely these days, I couldn't bear to bring anything else on him. But maybe if these evening classes are a huge success and he gets a lot of praise for that . . . then I could face him with the other thing. Were I to go ahead with it, of course."

Bill looked admiringly at Grania. Like himself she was more confident than her parents, and also like him she didn't want to upset them. "We have so much in common," he said suddenly. "Isn't it a pity that we don't fancy each other."

"I *know*, Bill." Grania's sigh was heartfelt. "And you're a very good-looking guy, 'specially in that new jacket. And you've got lovely shiny brown hair and you're young, you won't be dead when I'm forty. Isn't it awful that we couldn't fancy each other but I don't, not even a bit."

"I know," Bill said. "Neither do I, isn't it a crying shame?"

❧

As a treat he decided to take the family to lunch, out to the seaside. They took the train called the DART.

"We're darting out to the seaside," Olive told several people on the train, and they smiled at her. Everyone smiled at Olive, she was so eager. They explained to her that DART meant Dublin Area Rapid Transit, but she didn't take it in.

They walked down to look at the harbor and the fishing boats. There were still summer visitors around and tourists snapping the scene. They walked through the windy main street of the little town and looked at the shops. Bill's mother said it must be wonderful to live in a place like this.

"When we were young anyone could have afforded a place out here," Bill's father said. "But it seemed very far away in those days and the better jobs were nearer the city so we didn't come."

"Maybe Bill would live somewhere like this one day when he got a promotion," his mother suggested, almost afraid to hope.

Bill tried to see himself living in one of the new flats or the old houses here with Lizzie. What would she do all day as he commuted into Dublin City on the DART? Would she have friends out here as she had everywhere? Would they have children? She had said one boy and one girl, and then curtains. But that was a long time ago. Whenever he brought the subject up nowadays, she was much more vague. "Suppose you got pregnant now," Bill had suggested one night. "Then we'd have to advance our plans a bit."

"Absolutely wrong, Bill sweetheart," she had said. "We would have to cancel all our plans."

And he saw for the first time the hint of hardness behind her smile. But of course he dismissed this notion. Bill knew that Lizzie wasn't hard. Like any woman she feared the dangers and accidents of her own body. It wasn't fair, really, the way it was organized. Women could never be as relaxed about lovemaking, knowing it might result in something unexpected like pregnancy.

Olive was not a good walker, and his mother wanted to visit the church anyway, so Bill and his father walked up to the Vico Road, an elegant curved road that swept the bay, which had often been compared to the Bay of Naples. A lot of the roads here had Italian names like Vico and Sorrento, and there were houses called La Scala, Milano, Ancona. People who had traveled had brought back memories of similar seaside views. Also, it was full of hills like they said the Italian coastline was.

Bill and his father looked at the gardens and homes and admired them without envy. If Lizzie had been here, she would have said it was unfair for some people to have houses like that, with two big cars parked outside. But Bill, who worked as a bank clerk, and his father—who sliced bacon and wearing plastic gloves inserted it into little transparent bags and weighed them out at so many grams each—were able to see these properties without wanting them for themselves.

The sun shone and they looked far down. The sea was shimmering. A few yachts were out. They sat on the wall and Bill's father puffed a pipe.

"Did it all turn out as you wanted when you were young?" Bill said.

"Not *all,* of course, but most of it." His father puffed away.

"Like what bits?"

"Well, having such a good job and keeping it in spite of everything. That was something I'd never have bet money on if I was a gambling man. And then there was your mother accepting me, and being such a marvelous wife, and making us such a great home. And then there was Olive and you, and that was a great reward to us."

Bill felt a strange choking sensation. His father lived in an unreal world. All these things were blessings? Things to be delighted with? An educationally subnormal daughter? A wife who could barely fry an egg and this was called making a great home? A job that they would never get anyone of his competence to do, and to do so well . . .

"Dad, why am I part of the good bits?" Bill asked.

"Come on now, you're just asking for praise." His father smiled at him as if the lad had been teasing him.

"No, I mean it, why are you pleased with me?"

"Who could ask for a better son? Look at the way you take us all out for a day's trip today with your hard-earned money and you contribute to the house plenty, and you're so good to your sister."

"Everyone loves Olive."

"Yes they do, but you are especially good to her. Your mother and I have no fears and worries. We know that in the fullness of time when we've gone to Glasnevin cemetery, you'll look after Olive."

Bill heard himself speak in a tone he didn't recognize as his own. "Ah, don't you know Olive will always be looked after. You would never worry about a thing like that, would you?"

"I know there are plenty of homes and institutions, but we know that you'd never send Olive off to a place like that."

And as they sat in the sun with the sea shimmering below a little breeze came up and blew around them and it went straight into Bill Burke's heart. He realized what he had never faced in his twenty-three years of living. He knew now that Olive was his problem, not just theirs. That his big simple sister was his for life. When he and Lizzie married in two years time, when he went abroad with Lizzie to live, when their two children were born, Olive would be part of their family.

His father and mother might live for another twenty years. Olive would only be forty-five then, with the mind of a child. He felt very cold indeed.

"Come on, Dad, Mam will have said three rosaries in the church and they'll be in the pub waiting for us."

And indeed there they were, Olive's big face shining to see her brother come in.

"That's Bill, the bank manager," she said.

And everyone in the pub smiled. As they would always smile at Olive once they didn't have to take her on for life.

BILL WENT UP to Mountainview to register for the Italian lesson. He realized with a heavy heart how lucky he had been that his father had saved money to send him to a smaller and better school. In Bill's school there were proper games pitches, and the parents had paid a so-called voluntary subscription to maintain some of the frills and extras that would never be known in Mountainview.

He looked at the shabby paint and the ugly bicycle shed. Few boys who went to school here would find it easy to get into the bank as he had done. Or was he just being snobbish? Perhaps things had changed. Perhaps he was guiltier than others because he was trying to keep a system going in his mind. It was something he could talk to Grania about. Her father taught here, after all.

It was not something he could talk to Lizzie about.

Lizzie had become excited about the lessons. "I'm telling everyone that we'll be speaking Italian shortly." She laughed happily. For an instant she reminded him of Olive. The same innocent belief that once you mentioned something, that was it, it had happened, and you were somehow in command. But who could compare the beautiful feckless, wild-eyed Lizzie to poor Olive, the lumpen, slow, smiling sister that would be his forevermore?

Part of Bill hoped that Lizzie would change her mind about the lessons. That would be a few pounds saved anyway. He was beginning to feel panicky about the amount of his salary that was promised in debts before he took home anything at all at the end of the month. His new

jacket gave him pleasure but not *that* much pleasure. Possibly it had
been a foolish extravagance that he would live to regret.

"What a beautiful jacket, is it pure wool?" asked the woman at the
desk. She was old, of course, over fifty. But she had a nice smile and she
felt the sleeve just above his wrist.

"Yes it is," Bill said. "Light wool, but apparently you pay for the cut.
That's what I was told."

"Of course you do. It's Italian isn't it?" Her voice was Irish but
slightly accented, as if she had lived abroad. She seemed genuinely interested. Was she the teacher? Bill had been told that they were going to
have a real Italian. Was this the first cutback?

"Are you the teacher?" he asked. He hadn't parted with his money
yet. Possibly this was not the week to hand over fees from Lizzie and
himself. Suppose it was a cheapskate kind of thing. Wouldn't that have
been typical? Just to throw his money away foolishly without checking.

"Yes indeed. I am Signora. I lived twenty-six years in Italy, in Sicilia. I
still think in Italian and dream in it. I hope that I will be able to share all
this with you and the others who come to the class."

Now it was going to be harder still to back out. Bill wished he wasn't
such a Mister Nice Guy. There were people in the bank who would
know exactly how to get out of this situation. The sharks, he and Grania
called them.

Thinking of Grania reminded him of her father. "Do you have enough
numbers to make the class workable?" he asked. Perhaps this could be
his out. Maybe the class would never take place.

But Signora's face was alive with enthusiasm. "*Si si*, we have been so
fortunate. People from far and near have heard about it. How did you
hear, Signor Burke?"

"In the bank," he said.

"The bank." Signora's pleasure was so great, he didn't want to punc-
ture it. "Imagine, they know of us in the bank."

"Will I be able to learn bank terms do you think?" He leaned across
the table, his eyes seeking reassurance in her face.

"What kind exactly?"

"You know, the words we use in banking . . ." But Bill was vague,
he didn't know the terms he might use in banking in Italy one day.

"You can write them down for me and I could look them up for you,"

Signora explained. "But to be very truthful the course will not concentrate on banking terms. It will be more about the language and the feel of Italy. I want to make you love it and know it a little so that when you go there it will be like going home to a friend."

"That will be great," Bill said, and handed over the money for Lizzie and himself.

"*Martedì*," Signora said.

"I beg your pardon?"

"*Martedì* . . . Tuesday . . . now you know one word already."

"*Martedì*," Bill said, and walked to the bus stop. He felt that even more than his fine wool well-cut jacket, this was good money being thrown away.

"What will I wear for the evening class?" Lizzie asked him on Monday night. Only Lizzie would want to know that. Other people might want to know whether to bring notebooks or dictionaries or name badges.

"Something that won't distract everyone from their studies," Bill suggested.

It was a pretty vain hope and a foolish suggestion. Lizzie's wardrobe did not include clothes that would not distract. Even now, at the end of summer, she would have a short skirt that would show her long, tanned legs, she would have a tight top and a jacket loosely around her shoulders.

"But what exactly?"

He knew it wasn't a question of style. It was a matter of choosing a color. "I love the red," he said.

Her eyes lit up. It was very easy to please Lizzie. "I'll try it on now," she said, and got her red skirt and red-and-white shirt. She looked marvelous, fresh and young, like an advertisement for shampoo with her golden hair.

"I could wear a red ribbon in my hair?" She seemed doubtful.

Bill felt a huge protective surge well up in him. Lizzie really did need him. Owlish and obsessed with paying debts as he was, she would be lost without him.

"Tonight's the night," he told Grania at work next day.

"You'll tell me honestly, won't you? You'll tell me what it's like."

Grania seemed very serious. She was wondering how it would go for her father, whether he might look good or just foolish.

Bill assured her he would tell the truth, but somehow he knew it was unlikely. Even if it was a disaster, Bill would not feel able to blow the whistle. He would probably say that it was fine.

∽

BILL DID NOT recognize the dusty school annex when they arrived. The place had been transformed. Huge posters festooned the walls, pictures of the Trevi Fountain and the Coliseum. Huge images of the *Mona Lisa* and of Michelangelo's *David* and mixed among them mighty vineyards and plates of Italian food. There was a table covered in red, white, and green crepe paper that held paper plates covered with cling film.

They seemed to have real food on them, little pieces of salami and cheese. There were paper flowers, too, each one with a big label giving its name. Carnations were *garofani* . . . Somebody had taken immense pains and trouble.

Bill hoped that it would all work out well. For the strange woman with the odd-colored red-and-gray hair called simply Signora, to the kind man hovering in the background who must be Grania's father, to all the people who sat awkwardly and nervously around waiting for it to start. All of them with some hope or dream like his own. None of them, by the look of it, wanting to make a career in international banking.

Signora clapped her hands and introduced herself. *"Mi chiamo Signora. Come si chiama?"* she asked the man who must be Grania's father.

"Mi chiamo Aidan," he said. And so on around the classroom.

Lizzie loved it. *"Mi chiamo Lizzie,"* she cried, and everyone smiled admiringly as if she had achieved a great feat.

"Let's try to make our names more Italian. You could say: '*Mi chiamo Elisabetta.*' "

Lizzie loved that even more and could hardly be stopped from repeating it.

Then they all wrote *Mi chiamo* and their names on huge pieces of paper and pinned them on. And they learned how to ask each other how they were, what time it was, what day it was, what date, where they lived.

"*Chi è?*" pointing at Bill.

"*Guglielmo,*" the class all shouted back.

Soon they knew everyone's names in Italian and the class had visibly relaxed. Signora handed out pieces of paper. There were all the phrases they had been using, familiar to the sound but they would never have been able to pronounce them had they seen them written first.

They went through them over and over, what day, what time, what is your name and they answered them. People's faces were taking on a look of near smugness.

"*Bene,*" said Signora. "Now we have ten minutes more." There was a gasp. The two hours could not truly be over. "You have all worked so hard there is a little treat, but we have to pronounce the salami before we eat it, and the *formaggio.*"

Like children the thirty adults fell on the sausage and cheese and pronounced the words.

"*Giovedì,*" Signora was saying.

"*Giovedì,*" they were all chorusing. Bill began to put the chairs away neatly by the wall in a stack. Signora seemed to look at Grania's father as if to know whether this was what was needed. He nodded quietly. Then the others helped. In minutes the classroom was tidy. The porter would have little to do in terms of clearing up.

Bill and Lizzie went out to the bus stop.

"*Ti amo,*" she said to him suddenly.

"What's that?" he asked.

"Oh go on, you're the one with the brains," Lizzie said. She was smiling fit to break his heart. "Go on, guess. *Ti* . . . what's that?"

"It's 'you,' I think," said Bill.

"And what's *amo*?"

"Is it love?"

"It means *I love you.*"

"How do you know?" He was amazed.

"I asked her just before we left. She said they were the most beautiful two words in the world."

"They are, they are," said Bill.

Perhaps the Italian classes might work after all.

❧

"IT WAS REALLY and truly great," Bill told Grania next day.

"My father came home high as a kite, thank God," Grania said.

"And she's really good, you know, she makes you think you can speak the language in five minutes."

"So you're off to run the Italian section then," Grania teased.

"Even Lizzie liked it, she was really interested. She kept saying the sentences over and over on the bus, everyone was joining in."

"I'm sure they were." Grania was clipped.

"No, stop being like that. She took much more notice of it than I thought she would. She calls herself Elisabetta now." Bill was proud.

"I bet she does," Grania said grimly. "I'd also like to bet she'll have dropped out by lesson three."

❧

AS IT HAPPENED Grania was right, but not because Lizzie wasn't interested. It was because her mother came to Dublin.

"She hasn't been for ages and I have to meet her off the train," she said to Bill apologetically.

"But can't you tell her you'll be back at half past nine?" Bill begged. He felt sure that if Signorina Elisabetta was to miss out on one lesson, that would be it. She would claim that she was far too far behind to catch up.

"No honestly, Bill, she doesn't come to Dublin very often. I have to be there." He was silent. "You care about your mother enough to *live* with her for heaven's sake, why shouldn't I meet mine at Heuston Station? It's not much to ask."

Bill was very reasonable. "No," he agreed. "It's not."

"And Bill, could you lend me the money for a taxi? My mother hates traveling on a bus."

"Won't she pay for the taxi?"

"Oh don't be so mean, you're mean and tightfisted and penny-pinching."

"That's not fair, Lizzie. It's not true and it's not fair."

"Okay." She shrugged.

"What do you mean okay?"

"Just that. Enjoy the lesson, give my love to Signora."

"Have the money for the taxi."

"No, not like that, not with a bad grace."

"I'd love you and your mother to travel by taxi, I'd love it. It would make you feel happy and generous and welcoming. Please take it, Lizzie, please."

"Well, if you're sure."

He kissed her on the forehead. "Will I meet your mother this time?"

"I hope so, Bill, you know we wanted you to last time but she had so many friends around. They took all her time. She knows so many people, you see."

Bill thought to himself that Lizzie's mother might know a lot of people, but none of them well enough to meet her at the railway station with a car or taxi. But he didn't say it.

"*Dov'è la bella Elisabetta?*" Signora asked.

"*La bella Elisabetta è andata alla stazione,*" Bill heard himself say. "*La madre di Elisabetta arriva stasera.*"

Signora was overwhelmed. "*Benissimo, Guglielmo. Bravo, bravo.*"

"You've been cramming, you little sneak," said an angry-faced thickset fellow with *Luigi* on his blue name tag. His real name was Lou.

"We did *andata* last week, it was on the list, and we did *stasera* the first day. They're all words we know. I *didn't* cram."

"Oh Jesus, keep your shirt on," said Lou, who frowned more than ever and joined with the class shouting that in this piazza there were many beautiful buildings. "There's a lie for a start," he muttered, looking out the window at the barrack-like school yard.

"It's getting better, they are painting it up," Bill said.

"You're a real cheerful Charlie, aren't you?" Lou said. "Everything's always bloody marvelous as far as you're concerned."

Bill longed to tell him that everything was far from cheerful, he was trapped in a house where everyone depended on him, he had a girlfriend who didn't love him enough to introduce him to her mother, he had no idea how he was going to pay his term loan next month.

But, of course, he said none of these things. Instead he joined in the chorus chanting that *in questa piazza ci sono molti belli edifici.* He wondered where Lizzie and her mother had gone. He hoped beyond reason that she hadn't taken her mother to a restaurant and cashed a check. This time there would be real trouble in the bank.

They had little bits of bread with filling of some sort on them. Signora said they were *crostini.* "What about the *vino?*" someone asked.

"I wanted to have *vino, vino rosso, vino bianco.* But it's a school you see, they don't want any alcohol on the premises. Not to give a bad example to the children."

"A bit late for that round here," Lou said.

Bill looked at him with interest. It was impossible to know why a man like that was learning Italian. Although it was difficult to see why any of them were there, and he felt sure that a lot of them must puzzle about Lizzie, there seemed to be no reason that anyone could fathom why Lou, now transformed to Luigi, should come to something that he obviously despised, two nights a week, and glower at everyone from beginning to end. Bill decided he would have to regard it as part of the rich tapestry of life.

One of the paper flowers was broken and on the floor.

"Can I have this, Signora?" Bill asked.

"*Certo, Guglielmo,* is it for *la bellissima Elisabetta?*"

"No, it's for my sister."

"*Mia sorella, mia sorella* my sister," Signora said. "You are a kind, good man, Guglielmo."

"Yeah, but where does that get you these days?" Bill asked as he went out to the bus stop.

❧

OLIVE WAS WAITING for him at the door. "Speak in Italian," she cried.

"*Ciao, sorella,*" he said. "Have a *garofano.* I brought it for you."

The look of pleasure on her face made him feel worse than he had been feeling already, which had been pretty bad.

❧

BILL WAS TAKING sandwiches to work this week. There was no way he could afford even the canteen.

"Are you okay?" Grania asked him, concerned. "You look tired."

"Oh, we international linguists have to learn to take the strain," he said with a weak smile.

Grania looked as if she had been about to ask him about Lizzie but changed her mind. Lizzie? Where was she today? With her mother's friends maybe, having cocktails in one of the big hotels. Or somewhere down in Temple Bar discovering some new place that she would tell him about, eyes shining. He wished she would ring and speak to him, ask about last night at the class. He would tell her how she had been missed and called beautiful. He would tell her about the sentence he had made up, saying she had gone to the station to meet her mother. She would tell him what she did. Why this silence?

The afternoon seemed long and tedious. After work he began to worry. A whole day never passed like this without any contact. Should he go around to her flat? But then if she was entertaining her mother, might she not regard this as intrusive? She had said she hoped they would meet. He mustn't force it.

Grania was working late too. "Waiting for Lizzie?" she asked.

"No, her mother's in town, she's probably tied up. Just wondering what to do."

"I was wondering what to do too. Great fun being in the bank, isn't it? When the day ends you're such a zombie you can't think what to do next." Grania laughed at the whole notion of it.

"You're always rushing here and there, Grania." He sounded envious.

"Well, not tonight. I haven't a notion of going home. My mother will be on her way out to the restaurant, my father disappeared into his study, and Brigid like some kind of wild animal because she's put on weight again. She's kicking the scales and saying that the house is full of the smell of frying, and she talks about food for about five hours each evening. She'd make your hair go white overnight listening to her."

"Is she really worried about it?" Bill was always so kind and interested in people's problems.

"I don't know whether she is or not. She's always looked the same to me, a bit squarish but fine. When she has her hair done and she's smiling she's as good as anyone, but there's this dreary litany of a pound here or a kilo there or a zip that broke or tights that split. Jesus, she'd drive you insane. I'm not going home to listen to that, I tell you."

There was a pause. Bill was on the point of asking her to have a drink when he remembered his finances. This would be a good excuse to go home on his season ticket and spend not a single penny.

At that moment Grania said: "Why don't I take you to the pictures and chips, my treat?"

"I can't do that, Grania."

"Yes you can. I owe you for signing up for those classes, it was a great favor." She made it sound reasonable.

They went through the film listings in the evening paper and argued good-naturedly about what might be good and what might be rubbish. It would have been so easy to be with someone like this all the time, Bill thought yet again. And he felt sure that Grania was thinking the same thing. But when it wasn't there, it wasn't there. She would remain loving this awkward older man and endure the problems that lay ahead when her father found out. He would stay with Lizzie, who had his heart broken morning, noon, and night. That's what happened to people.

When he got back home, his mother had an anxious face. "That Lizzie's been here," she said. "Whatever time you came in you were to go to her flat."

"Is anything wrong?" He was alarmed. It wasn't like Lizzie to come to the house, not after her uncertain welcome on her one official visit.

"Oh, I'd say there's plenty wrong, she's a troubled girl," his mother said.

"But was she sick, had anything happened?"

"Troubled in herself, I mean," his mother repeated.

He knew he would get nothing but a general mood of disapproval, so he went down the road and caught a bus in the other direction.

She was sitting there in the warm September night outside the house where she had her bed-sitter. There were big stone steps leading up to the door, and Lizzie sat hugging her knees swaying backward and forward. To his relief she wasn't crying and didn't seem upset or in a state.

"Where were you?" she asked accusingly.

"Where were *you*?" Bill said. "*You* are the one who says I'm not to call you, not to turn up."

"I was here."

"Yes, well I was out."

"Where did you go?"

"To the pictures," he said.

"I thought we had no money, we weren't meant to be doing anything normal like going to the pictures."

"I didn't pay. Grania Dunne took me as a treat."

"Oh yes?"

"Yes. What's wrong, Lizzie?"

"Everything," she said.

"Why did you come to my house?"

"I wanted to see you, to make things right."

"Well, you succeeded in frightening the life out of my mother and out of me. Why didn't you ring me at work?"

"I was confused."

"Did your mother arrive?"

"Yes, she did."

"And did you meet her?"

"Yes." Her voice was very flat.

"And take the taxi?"

"Yes."

"So, what's wrong?"

"She laughed at my flat."

"Oh, Lizzie. Come *on*. You didn't drag me all the way here, twenty-four hours later, to tell me that, did you?"

"Of course." She laughed.

"It's her way, it's your way . . . people like you and your mother laugh all the time, it's what you do."

"No, not that kind of laughing."

"Well, what kind?"

"She just said it was too funny and asked could she go now that she'd seen it. She said I'd never let the taxi go and marooned her in this neck of the woods, had I?"

Bill was sad. Lizzie had obviously been very upset. What a thoughtless bloody woman. She hardly ever saw her daughter, couldn't she have been nice for the few hours she *was* in Dublin.

"I know, I know," he said soothingly. "But people always say the wrong thing, they're known for it. Come on, let's not worry about it, let's go upstairs. Hey, come on."

"No, we can't."

She was going to need a bit of persuading.

"Lizzie, I have people in the bank all day from nine o'clock in the morning saying the wrong thing, they're not evil people, they just upset others. The trick is not to let them. And then when I go home my mother tells me she's worn out pouring tinned sauce over the frozen chicken, and my father tells me of all the chances he never had as a boy and Olive tells anyone who will listen that I am the head of the bank. And sometimes it's a bit hard to take, but you just put up with it, that's what it's all about."

"For you, yes, but not for me." Again her voice was very dead.

"So did you have a row? Is that it? It'll pass, family rows always do. Honestly, Lizzie."

"No, we didn't exactly have a row."

"Well?"

"I had her supper ready. It was chicken livers and a miniature of sherry, and I had the rice all ready too. I showed it to her and she laughed again."

"Yes, well, as I said . . ."

"She wasn't going to stay, Bill, not for supper. She said she had only called in to keep me quiet. She was going to some art gallery, some opening, some exhibition. She'd be late. She tried to push past me."

"Um . . . yes . . . ?" Bill didn't like this at all.

"So, I couldn't take it anymore."

"What did you do, Lizzie?" He was amazed that he could keep so calm.

"I locked the door and threw the key out the window."

"You *what*?"

"I said, now you *have* to stay and sit and talk to your daughter. I said, now you can't get out and run away as you've run away from us all, all your life, from Daddy and from the rest of us."

"And what did she do?"

"Oh, she got into a terrible temper and kept screaming and beating the door and saying I was cracked and like my father and you know, the usual."

"No, I don't know. What else?"

"Oh, what you'd expect."

"And what happened then?"

"Well, she wore herself out, and eventually she did have supper."

"And was she still shouting then?"

"No, she was just worried in case the house went on fire and we'd be burned to a crisp. That's what she kept saying, burned to a crisp."

Bill's mind was working slowly but surely. "You *did* let her out eventually."

"No I didn't. Not at all."

"But she's not still there?"

"Yes she is."

"You can't be serious, Lizzie."

She nodded several times. "I'm afraid I am."

"How did you get out?"

"The window. When she was in the bathroom."

"She slept there?"

"She had to. I slept in the chair. She had the whole bed." Lizzie sounded defensive.

"Let me get this straight. She came here yesterday, Tuesday at seven o'clock, and it's now eleven o'clock at night on Wednesday and she's *still* here, locked in against her will?"

"Yes."

"But God Almighty, why?"

"So that I could talk to her. She never makes time to talk to me. Never, not once."

"And *has* she talked to you? I mean now that she's locked in?"

"Not really, not in a satisfactory way, she just keeps giving out and saying I'm unreasonable, unstable, whatever."

"I don't believe this, Lizzie, I don't. She's been there not only all night but all day and all tonight?" His head was reeling.

"What else could I do? She never has a moment, always in a rush . . . to go somewhere else, to meet other people."

"But you can't do this. You can't lock people in and expect them to talk."

"I know it mightn't have been the right thing to do. Listen, I was wondering could you come and talk to her . . . she doesn't seem very reasonable."

"Me talk to her? *Me*?"

"Well you did say you wanted to meet her, Bill. You asked several times."

He looked into the beautiful troubled face of the woman he loved. Of course he had wanted to meet his future mother-in-law. But not when she was locked into a bed-sitter. Not when she had been kidnapped for over thirty hours and was about to call the Guards. This was going to be a meeting that called for diplomacy like Bill Burke had never known to exist.

He wondered how his heroes in fiction would have handled it, and knew with a great certainty that nobody would ever have put them in a position where they might have to.

They walked up the stairs to Lizzie's flat. No noise came from inside. "Could she have got out?" Bill whispered.

"No. There's a sort of bar under the window. She couldn't have opened it."

"Would she have broken the glass?"

"No, you don't know my mother."

True, Bill thought, but he was about to get to know her under very strange circumstances indeed. "Will she be violent, rush at me or anything?"

"No, of course not." Lizzie was scornful of his fears.

"Well, speak to her or something, tell her who it is."

"No, she's cross with me, she'd be better with someone new." Lizzie's eyes were huge with fear.

Bill squared his shoulders. "Um, Mrs. Duffy, my name is Bill Burke, I work in the bank," he said. It produced no response. "Mrs. Duffy are you all right? Can I have your assurance that you are calm and in good health?"

"Why should I be either calm or in good health? My certifiably insane daughter has imprisoned me in here and this is something she will regret every day, every hour from now until the end of her life." The voice sounded very angry, but strong.

"Well, Mrs. Duffy, if you just stand back from the door I will come in and explain this to you."

"Are you a friend of Elizabeth's?"

"Yes, a very good friend. In fact I am very fond of her."

"Then you must be insane too," said the voice.

Lizzie raised her eyes. "See what I mean," she whispered.

"Mrs. Duffy, I think we can discuss this much better face-to-face. I am coming in now so please stand well away."

"You are not coming in. I have put a chair under the door handle in case she was going to bring back some other drug addicts or criminals like you. I am staying here until somebody comes to rescue me."

"I have come to rescue you," Bill said desperately.

"You can turn the key all you like, you won't get in."

It was true, Bill found. She had indeed barricaded herself in.

"The window?" he asked Lizzie.

"It's a bit of a climb but I'll show you."

Bill looked alarmed. "I meant *you* to go in the window."

"I can't, Bill, you've heard her. She's like a raging bull. She'd kill me."

"Well, what will she do to me, suppose I did get in? She thinks I'm a drug addict."

Lizzie's lip trembled. "You said you'd help me," she said in a small voice.

"Show me the window," said Bill. It was a bit of a climb and when he got there he saw the pole that Lizzie had wedged under the top part of the window. He eased it out, opened the window, and pulled the curtain back. A blond woman in her forties, with a mascara-stained face, saw him just as he got in and ran at him with a chair.

"Stay away from me, get off, you useless little thug," she cried.

"Mummy, Mummy," Lizzie shouted from outside the door.

"Mrs. Duffy, please, please." Bill took up the lid of the bread bin to defend himself. "Mrs. Duffy, I've come to let you out. Look, here's the key. Please, please put the chair down."

He did indeed seem to be offering her a key, her eyes appeared to relax slightly. She put down the chair and watched him warily.

"Just let me open the door, and Lizzie can come in and we can all discuss this calmly," he said, moving toward the door.

But Lizzie's mother had picked up the kitchen chair again. "Get away from that door. Who knows what kind of a gang there is? I've told Lizzie I have no money, I have no credit cards . . . it's useless kidnapping *me*. No one will pay a ransom. You've really picked the wrong woman." Her lip was trembling, she looked so like her daughter that Bill felt the familiar protective attitude sweeping over him.

"It's only Lizzie outside, there's no gang. It's all a misunderstanding." His voice was calming.

"You can say that again. Locked in here with that lunatic girl since last night and then she goes off and leaves me here, all on my own, wondering what's next in the door, and you come in the window with a bread bin coming at me."

"No, no, I just picked that up when you picked up the chair. Look I'll put it down now." His voice was having a great effect. She seemed ready to talk reason. She put the red kitchen chair down and sat on it, exhausted, frightened, and unsure what to do next.

Bill began to breathe normally. He decided to let the moment last rather than introduce any new elements into it like opening the door. They looked at each other warily.

Then there was a cry from outside. "Mummy? Bill? What's happening? Why aren't you talking, shouting?"

"We're resting," Bill called. As an explanation he wondered was it adequate.

But Lizzie seemed to think so. "Okay," she said from outside.

"Is she on some kind of drugs?" her mother asked.

"No. Heavens no, not at all."

"Well, what was it all about? All this locking me in, saying she wanted to talk and then not talking any sense."

"I think she misses you," Bill said slowly.

"She'll be missing me a lot more from now on in," said Mrs. Duffy.

Bill looked at her, trying to take her in. She was young and slim, she looked a different generation to his own mother. She wore a floaty kind of caftan dress, with some glass beads around the neckline. It was the kind of thing you saw in pictures of New Age people, but she didn't have open sandals or long, flowing hair. Her curls were like Lizzie's, but with little streaks of gray. Apart from her tear-stained face she could have been going to a party. Which was of course what she *had* been doing when she was waylaid.

"I think she was sorry that you had grown a bit apart," Bill said. There was a snort from the figure in the caftan. "Well, you know, you live so far away and everything."

"Not far enough I tell you. All I did was ask the girl to come out and meet me for a quick drink and she insists on coming to the station in a taxi, and bringing me here. I said, well only for a little while because we had to go to Chester's opening . . . where Chester thinks I am now is beyond worrying about."

"Who is Chester?"

"He's a friend, for God's sake, a friend, one of the people who lives near where I live, he's an artist. We all came up, no one will know what happened to me."

"Won't they think of looking for you here . . . in your daughter's house?"

"No, of course not, why would they?"

"They know you have a daughter in Dublin?"

"Yes, well maybe. They know I have three children but I don't bleat on and on about them, they wouldn't know where Elizabeth *lived* or anything."

"But your other friends, your real friends?"

"These are my real friends," she snapped.

"Are you all right in there?" Lizzie called.

"Leave it for a bit, Lizzie," Bill said.

"By God you're going to pay for this, Elizabeth," her mother called.

"Where are they staying . . . your friends?"

"I don't know, that's the whole bloody problem, we said we'd see how it went at the opening and maybe if Harry was there we might all go to Harry's. He lives in a big barn, we once stayed there before. Or if all else failed Chester would know some marvelous little B and B's for half nothing."

"And will Chester have called the Guards, do you think?"

"Why on earth should he have done that?"

"To see what had happened to you."

"The Guards?"

"Well, if he was expecting you and you had disappeared."

"He'll think I just drifted off with someone at the exhibition. He might even think I hadn't bothered to come up at all. That's what's so bloody maddening about it all."

Bill let out a sigh of relief. Lizzie's mother was a floater and a drifter. There would not be a full-scale alert looking for her. No Garda cars would cruise by, eyes out for a blonde in a caftan. Lizzie would not spend the rest of the night in a Garda station in a cell.

"Will we let her in, do you think?" He managed to make it appear that they were together in this.

"Will she go on with all that stuff about never talking and never relating and running away."

"No, I'll see to it that she doesn't, believe me."

"Very well. But don't expect me to be all sunshine and light after this trick she's pulled."

"No, you have every right to be upset." He moved past her to the door. And there was Lizzie cowering outside in the dark corridor. "Ah, Lizzie," Bill said in the voice you would use if you found an unexpected but delightful guest on your doorstep. "Come in, won't you. And perhaps you could make us all a cup of tea."

Lizzie scuttled by him into the kitchen, avoiding the eye of her mother.

"Wait until your father hears about this carry-on," her mother said.

"Mrs. Duffy, do you take your tea with milk and sugar?" Bill interrupted.

"Neither, thank you."

"Just black for Mrs. Duffy," Bill called, as if he were giving a command to the staff. He moved around the tiny flat tidying things up, straightening the counterpane on the bed, picking up objects from the floor, as if establishing normality in a place that had temporarily abandoned it. Soon they were sitting, an unlikely threesome, drinking mugs of tea.

"I bought a tin of shortbread," Lizzie said proudly, taking out a tartan-colored box.

"They cost a fortune," Bill said, aghast.

"I wanted to have something for my mother's visit."

"I *never* said I was coming to visit, that was all your idea. Some idea it was too."

"Still, they're in a tin," Bill said. "They could last for a long time."

"Are you soft in the head?" Lizzie's mother suddenly asked Bill.

"I don't think so. Why do you ask?"

"Talking about biscuits at a time like this. I thought you were meant to be the one in charge."

"Well, isn't it better than screaming and talking about needing and relating and all the things you said you didn't want talked about?" Bill was stung with the unfairness of it.

"No it's not, it's insane if you ask me. You're just as mad as she is. I've got myself into a lunatic asylum."

Her eyes darted to the door, and he saw her grip bag beside it. Would she make a run for it? Would that perhaps be for the best? Or had they gone so far into this that they had better see it through to the end. Let Lizzie tell her mother what was wrong, let her mother accept or deny all this. His father had always said that they should wait and see. It seemed a poor philosophy to Bill. What were you waiting for? What would you see? But his father seemed pleased with the end product, so perhaps it had its merits.

Lizzie munched the biscuit. "These are beautiful," she said. "Full of butter, you can tell." She was so endearing, like a small child. Could her mother not see that in her too?

Bill looked from one to the other. He hoped he wasn't imagining that the mother's face seemed to be softening a little.

"It's quite hard, Lizzie, in ways, a woman alone," she began.

"But you didn't have to be alone, Mummy, you could have had us all with you, Daddy and me and John and Kate."

"I couldn't live in a house like that, trapped all day waiting for a man to come home with the wages. And then your father often *didn't* come home with the wages, he went to the betting shop with them. Like he does still over in Galway."

"You didn't have to go."

"I had to go because otherwise I would have killed somebody, him, you, myself. Sometimes it's safer to go and get a bit of air to breathe."

"When *did* you go?" Bill asked conversationally, as if he were inquiring about the times of trains.

"Don't you know, don't you know every detail of the wicked witch who ran away abandoning everyone?"

"No I don't, actually. I didn't even know you *had* ever gone until this moment. I thought you and Mr. Duffy had separated amicably and that all your children had scattered. It seemed very grown up and what families should do."

"What do you mean what families should do?" Lizzie's mother looked at him suspiciously.

"Well you see I live at home with my mother and father and I have a handicapped sister, and honestly I can't ever see any way of *not* being there or nearby anyway, so I thought what Lizzie's family had was very free . . . and I kind of envied it." He was so transparently honest. Nobody could put on an act like that.

"You could just get up and go," Lizzie's mother suggested.

"I suppose so, but I wouldn't feel easy about it."

"You've only one life." They were both ignoring Lizzie now.

"Yes that's it. I suppose, if we had more than one then I wouldn't feel so guilty."

Lizzie tried to get back into the conversation. "You never write, you never stay in touch."

"What's there to write *about*, Lizzie? You don't know my friends. I don't know yours. I don't know John's or Kate's. I still love you and want the best for you even though we don't see each other all the time." She stopped, almost surprised at herself that she had said this much.

Lizzie was not convinced. "You couldn't love us, otherwise you'd come to see us. You wouldn't laugh at me and this place I live in, and laugh at the idea of staying with me, not if you loved us."

"I think what Mrs. Duffy means . . ." Bill began.

"Oh, for Jesus sake call me Bernie." Bill was so taken aback, he forgot his sentence. "Go on, you were saying what I meant was . . . what *do* I mean?"

"I think you mean that Lizzie *is* very important to you, but you have sort of drifted away a bit, what with West Cork being so far from here . . . and that last night was a bad time to stay because your friend Chester was having an art exhibition, and you wanted to be there in time to give him moral support. Was it something like that?" He looked from one to the other with his round face creased in anxiety. Please may she have meant something like this, and not have meant that she was going for the Guards or that she was never going to see Lizzie as long as she lived.

"It was a *bit* like that," Bernie agreed. "But only a bit."

Still, it was something, Bill thought to himself. "And what Lizzie meant when she threw away the key was that she was afraid life was passing too quickly and she wanted a chance to get to know you and talk properly, make up for all the lost time, wasn't that it?"

"That was it." Lizzie nodded vigorously.

"But God Almighty, whatever your name is . . ."

"Bill," he said helpfully.

"Yes, well Bill, it's not the act of a sane person to lure me here and lock me in."

"I didn't lure you here. I borrowed the money from Bill to get a taxi for you. I invited you here, I bought shortbread and bacon and chicken livers and sherry. I made my bed for you to sleep in. I wanted you to stay. That wasn't all that much, was it?"

"But I couldn't." Bernie Duffy's voice was gentler now.

"You could have said you'd come back the next day. You just laughed. I couldn't bear that, and then you got crosser and crosser and said awful things."

"I wasn't talking normally because I wasn't talking to a normal person. I was really shaken by you, Lizzie. You seemed to be losing your mind. Truly. You weren't making any sense. You kept saying that the last six years you had been like a lost soul . . ."

"That's just the way it was."

"You were seventeen when I left. Your father wanted you to go to Galway with him, you wouldn't . . . You insisted you were old enough to live in Dublin, you got a job in a dry cleaner's, I remember. You had your own money. It was what you wanted. That was what you said."

"I stayed because I thought you'd come back."

"Back to where? Here?"

"No, back to the house. Daddy didn't sell it for a year, remember?"

"I remember and then he put every penny he got for it on horses that are still running backwards somewhere on English racetracks."

"Why didn't you come back, Mummy?"

"What was there to come back *to*? Your father was only interested in a form book, John had gone to Switzerland, Kate had gone to New York, you were running with your crowd."

"I was waiting for you, Mummy."

"No, that's not true, Lizzie. You can't rewrite the whole thing. Why didn't you write and tell me if that was the way it was."

There was a silence.

"You only liked hearing from me if I was having a good time, so I told you about the good times. On postcards and letters. I told you when I went to Greece, and to Achill Island. I didn't tell you about wanting you to come back, in case you got annoyed with me."

"I would have liked it a hell of a lot more than being hijacked, imprisoned . . ."

"And is it nice where you are in West Cork?" Again Bill was being conversational and interested. "It always sounds a lovely place to me, the pictures you see of the coastline."

"It's very special. There are a lot of free spirits there, people who have gone back to the land, people who paint, express themselves, make pottery."

"And do you specialize in any of the arts . . . er . . . Bernie?" He was owlish and interested, she couldn't take offense.

"No, not myself personally, but I have always been interested in artistic people, and places. I find myself stifled to be cooped up anywhere. That's why this whole business . . ."

Bill was anxious to head her off the subject. "And do you have a house of your own or do you live with Chester?"

"No, heavens no." She laughed just like her daughter laughed, a happy peal of mirth. "No, Chester is gay, he lives with Vinnie. No, no. They're my dearest friends. They live about four miles away. No, I have a room, a sort of studio I suppose, an outbuilding it once was, off a bigger property."

"That sounds nice, is it near the sea?"

"Yes, of course. Everywhere's near the sea. It's very charming. I love it. I've been there for six years now, made a real little home of it."

"And how do you get money to live, Bernie? Do you have a job?"

Lizzie's mother looked at him as if he had made a very vulgar noise. "I beg your pardon?"

"I mean, if Lizzie's father didn't give you any money you have to earn a living. That's all." He was unrepentant.

"It's because he works in a bank, Mummy," Lizzie apologized. "He's obsessed with earning a living."

Suddenly it became too much for Bill. He was sitting in this house in the middle of the night trying to keep the peace between two madwomen and they thought that *he* was the odd one because he actually had a job and paid his bills and lived according to the rules. Well, he had had just about enough. Let them sort it out. He would go home, back to his dull house, with his sad family.

He would never be transferred into international banking no matter how much he learned about "How are you and beautiful buildings and red carnations." He would not try anymore to make selfish people see some good in each other. He felt an entirely unfamiliar twitching in his nose and eyes as if he were about to cry.

There was something about his face that both women noticed at the same time. It was as if he had opted out, left them.

"I didn't mean to laugh at your question," Lizzie's mother said. "Of course I have to earn money. I do some help in the home where I have my studio, you know, cleaning, light housework, and when they have parties I help with the . . . well with the clearing up. I love ironing, I always have, so I do all their ironing too, and for this I don't have to pay any rent. And of course they give me a little spending money too."

Lizzie looked at her mother in disbelief. This was the arty lifestyle, mixing with the great and the rich, the playboys and the glittery set who had second homes in the southwest of Ireland. Her mother was a maid.

Bill was in control of himself again. "It must be very satisfying," he said. "Means you can have the best of both worlds, a nice place to live, independence and no real worries about how to put food on the table."

She searched his face for sarcasm, but did not find any. "That's right," Bernie Duffy said eventually. "That's the way it is."

Bill thought he must speak before Lizzie blurted out something that would start them off again. "Perhaps sometime when the weather gets finer Lizzie and I could come down and see you there. It would be a real treat for me. We could come on the bus, and change at Cork City." Eager, boyish, and planning it as if this was a social call long overdue.

"And, are you two . . . I mean, are you Lizzie's boyfriend?"

"Yes, we are going to get married when we are twenty-five, two years time. We hope to get a job in Italy so we are both learning Italian at night."

"Yes, she told me that amongst all the other ramblings," Bernie said.

"That we were getting married?" Bill was pleased.

"No, that she was learning Italian. I thought it was more madness."

There seemed little more to be said. Bill stood up as if he were a normal guest taking his leave of a normal evening. "Bernie, as you may have noticed it's very late now. There won't be more buses running, and it might be difficult to find your friends even if there were buses. So I suggest that you stay here tonight, at your own wish, of course, with the key in the door. And then tomorrow when you've both had a good rest, you and Lizzie, say good-bye to each other nice and peaceably and I probably won't see you until next summer when it would be lovely if we could come and see you in West Cork."

"Don't go," Bernie begged. "Don't go. She's nice and quiet while you're here but the moment you are out the door she'll be ranting and raving and saying she was abandoned."

"No, no. It won't be a bit like that now." He spoke with conviction. "Lizzie, could you give your mother the key? Now Bernie, you keep that and then you know you can come and go as you please."

"How will *you* get home, Bill?" Lizzie asked.

He looked at her in surprise. She never usually asked or seemed to care that he had to walk three miles when he left her at night.

"I'll walk, it's a fine starry night," he said. They were both looking at him. He felt an urge to say something more, to make the peaceful moment last. "At Italian class last night Signora taught us a bit about the weather, how to say it's been a great summer. *È stata una magnifica estate.*"

"That's nice," Lizzie said. "*È stata una magnifica estate.*" She repeated it perfectly.

"Hey, you got it in one, the rest of us had to keep saying it over." Bill was impressed.

"She always had a great memory, even as a little girl. You said a thing once and Elizabeth would remember it always." Bernie looked at her daughter with something like pride.

On the way home Bill felt quite lighthearted. A lot of the obstacles that had seemed huge were less enormous now. He didn't need to fear some classy mother in West Cork who would regard a lowly bank clerk as too humble for her daughter. He didn't have to worry anymore that he might be too dull for Lizzie. She wanted safety and love and a base, and he could give her all of those things. There would, of course, be problems ahead. Lizzie would not find it easy to live on a budget. She would never change in her attitude to spending and wanting things now. All he had to do was try to make it happen somehow within reason. And to head her toward work. If her dizzy mother actually earned a living doing other people's ironing and cleaning then perhaps Lizzie's own goalposts might move.

Attitudes might change.

They might even go to Galway and visit her father sometime. Let her know that she was already part of a family, she didn't have to pretend and wish. And that soon she would be part of his family.

Bill Burke walked on through the night as other people drove by in cars or hailed taxis. He had no envy for any of them. He was a lucky man. So all right, he had people who needed him. And people who relied on him. But that was fine. That meant he was just that sort of person, and maybe in the years to come his son would be sorry for him and pity him as Bill pitied his own father. But it wouldn't matter. It would only mean that the boy wouldn't understand. That was all.

KATHY

Kathy Clarke was one of the hardest-working girls in Mountainview. She frowned with concentration in class, she puzzled things out, she hung back and asked questions. In the staff room they often made good-natured fun of her. "Doing a Kathy Clarke" meant screwing up your eyes at a notice on the bulletin board trying to understand it.

She was a tall, awkward girl, her navy school skirt a bit too long, none of the pierced ears and cheap jewelry of her classmates. Not really bright but determined to do well. Almost too determined. Every year they had parent–teacher meetings. Nobody could really remember who came to ask about Kathy.

"Her father's a plumber," Aidan Dunne said once. "He came and put in the cloakroom for us, great job he made of it too, but of course it had to be paid for in cash. Didn't tell me till the end . . . nearly passed out when he saw the checkbook."

"I remember her mother never took the cigarette out of her mouth during the whole chat," said Helen the Irish teacher. "She kept saying what *good* will all this do her, will it earn her a living."

"That's what they all say." Tony O'Brien the principal-elect was resigned. "You're surely not expecting them to talk about the sheer intellectual stimulation of studying for its own sake."

"She has a big sister who comes too," someone else remembered. "She's the manageress in the supermarket. I think she's the only one who understands about poor Kathy."

"God, wouldn't it be a great life if the only worries we had were about them working too hard and frowning too much with concentration," said Tony O'Brien, who as principal-elect had many more trying problems on his desk every day. And not only on his desk.

In his life of moving on from one woman to another there had been very few women he had wanted to stay with, and now that it had finally happened and he had met one, there was this goddamned complication. She was the daughter of poor Aidan Dunne, who had thought that he was going to be principal. The misunderstanding and the confusions would have done credit to a Victorian melodrama.

Now young Grania Dunne wouldn't see him because she accused him of having humiliated her father. It was farfetched and wrong, but the girl believed it. He had left the decision to her, saying for the first time in his life that he would remain unattached waiting until she came back to him. He sent her jokey postcards to let her know that he was still there, but there was no response. Perhaps he was stupid to go on hoping. He knew how many other fish there were in the sea, and he had never been short of female fishes in his life.

But somehow none of them had the appeal of this bright, eager girl with the dancing eyes and the energy and quick response that made him feel genuinely young again. She hadn't thought he was too old for her, not that night she had stayed. The night before he knew who she was and that her father had expected the job that could never be his.

The last thing Tony O'Brien had expected as principal of Mountainview was that he would live a near monastic life at home. It was doing him no harm, early nights, less clubbing, less drinking. In fact he was even trying to cut down on his smoking in case she came back. At least he didn't smoke in the mornings now. He didn't reach out of the bed, eyes closed, hands searching for the packet, he managed to wait till break and have his first drag of the day in the privacy of his own office with a coffee. That was an advance. He wondered should he send her a card with a picture of a cigarette on it saying Not *still smoking,* but then she might think he was totally cured, which he was far from being. It was absurd how much of his thoughts she took up.

And he had never realized what an exhausting job it was running a school like Mountainview, the parent–teacher meetings and Open Nights were only one of the many things that cried out for his being there.

He had little time left to worry about the Kathy Clarkes of this world. She would leave school, get some kind of a job; maybe her sister might get her into the supermarket. She would never get third-level education. There wasn't the background, there weren't the brains. She would survive.

⟨∼⟩

NONE OF THEM knew what Kathy Clarke's home life was like. If they thought at all, they might have assumed it was one of the houses on the big sprawling estate with too much television and fast food and too little peace and quiet, too many children and not enough money coming in. That would be the normal picture. They could not know that Kathy's bedroom had a built-in desk and a little library of books. Her elder sister, Fran, sat there every evening until homework was finished. In winter there was a gas heater with portable cylinders of bottled gas that Fran bought at a discount in the supermarket.

Kathy's parents laughed at the extravagance, all the other children had done their homework at the kitchen table and hadn't it been fine. But Fran said it had not been fine. She had left school at fifteen with no qualifications, it had taken her years to build her way up to a position of seniority, and there were still huge gaps in her education. The boys had barely scraped by, two working in England and one a roadie with a pop group. It was as if Fran had a mission to get Kathy to make more of herself than the rest of the family.

Sometimes Kathy felt she was letting Fran down. "You see I'm not really very bright, Fran. Things don't come to me like they do to some of them in the class. You wouldn't believe how quick Harriet is."

"Well, her father's a teacher, why wouldn't she be bright?" Fran sniffed.

"Yes, this is what I mean, Fran. You're so good to me. When you should be dancing you give time to me hearing my homework, and I'm so afraid I'll fail all my exams and be a disgrace to you after all your work."

"I don't want to go dancing," Fran would sigh.

"But you're still young enough surely to go to discos?" Kathy was sixteen, the baby of the family, Fran was thirty-two, the eldest. She really should be married now with a home of her own like all her friends were, and yet Kathy never wanted Fran to leave. The house would be unthinkable without her. Their mam was out a lot in town, getting things done was what it was called. In fact it was playing slot machines.

There would have been very few comforts in this house if Fran were not there to provide them. Orange juice for breakfast, and a hot meal in the evening. It was Fran who bought Kathy's school uniform and who taught the girl to polish her shoes and to wash her blouses and underwear every night. She would have learned nothing like this from her mother.

Fran explained the facts of life to her and bought her the first packet of Tampax. Fran said that it was better to wait until you found someone you liked a lot to have sex with, rather than having it with anyone just because it was expected.

"Did you find someone you liked a lot to have it with?" the fourteen-year-old Kathy had asked with interest.

But Fran had an answer for that one too. "I've always thought it best not to talk about it, you know the magic sort of goes out of it once you start speaking about it," she said, and that was that.

Fran took her to the theater, to plays in the Abbey, the Gate, and the Project. She brought her up and down Grafton Street and through the smart shops as well. "We must learn to do everything with an air of confidence," Fran said. "That's the whole trick, we mustn't look humble and apologetic as if we hadn't a right to be here."

There was never a word of criticism from Fran about their parents. Sometimes Kathy complained: "Mam takes you for granted, Fran, you bought her a lovely new cooker and she still never makes anything in it."

"Ah, she's all right," Fran would say.

"Dad never says thank you when you bring him home beer from the supermarket. He never brings you home a present."

"He's not the worst," Fran said. "It's not a great life with your head stuck down pipes and round S bends all the time."

"Will you get married do you think?" Kathy asked her once anxiously.

"I'll wait until you're a grown-up then I'll put my mind to it." Fran laughed when she said it.

"But won't you be too old?"

"Not at all. By the time you're twenty I'll only be thirty-six, in my prime," she assured her sister.

"I thought you were going to marry Ken," Kathy had said.

"Yes, well I didn't. And he went to America, so he's out of the picture." Fran was brisk.

Ken had worked in the supermarket too and was very go-ahead. Mam and Dad said that he and Fran were sure to make a go of it. Kathy had been very relieved when Ken had left the picture.

∽

AT THE SUMMER parent–teacher meeting Kathy's father wasn't able to go. He said he had to work late that night.

"Please, Dad, please. The teachers want a parent there. Mam won't come, she never does, and you wouldn't have to do anything only listen and tell them it's all fine."

"God, Kathy, I hate going into a school, I feel out of place."

"But Dad, it's not as if I had done anything bad and they were giving out about me, I just want them to think you're all interested."

"And we are, we are, child . . . but your mother's not herself these days and she'd be worse than useless and you know the way they go on about smoking up there, it sets her back . . . maybe Fran will go again. She'd know more than we would anyway."

So Fran went and spoke about her little sister to the tired teachers, who had to see legions of parents in a confessional situation and give a message of encouragement laced with caution to all of them.

"She's too serious," they told Fran. "She tries too hard, she might take more in if she were to relax more."

"She's very interested, really she is," Fran protested. "I sit with her when she does her homework, she never neglects any of it."

"She doesn't play any games does she?" The man who was going to be the new headmaster was nice. He seemed to have the vaguest knowledge of the children and spoke in generalities. Fran wondered if he really remembered them all or was making wild guesses.

"No, she doesn't want to take the time from her studying, you see."

"Maybe she should." He was brusque and good-natured about it.

"I don't think she should continue with Latin," the nice, pleasant Mr. Dunne said.

Fran's heart fell. "But Mr. Dunne, she tries so hard. I never studied it myself and I'm trying to follow it in the book with her and she really does put in hours on it."

"But you see, she doesn't understand what it's about." Poor Mr. Dunne was trying hard not to offend her.

"Could I get her a couple of private lessons? It would be great for her to have Latin in her Leaving. Look at all the places she could go with a subject like that."

"She may not get the points for university." It was as if he was letting her down lightly.

"But she *has* to. None of us have got anywhere, she must get a start in life."

"You have a very good job yourself, Miss Clarke. I see you when I go to the supermarket, couldn't you get Kathy a job there?"

"Kathy will *never* work in the supermarket." Fran's eyes were blazing.

"I'm sorry," he said quietly.

"No, I'm sorry, it is very kind of you to take such an interest. Please forgive me for shouting like this. Just advise me what would be best for her."

"She should do something that she would enjoy, something she wouldn't have to strain at," Mr. Dunne said. "A musical instrument, has she shown any interest?"

"No." Fran shook her head. "Nothing like that. We're all tone-deaf, even the brother who's working for a pop group."

"Or painting?"

"I can't see it myself, she'd only fret over that, too, to know was she getting it right." It was easy to talk to this kind man, Mr. Dunne. It was probably hard for him to tell parents and family that a child wasn't bright enough to get third-level education. Maybe his own children were at university and he wished that others would also get the chance. And it was good of him to care that poor Kathy should be happy and relaxed. She hated being so negative to all his suggestions. The man meant so well. He must have great patience, too, being a teacher.

Aidan looked back at the thin, handsome face of this girl who showed much more interest in her sister than either of the parents could summon up. He hated having to say that a child was slow, because truthfully he felt guilty about it. He always thought that if the school were smaller, or there were better facilities, if there were bigger libraries, extra tuition when called for, maybe then there would be far fewer slow pupils. He had discussed this with Signora when they planned the Italian classes. She said it had a lot to do with people's expectations. It took more than a generation of free education to stop people believing there were barriers and obstacles in the way.

It had been the same in Italy, she said. She had seen the children of a local hotelier and his wife grow up. The village had been small and poor, nobody ever thought that the children from the little school there should do more than their fathers or mothers had. She had taught them English only so that they could greet tourists and be chambermaids or waiters. She had wanted so much more for them. Signora understood what Aidan wanted for the people around Mountainview school.

She was such an easy person to talk to. They had many a coffee as they planned the evening classes. She was undemanding company, asking no questions about his home and family, telling little of her own life in that Jerry Sullivan household. He had even told her about the study he was making for himself.

"I'm not very interested in possessions," Signora said. "But a lovely quiet room with light coming in a window and a desk in good wood, and all your memories, and books and pictures on a wall . . . that would be very satisfying indeed." She spoke as if she were a gypsy or a bag lady who might never aspire to something so wonderful, but would appreciate it as a reward for others.

He would tell her about this Kathy Clarke, the girl with the anxious face trying hard because her sister expected so much and thought she was clever. Maybe Signora would come up with an idea, she often did.

But he took his mind away from the pleasant chats he had with her and so enjoyed and back to the present. There was a long night ahead of him. "I'm sure you'll think of something, Miss Clarke." Mr. Dunne looked beyond her to the line of parents still to be seen.

"I'm very grateful to you all here." Fran sounded as if she meant it. "You really do give your time, and care about the children. Years ago when I was at school it wasn't like that, or maybe I'm only making excuses." She was serious and pale-faced. Young Kathy Clarke was lucky to have such a concerned sister.

Fran went to the bus stop hands in pockets and head down. She had to pass an annex on the way out and saw a notice up advertising Italian lessons next September. A course to introduce you to the colors and paintings and music and language of Italy. It promised to be fun as well as educational. Fran wondered whether something like that might be a good idea. But it was too dear. She had so many outgoings. It would be very hard to pay a whole term in advance. And suppose Kathy decided to take the whole thing too seriously, as she had taken everything else. Then it might be a case of the cure being worse than the disease. No, she would have to think of something else. Fran sighed and walked to the bus stop.

There she met Peggy Sullivan, one of the women who worked at the checkout. "They'd put years on you these meetings, wouldn't they?" said Mrs. Sullivan.

"There's a lot of hanging about certainly, but it's better than when we were young and no one knew where we were half the time. How's your own little fellow getting on?" As manageress Fran had made it her business to know personally as many of the staff as possible. She knew that Peggy had two children, both of them severe trials. A grown-up daughter who didn't get on with the father and a youngster who wouldn't open a book.

"Well, Jerry's not going to believe this but apparently he's much improved. They all said it. He's started to join the human race again, as one of them put it."

"That's a bit of good news."

"Well, it's all down to this cracked one we have living with us. Not a word to anyone, Miss Clarke, but we have a lodger, half Italian half Irish. Says she was married to an Italian and he died, but that's not true at all. I think she's a nun in disguise. But anyway didn't she take an interest in Jerry and she has him a changed man it would appear." Peggy Sullivan explained that Jerry hadn't understood that poetry was meant to *mean* something until Signora came to the house and this had made all the difference. His English teacher was delighted with him, and he hadn't understood that history really happened and now he did, and *that* had made all the difference.

Fran thought sadly that her own sister, on whom she had lavished such attention, had not realized that Latin was a language people spoke. Perhaps this Signora might open doors for her, too. "What does she do for a living, your lodger?" she asked.

"Oh, you'd need a fleet of detectives to find out. A bit of sewing here and a bit of work up in a hospital, I believe, but she's going to be teaching an Italian class here in the school next term and she's high as a kite over it. You'd think it was the World Cup she'd won all by herself, singing little Italian songs. She's spending the whole summer getting ready for it. Nicest woman that ever wore shoe leather, but off-the-wall I tell you, off-the-wall."

Fran decided there and then. She would sign up for the course. She and Kathy would go there every Tuesday and Thursday, they'd bloody learn Italian, that's what they'd do, and they'd enjoy doing it, with this madwoman who was singing songs and getting ready for it so excitedly. It might make the poor nervous, tense Kathy relax a bit, and it might help Fran to forget Ken, who had gone to America without her.

"They said Kathy was a great girl," Fran said proudly at the kitchen table.

Her mother, despondent over some heavy losses at the machines, tried to show enthusiasm. "Well, why wouldn't they? She *is* a great girl."

"They didn't say anything bad about me?" Kathy asked.

"No, they didn't. They said you were great at your homework and that it was a pleasure to teach you. So now!"

"I'd like to have been there, child, it's just that I didn't think I'd get off in time." Kathy and Fran forgave him. It didn't matter now.

"I have a great treat for you, Kathy, we're going to learn Italian. Yourself and myself."

If she had suggested they fly to the moon, nothing could have surprised the Clarke family more.

Kathy flushed with pleasure. "The two of us?"

"Why not? I always fancied going to Italy and wouldn't my chances of picking up an Italian fellow be much better if I could speak the language!"

"Would I be able for it?"

"Of course you would, it's for eejits like myself who haven't learned anything, you'd probably be top of the class, but it's meant to be fun. There's this woman and she's going to play us operas and show us pictures and give us Italian food. It'll be terrific."

"It's not very expensive, is it, Fran?"

"No, it's not, and look at the value we'll get from it," said Fran, who was already wondering was she verging on madness to have made such an announcement.

During the summer Ken settled himself in the small town in New York State. He wrote again to Fran. "I love you, I will always love you. I do understand about Kathy but couldn't you come out here? We could have her out for the holidays, you could teach her then. Please say yes before I get a little service flat for myself. Say yes and we'll get a little house. She's sixteen, Fran, I can't wait another four years for you."

SHE WEPT OVER the letter, but she couldn't leave Kathy now. This had been her dream, to see one of the Clarkes get to university. True, Ken had said wait until their children were born, then they could plan it from the word go, to give them all the chances in the world, but Ken didn't understand. She had invested too much in Kathy. The girl was not an intellectual, but she was not stupid. If she had been born to wealthy parents, she would have had all the advantages that would cushion her. She would get her place in university merely because there would be enough time, there would be books in the house, people would have expectations. Fran had raised Kathy's hopes. She couldn't go now and leave her to her mother, who would look up vaguely from the gambling machines, and her father, who would mean well but see no further than the next cash-in-hand job for the few simple comforts he wanted from life.

Kathy would drown without her.

IT WAS A warm summer, visitors came to Ireland in greater numbers than before. The supermarket arranged special picnic lunches that people could take out to the park. It had been Fran's idea, it was a great success.

Mr. Burke at the bacon counter had been doubtful. "I don't want to go on about being in this business man and boy, Miss Clarke, but really I can't think it's a good idea to slice bacon and fry it and serve it cold in a sandwich. Why wouldn't they make do with nice lean ham like they always did?"

"There's a taste now, Mr. Burke, that people like their bacon crispy and you see if we keep the pieces nice and warm and fill the sandwiches as they come in, I can tell you they'll want more and more."

"But suppose I cut it and it's fried and nobody buys it, what then, Miss Clarke?" He was such a nice man, anxious and very willing to please but fearful of change.

"Let's give it a three-week trial, Mr. Burke, and see," she said.

She had been totally correct. People flocked for the great sandwiches. They lost money on them, of course, but that didn't matter; once you got people into the supermarket they bought other things on the way to the checkout.

She took Kathy to the Museum of Modern Art, and on her day off they went on a three-hour bus tour of Dublin. Just so that we know about where we live, Fran had said. They loved it, the two Protestant cathedrals that they had never been inside, and they drove around the Phoenix Park and they looked on proudly as the Georgian doors and fanlight windows were pointed out.

"Imagine we're the only Irish people on the bus," Kathy whispered. "This is all ours, the others are visitors."

And without being too bossy Fran organized the sixteen-year-old to get a smart yellow cotton dress, and to get her hair cut. At the end of the summer she was tanned and attractive-looking, her eyes had lost the haunted look.

Kathy did have friends, Fran noticed, but not close, giggly friends as she had known when she was young, what seemed like a whole generation ago. Some of these friends went to a noisy disco on a Saturday, a place that Fran knew about from the youngsters at work.

She knew enough to know it was not at all well run and that drugs circulated freely. She always happened to be passing by at one o'clock in the morning to collect her sister. She asked Barry, one of the young van drivers in the supermarket, to pick her up on several of these Saturdays and to drive past the disco. He had said it wasn't a place for a youngster.

"What can I do?" Fran shrugged at him. "Tell her not to go and she feels a victim. I think I'm lucky that I can have you to act as an excuse to get her home." Barry was a great kid, mad for overtime since he wanted to buy a motorbike. He said he had saved enough for one third of it, as soon as he had half the price he'd go and choose it, and then when he had two thirds he would buy it and pay the rest later.

"And what do you want it for, Barry?" Fran asked.

"For freedom, Miss Clarke," he said. "You know, freedom, all that air rushing past and everything."

Fran felt very old. "My sister and I are going to learn Italian," she told him one night as they waited outside the disco edging the advent of his motorbike nearer.

"Oh that's great, Miss Clarke. I'd like to do that myself. I went to the World Cup, I made the greatest of friends, the nicest people you'd meet in a day's walk, Miss Clarke, much the way we'd be, I often think, if we had the weather."

"Maybe you'll learn Italian too." She spoke absently. She was watching tough-looking people come out of the disco. Why did Kathy and her friends want to go there? Imagine the freedom they had at sixteen to go to such places compared to her day.

"I might if I have the bike paid for because one of the first places I'm going to take it is Italy," Barry said.

"Well, it's up in Mountainview school and it begins in September." She spoke in a slightly distracted tone because she had just seen Kathy, Harriet, and their friends come out. She leaned over and hooted the horn. Immediately they looked over. The regular Saturday lift home was becoming part of the scene. What about the parents of all these girls, she thought? Did any of them care? Was she just a fusspot herself? Lord, but it would be such a relief when the term started again and all these outings were over.

THE ITALIAN CLASSES began on a Tuesday at seven o'clock. There had been a letter from Ken that morning. He was settled in his little apartment; a flat didn't mean a flat, it meant a flat tire over there. The stock control was totally different. There were no deals with suppliers; you paid what was asked. People were very friendly, they invited him around to their homes. Soon it would be Labor Day and they would have a picnic to define that the summer was over. He missed her. Did she miss him?

There were thirty people in the class. Everyone got a huge piece of cardboard to put their names on, but this marvelous woman said they should be called by the Italian version. So Fran became Francesca, and Kathy, Caterina. They had great games of shaking hands and asking people what their names were. Kathy seemed to be enjoying it hugely. It would be worth it in the end, Fran said, putting the memory of Ken going to Labor Day picnics out of her mind.

"Hey, Fran, do you see that guy who says *Mi chiamo Bartolomeo?* Isn't that Barry from your supermarket?" It was indeed. Fran was pleased, the overtime must have been good enough to sort out the bike. They waved at each other across the room.

What an extraordinary assortment of people. There was that elegant woman, surely she was the one who gave those huge lunches at her house. What on earth could she be doing at a place like this? And the beautiful girl with the golden curls, *Mi chiamo Elisabetta,* and her nice staid boyfriend in his good suit. And the dark, violent-looking Luigi and the older man called Lorenzo. What an amazing mixture.

Signora was delightful. "I know your landlady," Fran said to her when they were having little snacks of salami and cheese.

"Yes, well, Mrs. Sullivan is a relation, I am a relation," Signora said nervously.

"Of course. How stupid, yes I know she is." Fran was reassuring. It was her own father's lifestyle, she knew it well. "She said you were very helpful to her son."

Signora's face broke into a wide smile. She was very beautiful when she smiled. Fran didn't think she could be a nun. She was sure Peggy Sullivan had got it wrong.

❧

THEY LOVED THE lessons, Fran and Kathy. They went together on the bus laughing like children at their mispronunciations and at the stories Signora told them. Kathy told the girls at school and they could hardly believe it.

There was an extraordinary bond among the people in the class. It was as if they were on a desert island and their only hope of rescue was to learn the language, and remember everything they were taught. Possibly because Signora believed that they were all capable of great feats, they began to believe it too. She begged them to use the Italian words for everything, even if they couldn't form the whole sentence. They found themselves saying that they had to get back to the *casa* or that the *camera* was very warm or that they were *stanca* instead of tired.

And all the time Signora watched and listened, pleased but not surprised. She had never thought that anyone faced with the Italian language would feel anything but delight and enthusiasm for it. With her was Mr. Dunne, whose special project all this was. They seemed to get on together very well.

"Maybe they were friends from way back," Fran wondered.

"No, he's got a wife and grown-up children," Kathy explained.

"He could still have a wife and be her friend," Fran said.

"Yes, but I think he could be having it off with her, they're always giving special little smiles. Harriet says that's a dead giveaway." Harriet was Kathy's friend at school who was very interested in sex.

❧

AIDAN DUNNE WATCHED the flowering of the Italian class with a pleasure that he had not known possible. Week after week they came to the school, bicycles, motorbikes, vans, and bus, even the amazing woman in the BMW. And he loved planning the various surprises for them too. The paper flags they made, she would give everyone a blank flag then call out colors that they were to fill in. Each person would hold up a flag and the rest of the class had to call out the colors. They were like children, eager, enthusiastic pupils. And when the class was over, that tough-looking fellow, called Lou or Luigi or whatever, used to help tidy up, tough type, the last one you'd ever think would be hanging around to tidy up, put away boxes and stack chairs.

But that was Signora for you. She had this simple way of expecting the best and getting it. She had asked him if she could make cushion covers for him.

"Come and see the room," Aidan suggested suddenly.

"That's a good idea. When will I come?"

"Saturday morning. I've no school, would you be free?"

"I can be free anytime," she said.

He spent all of Friday evening cleaning and polishing his room. He took out the tray with the two little red glasses that came from Murano beside Venice. He had bought a bottle of marsala. They would toast the success of the room and the classes.

She came at midday and brought some sample fabrics. "I thought that yellow would be right from what you told me," she said, holding up a glowing rich color. "It costs a little more a meter than the others, but then it's a room for life, isn't it?"

"A room for life," Aidan repeated.

"Do you want to show it to your wife before I begin?" she asked.

"No, no. Nell will be pleased. I mean, this is *my* room really."

"Yes, of course." She never asked questions.

Nell was not at home that morning, nor were either of his daughters. Aidan hadn't told them of the visit, and he was glad they weren't there. Together he and Signora toasted the success of the Italian class and the Room for Life.

"I wish you could teach in the school itself, you can create such enthusiasm," he said admiringly.

"Ah. That's only because they want to learn."

"But that girl Kathy Clarke, they say she's as bright as a button these days, all due to the Italian classes."

"Caterina . . . a nice girl."

"Well, I hear that she has them all entertained in the classroom with stories of your class, they all want to join."

"Isn't that wonderful?" said Signora.

What Aidan did not report, because he didn't know it, was that Kathy Clarke's description of the Italian class included an account of his playing footsie with the ancient Italian teacher, and that he looked at her with the adoring eyes of a puppy. Kathy's friend Harriet said she had always suspected it. It was the quiet ones that you had to watch. That's where real passion and lust were lurking.

❧

MISS HAYES WAS taking a history class and was anxious to relate things to the modern day. Something the children might recognize. Telling them the Medicis were patrons of the arts was no use, she called them sponsors. That would mean something.

"Can anyone think of the people that they sponsored?" she asked.

They looked at each other blankly.

"Sponsor?" Harriet asked. "Like a drinks company or an insurance company?"

"Yes. You must know the names of some of the famous artists of Italy, don't you?" The history teacher was young, she was not yet hardened to how much children had forgotten or what they had never known.

Quietly Kathy Clarke stood up. "One of the most important was Michelangelo. When one of the Medicis was Pope Sixtus V he asked Michelangelo to do the roof of the Sistine Chapel, and he wanted all the different scenes." In a calm, confident voice she told the class about the scaffolding that was built, the rows and the fallings-out. The problems that there still were in keeping the colors alive.

There was no frown, there was just enthusiasm. Since she had obviously gone further than Miss Hayes the young history teacher could have attempted, it was soon time to bring it to an end.

"Thank you for that, Katherine Clarke, now can anyone else name any other artist of the period?"

Kathy's hand went up again. The teacher looked around to see if there was any other taker, but there was no one. The boys and girls looked on amazed as Kathy Clarke explained about Leonardo da Vinci's notebooks, five thousand pages of them, all in mirror writing, maybe because he was left-handed or maybe because he wanted them kept secret. And how he applied to the Duke of Milan for a job saying he could design cannon-proof ships in wartime and statues in peacetime.

Kathy knew all this and was telling it as if it were a story.

"Jesus, Mary, and Joseph, those Italian culture classes must be something else," said Josie Hayes in the staff room.

"What do you mean?" they asked.

"I've had Kathy Clarke standing up giving me a rundown of the Renaissance like nobody's ever heard."

Across the room Aidan Dunne, who had dreamed up the classes, stirred his coffee and smiled to himself. A big happy smile.

IT BROUGHT THEM even closer together, Kathy and Fran, the hours spent at the Italian class. Matt Clarke came home from England in the autumn to tell them that he was getting married to Tracey from Liverpool but that they weren't having much of a do, they were going to go to the Canaries instead. Everyone was relieved that it didn't mean a trek to England for the wedding. They giggled a bit when they heard that the honeymoon was going to be before not after the marriage.

Matt thought it was sensible. "She wants a suntan for the wedding snaps and of course if we hate each other out there then we can call it off," he said cheerfully.

Matt gave his mother money for the slot machines and took his father for a few pints. "What's all this business about learning Italian?" he asked.

"Search me," said his father. "I can't make head nor tail of it. Fran is worn out above in the supermarket early mornings, late nights. The fellow she was going with has gone off to the States. I haven't a notion why she wants to bring all this on herself, specially since they say over in the school that young Kathy works too hard already. But they're mad about it. Planning to go there next year and all. So let them at it."

"Kathy's turning into a grand little looker, isn't she?" Matt said.

"I suppose she is. Do you know, seeing her every day I never noticed," his father said with an air of surprise.

Kathy was indeed becoming more attractive. At school her friend

Harriet commented on it. "Do you have a fellow or something at this Italian class? You seem different somehow."

"No, but there are lots of older men there all right." Kathy laughed. "Very old, some of them. We have to pair into couples to do the asking-for-a-date bit. It's a scream. I had this man, he must be about a hundred, called Lorenzo. Well, I think it's Laddy in real life. Anyway Lorenzo says to me '*È libera questa sera*' and he rolls his eyes and twirls an imaginary mustache and everyone was sick with laughter."

"Go on. And does she teach you anything really useful like How's about it and what you'd say?"

"Sort of." Kathy searched her memory for the phrase. "There's things like *Vive solo* or *sola,* that's Do you live alone. And there's one I can't quite remember . . . *Deve rincasare questa notte,* Do you have to go home tonight."

"And she's the old one we see in the library sometimes with the funny-colored hair?"

"Yes, Signora."

"Imagine," said Harriet. Things were getting stranger all the time.

"DO YOU STILL go to those classes in Mountainview, Miss Clarke?" Peggy Sullivan was handing in her till's takings.

"They're really terrific, Mrs. Sullivan. Do pass that on to Signora, won't you? Everyone just loves them. Do you know that nobody at all has fallen out of the class. That must be unheard of."

"Well, she sounds very cheerful about them, I must say. An extraordinarily secretive person, of course, Miss Clarke. Claims she was married to some Italian for twenty-six years in a village out there . . . never a letter from Italy . . . not a picture of him in sight. *And* it turns out she has a whole family living in Dublin, a mother in those expensive flats down by the sea, a father in a home and brothers and sisters all over the place."

"Yes, well . . ." Fran didn't want to hear anything even mildly critical or questioning about Signora.

"It just seems odd, doesn't it. What's she living in one room in our estate for if she has all this family dotted all over the place?"

"Maybe she doesn't get on with them. It could be as simple as that."

"She goes to see her mother every Monday and her father twice a week up in the home. She wheels him out in his chair, one of the nurses told Suzi. She sits and reads to him under a tree and he just sits and stares ahead, even though he makes an effort to talk to the others who only come once in a blue moon."

"Poor Signora," said Fran suddenly. "She deserves better than that."

"Well she does, now that you say it, Miss Clarke," said Peggy Sullivan.

❧

SHE HAD GOOD reason to be grateful to this strange visitor, nun or not a nun. She had been a great influence on their lives. Suzi got on great with her and came home much more regularly, Jerry regarded her as his own private tutor. She had made net curtains for them and matching cushion covers. She had painted the dresser in the kitchen and planted window boxes. Her room was immaculate and neat as a new pin. Sometimes Peggy Sullivan had gone in to investigate. As one would. But Signora seemed to have acquired no more possessions than those she had when she arrived. She was an extraordinary person. It was good that they all liked her in the class.

❧

KATHY CLARKE WAS the youngest of her students by far. The girl was eager to learn and asked about the grammar, which the others didn't know or didn't bother about. She was attractive, too, in that blue-eyed, dark-haired way that she had never seen in Italy. There the dark beauties all had huge brown eyes.

She wondered what Kathy would do when she left school. Sometimes she saw the girl studying in the library. She must have hopes of getting a third-level education.

"What does your mother think you might do when you leave school?" she asked Kathy one evening when they were all tidying up the chairs after the lesson. People stayed and chatted, no one was anxious to run away, which was good. She knew for a fact that some of them went for a drink in a pub up the hill and others for coffee. It was all as she had hoped.

"My mother?" Kathy seemed surprised.

"Yes, she seems so eager and enthusiastic about everything," Signora said.

"No, she doesn't really know much about the school or what I'm doing. She doesn't go out much, she'd have no idea what there was to do or study or anything."

"But she comes here to the class with you, doesn't she, and she goes out to work in the supermarket? Mrs. Sullivan where I stay says she's the boss."

"Oh, that's Fran. That's my *sister*," Kathy said. "Don't let her hear you said that, she'd go mad."

Signora looked puzzled. "I'm so sorry, I get everything wrong."

"No, it's an easy mistake." Kathy was anxious for the older woman not to be embarrassed. "Fran's the oldest of the family, I'm the youngest. Of course you thought that."

She didn't say anything to Fran about it. No point in making Fran go to the mirror to look for lines. Poor Signora was a bit absentminded, and she did get a lot of things wrong. But she was so marvelous as a teacher. Everyone in the class, including Bartolomeo, the one of the motorbike, loved her.

Kathy liked Bartolomeo, he had a lovely smile and he told her all about football. He asked where she went dancing, and when she told him about the disco in the summer he said it was a date when it came to half term and they could go out dancing again, he'd tell her a good place.

She reported this to Harriet. "I knew you joined that class just for sex," Harriet said. And they laughed and laughed over it long after anyone else would have thought it remotely funny.

❧

THERE WAS A bad rainstorm in October and a leak came in the roof of the annex where the evening class was held. With huge solidarity they all managed to cope with it by getting newspapers, and moving tables out of the way and finding a bucket in one of the cloakrooms. All the time they shouted *Che tempaccio* at each other and *Che bruto tempo*. Barry said he would wait outside in his rain gear at the bus stop and flash his lights when the bus arrived so that everyone would not get soaked to the skin.

Connie, the woman with the jewelry that Luigi said would buy a block of flats, said she could give four people a lift. They scrambled into her beautiful BMW—Guglielmo, the nice young man from the bank, his dizzy girlfriend, Elisabetta, Francesca, and young Caterina. They went first to Elisabetta's flat and there was a lot of chorusing of *ciao* and *arrivederci* as the two young lovers scampered up the steps in the rain.

And then it was on to the Clarkes' house. Fran in front gave directions. This was not the kind of territory that would be familiar to Connie. When they got there, Fran saw her mother putting out the dustbin, a cigarette still in her mouth despite the rain that would fall on it and make it soggy, the same scuffed slippers and sloppy housecoat that she wore all the time. She then felt ashamed of herself for feeling ashamed of her mother. Just because she was getting a lift in a smart car didn't mean that she should change all her values. Her mother had had a hard life and had been generous and understanding when it was needed.

"There's Mam getting drenched. Wouldn't the bins have done in the morning?" Fran said.

"*Che tempaccio, che tempaccio,*" Kathy said dramatically.

"Go on, Caterina. Your granny's holding the door open for you," Connie said.

"That's my mother," Kathy said.

There was so much rain, so much confusion of banging doors and clattering dustbins, nobody seemed to take much notice.

Inside the house Mrs. Clarke was looking with surprise and disgust at her wet cigarette. "I got drowned waiting for you to come in from that limousine."

"God, let's have a cup of tea," said Fran, running to the kettle.

Kathy sat down suddenly at the kitchen table.

"*Due tazze di tè,*" Fran said in her best Italian. "Come on, Kathy. *Con latte? Con zucchero?*"

"You know I don't take milk and sugar." Kathy's voice was remote. She looked very pale. Mrs. Clarke said there was no point in a person staying up if this is all you were to hear, she was going off to her bed and

to tell that husband of hers when and if he ever came in from the pub not
to be leaving any frying pan to clean up in the morning.

She was gone, complaining, coughing, and creaking up the stairs.

"What is it, Kathy?"

Kathy looked at her. "Are you my mother, Fran?" she asked.

There was a silence in the kitchen. They could hear the flushing of the
lavatory upstairs and the rain falling on the concrete outside.

"Why do you ask this now?"

"I want to know. Are you or aren't you?"

"You know I am, Kathy." A long silence.

"No I didn't know. Not until now." Fran came toward her, reaching
out. "No, go away from me. I don't want you to touch me."

"Kathy you knew, you felt it, it didn't need to be said, I thought you
knew."

"Does everyone else know?"

"What do you mean everyone else? The people who need to, know.
You know how much I love you, how I'd do everything on earth for you
and get you the best that I could get."

"Except a father and a home and a name."

"You have a name, you have a home, you have another father and
mother in Mam and Dad."

"No I haven't. I'm a bastard that you had and never told me about."

"There's no such word as 'bastard,' as you well know. There's no
such thing anymore as an illegitimate child. And you were legally part of
this household since the day you were born. This is your home."

"How could you . . ." Kathy began.

"Kathy, what are you saying . . . that I should have given you away
to strangers for adoption, that I should have waited until you were eighteen before I got to know you and only then if you sought me out?"

"And all of these years letting me think that Mam was my mother. I
can't believe it." Kathy shook her head as if to clear it, to take this new
and frightening idea out of her mind.

"Mam was a mother to you and to me. She welcomed you from the
day she knew about you. She said won't it be grand to have another
baby round here. That's what she said and it was. And, Kathy, I thought
you knew."

"How would I have known? We both called Mam and Dad Mam and

Dad. People said you were my sister and that Matt and Joe and Sean were my brothers. How was I to know?"

"Well, it wasn't a big thing. We were all together in the house, you were only seven years younger than Joe, it was the natural way to do things."

"Do all the neighbors know?"

"Some of them maybe, they've forgotten I imagine."

"And who was my father? Who was my real father?"

"Dad is your real father in that he brought you up and looked after both of us."

"You know what I mean."

"He was a boy who was at a posh school and his parents didn't want him to marry me."

"Why do you say 'was'? Is he dead?"

"No, he's not dead, but he's not part of our lives."

"He's not part of your life, he might be part of mine."

"I don't think that's a good idea."

"It doesn't matter what you think. Wherever he is, he's still my father. I have a right to know him, to meet him, to tell him I'm Kathy and that I exist because of him."

"Please have some tea. Or let me have some anyway."

"I'm not stopping you." Her eyes were cold.

Fran knew she needed more tact and diplomacy than had ever been called on in work. Even the time when one of the director's children, there on a holiday job, was found pilfering. This was vastly more important.

"I'll tell you every single thing you want to know. Everything," she said, in as calm a voice as she could manage. "And if Dad comes in in the middle of it I suggest we move up to your room."

Kathy's room was much bigger than Fran's. It had the desk, the bookshelf, the handbasin that had been put in lovingly by the plumber in the house years ago.

"You did it all from guilt, didn't you, the nice room, the buying my uniform, and the extra pocket money and even the Italian classes. You paid for it all because you were so guilty about me."

"I have never had a day's guilt about you in my life," Fran said calmly. She sounded so sure that she stopped Kathy in the slightly hysterical tone she was taking. "No, I have felt sad for you sometimes, because you work so hard and I hoped I would be able to give you everything to start you off well. I worked hard so that I could always provide a good living for you. I've saved a little every single week in a building society, not much but enough to give you independence. I have loved you every day of my life, and honestly it got kind of blurred whether you were my sister or my daughter. You're just Kathy to me and I want the very, very best for you. I work long and hard to get it and I think about it all the time. So I assure you whatever I feel I don't feel guilty."

Tears came into Kathy's eyes. Fran reached her hand over tentatively and patted the hand that clutched the mug of tea.

Kathy said: "I know, I shouldn't have said that. I got a shock, you see."

"No, no it's all right. Ask me anything."

"What's his name?"

"Paul. Paul Malone."

"Kathy Malone?" she said wonderingly.

"No, Kathy Clarke."

"And how old was he then?"

"Sixteen. I was fifteen and a half."

"When I think of all the bossy advice you gave me about sex and how I listened."

"Look back on what I said you'll find that I didn't preach what I didn't practice."

"So you loved him, this Paul Malone?" Kathy's voice was very scornful.

"Yes, very much. Very much indeed. I was young but I thought I knew what love was and so did he, so I won't dismiss it and say it was nonsense. It wasn't."

"And where did you meet him?"

"At a pop concert. We got on so well then I used to sneak out to meet him from school sometimes and we'd go to the pictures, and he was meant to be having extra lessons so he could skip that. And it was a wonderful happy time."

"And then?"

"And then I realized I was pregnant, and Paul told his mother and father and I told Mam and Dad and all hell broke out everywhere."

"Did anyone talk about getting married?"

"No, nobody talked about it. I thought about it a lot up in the room that's your room now. I used to dream that one day Paul would come to the door with a bunch of flowers and say that as soon as I was sixteen we would marry."

"But it didn't happen obviously?"

"No, it didn't."

"And why did he not want to stay around and support you even if you didn't marry?"

"That was part of the deal."

"Deal?"

"Yes. His parents said that since this was an unlikely partnership and that there was no future in it, it might be kindest for everyone to cut all ties. That's what they said. Cut all ties or maybe sever all ties."

"Were they awful?"

"I don't know, I'd never met them until then, any more than Paul had met Mam and Dad."

"So the deal was that he was to get away with it, father a child and never see her again."

"They gave four thousand pounds, Kathy, it was a lot of money then."

"They bought you off!"

"No, we didn't think it was like that. I put two thousand in a building society for you. It's grown a lot as well as what I added myself, and we gave the other two thousand pounds to Mam and Dad because they would be bringing you up."

"And did Paul Malone think that was fair? To give four thousand pounds to get rid of me?"

"He didn't know you. He listened to his parents, they told him sixteen was too young to be a father, he had a career ahead of him, it was a mistake, he must honor his commitment to me. That's the way they saw it."

"And did he have a career?"

"Yes, he's an accountant."

"My father the accountant," Kathy said.

"He married and he has children now, his own family."

"You mean he has other children?" Kathy's chin was in the air.

"Yes, that's right. Two, I believe."

"How do you know?"

"There was an article about him in a magazine not long ago, you know, lifestyles of the rich and famous, that is."

"But he's not famous."

"His wife is, he married Marianne Hayes." Fran waited to see the effect this would have.

"My father is married to one of the richest women in Ireland."

"Yes."

"And he gave a measly four thousand pounds to get rid of me."

"That's not the point. He wasn't married to her then."

"It is the point. He's rich now, he should give something."

"You have enough, Kathy, we have everything we want."

"No of course I haven't everything I want, and neither do you," Kathy said, and suddenly the tears that were waiting came and she cried and cried, while Fran, who she had thought for sixteen years was her sister, stroked her head and her wet cheeks and her neck with all the love a mother could give.

The next morning at breakfast Joe Clarke had a hangover.

"Will you give me a can of cold Coca-Cola from the fridge, Kathy, like a good girl? I've a bugger of a job to do today out in Killiney and the van will be here for me any minute."

"You're nearer to the fridge than I am," Kathy said.

"Are you giving me cheek?" he asked.

"No, I'm just stating a fact."

"Well, no child of mine is going to be stating facts in that tone of voice, let me tell you," he said, face flushed with anger.

"I'm not a child of yours," Kathy said coldly.

They didn't even look up startled, her grandparents. These old people she had thought of as her mother and father. The woman went on reading the magazine and smoking, the man grumbled. "I'm as good as any other goddamn father you ever had or will have, go on child give me the Coke now to save me getting up, will you."

And Kathy realized that they weren't in the business of secrecy or pretending. Like Fran, they had assumed she knew the state of affairs.

She looked across at Fran standing with a rigid back looking out the window.

"All right, Dad," she said, and got him the can and a glass to pour it into.

"There's a good girl," he said, smiling at her as he always did. For him nothing had changed.

❧

"WHAT WOULD YOU do if you discovered you weren't your parents' child?" Kathy asked Harriet at school.

"I'd be delighted, I tell you that."

"Why?"

"Because then I won't grow up to have an awful chin like my mother and my grandmother, and I wouldn't have to listen to Daddy droning on and on about getting enough points in the Leaving." Harriet's father, a teacher, had great hopes that she would be a doctor. Harriet wanted to own a nightclub.

They let the matter drop.

"What do you know about Marianne Hayes?" Kathy asked later.

"She's like the richest woman in Europe or is it only Dublin? And she's good-looking too. I suppose she bought all those things like good teeth and a suntan and all that shiny hair."

"Yeah, I'm sure she did."

"Why are you interested in her?"

"I dreamed about her last night," Kathy said truthfully.

"I dreamed that I had sex with a gorgeous fellow. I think we should get started on it, you know we are sixteen."

"You're the one who said we should concentrate on our studies," Kathy complained.

"Yeah, that was before this dream. You look awful pale and tired and old, don't dream about Marianne Hayes again, it's not doing you any good."

"No, it's not," Kathy agreed, thinking suddenly of Fran with her white face and the lines under her eyes, and no suntan and no holidays abroad. She thought of Fran saving money every week for her for sixteen years. She remembered Fran's boyfriend Ken going off to America, had he, too, found some rich woman? Someone who wasn't a plumber's daughter who had dragged herself up to the top in a supermarket, someone who wasn't struggling to support an illegitimate child. Ken had known about her. It didn't appear that Fran had gone to any trouble to keep it all a secret.

As she had said last night, there were many, many households all over Dublin where the youngest child was really a grandchild. And Fran had said that in many cases the mother had not stayed at home, the eldest sister had left to start a new life. It wasn't fair.

It just wasn't fair that Paul Malone should have his pleasure and no responsibility. Three times that day in class she was reprimanded for not paying attention. But Kathy Clarke had no interest in her studies. She was planning how she should best visit Paul Malone.

❧

"TALK TO ME," Fran said that evening.

"What about? You said there was nothing more to say."

"So nothing's changed?" Fran asked. Her eyes were anxious. She didn't have expensive creams to take away the lines on her face. She never had anyone to help her bring up a child. Marianne Hayes, now Marianne Malone, must have had help everywhere. Nurses, nannies, au pairs, chauffeurs, tennis coaches. Kathy looked at her mother with a level glance. Even though her world had turned upside down, she wouldn't add this to Fran's trouble.

"No, Fran," she lied. "Nothing's changed."

❧

IT WASN'T HARD to find out where Paul and Marianne lived.

There was something about them in a paper almost every week. Everyone knew of their house. But she didn't want to go and see him at home. She must go to his office. Talk to him in a businesslike way. There was no need to involve his wife in what she wanted to say.

Armed with a phone card, she began to telephone large accountancy firms. On the second call she got the name of where he worked. She had heard of the company, they were accountants to all the film stars and theater people. This was a show business kind of place. Not only did he have all the money, he had all the fun too.

Twice she went to the offices and twice her courage failed. The building was so enormous. She knew they only occupied floors five and six, but somehow she didn't have the confidence. Once in she could talk to him, tell him who she was, how her mother had worked and saved. She would beg for nothing. She would point out the injustice, that was all. But the place was too impressive. It overawed her. The commissionaire in the foyer, the girls at the information desk downstairs who called up to see if you were allowed access to the prestigious offices above.

She would need to look different to get past these groomed dragons at the desk if she was to meet Paul Malone. They wouldn't let a schoolgirl in a navy skirt up to see a senior accountant, particularly one married to a millionaire.

She telephoned Harriet.

"Can you bring in some posh clothes of your mother's tomorrow to school?"

"Only if you tell me why."

"I'm going to have an adventure."

"A sexual adventure?"

"Possibly."

"Do you want nighties and knickers then?" Harriet was very practical.

"No, a jacket. And gloves even."

"God Almighty," said Harriet. "This must be something very kinky altogether."

Next day the clothes arrived slightly crushed in a games bag. Kathy tried them on in the girls' cloakroom. The jacket was fine, but the skirt seemed wrong.

"Where's the adventure?" Harriet was breathless with excitement.

"In an office, a smart office."

"You could sort of hitch your skirt up, you know the school one. It would look okay if it was meant to be short. Will he be undressing you or will you be doing it yourself?"

"What? Oh, yes I'll be doing it myself."

"That's all right then." Together they made Kathy look like someone who might gain access anywhere. She had already taken Fran's lipstick and eyeshadow.

"Don't put it all on now," Harriet warned.

"Why not?"

"I mean you've got to go to class, they'll know something's up if you go in like that."

"I'm not going to class. You're to say you got a message that I had the flu."

"No, I don't believe it."

"Go on, Harriet. I did it for you when you wanted to go down and see the pop stars."

"But where are you going at nine o'clock in the morning?"

"To the office to have the adventure," Kathy said.

"You are something else," said Harriet, whose mouth was round in admiration.

This time she didn't falter.

"Good morning. Mr. Paul Malone, please."

"And the name?"

"The name will mean nothing to him, but if you could say it is Katherine Clarke, come here about the matter of Frances Clarke, a client from a long time ago." Kathy felt that this was an office where people had full names, not Kathys and Frans.

"I'll speak to his secretary. Mr. Malone doesn't see anyone without an appointment."

"You may tell her that I will wait until he's free." Kathy spoke with a quiet intensity that was far more effective than her attempts to dress for the part.

One of the gorgeous receptionists seemed to shrug slightly at the other and make the call in a low voice.

"Miss Clarke, would you care to speak to Mr. Malone's secretary?" she said eventually.

"Certainly."

Kathy walked forward, hoping that her school skirt would not fall suddenly below Harriet's mother's jacket.

"It's Penny here. Can I help you?"

"Have you been given the relevant names?" Kathy said. How wonderful that she remembered that word "relevant." It was a great word, it covered everything.

"Well yes . . . but this is not actually the point."

"Ah, but I think it is. Please mention these names to Mr. Malone and please tell him that it will not take very long. Only ten minutes at the very most of his time, but I will wait here until he can see me."

"We don't make appointments like this."

"Please give him the names." Kathy felt almost dizzy with excitement. She waited politely for three more minutes, then there was a buzz.

"Mr. Malone's secretary will meet you on the sixth floor," said one of the goddesses at the desk.

"Thank you so much for your help," said Kathy Clarke, hitching up her school skirt and going into the lift that would take her to meet her father.

"Miss Clarke?" Penny said. Penny was like someone from a beauty contest. She wore a cream-colored suit and had very high-heeled black shoes. Around her neck she wore a thick black necklace.

"That's right." Kathy wished she were better-looking and older and well dressed.

"Come this way, please. Mr. Malone will see you in the conference room. Coffee?"

"That would be very nice, thank you."

She was shown into a room with a pale wood table, and eight chairs around it. There were paintings on the wall, not just pictures behind glass like they had in school, but real paintings. There were flowers on the windowsill, fresh flowers, arranged that morning. She sat and waited.

In he came, young, handsome, younger-looking than Fran, although he had been a year older.

"Hallo," he said, with a big smile from ear to ear.

"Hallo," she said. There was a silence.

At that moment Penny arrived with the coffee. "Shall I leave it?" she asked, dying to stay.

"Thanks, Pen," he said.

"Do you know who I am?" she asked when Penny had left.

"Yes," he said.

"Were you expecting me?"

"Not for about two or three more years, to be honest." His grin was attractive.

"And what would you have done then?"

"What I'll do now—listen . . ."

It was a clever thing to say, he was leaving it all to her.

"Well, I just wanted to come and see you," she said a little uncertainly.

"Absolutely," he said.

"To know what you looked like."

"And now you do." He was warm as he said it, he was warm and welcoming. "What do you think?" he asked.

"You look fine," she said reluctantly.

"And so do you, very fine," he said.

"I only just found out, you see," she explained.

"I see."

"So, that's why I had to come and talk to you."

"Sure, sure." He had poured them coffee and left her to add milk and sugar if she wished.

"You see, until this week I honestly thought I was Mam and Dad's daughter. It's been a bit of a shock."

"Fran didn't tell you that she was your mother?"

"No, she didn't."

"Well, when you were younger I can understand, but when you were older surely . . . ?"

"No, she thought I sort of understood, but I didn't. I thought she was just a marvelous elder sister. I wasn't too bright, you see."

"You look fine and bright to me." He seemed genuinely to admire her.

"I'm not as it happens. I'm a hard worker and I'll get there in the end, but I don't have quick leaps of understanding, not like my friend Harriet. I'm a bit of a plodder."

"So am I as it happens. You take after your father then."

It was such an extraordinary moment there in this office. He was admitting he was her father. She felt almost light-headed. But she had no idea where to go now. He had taken away all her arguments. She thought he would have blustered, and denied things and excused himself. But he had done nothing like this.

"You wouldn't have got a job like this if you were just a plodder."

"My wife is very wealthy, I am a charming plodder, I don't upset people. In a way that's why I am here."

"But you got to be an accountant all by yourself before you met her, didn't you?"

"Yes, I got to be an accountant, not here exactly. And I hope you'll meet my wife one day, Katherine. You'll like her, she's a very, very nice woman."

"It's Kathy, and I couldn't like her. I am sure she is very nice, but she wouldn't want to meet me."

"Yes, if I tell her I would like it. We do things to please each other, I would meet someone to please her."

"But she doesn't know I exist."

"Yes she does. I told her, a long time ago. I didn't know your name, but I told her that I had a daughter, a daughter I didn't see but would probably meet when she was grown up."

"You didn't know my name?"

"No. When all the business happened Fran said she would just tell me if it was a girl or a boy, that was all."

"That was the deal?" Kathy said.

"You put it very well. That was the deal."

"She's very kind about you, she thinks you were great in all this."

"And what message does she send me?" He was very relaxed, gentle, not watchful or anything.

"She has no idea I'm here."

"Where does she think you are?"

"At school up in Mountainview."

"Mountainview? Is that where you are?"

"There isn't much money out of four thousand pounds sixteen years ago to send me to a posh place," Kathy said with spirit.

"So you know about the deal?"

"I heard it all at the same time, in one night. I realized she was not my sister and that you had sold me."

"Is that how she put it?"

"No. It's how it is, she puts it differently."

"I'm very sorry. It must have been a bad, bleak kind of thing to hear."

Kathy looked at him. That's exactly what it had been. Bleak. She had thought about the unfairness of the deal. Her mother was poor, and could be paid off. Her father was the son of privileged people and didn't have to pay for his fun. It had made her think the system was always loaded against people like her, and always would be. Odd that he understood exactly the feeling.

"Yes it was. It is."

"Well, tell me what you want from me. Tell me and we can talk about it."

She had been going to demand everything under the sun for Fran and for herself. She had been going to make him realize that it was too late in the twentieth century for the rich to get away with everything. But somehow it wasn't easy to say all this to the man who sat easily and warmly giving every impression of being pleased to see her rather than horrified.

"I'm not sure yet what I want. It's all a bit soon."

"I know. You haven't had time to work out how you feel yet." He didn't look relieved or off the hook, he sounded sympathetic.

"It's still hard for me to take in, you see."

"And for me, meeting you too. That's hard to take in." He was putting himself in the same boat.

"Aren't you annoyed I came?"

"No, you couldn't be more wrong. I'm delighted you came to see me. I'm only sorry that life was hard up to now and then it got worse with this shock. That's what I feel."

She felt a lump in her throat. He couldn't have been more different than she had thought. Was it possible that this man was her father? That if things had been different he and Fran would have been married and she would be their eldest girl?

He took out a business card and wrote a number on it. "This is my direct line. Ring this and you won't have to go through the whole system," he said. It seemed almost too slick, as if he was arranging not to have explanations. Avoiding the people at work knowing about his nasty little secret.

"Aren't you afraid I might ring you at home?" she asked, sorry to break the mood of his niceness but determined that she would not allow herself to be conned by him.

He still had his pen in his hand. "I was about to write down my home number as well. You can call me anytime."

"And what about your wife?"

"Marianne will be happy to speak to you too of course. I shall tell her tonight that you came to see me."

"You're very cool, aren't you?" Kathy said with a mixture of admiration and resentment.

"I'm calm, I suppose, on the exterior, but inside I'm very excited. Who wouldn't be? To meet a handsome grown-up daughter for the first time and to realize that it was because of me you came into the world."

"And do you ever think of my mother?"

"I thought of her for a while, as we all think of our first love, and more than that because of what happened and because you had been born. But then since it wasn't going to happen, I went on and thought of other things and other people."

It was the truth, Kathy couldn't deny that.

"What will I call you?" she asked suddenly.

"You call Fran, Fran, can't you call me Paul?"

"I'll come and see you again, Paul," she said, standing up to leave.

"Anytime you want me I'll be here, Kathy," said her father.

They put out a hand each, but when they touched he drew her to him and hugged her. "It will be different from now on, Kathy," he said, "Different and better."

As she went back to school in the bus Kathy scraped off her lipstick and eyeshadow. She rolled up Harriet's mother's jacket into the canvas bag and went along to rejoin the classes.

"Well?" demanded Harriet.

"Nothing."

"What do you mean 'nothing'?"

"Nothing happened."

"You mean you took all that gear and went to his office and he didn't touch you?"

"He sort of hugged me," Kathy said.

"I expect he's impotent," Harriet said wisely. "In the magazines you always hear of women writing in about that sort of thing, there seems to be a lot of it about."

"It could be, I suppose," said Kathy, and took out her geography textbook.

Mr. O'Brien, who still took senior geography even though he was principal, looked at her over his half glasses. "Your flu better all of a sudden, Kathy?" he said suspiciously.

"Yes, thank God, Mr. O'Brien," Kathy said. It wasn't actually rude or defiant, but she spoke to him as an equal not a pupil.

That child has come on a lot since the beginning of term, he said to himself. He wondered had it anything to do with the Italian classes, which by some miracle had proved not to be the total disaster he had predicted but a huge success.

❧

MAM HAD GONE to Bingo, Dad was at the pub. Fran was at home in the kitchen.

"You're a bit late, Kathy. Everything all right?"

"Sure, I took a bit of a walk. I learned all the parts of the body for class tonight. You know she's going to put us into pairs and ask *Dov'è il gomito* and you have to touch your partner's elbow."

Fran was pleased to see her happy. "Will I make us a toasted sandwich to give us energy for all this?"

"Great. Do you know the feet?"

"*I piedi.* I learned them at lunchtime." Fran grinned. "We're going to be teacher's pets, you and I."

"I went to see him today," Kathy said.

"Who?"

"Paul Malone."

Fran sat down. "You're not serious."

"He was very nice, very nice indeed. He gave me his card. Look, he gave me his direct line and his home number."

"I don't think it was a wise thing to do," Fran said eventually.

"Well, he seemed quite pleased. In fact he said he was glad I did."

"He did?"

"Yes. And he said I could come anytime and go to his house and meet his wife if I wanted to." Fran's face seemed empty suddenly. As if all the life had gone out of it. It was as if someone had put a hand into her head and switched something off. Kathy was puzzled. "Well, aren't you pleased? There was no row, no scene, just normal and natural as you said it was. He understood that it had all been a bit of a shock, and he said from now on it would be different. Different and better, those were his words."

Fran nodded, it was as if she wasn't able to speak. She nodded again and got out the words. "Yes, that's good. Good."

"Why aren't you glad? I thought this is what you'd like."

"You have every right to get in touch with him and to be part of all he has. I never meant to deny you that."

"It isn't a question of that."

"It is a question of that. You're right to feel shortchanged when you see a man like that who has everything—tennis courts, swimming pools, chauffeurs probably."

"That's not what I was looking for," Kathy began.

"And then you come back to a house like this, and go to a school like Mountainview and you're meant to think that going to some bloody evening class that I scrimp and save for is a treat. No wonder you hope things are going to be . . . what is it, different and better?"

Kathy looked at her in horror. Fran thought she wanted Paul Malone instead of her. That she had been swayed and dazzled by a momentary meeting with a man she had not heard of until a few days ago.

"It's only better because now I know everything. Nothing else will change," she tried to explain.

"Of course." Fran was clipped and tight now. She was spreading the cheese on bread, with two slices of tomato each, and putting it under the grill as if she were a robot.

"Fran, stop. I don't want any of that. Listen. Don't you understand? I had to see him. You were right, he's not a monster, he's nice."

"I'm glad I told you."

"But you've got it wrong. Look, ring him yourself, ask him. It's not that I want to be with him rather than you. It's only just to see him the odd time. That's all. Talk to him on the phone then you'll understand."

"No."

"Why? Why not? Now that I've sort of paved the way."

"Sixteen years ago I made a bargain. There was a deal, I would not contact them again and I never did."

"But I didn't make that deal."

"No, and am I criticizing you? I said you had every right. Isn't that what I said?" Fran served them the cheese on toast and poured a glass of milk each.

Kathy felt inexpressibly sad. This kind woman had slaved for her, making sure that there was everything she needed. There would have been no pints of nice cold milk at the ready, no hot suppers cooked, if it were not for Fran. Now she had even let slip that she had scrimped and saved for the Italian classes. No wonder she was hurt and upset at the thought that Kathy might, after all this sacrifice, be prepared to forget the years of love and commitment. That she might be blinded by the unaccustomed thought of access to real wealth and comfort.

"We should go now for the bus," Kathy said.

"Sure, if you want to."

"Of course I want to."

"Right then." Fran put on a coat that had seen better days. She changed into her good shoes, which weren't all that good. Kathy remembered the soft Italian leather shoes that her father wore. She knew that they were very, very expensive.

"*Avanti,*" she said. And they ran for the bus.

❧

AT THE LESSON Fran was paired with Luigi. His dark, menacing frown seemed somehow more sinister than ever tonight.

"*Dov'è il cuore?*" Luigi asked. His Dublin accent made it hard to know which part of the body he was talking about. "*Il cuore,*" said Luigi again, annoyed.

"*Il cuore,* the most important part of the body for God's sake."

Fran looked at him vaguely. "*Non so,*" she said.

"Of course you know where your bloody *cuore* is." Luigi was getting more unpleasant by the moment.

Signora helped her out. "*Con calma per favore,*" Signora came in to make the peace. She lifted Fran's hand and put it on her heart. "*Ecco il cuore.*"

"It took you long enough to find it," Luigi grumbled.

Signora looked at Fran. She was quite different tonight. Normally she was part of everything and encouraging the child to participate as well.

Signora had checked with Peggy Sullivan. "Did you tell me that Miss Clarke was the mother of the sixteen-year-old girl?" she asked.

"Yes, she had her when she was only that age herself. Her mam brought the girl up, but she's Miss Clarke's child, it's well known."

Signora realized that it had not been known to Kathy. But they were both different this week. Perhaps it was known now. Guiltily she hoped she had played no part in it.

❧

KATHY WAITED A week before she called Paul Malone on his private line.

"Is this a good time to talk?" she asked.

"I have someone with me at the moment but I do want to speak, so please can you hold on a moment?" She heard him getting rid of someone else. An important person maybe. A well-known personality, for all she knew.

"Kathy?" His voice was warm and welcoming.

"Did you mean it that we could meet somewhere sometime, not rushed like in an office?"

"Of course I meant it. Will you have lunch with me?"

"Thank you, when?"

"Tomorrow. Do you know Quentin's?"

"I know where it *is*."

"Great. Will we say one o'clock? Does that fit in with school?"

"I'll make it fit in with school." She was grinning and she felt him smile too.

"Sure, but I don't want you getting into trouble."

"No, I'll be fine."

"I'm glad you rang," he said.

❧

SHE WASHED HER hair that night and dressed with care, her best school blouse and she had taken the stain remover to her blazer.

"You're meeting him today," Fran said as she watched Kathy polish her shoes.

"I've always said you should have been in Interpol," Kathy said.

"No, you've never said that."

"It's just for lunch."

"I told you, it's your right if you want to. Where are you going?"

"Quentin's." She had to tell the truth. Fran would have to know sooner or later. She wished he hadn't picked somewhere quite as posh, somewhere so far from their ordinary world.

Fran managed to find the words of encouragement. "Well, that will be nice, enjoy it. All of it."

KATHY REALIZED HOW little part in their lives Mam and Dad seemed to play these days, they were just there in the background. Had it always been like that and she just hadn't noticed? She told the duty teacher that she had a dentist's appointment.

"You have to show these in writing," the teacher said.

"I know but I was so frightened thinking about it I forgot to take the card. Can I bring it to you tomorrow?"

"All right, all right."

Kathy realized that it had paid off to have been a good hardworking pupil all those years. She was not one of the school troublemakers. She could get away with anything now.

Naturally she told Harriet that she was skipping classes.

"Where are you going this time? To dress up as a nurse for him?" Harriet wanted to know.

"No, just to lunch in Quentin's," she said proudly.

Harriet's jaw fell open. "Now you *are* joking."

"Not a bit of it, I'll bring you back the menu this afternoon."

"You have the most exciting sex life of anyone I ever met," Harriet said in envy.

IT WAS DARK and cool and very elegant.

A good-looking woman in a dark suit came forward to meet her.

"Good afternoon, I'm Brenda Brennan and you're most welcome. Are you meeting somebody?"

Kathy wished she could be like this, she wished that Fran could. Confident and assured. Maybe her father's wife was like this. Something you had to be born to, not something that could be learned. Still, you could learn to pretend to be confident.

"I am meeting a Mr. Paul Malone. He said he'd book a table for one o'clock, I'm a little early."

"Let me show you to Mr. Malone's table. A drink while you're waiting?"

Kathy ordered a Diet Coke. It came in a Waterford crystal glass with ice and slices of lemon. She must remember every moment of it for Harriet.

He came in nodding to this table and smiling at that one. A man stood up to shake his hand. By the time he got to her, he had greeted half the place.

"You look different, lovely," he said.

"Well at least I'm not wearing my friend's mother's jacket and a ton of makeup to get past reception." She laughed.

"Should we order quickly? Do you have to rush back?"

"No, I'm at the dentist, it can take ages. Do you have to rush back?"

"No, not at all."

They got the menus and Ms. Brennan came to explain the dishes of the day. "We have a nice *insalata di mare*," she began.

"*Gamberi, calamari?*" Kathy asked before she could stop herself. Only last night they had been doing all the seafood . . . *Gamberi* prawns, *calamari* squid . . .

Both Paul and Brenda Brennan looked at her in surprise.

"I'm showing off. I go to Italian evening classes."

"I'd show off if I knew all that off the top of my head," Ms. Brennan said. "I had to learn them from my friend Nora who helps us write the menus when we have Italian dishes." They seemed to look at her admiringly, or maybe she was just getting bigheaded.

Paul had his usual, which was a glass of wine mixed with mineral water.

"You didn't have to bring me to somewhere as smart as this," she said.

"I'm proud of you. I wanted to show you off."

"Well, it's just Fran thinks . . . I suppose she's jealous that I can go to somewhere like this with you. I'd never go anywhere except Colonel Sanders or McDonald's with her."

"She'd understand. I just wanted to bring you somewhere nice to celebrate."

"She says it's my right and she said I was to enjoy it all. That's what she said this morning, but I think in her heart she's a bit upset."

"Does she have anyone else, any boyfriend or anything?" he asked. Kathy looked up surprised. "What I'm trying to say . . . it's none of my business but I hope she has. I'd hoped she would have married and given you sisters and brothers. But if you don't want to tell me then don't, because as I say I don't have any right to ask."

"There was Ken."

"And was it serious?"

"You'd never know. Or at least I'd never know because I see nothing, understand nothing. But they went out a lot, and she used to laugh when he came to the house in the car to collect her."

"And where is he now?"

"He went to America," Kathy said.

"Was she sorry, do you think?"

"Again I don't know. He writes from time to time. Not so much lately but he did a lot in the summer."

"Could she have gone?"

"It's funny you should say that . . . she asked me once if I'd like to go and live in some small town in the backwoods of America. It's not New York City or anywhere. And I said Lord no, give me Dublin any day, at least it's a capital city."

"Do you think she didn't go with Ken because of you?"

"I never thought of that. But then all that time I thought she was my sister. Perhaps that could have had something to do with it." She looked troubled now, and guilty.

"Stop worrying about it, if it's anyone's fault it's mine." He had read her thoughts.

"I asked her to ring you but she won't."

"Why? Did she give a reason?"

"She said because of the deal . . . she was going to keep her part of the bargain, you kept yours."

"She was always straight as a die," he said.

"So it looks as if you two will never talk."

"We'll never get together and walk into the sunset that's for sure, because we're both different people now. I love Marianne and she may or may not love Ken or she'll love someone else. But we will talk, I'll see to that. Now you and I are going to have a real lunch as well as solving the problems of the world."

He was right, there wasn't much more to be said. They talked of school and show business, and the marvelous Italian classes, and his two children, who were seven and six.

As they paid the bill the woman at the cash desk looked at her with interest. "Excuse me, but is that a Mountainview blazer you're wearing?" Kathy looked guilty. "It's just that my husband teaches there, that's how I recognize it," she continued.

"Oh really, what's his name?"

"Aidan Dunne."

"Oh, Mr. Dunne's very nice, he teaches Latin and he set up the Italian classes," she told Paul.

"And your name . . . ?" the woman behind the desk asked.

"Will be forever a mystery. Girls who take time off for lunch don't want tales brought back to their teachers." Paul Malone's smile was charming, but his voice was steely. Nell Dunne at the cash desk knew she was being criticized for taking too much interest. She just hoped that Ms. Brennan hadn't overheard.

⁊

"DON'T TELL ME about it." Harriet yawned. "You had oysters and caviar."

"No. I had *carciòfi* and lamb. Mr. Dunne's wife was on the cash desk, she recognized the blazer."

"Now you're done for," said Harriet with a smirk.

"Not a bit of it, I didn't tell her who I was."

"She'll know. You'll be caught."

"Stop saying that, you don't want me to be caught you want me to go on having these adventures."

"Kathy Clarke, I tell you if I had been burned at the stake I'd have said you were the last person on earth to have adventures."

"That's the way it goes," said Kathy cheerfully.

～

"PERSONAL CALL FOR Miss Clarke on line three," went the loud-speaker. Fran looked up in surprise. She moved into the surveillance room, a place where they could see shoppers without being seen themselves.

She pressed the button and got line three. "Miss Clarke, Supervisor," she said.

"Paul Malone," said the voice.

"Yes?"

"I'd love to talk. I don't suppose you'd like to meet?"

"You're right, Paul. No bitterness, just no point."

"Fran, can I talk to you a little on the phone?"

"It's a busy time."

"It's always a busy time for busy people."

"Well, you've said it."

"But what's more important than Kathy?"

"To me, nothing."

"And she is hugely important to me too but . . ."

"But you don't want to get too involved."

"Absolutely wrong. I would love to get as involved as I can, but you brought her up, you made her what she is, you are the person who cares for her most in the world. I don't want to muscle in suddenly. I want you to tell me what would be best for her."

"Do you think I know? How could I know? I want everything in the world for her, but I can't get it. If you can get more, then do it, get it, give it to her."

"She thinks the world of you, Fran."

"She's pretty taken with you too."

"She only knows about me a week or two, she's known you all her life."

"Don't break her heart, Paul. She's a great girl, she's had such a shock. I thought she sort of knew, guessed, absorbed it or something. It's not such an unusual situation around here. But apparently not."

"No, but she's coped with it. She's got your genes. She can cope with things, fair or unfair."

"And yours too, lots of courage."

"So what will we do, Fran?"

"We have to leave it to her."

"She can have as much of me as she wants, but I promise you I won't try to take her away from you."

"I know." There was a silence.

"And are things . . . well, all right?"

"Yeah, they're, well, all right."

"She tells me you're both learning Italian, she spoke Italian in the restaurant today."

"Good for her." Fran sounded pleased.

"Didn't we do well in a way, Fran?"

"We sure did," she said, and hung up before she burst into tears.

❧

"WHAT ARE *carciòfi*, Signora?" Kathy asked at Italian class.

"Artichokes, Caterina. Why do you ask?"

"I went to a restaurant and they had them on the menu."

"I wrote that menu for my friend Brenda Brennan," Signora said proudly. "Was it Quentin's?"

"That's right, but don't tell Mr. Dunne. His wife works there, a bit of a prune I think."

"I believe so," said Signora.

"Oh by the way, Signora, you know the way you said you thought Fran was my mother and I said she was my sister?"

"Yes, yes . . ." Signora was ready to apologize.

"You were quite right, I hadn't understood," Kathy said as if it were the most natural mistake in the world anyone could have made, mistaking a mother for a sister.

"Well, it's good to have it all sorted out."

"I think it *is* good," Kathy said.

"It must be." Signora was serious. "She's so young, and so nice, and you'll have her around for years and years, much longer than if she were an older mother."

"Yes. I wish she'd get married, then I wouldn't feel so responsible for her."

"She may in time."

"But I think she missed her chance. He went to America. I think she stayed because of me."

"You could write to him," said Signora.

~⋚⋚)

SIGNORA'S FRIEND BRENDA Brennan was thrilled to hear how well the classes were going. "I had one of your little pupils in the other day, well, she was wearing a Mountainview blazer and said that she was learning Italian."

"Did she have artichokes?"

"How do you know these things, you must be psychic!"

"That's Kathy Clarke . . . she's the only child, the rest of them are grown-ups. She said that Aidan Dunne's wife works there. Is that right?"

"Oh, this is the Aidan you talk about so much. Yes, Nell is the cashier. Odd sort of woman, I don't know what she's at, to be honest."

"What do you mean?"

"Well, highly efficient, honest, quick. Nice mechanical smile at the customers, remembers their names. But she's miles away."

"Miles away where?"

"I think she's having an affair," Brenda said eventually.

"Never. Who with?"

"I don't know, she's so secretive and she meets someone after work often."

"Well, well."

Brenda shrugged it off. "So if you're thinking of making a play for her husband, go ahead, the wife isn't going to be able to cast any stones at you."

"Heavens, Brenda, what an idea. At my age. But tell me, who was Kathy Clarke having lunch with in your elegant restaurant?"

"It's funny . . . she was with Paul Malone, you know, or maybe you wouldn't, very trendy accountant married to all that Hayes money. Buckets of charm."

"And Kathy was with him?"

"I know. She could have been his daughter," Brenda said. "But honestly, the longer I work in this business the less surprised I am about anything."

⟨∾⟩

"Paul?"

"Kathy, it's been ages."

"Will you come to have lunch with me, my treat. Not Quentin's."

"Sure where do you suggest?"

"I won a voucher at Italian class to this place, lunch for two including wine."

"I can't have you missing school like this."

"Well, I was going to suggest a Saturday unless that's a problem."

"It's never a problem, I told you that."

⟨∾⟩

She showed him the prize she had won at the Italian class. Paul Malone said he was very pleased to have been chosen as her guest.

"I want to put something to you. It's got a bit to do with money but it's not begging."

"You put it to me," he said.

She told him about this flight to New York for Christmas. Ken would pay most of it, but he literally didn't have all of it and he couldn't borrow out there; it wasn't like here where people sort of lived on credit.

"Tell me about it," said Paul Malone the accountant.

"He was so pleased when I wrote and told him that I knew about everything now, and I was so sorry if I had stood in their way. He wrote back and said that he loved Fran to bits and that he had been thinking of coming back to Ireland for her but he felt he would have messed it up all ways if he did that. Honestly, Paul, I couldn't let you see the letter because it's private, but you'd love it, you really would, you'd be pleased for her."

"I know I would."

"So I'll tell you exactly how much it is. It's about three hundred pounds. I know it's enormous. And I know all that's in this building society account Fran has for me, so you see it's only a loan. When we get them together I can give it straight back to you."

"How will we give it so that it doesn't look the way it is?"

"You'll do it."

"I'd give you anything, Kathy, and your mother too. But you can't take away people's pride."

"Could we send it to Ken?"

"That might be taking away his pride."

There was a silence. The waiter came to ask were they enjoying the meal.

"*Benissimo,*" Kathy said.

"My . . . my young friend has taken me here on a voucher she won at Italian class," Paul Malone said.

"You must be clever," said the waiter.

"No, I'm just good at winning things," Kathy said.

Paul looked as if an idea had just struck him. "That's it, you could win a couple of air tickets," he suggested.

"How could I do that?"

"Well, you won us two lunches here."

"That's because Signora organized it that someone in the class should get a prize."

"Well, maybe I could organize it that someone could win two air tickets."

"It would be cheating."

"It would be better than being patronizing."

"Can I think about it?"

"Don't think too long, we have to set up this imaginary competition."

"And should we tell Ken?"

"I don't think so," said Paul. "What do you think?"

"I don't think he has any need to know the whole scenario," Kathy said. It was a phrase Harriet used a lot.

Lou

When Lou was fifteen, three men with sticks had come into his parents' shop, taken all the cigarettes, the contents of the till, and as the family cowered behind the counter there came the noise of a Garda car.

Quick as a flash Lou said to the biggest of the men: "Out the back, over the wall."

"What's in it for you?" the fellow hissed.

"Take the fags, leave the money. Go."

And that's exactly what they did.

The Guards were furious. "How did they know there was a back way?"

"They must have known the area." Louis shrugged.

His father was very angry indeed. "You let them away with it, you bloody let them away, the Guards could have had them in jail if it hadn't been for you."

"Get real, Da." Lou always spoke like a gangster anyway. "What's the point? The prisons are full, they'd get the probation act, and they'd come back and smash the place up. This way they owe us. It's like paying protection money."

"Living in a bloody jungle," his father said. But Lou was certain he had done the right thing, and secretly his mother agreed with him.

"No point in attracting trouble" was her motto. Delivering aggressive thieves with sticks to the Guards would have been attracting trouble as far as she was concerned.

Six weeks later a man came in to buy cigarettes. About thirty, burly with a nearly shaved head. It was after school and Lou was serving.

"What's your name?" the man asked.

Lou recognized the voice as the one that had asked him what was in it for him. "Lou," he said.

"Do you know me, Lou?"

Lou looked him straight in the eye. "Not from a bar of soap," he said.

"Good lad, Lou, you'll be hearing from us." And the man who had taken more than fifty packets of cigarettes six weeks ago while waving a stick paid nice and politely for his packet. Not long after, the big man came in with a plastic bag. "Leg of lamb for your mother, Lou," he said, and left.

"We won't say a thing to your father," she said, and cooked it for their Sunday lunch.

Lou's father would have said that they would not appreciate someone distributing the contents of *their* shop around the neighborhood like some modern-day Robin Hood, and presumably the butcher's shop that had been done over felt the same.

Lou and his mother thought it easier not to go too far down that road. Lou thought of the big man as Robin Hood, and when he saw him around the place he would just nod at him. "Howaya."

And the big man would laugh back at him and say: "How's it going, Lou?"

In a way Lou hoped that Robin would get in touch again. He knew that the debt had been paid by the gift of the lamb. But he felt excited at the thought of being so close to the underworld. He wished Robin would give him some kind of task. He didn't want to do a smash-and-grab himself. And he couldn't drive a getaway car. But he did want to be involved in something exciting.

THE CALL DIDN'T come while he was at school. Lou was not a natural student, at sixteen he was out of the classroom and into the job center without very much hope there either. One of the first people he saw was Robin studying the notices on the board.

"Howaya, Robin," Lou said, forgetting that was only a made-up name.

"What do you mean, Robin?" the man asked.

"I have to call you something. I don't know your name so that's what I call you."

"Is it some kind of a poor joke?" The man looked very bad-tempered indeed.

"No, it's like Robin Hood, you know the fellow . . ." His voice trailed away. Lou didn't want to talk about Merry Men in case Robin thought he might be saying he was gay, he didn't want to say a band or a gang. Why had he ever said the name at all?

"As long as it's not a reference to people robbing things . . ."

"Oh God *no, no,*" Lou said, as if such an idea was utterly repulsive.

"Well then." Robin seemed mollified.

"What is your real name?"

"Robin will do fine, now that we know there's no misunderstanding."

"None, none."

"Good, well how are things, Lou?"

"Not great, I had a job in a warehouse but they had stupid rules about smoking."

"I know, they're all the same." Robin was sympathetic. He could read the story of a boy's first job ending in being fired after a week. It was probably his own.

"I'll tell you, there's a job here." He pointed at an advertisement offering a cleaning job in a cinema.

"It's for girls isn't it?"

"It doesn't say, you can't say nowadays."

"But it would be a desperate job." Lou was disappointed that Robin thought so little of him as to point him in such a lowly direction.

"It could have its compensations," Robin said, looking vaguely into the distance.

"What would they be?"

"It could mean leaving doors open."

"Every night? Wouldn't they cop on?"

"Not if the bolt was just pulled slightly back."

"And then?"

"And then if other people, say, wanted to go in and out they would have a week to do so."

"And after that?"

"Well, whoever had that cleaning job could move on in a bit, not too quickly, but in a bit. And would find that people were very grateful to him."

Lou was so excited, he could hardly breathe. It was happening. Robin was including him in his gang. Without another word he went up to the counter and filled in the forms for the post as cleaner.

"Whatever made you take a job like that?" his father said.

"Someone's got to do it." Lou shrugged.

He cleaned the seats and picked up the litter. He cleaned the lavatories and used scouring powder to get rid of the graffiti. Each evening he loosened the bolt on the big back door. Robin didn't even have to tell him which, it was quite obvious that this was the only way that people could get in.

The manager was a nervous fussy little man. He told Lou that the world was a wicked place now, totally different to when he was growing up.

"True enough," Lou said. He didn't engage in much conversation. He didn't want to be remembered one way or another after the event.

The event happened four days later. Thieves had got in, broken into the little covered-in cash desk and got away with the night's takings. They had sawed through a bolt, apparently. They must have been able to reach through a crack in the door. The Guards asked was there any way that the door could have been left unlocked, but the nervous fussy manager, who was by this stage nearly hysterical and confirmed in his belief of the wickedness of the world, said that was ridiculous. He always checked at night, and why would they have had all the sawing if they had got in an open door. Lou realized they organized that to protect him. Nobody could finger the new cleaner as being the inside contact.

He stayed on at the cinema, carefully locking the newly fitted bolt for two weeks to prove that he was in no way connected. Then he told the manager he had got a better position.

"You weren't the worst of them," the manager said, and Lou felt slightly ashamed because he knew that in a way he was the worst of them. His predecessors hadn't opened the doors to admit the burglars. But there was no point whatsoever in feeling guilty about that now. What was done was done. It was a matter of waiting to see what happened next.

What happened next was that Robin came in to buy a pack of cigarettes and handed him an envelope. His father was in the shop, so Lou took it quietly without comment. Only when he was alone did he open it. There were ten ten-pound notes. A hundred pounds for loosening a bolt four nights in succession. As Robin had promised, people were being grateful to him.

❧

LOU NEVER ASKED Robin for a job. He went about his own work, taking bits here and there. He felt sure that if he was needed, he would be called on. But he longed to run into the big man again. He never saw Robin anymore at the job centre.

He felt sure that Robin was involved in the job at the supermarket where they had got almost the entire contents of the liquor store into a van and away within an hour of late closing. The security firm just couldn't believe it. There was no evidence of an inside job.

Lou wondered how Robin had managed it, and where he stashed what he stole. He must have premises somewhere. He had gone up in the world since the time years ago when he had come into their shop. Lou had only been fifteen. Now he was nearly nineteen. And in all that time he had only done one job for big Robin.

❧

HE MET HIM again unexpectedly at a disco. It was a noisy place and Lou hadn't met any girls he fancied. More truthfully, he hadn't met any girls who fancied him. He couldn't understand it, he was being as nice as anything, smiling, buying them drinks, but they went for mean-looking fellows, people who scowled and frowned. It was then he saw Robin dancing with a most attractive girl. The more she smiled and shimmered at him, the deeper and darker and more menacing Robin appeared to be. Maybe this was the secret. Lou practiced his frown as he stood at the bar, scowling at himself in the mirror, and Robin came up behind him.

"Looking well, Lou?"

"Good to see you again, Robin."

"I like you, Lou, you're not a pushy person."

"Not much point. Take it easy I always say."

"I hear there was a bit of trouble in your parents' shop the other day."

How had Robin heard that? "There was, kids, brats."

"Well, they've been dealt with, the hide has been beaten off them, they won't touch the place again. Small call to our friends the Gardai telling them where the stuff can be found, should be sorted out tomorrow."

"That's very good of you, Robin, I appreciate it."

"Not at all, it's a pleasure," he said. Lou waited. "Working at the moment?"

"Nothing that can't be altered if needs be," Lou said.

"Busy place here, isn't it?" Robin nodded at the bar where they stood. Ten-pound notes and twenty-pound notes were flashing back and forward. The night's takings would be substantial.

"Yeah, I'd say they have two guys and an Alsatian to take all that to a night safe."

"As it happens they don't," said Robin. Lou waited again. "They have this van that drives the staff home, about three in the morning, and the last to be left off is the manager, who looks as if he's carrying a duffel bag with his gear in it, but that's the takings."

"And does he put it in a safe?"

"No, he takes it home and someone comes to his house to pick it up a bit later and they put it in a safe."

"Bit complicated, isn't it?"

"Yeah, but this is a tough kind of an area." Robin shook his head disapprovingly. "No one would want to be driving a security van round here, too dangerous." Robin frowned darkly as if this was a monstrous shadow over their lives.

"And most people don't know this setup, about the manager with the sports bag?"

"I don't believe it's generally known at all."

"Not even to the driver of the van?"

"No, not at all."

"And what would people need, do you think?"

"Someone to reverse in front of the van accidentally, and prevent the van leaving the lane for about five minutes." Lou nodded. "Someone who has a car and a clean driving license and a record of coming here regularly."

"That would be a good idea."

"You have a car?"

"Sadly no, Robin, a license yes, a record of coming here, but not a car."

"Were you thinking of buying one?"

"I was indeed, a secondhand car . . . thinking a lot, but it hasn't been possible."

"Until now." Robin raised a glass to him.

"Until now," Lou said. He knew he must do nothing until he heard from Robin. He felt very pleased that Robin had said he liked him. He frowned vaguely at a girl nearby, and she asked him to dance. Lou hadn't felt so good for a long time.

Next day his father said that you wouldn't believe it but the Guards had found every single thing that had been taken by those young pups. Wasn't it a miracle? Three days later a letter and hire-purchase agreement form came from a garage. Mr. Lou Lynch had paid a deposit of two thousand pounds and agreed to pay a monthly sum. The car could be picked up and the agreement signed within the next three days.

"I'm thinking of getting a car," Lou told his parents.

"That's great," said his mother.

"Bloody marvelous what people can do on the dole," his father said.

"I'm not on the dole as it happens," Lou said, stung.

He was working in a big electrical appliances store, carrying fridges and microwaves out to the backs of people's cars. He had always hoped it might be the kind of place where Robin would come and find him. How could he have guessed it would be in a discotheque?

He drove his car around proudly. He took his mother out to Glendalough one Sunday morning, and she told him that when she was a young girl she always dreamed that she might meet a fellow with a car, but it never happened.

"Well, it's happened now, Mam," he said soothingly.

"Your Da thinks you're on the take, Lou, he says there's no way you could have a car like this on what you earn."

"And what do you think, Ma?"

"I don't think at all, Son," she said.

"And neither do I, Ma," he said.

It was six weeks before he ran into Robin again. He called to the big store and bought a television. Lou carried it to his car for him.

"Been going to that disco regularly?"

"Twice, three times a week. They know me by name now."

"Bit of a dump though."

"Still. You've got to dance somewhere, drink somewhere." Lou knew that Robin liked people to be relaxed.

"Very fair point. I was wondering if you'd be there tonight?"

"Certainly I will."

"And maybe not drink anything because of Breathalyzers."

"I think a night on the mineral water's very good for everyone from time to time."

"Maybe I'd show you a good place to park the car there tonight."

"That would be great." He asked no other details, that was his strength. Robin seemed to like him wanting as little information as possible.

About ten o'clock that night he parked the car where Robin indicated. He could see how it would obstruct the exit from the alley into the main road if he pulled out. He realized he would be in full view of everyone in the staff van. The car would have to stall. And refuse to start despite his apparent best efforts. But there were about five hours before that happened.

So he went into the disco, and within fifteen minutes he met the first girl he ever thought he could love and live with for the rest of his life. Her name was Suzi and she was a tall, stunning redhead. It was her first time at the disco, she told him. But she was beginning to vegetate at home in her flat, and she decided she would go out and see what the night brought.

And the night had brought Lou. They danced and they talked, and she said she loved that he drank mineral water, so many fellows just stank of beer. And he said he did drink beer sometimes, but not in great quantities.

She worked in a cafe in Temple Bar, she told him. They liked the same kinds of films and they liked the same music and they loved curries and they didn't mind swimming in the cold sea in the summer and they each hoped to go to America one day. You can learn a lot about other people in four and a half hours if you are sober. And everything that Lou learned about Suzi he liked. Under normal circumstances he would have driven her home.

But these were not normal circumstances. And the only reason that he had a car at all was that the circumstances were so very far from normal.

I'd offer you a lift home but I have to meet this guy here a bit later. Could he say that, or would it be suspicious later when he was questioned? Because questioned he would be. Could he walk her home and then come back? That might have been possible, but Robin wanted him to establish his presence as being on the scene all night.

"I'd really like to see you again, Suzi," he said.

"Well I'd like that too."

"So will we say tomorrow night? Here or somewhere quieter?"

"So is tonight over now?" Suzi asked.

"For me it is, but listen, tomorrow night can go on as long as we like it to."

"Are you married?" Suzi asked.

"No, of course I'm not. Hey, I'm only twenty. Why would I be married?"

"Some people are."

"I'm not. Will I see you tomorrow?"

"Where are you going now?"

"To the men's room."

"Do you do drugs, Lou?"

"Jesus I don't. What is this, an interrogation?"

"It's just that you've been going to the loo all night." It was true he had, just to get himself noticed, seen, remembered.

"No, I don't. Listen, sweetheart, you and I'll have a great night out tomorrow, go wherever you want, I mean it."

"Yeah," she said.

"No, not Yeah . . . Yes. I mean it."

"Good night, Lou," she said, hurt and annoyed. And picked up her jacket and walked out into the night.

He longed to run after her. Was there ever such bad timing? How miserably unfair it all was.

෴

THE MINUTES CREPT by until it was time for action, then he went to his car, the last to leave the club. He waited until the minivan filled and the lights went on. At that very moment he shot backward in its path. Then he revved the engine over and over, flooding it, ensuring that it wouldn't start.

The operation worked like clockwork. Lou looked at none of it, all the time he played the part of a man desperate to start his car, and when he realized that dark figures had climbed a wall and got away, he watched astounded as the scarlet-faced manager came running out crying help and wanting the Guards and panicking utterly.

Lou sat helpless in the car. "I can't get it out of here, I'm trying."

"He's one of them," shouted somebody, and strong hands held him, bouncers, barmen, until they realized who it was.

"Hey, that's Lou Lynch," they said, releasing him.

"What *is* all this, first my car won't start and then you all jump on me. What's happening?"

"The takings have been snatched, that's what's happened." The manager knew his career was over. He knew there would be hours ahead with the Guards. And there were, for everybody.

One of the Guards recognized Lou's address. "I was up there not long back, a crowd of kids broke in and stole all before them."

"I know, Guard, and my parents were very grateful you retrieved it all."

The Guard was pleased to be so publicly praised for what had been

after all a tip-off out of the blue. Lou was regarded as the most unlucky
accident to have happened for a long time. The staff told detectives that
he was a very nice fellow, couldn't be involved in anything like that. He
got a good report from the big electrical store, his car payments were up-
to-date, he hadn't an ounce of alcohol in his body. Lou Lynch was in the
clear.

But he didn't spend all the next day thinking about Robin and wondering when the next envelope would come and how much it would
contain. He thought instead about the beautiful Suzi Sullivan. He would
have to lie to her and tell her the official account of what had happened.
He hoped she wasn't too annoyed with him.

He went to her restaurant in his lunch break with a red rose. "Thank
you for last night."

"There wasn't much *of* last night," Suzi complained. "You were such
a little Cinderella, we all had to come home early."

"It won't happen tonight," he said. "Unless you want to, of course."

"We'll see," said Suzi darkly.

THEY MET ALMOST every night after that.

Lou wanted them to go back to the disco where they had met. He said
that it was for sentimental reasons. In reality it was because he didn't
want the staff to think that he never came back again after the Incident.

He heard all about the Incident. Apparently four men with guns had
got into the van and told them to lie down. They had taken everyone's
carrier bag and left in minutes. Guns. Lou felt a bit sick in his stomach
when he heard that. He had thought that Robin and his friends were still
in sticks. But, of course, that was all five years ago, and the world had
moved on. The manager lost his job, the system of banking the takings
was changed, a huge van with barking dogs picked them up each night.
You'd need an army to take that on.

It was three weeks later when he was leaving work that he saw Robin
in the car park. There was again an envelope. Again Lou pocketed it
without looking.

"Thank you very much," he said. "Aren't you going to see what's in
it?" Robin seemed disappointed.

"No need to. You've treated me well in the past."

"There's a thousand quid," Robin said proudly.

That was something to get excited about. Lou opened the envelope and saw the notes. "That's absolutely terrific," he said.

"You're a good man, Lou, I like you," said Robin, and drove away.

A thousand pounds in his pocket and the most beautiful redhead in the world waiting for him, Lou Lynch knew he was the luckiest man in the world.

HIS ROMANCE WITH Suzi developed nicely. He was able to buy her things and take her to good places with his stash of money. But it seemed to alarm her when he pulled out twenty-pound notes.

"Hey Lou, where do you get money like that to throw around?"

"I work, don't I?"

"Yeah, and I know what they pay you in that place. That's the third twenty you've split this week."

"Are you watching me?"

"I like you, of course I watch you," she said.

"What are you looking for?"

"I'm hoping not to find that you're some sort of a criminal," she said quite directly.

"Do I look the type?"

"That's not a yes or a no."

"And there are some questions to which there are no yes-and-no answers," Lou said.

"Okay, let me ask you this, are you involved in anything at the moment?"

"No." He spoke from the heart.

"And do you plan to be?" There was a pause. "We don't need it, Lou, you've got a job, I've got a job. Let's not get caught up in something messy." She had beautiful creamy skin and huge dark green eyes.

"All right, I won't get involved in anything again," he said.

And Suzi had the sense to let it rest there. She asked no questions about the past. The weeks went on and they saw more and more of each other, Suzi and Lou. She brought him to meet her parents one Sunday lunchtime.

He was surprised where they lived.

"I thought you were posher than this place," he said.

"I made myself seem posher to get the job in the restaurant."

Her father was not nearly as bad as she had said he was, he supported the right football team and he had cans of beer in the fridge.

Her mother worked in that supermarket that Robin and his friends had done over a while back. She told them the story, and how Miss Clarke the supervisor had always thought there must be someone in the shop who had left the door open for them, but nobody knew who it was.

Lou listened, shaking his head at it all. Robin must have people all over the city loosening bolts, parking cars in strategic places. He looked at Suzi, smiling and eager. For the first time he hoped that Robin wouldn't contact him again.

❧

"They liked you," Suzi said, surprised, afterward.

"Well, why not? I'm a nice fellow," Lou said.

"My brother said you had a terrible frown but I told him it was a nervous tic and he was to shut up about it."

"It's *not* a nervous tic, it's a deliberate attempt to look important," Lou said crossly.

"Well, whatever it is, it was all they could find fault with so that's something. When am I going to meet yours?"

"Next week," he said.

His mother and father were alarmed that he was bringing a girl to lunch. "I suppose she's pregnant," his father said.

"She most certainly is not, and there'll be none of that talk when she comes to the house."

"What kind of things would she eat?" His mother was doubtful.

He tried to remember what he had to eat at the Sullivans' house. "Chicken," he said. "She just loves a bit of chicken." Even his mother could hardly destroy a chicken.

"They liked you," he said to her afterward, putting on exactly the same note of surprise as she had.

"That's good." She pretended indifference, but he knew she was pleased.

"You're the first, you see," he explained.

"Oh yeah?"

"No, I mean the first I brought home."

She patted him on the hand. He was very, very lucky to have met a girl like Suzi Sullivan.

❦

AT THE BEGINNING of September he met Robin by accident. But, of course, it wasn't by accident. Robin was parked near his parents' shop and just got out of the car.

"A half pint to end the day?" Robin said, jerking his head toward the nearby pub.

"Great," Lou said with fake enthusiasm. He sometimes feared Robin could read minds; he hoped he couldn't see the insincerity in Lou's tone.

"How are things?"

"Great, I've got a smashing girl."

"So I see, she's a real looker, isn't she?"

"Absolutely. We're quite serious about it all."

Robin punched him on the arm. It was meant to be a punch of solidarity, but somehow it hurt. Lou managed not to rub where it felt bruised. "So you'll be needing a deposit on a house soon?" Robin asked casually.

"We're not in any hurry with that, she's got a grand bed-sit."

"But *eventually* of course?" Robin wasn't taking any argument.

"Oh yes, way down the line." There was a silence. Did Robin know that Lou was trying to get off the hook?

Robin spoke. "Lou, you know I always said I liked you."

"Yes, and I always liked you too. It was mutual. And is mutual," Lou added hastily.

"Considering how we met, as it were."

"You know the way it is, you forget how you met people."

"Good, good." Robin nodded. "What I'm looking for, Lou, is a place."

"A place. To live in?"

"No, no. I've got a place to live in, a place that our friends the Guards turn over with great regularity. They sort of regard it as part of their weekly routine, go in and search my place."

"It's harassment."

"I know it is, they know it is. They never find anything, so they know well it's harassment."

"So if they don't find anything . . . ?" Lou had no idea where all this was going.

"It means that things have to be somewhere else and that's getting increasingly difficult," Robin said. In the past Lou had always waited. Robin would say what he wanted in time. "The kind of place I want is somewhere that there's a lot of activity two or three times a week, a place where people wouldn't be noticed going in and out."

"Like the warehouse where I work?" Lou asked nervously.

"No, there's proper security there."

"What would this place have to have, in terms of facilities?"

"Not very much space at all, like enough for . . . imagine five or six cases of wine . . . packages about that size, in all."

"That shouldn't be hard, Robin."

"I'm watched like a hawk. I'm spending weeks going round talking to everyone I know that they don't have a file on, just to confuse them. But there's something coming in soon, and I really do need a place."

Lou looked anxiously out the door of the pub in the direction of his parents' shop.

"I don't think it would be possible in Ma and Da's place."

"No, no, that's not what I want at all, it's a place with bustle, doors in and out, lots of people moving through."

"I'll think," Lou said.

"Good, Lou. Think this week will you, and then I'll give you the instructions. It's very easy, no driving cars or anything."

"Well actually, Robin, this is something I meant to bring up, but I'm thinking of . . . um . . . well, not being involved anymore."

Robin's frown was terrible to see. "Once you're involved you're *always* involved," he said. Lou said nothing. "That's the way it is," Robin added.

"I see," said Lou, and he frowned hard in response to show how seriously he took it.

❧

THAT NIGHT SUZI said she wasn't free, she had promised to help the mad old Italian woman who lived as a lodger in their house to do up an annex in Mountainview school for some evening class.

"*Why* do you have to do that?" Lou grumbled. He had wanted to go to the pictures and then for some chips and then back to bed with Suzi in her little bed-sitter. He did not want to be on his own thinking about the fact that once you were involved, you could never get uninvolved again.

"Come with me," Suzi suggested, "that'll make it quicker."

Lou said he would, and they went to this annex attached to the school but slightly separate from it. It had an entrance hall, a big classroom, two lavatories, and a small kitchen space. In the hall there was a store-room with a few boxes in it. Empty boxes.

"What are all these?" he asked.

"We're trying to tidy up the place so it looks more festive and not so much like a rubbish dump for when the classes start," said the deranged woman they called Signora. Harmless but very odd, and some most peculiar-colored hair, like a piebald mare.

"Should we throw out the boxes?" Suzi suggested.

Slowly Lou spoke. "Why don't I just tidy them up and leave them in a neat stack in there. You'd never know when you might need a few boxes."

"For Italian classes?" Suzi said in disbelief.

But at this moment Signora interrupted. "No, he's right. We could use them to be tables when we are learning the section on what to order in an Italian restaurant, they could be counters in the shops, or a car at the garage." Her face seemed radiant at all the uses there would be for boxes.

Lou looked at her with amazement. She was obviously missing her marbles, but at this moment he loved her. "Good woman, Signora," he said, and tidied the boxes into neat piles.

❧

He couldn't contact Robin, but he wasn't surprised to get a phone call at work.

"Don't want to come and see you, the toy soldiers are going mad with excitement these days. I can't move without five of them padding after me."

"I found somewhere," said Lou.

"I knew you would, Lou."

Lou told him where it was, and about the activity every Tuesday and Thursday, thirty people.

"Fantastic," Robin said. "Have you enrolled?"

"For what?"

"For the class, of course."

"Oh Jesus, Robin, I scarcely speak English, what would I be doing learning Italian?"

"I'm relying on you," said Robin, and he hung up.

There was an envelope waiting for him at home that night. It contained five hundred pounds and a note. "Incidental expenses for language learning." He had been serious.

&

"You're going to do *what*?"

"Well, you're the one who said I should better myself, Suzi. Why not?"

"When I said better yourself, I meant smarten yourself up, get a better-paid job. I didn't mean go mad and learn a foreign language." Suzi was astounded. "Lou, you have to be off your head. It costs a fair amount. Poor Signora is afraid that it will be too dear for people, and suddenly out of the blue, you decide to take it up. I can't take it in."

Lou frowned a mighty frown. "Life would be very dull if we all understood everyone," he said.

And Suzi said that it would be a lot easier to get on with.

Lou went to the first Italian lesson as a condemned man walks to Death Row. His years in the classroom had not been glorious. Now he would face further humiliation. But it had been surprisingly enjoyable. First the mad Signora asked them all their names and gave them ridiculous pieces of colored cardboard to write them on, but they had to write Italianized versions.

Lou became Luigi. In a way he liked it. It was important.

"Mi chiamo Luigi," he would say and frown at people, and they seemed impressed.

They were an odd bunch, a woman dripping in jewelry that no one in their sane senses would have worn to Mountainview school, and driving a BMW. Lou hoped that Robin's friends wouldn't steal the BMW. The woman who drove it was nice, as it happened, and she had sad eyes.

There was a very nice old fellow, a hotel porter called Laddy, though he had Lorenzo written on his badge, a mother and daughter, a real dizzy blonde called Elisabetta who had a serious boyfriend with a collar and tie, and dozens of others that you'd never expect to find at a class like this. Perhaps they wouldn't think it odd that he was there. They might not even question it for a moment why he was there.

For two weeks he questioned it himself, then he heard from Robin. Some boxes would be coming in on Tuesday, just around seven-thirty when the classroom was filling up. Maybe he could see to it that they got into the store cupboard in the hall.

He didn't know the man in the anorak. He just looked out for the van. There were so many people arriving, parking bikes, motorbikes, the dame with the BMW, two women with a Toyota Starlet . . . the van didn't cause any stir.

There were four boxes, they were in in a flash, the van and the man in the anorak were gone.

On Thursday he had the four boxes ready to be pulled out quickly. The whole thing was done in seconds. Lou had made himself teacher's pet by helping with the boxes. Sometimes they covered them with red crepe paper and put cutlery on them.

"Quanto costa il piatto del giorno?" Signora would ask, and they would all repeat it over and over until they could ask for any damn thing and lift knives and say *"Ecco il coltello!"*

Babyish it might have been, but Lou liked it, he even saw himself and Suzi going to Italy one day and he would order her a *bicchiere di vino rosso* as quick as look at her.

Once Signora lifted a heavy box, one of the consignment.

Lou felt his heart turn over, but he spoke quickly. "Listen, Signora, will you let *me* lift those for you, it's the empty ones we want."

"But what's in it, this is so heavy."

"Could you be up to them in a school? Come on, here we are. What are they going to be today?"

"They are doing hotels, *alberghi. Albergo di prima categoria, di seconda categoria.*"

Lou was pleased that he understood these things. "Maybe I wasn't just thick at school," he told Suzi. "Maybe I was just badly taught."

"Could be," Suzi said. She was preoccupied. There had been some trouble with Jerry; her mam and dad had been called to see the headmaster. They said it sounded serious. And just after he had been getting on so well and doing so well since Signora had come to the house, and actually doing his homework and everything. It couldn't have been stealing, or anything. They had been very mysterious up at the school.

~∾⁓

ONE OF THE nice things about working in a cafe was listening to people's conversations. Suzi said that she could write a book about Dublin just from the bits of overheard conversation.

People were talking about secret weekends, and plans for further dalliances, and cheating on their income tax. And incredible scandal about politicians and journalists and television personalities . . . maybe none of it true, but all of it hair-raising. But it was often the most ordinary conversations that were the most fascinating. A girl of sixteen determined to get pregnant so that she could leave home and get a council flat, a couple who made fake I.D. cards explaining the economics of buying a good laminator. Lou hoped that Robin and his friends would never use this cafe to discuss their plans. But then it was a bit up-market for them, he was probably in the clear as regards this.

Suzi would spend a lot of time clearing a nearby table when people were saying interesting things. A middle-aged man and his daughter came in, good-looking blond girl with a bank uniform. The man was craggy and had longish hair, hard to know what he did, maybe a journalist or a poet. They seemed to have had a row. Suzi hovered nearby.

"I'm only agreeing to meet you because it's a half hour off work and

I'd love a cup of good coffee compared to that dishwater we get in the canteen," the girl said.

"There's a new and beautiful percolator with four different kinds of coffee waiting for you anytime you would like to call," he said. He didn't sound like a father, he sounded more like a lover. But he was so old. Suzi kept shining up the table so that she could hear more.

"You mean you've used it?"

"I keep practicing, waiting for the day you'll come back and I can make you Blue Mountain or Costa Rica."

"You'll have a long wait," said the girl.

"Please, can't we talk?" He was begging. He was quite a handsome old man, Suzi admitted.

"We are talking, Tony."

"I think I love you," he said.

"No you don't, you just love the memory of me and you can't bear that I don't just troop back there like all the others."

"There are no others now." There was a silence. "I never said I loved anyone before."

"You didn't say you loved me, you only said you *thought* you loved me. It's different."

"Let me find out. I'm almost certain." He smiled at the girl.

"You mean let's get back into bed together until you test it?" She sounded very bitter.

"No I don't, as it happens. Let's go out for dinner somewhere and talk like we used to talk."

"Until bedtime and then it's let's get back into bed like we used to do that."

"We only did that once, Grania. It's not just about that." Suzi was hooked now. He was a nice old guy, the girl Grania should give him a chance, just for dinner. She was dying to suggest it but knew she had to say nothing.

"Just dinner then," Grania said, and they smiled at each other and held hands.

IT WAS NOT always the same man, the same van, or the same anorak. But the contact was always minimal and the speed great.

The weather became dark and wet, and Lou provided a big hanging rail for the wet coats and jackets that might otherwise have been stacked in the hall cupboard. "I don't want to drip all over Signora's boxes," he would say.

Weeks of boxes in on Tuesday and out on Thursday. Lou didn't want to think about what was in them. It wasn't bottles, that was for sure. If Robin were involved in bottles, it would be a whole liquor store full of them like the time in the supermarket. Lou couldn't deny it anymore. He knew it must be drugs. Why else was Robin so worried? What other kind of business involved one person delivering and another collecting? But God Almighty, drugs in a school. Robin must be mad.

⁊⁊

AND THEN BY chance there was this matter of Suzi's young brother, a young redhead with an impudent face. He had been found with a crowd of the older boys in the bicycle shed. Jerry had sworn that he was only being their delivery boy, they had asked him to pick up something at the school gates because they were being watched by the headmaster. But the Mr. O'Brien who terrorized them all nearly lifted the head off Suzi's entire family about the whole thing.

Only the pleas of Signora had succeeded in keeping Jerry from being expelled. He was so very young, the whole family would ensure that he didn't hang around after school but came straight home to do his lessons. And in fact, because he had shown such improvement and because Signora gave her personal guarantee, Jerry had been spared.

The older boys were out, expelled that day. Apparently Tony O'Brien said that he didn't give one damn about what happened to their futures. They didn't have much of a future, but what they had of it would not be spent in his school.

Lou wondered what hell would break loose if it were ever discovered that the school annex was acting as a receiving depot for drugs every Tuesday and passing them on the next stage of their journey on a Thursday. Perhaps some of these very consignments were the ones that had been handled by young Jerry Sullivan, his future brother-in-law.

Suzi and he decided that they would marry next year.

"I'll never like anyone more," Suzi said.

"You sound fed up, as if I'm only the best of a bad bunch," Lou said.

"No, that's not true." She had become even fonder of him since he had taken up Italian. Signora always spoke of how helpful he was at the class. "He's full of surprises certainly," Suzi had said. And indeed he was. She used to hear him recite his Italian homework, the parts of the body, the days of the week. He was so earnest about it, he looked like a little boy. A good little boy.

IT WAS JUST when he was thinking of getting a ring that he heard from Robin.

"Maybe a nice jewel for your red-haired girlfriend, Lou," he said.

"Yes, well Robin, I was thinking of buying it myself, you know, wanting to take her to the shop so that we could discuss . . ." Lou didn't know if there was to be further payment for his work up in the school. In one way it was so simple that he didn't really *need* any more. In another he was doing something so *dangerous* that he really should be paid very well for it. To make it worth the risk.

"I was going to say that if you went into that big place near Grafton Street and chose her a ring, you'd only have to leave a deposit on it, the rest would be paid."

"She'd know, Robin. I don't tell her anything."

Robin smiled at him. "I know you don't, Lou, and she wouldn't know. There's this guy who'd show you a tray of really good stuff, no prices mentioned, and then she'd always have something really nice on her finger. And paid for absolutely legitimately because the balance would be sorted out."

"I don't think so, listen I know how good this is but I think . . ."

"Think when you have a couple of kids and things are hard how glad you were that you once met a fellow called Robin and got a deposit for a house and your wife is wearing a rock that cost ten big ones on her finger."

Did Robin really mean ten thousand pounds? Lou felt dizzy. And there was the mention of a deposit for a house as well. You'd have to be stark staring mad to fly in the face of this.

They went into the jeweler's. He asked for George.

George brought a tray. "These are all in your price range," he said to Lou.

"But they're enormous," hissed Suzi. "Lou, *you* can't afford these."

"Please don't take away the pleasure of giving you a nice ring," he said, his eyes big and sad.

"No, but Lou, listen to me. We save twenty-five a week between us and we find it hard going. These must be two hundred and fifty pounds at least, that's ten weeks saving. Let's get something cheaper, really." She was so nice, he didn't deserve her. And she didn't have an idea she was looking at serious jewelry.

"Which one do you like best?"

"This isn't a real emerald is it, Lou?"

"It's an emerald-*type* stone," he said solemnly.

Suzi waved her hand backward and forward, it caught the light and it flashed. She laughed with pleasure. "God you'd swear it was the real thing," she said to George.

Lou went into a corner with George, where he paid more than two hundred and fifty in notes and saw that an extra nine and a half thousand pounds had already been paid toward a ring to be bought by a Mr. Lou Lynch on that day.

"I wish you every happiness, sir," said George without changing a line of the expression on his face.

What did George know or not know? Was George someone who once got involved and now couldn't get uninvolved? Had Robin really been in to a respectable place like this and paid all that money in cash? Lou felt faint and dizzy.

⟨∾⟩

SIGNORA ADMIRED SUZI'S ring. "It's very, very beautiful," she said.

"It's only glass, Signora, but wouldn't you think it was an emerald?"

Signora, who had always loved jewelry but never owned any knew it was an emerald. In a very good setting. She began to worry about Luigi.

❦

S UZI SAW THE good-looking blond girl called Grania come in. She wondered how the dinner with the older man had gone. As usual she longed to ask but couldn't.

"Table for two?" she inquired politely.

"Yes, I'm meeting a friend."

Suzi was disappointed that it wasn't the old man. It was a girl, a small girl with enormous glasses. They were obviously old friends.

"I must explain, Fiona, that nothing is settled, nothing at all. But I might be calling on you in the weeks ahead to say that I am staying with you, if you know what I mean."

"I know only too well what you mean. It's been ages since either of you called on me to be the alibi," Fiona said.

"Well, it's just that this fellow . . . well it's a very long story. I really do fancy him a lot but there are problems."

"Like he's nearly a hundred, is that it?" Fiona asked helpfully.

"Oh Fiona, if only you knew . . . that's the least of the problems. His being nearly a hundred isn't a problem at all."

"You live very mysterious lives, you Dunnes," Fiona said in wonder. "You're going out with a pensioner and you don't notice what age he is. Brigid is obsessed with the size of her thighs, which seem perfectly ordinary to me."

"It's all because of that holiday she went on where they had a nudist beach," Grania explained. "Some eejit said that if you could hold a pencil under your boobs and it didn't fall down then you were too floppy and you shouldn't go topless."

"And . . . ?"

"Brigid said that she could hold a telephone directory under hers and it wouldn't fall."

They giggled at the thought.

"Well, if she said it herself," said the girl in the enormous spectacles.

"Yeah, but the awful point was that nobody denied it, and now she's got a complex the size of a house." Suzi tried not to laugh aloud. She offered them more coffee. "Hey, that's a beautiful ring," Grania said.

"I just got engaged." Suzi was proud.

They congratulated her and tried it on.

"Is it a real emerald?" Fiona asked.

"Hardly. Poor Lou works as a packer up in the big electrical place. No, but it's terrific glass, isn't it?"

"It's gorgeous, where did you get it?"

Suzi told her the name of the shop.

When she was out of hearing, Grania said in a whisper to Fiona: "That's funny, they only sell precious stones in that shop. I know because they have an account with us. I bet that's not glass, I bet it's the real thing."

IT WAS COMING up to the Christmas party in the Italian class. They wouldn't be seeing each other for two weeks. Signora asked them all to bring something to the last lesson and they would make it into a party. Huge banners with *Buon Natale* hung all over the room, and banners for the New Year too. They had all dressed up. Even Bill, the serious fellow from the bank, Guglielmo as they all called him, had entered into the spirit of it all and had brought paper hats.

Connie, the woman with the car and the jewelry, brought six bottles of Frascati that she said she found in the back of her husband's car, and she felt that he might have been taking them off somewhere for his secretary, so they had better be drunk. No one quite knew whether or not to take her seriously, and there had been this restriction about drink earlier. But Signora said it had all been cleared with Mr. O'Brien, the principal, so they needn't worry about that aspect of things.

Signora didn't feel it necessary to add that Tony O'Brien had said that since the school seemed to be crawling with hard drugs and kids laying their hands on crack with ease, it seemed fairly minor if some adults had a few glasses of wine as a Christmas treat.

"What did you do last Christmas?" Luigi asked Signora for no reason except that he was sitting near her when all the *salute* and *molte grazie* and *va bene* were going on around them.

"Last year I went to midnight Mass at Christmas and watched my husband, Mario, and his children from the back of the church," Signora said.

"And why weren't you sitting with them?" he asked.

She smiled at him. "It wouldn't have been proper," she said.

"And then he went and died," Lou said. Suzi had filled him in on Signora, a widow apparently, even though Suzi's mother thought she was a plainclothes nun.

"That's right, Lou, he went and died," she said gently.

"*Mi dispiace,*" Lou said. "*Troppo triste,* Signora."

"You're right, Lou, but then life was never going to be easy for anyone."

He was about to agree with her when a horrifying thought struck him.

It was a Thursday and there had been no man with an anorak. No van. The school would be locked up for two weeks with all of whatever it was in the store cupboard in the hall. What in the name of God was he to do now?

Signora had brought them the words of "Silent Night" in Italian, and the evening was coming to a close. Lou was frantic. He had no car; even if he could get a taxi at this late stage, what on earth would he do to explain why he was carrying four heavy boxes from the store cupboard. There was no way that he could come in here again until the first week of January. Robin would kill him.

But then, it was Robin's fault. He had given no contact number, no fallback position. Something must have happened to whoever was due to pick up. That was where the weak link was. It wasn't Lou's fault. No one could blame him. But he was paid, very well paid, to think quickly and stay cool. What would he do?

The clear up was beginning. Everyone was shouting their good-byes.

Lou offered to get rid of the rubbish. "I can't have you do all that, Luigi, you're far too good already," said Signora.

Guglielmo and Bartolomeo helped him. In no other place would he have been friendly with two fellows like this, a serious bank clerk and a van driver. Together they carried black sacks of rubbish out into the night and found the big school bins.

"She's terribly nice, your one, Signora, isn't she?" said Bartolomeo.

"Lizzie thinks she's having a thing with Mr. Dunne, you know, the man in charge of the whole thing," Guglielmo whispered.

"Get away." Lou was amazed. The lads speculated about it.

"Well, wouldn't it be great if it were true."

"But at their age . . ." Guglielmo shook his head.

"Maybe when we get to their age we'll think it the most natural thing in the world." Lou somehow wanted to stand up for Signora. He didn't know whether he should deny this ridiculous suggestion or confirm it as the most normal thing in the world.

His heart was still racing about the boxes. He knew he had to do something he hated; he had to deceive this nice kind woman with the amazing hair. "How are you getting home, will Mr. Dunne be picking you up?" he asked casually.

"Yes, he did say he might drop by." She looked a little pink and flustered. The wine, the success of the evening, and the directness of his question.

Signora thought that if Luigi, not the brightest of pupils, had seen something in the way she related to Aidan Dunne, then it must be very well known in the class. She would hate it to be thought that she was his lady friend. After all, it wasn't as if words or anything else except companionship had been exchanged between them. But if his wife were to find out, or his two daughters. If they were to be a subject of gossip that Mrs. Sullivan would hear about, as she well might, considering how her daughter was engaged to Luigi.

Having lived so discreetly for years, Signora was nervous of stepping out of her role. And also, it was so unnecessary. Aidan Dunne didn't think of her as anything except a good friend. That was all. But it might not look that way to people who were, how would she put it, more basic, people like Luigi.

He was looking at her quizzically. "Right, will I lock up for you? You go ahead and I'll catch you up, we're all a bit late tonight."

"*Grazie, Luigi. Troppo gentile.* But be sure you *do* lock it. You know there's a watchman comes round an hour after we've all gone. Mr. O'Brien is a stickler for this. So far we've never been caught leaving it unlocked. I don't want to fall at the last fence."

So he couldn't leave it open and come back when he thought up a plan. He *had* to lock the bloody thing. He took the key. It was on a big heavy ring shaped like an owl. It was a silly childish thing, but at least it was big, no one would be able to forget it, or think they had it in a handbag if it wasn't there.

Like lightning he put his own key onto the silly owl ring and took off Signora's. Then he locked the school, ran after her, and dropped the key into her handbag. She wouldn't need it until next term, and even if before, he could always manage to substitute something, get the real key back into her handbag somehow. The main thing was to get her home thinking she had the key.

He did not see Mr. Dunne step out of the shadows and take her arm tonight, but wouldn't it be amazing if it were true. He must tell Suzi. Which reminded him, he had better stay with Suzi tonight. He had just given away his mother and father's key.

❧

"I'LL BE STAYING with Fiona tonight," Grania said.

Brigid looked up from her plate of tomatoes.

Nell Dunne didn't look up from the book she was reading. "That's nice," she said.

"So, I'll see you tomorrow evening then," Grania said.

"Great." Her mother still didn't look up.

"Great altogether," Brigid said sourly.

"You could go out too if you wanted to, Brigid. You don't have to sit sighing over tomatoes, there are plenty of places to go and you could stay in Fiona's too."

"Yes, she has a mansion that will fit us all," Brigid said.

"Come on, Brigid, it's Christmas Eve tomorrow. Cheer up."

"I can cheer up without getting laid," Brigid muttered.

Grania looked across anxiously, but her mother hadn't registered it. "Yes, so can we all," Grania said in a low voice. "But we don't go round attacking everyone over the size of our thighs, which, it may be said in all cases, are quite normal."

"Who mentioned my thighs to you?" Brigid was suspicious.

"A crowd of people came by the bank today to protest about them. Oh Brigid, do shut up, you're gorgeous, stop all this anorexic business."

"Anorexic?" Brigid gave a snort of laughter. "Suddenly you're all sweetness and light because lover boy has materialized again."

"Who is lover boy? Come on, who? You know nothing." Grania was furious with her younger sister.

"I know you've been moping and moaning. And you talk of *me* sighing over tomatoes, you sigh like the wind over everyone and you leap ten feet in the air when the phone rings. Whoever it is he's married. You're as guilty as hell."

"You have been wrong about everything since you were born," Grania told her. "But you were never more wrong in your life about this. He is not married, and I would lay you a very good bet that he never will be."

"That's the kind of crap people talk when they're dying for an engagement ring," said Brigid, turning the tomatoes over with no enthusiasm.

"I'm off now," Grania said. "Tell Dad I'll not be coming in so that he can lock the door."

Their father was hardly ever at the kitchen supper anymore. He was either away in his room planning colors and pictures for the wall, or up in the school talking about the evening class.

❦

AIDAN DUNNE HAD gone to the school in case Signora might be there, but the place was all locked up. She never went to the pub on her own. The coffee shop would be too crowded with last-minute shoppers. He had never telephoned her at the Sullivans' house, he couldn't start now.

But he really wanted to see her before Christmas to give her a little gift. He had found a locket with a little Leonardo da Vinci face inside. It wasn't expensive but it seemed entirely suitable. He hoped she would have it for Christmas Day. It was wrapped up with *Buon Natale* printed on the gold paper. It wouldn't be the same afterward.

Or perhaps it would, but he felt like talking to her for a while. She had once said to him that at the end of the road where she lived there was a wall where she sat sometimes and looked across at the mountains, and thought how different her life had become, and how *vista del monte* meant the school to her now. Perhaps she might be there tonight.

Aidan Dunne walked up through the busy estate. There were Christmas lights in the windows, cartons of beer being delivered at houses. It must be so different to Signora from last year, when she had spent Christmas with all those Italians in the village in Sicily.

She was sitting there very still. She didn't seem a bit surprised. He sat down beside her.

"I brought your Christmas present," he said.

"And I brought yours," she said, holding a big parcel.

"Will we open them now?" He was eager.

"Why not?"

They unwrapped the locket and the big colored Italian plate with yellow and gold and a dash of purple, perfect for his room. They thanked each other and praised the gifts. They sat like teenagers with nowhere to go.

It got cold and somehow they both stood up at the same time.

"*Buon natale,* Signora." He kissed her on the cheek.

"*Buon natale,* Aidan, *caro mio,*" she said.

❧

CHRISTMAS EVE THEY worked long, hard hours in the electrical store. Why did people wait until then to decide on the electric carving knife, the video, the electric kettle? Lou toiled all day, and it was at closing time that Robin came into the warehouse with a sales receipt. Lou had somehow expected him.

"Happy Christmas, Lou."

"*Buon natale,* Robin."

"What do you mean?"

"It's the Italian you made me learn, I can hardly think in English anymore."

"Well, I came to tell you that you can give it up any time you like," Robin said.

"*What?*"

"Sure. Another premises has been located, but the people have been very grateful indeed for the smooth way your premises were organized."

"But the last one?" Lou's face was white.

"What about the last one?"

"It's still in there," Lou said.

"You are joking me in this matter."

"Would I joke about a thing like this? Nobody ever came on the Thursday. Nothing was picked up."

"Hurry along there, get the man his appliance." The foreman wanted to close up.

"Give me your receipt," hissed Lou.

"It's a television for you and Suzi."

"I can't take it," Lou said. "She'd know it was nicked."

"It's not nicked, haven't I just paid for it?" Robin was hurt.

"No, but you know what I mean. I'll go and put it into your car."

"I was going to drive you back to her flat with the surprise Christmas present."

It *was*, as Lou would have guessed, the most expensive in the whole store. The top of the range. Suzi Sullivan would never have accepted any explanation for something like that being carried up the stairs into her bed-sitter.

"Listen we've much bigger problems than the telly, wait till I get my wages and then we'll see what we're going to do about the school."

"I presume you have taken some steps."

"Some, but they mightn't be the right ones."

Lou went in and stood with the lads. They got their money, a drink, and a bonus, and after what seemed forever he came to where the big man sat in his station wagon, the huge television set in the back.

"I have the key to the school but God knows what kind of lunatics they employ to walk round and test doors at odd times. The principal there is some kind of maniac apparently."

He produced the key, which he had carried with him at all times since the day he took it from Signora's key ring.

"You're a bright boy, Lou."

"Brighter than those who didn't tell me what to do if a bloody man in an anorak doesn't turn up." He was angry and aggrieved and frightened now. He was sitting with a criminal in the car park of his workplace with a giant television set that he could not accept. He had stolen a key, left a shipment of drugs in a school. He didn't feel like a bright man, he felt like a fool.

"Well, of course there are always problems with people," Robin said. "People let you down. Somebody has let us down. He will not work again."

"What will happen to him?" Lou asked fearfully. He had visions of the offending anorak who hadn't turned up ending up dead, weighed down with cement blocks in the River Liffey.

"As I said, he will never work again for people."

"Maybe he had a car crash, or maybe his child went to hospital." Why was Lou defending him? This was the man who had broken all their hearts.

He could have been off the hook if it hadn't been for this. Robin's people had found new premises. Oddly, he thought he might have continued with the lessons. He enjoyed them anyway. He might even have gone on the trip that Signora was planning to Italy next summer. There would have been no need to stay on as a cover. Nothing had been proved. It had been a successful resting place. No accusation of an inside job would have been made because nothing had been discovered, apart from this fool who had not turned up on the last Thursday.

"His punishment will be that he never works again." Robin shook his head in sorrow.

Lou saw a chink of light at the end of the tunnel. That was what you had to do to get uninvolved. Just screw up on a deal. Just do one job badly and you were never called again. If only he had known it would be so simple. But this job wasn't his to falter on. The anorak man was already suffering for this, and Lou had got the key and probably saved the day. It would have to be the next one.

"Robin, is this your car?"

"No, of course it isn't. You know that. I got it off a friend just so that I could transport the television to you and Suzi. But there you are." He looked sulky, like a child.

"The Guards won't be watching for you in this car," Lou said. "I have an idea. It might not work but it's all I can think of."

"Tell it to me."

And Lou told him.

It was almost midnight when Lou drove up to the school. He reversed the station wagon up to the door of the school annex, and looking left and right to see was he being watched, he let himself into the building.

Almost afraid to breathe, he went to the store cupboard and there they were, four boxes. Just as they always were, looking indeed as if they held a dozen bottles of wine each, but there was no sign saying *This Way Up*. Nothing saying *Handle with Care*. Tenderly he lifted them one by one outside the door. Then, straining and panting, he carried the huge television into the classroom. It had a built-in video, it was state of the art. He had written the note already in colored pencils, which he had bought in a late-night shop.

Buon natale a lei, Signora, e a tutti, it said.

The school would have a television. The boxes had been rescued. He would drive them in Robin's car to a place where a different man in a different van would meet him and take them silently.

Lou wondered about the lifestyle of people who were suddenly available on Christmas Eve. He hoped he would never be one of them.

He wondered what Signora would say when she saw it. Would she be the first in? Perhaps that madman Tony O'Brien, who seemed to prowl the place night and day, would find it first. They would wonder about it forever. The number had been filed off it. It could have been bought in any of two dozen stores.

The box revealed nothing of its origin. They would realize it had not been stolen when they began to inquire. They would guess forever and not be able to come up with a solution. The mystery of how the place had been entered would fade in time. After all, nothing had been stolen. There had been no vandalism.

Even tetchy Mr. O'Brien would have to give up eventually.

Meanwhile, there would be a great television and video for the use of the school and presumably the evening class where it had appeared.

And the next job that Robin asked Lou to do would be botched. And then sadly Lou would be told that he could never work again, and he could get on with his life.

❧

It was Christmas morning and he was exhausted. He went around to Suzi's parents' house for tea and Christmas cake. Signora was there quietly in the background playing chess with Jerry.

"Chess!" whispered Suzi in amazement. "That fellow can understand the pieces and the moves of chess. Wonders will never cease."

"Signora!" he said.

"Luigi." She seemed delighted to see him.

"You know, I got a present of a key ring just like yours," he said.

They weren't all that uncommon, it was hardly something to be marveled at.

"My owl key ring." Signora was always pleasant and responded to any conversation that was presented to her.

"Yeah, let me see, are they the same?" he said.

She took it from her bag and he pretended to make a comparison as he made the switch. He was safe now, and so was she. No one would ever remember this harmless little conversation. He must talk about other gifts and confuse them.

∾

"GOD, I THOUGHT that Lou would never stop talking tonight," Peggy Sullivan said as she and Signora washed up. "Do you remember when they used to say people were vaccinated with a gramophone needle, they can't say that today I suppose what with CDs and tapes."

"I remember that phrase. I once tried to explain it to Mario, but like so many things it got lost in the translation and he never knew what I meant."

It was a moment for confidences. Peggy never dared to ask this odd woman a personal question, but she had sort of lowered the guard here. "And did you not think of being with your own people at all, Signora, on Christmas Day?" she asked.

Signora did not look at all put out. She answered the question thoughtfully, with deliberation, as she answered Jerry's questions. "No, you know, it wasn't something I would have liked. It would have been artificial. And I have seen my mother and sisters many times and none of them suggested it. They have their own ways and customs now. It would be hard to try and add me to them. It would have been very false. None of us would have enjoyed it. But I did enjoy myself here today with your family." She stood there calm and untroubled. She wore a new locket around her neck. She had not said where she got it and nobody had liked to ask. She was much too private a person.

"And we liked having you very, very much, Signora," said Peggy Sullivan, who wondered nowadays what she had ever done before this odd woman had come to live there.

THE CLASS BEGAN again on the first Tuesday of January. A cold evening, but they were all there. Nobody was missing from the thirty who had signed on in September. It must be a record in any evening class.

And all the top brass were there, the principal, Tony O'Brien, and Mr. Dunne, and they were beaming all over their faces. The most extraordinary thing had happened. The class had been given a gift. Signora was like a child, almost clapping her hands with pleasure.

Who could have done it? Was it anyone here? Was it one of the class? Would they say, so that they could thank him or her? Everyone was mystified, but of course they all thought it was Connie.

"No, I wish it had been. I really do wish I had been nice enough to think of it." Connie seemed almost embarrassed now that she hadn't been responsible.

The principal said he was delighted, but he was anxious in terms of security. If nobody owned up to having given this generous present, then they would have to have the locks changed because somebody somewhere must have a key to the place. There had been no sign of a break-in.

"That's not the way the bank would look at it," Guglielmo said. "They'd say leave things as they are, whoever it is might give us a hi-fi next week."

Lorenzo, who was actually Laddy the hotel porter, said that you'd be surprised how many keys there were walking round the city of Dublin that would open the same doors.

And suddenly Signora looked up and looked at Luigi and Luigi looked away.

Please may she say nothing, he said to himself. Please may she know it will do no good, only harm. He didn't know if he was praying to God or just muttering to himself, but he meant it. He really meant it.

And it seemed to have worked. She looked away too.

The class began. They were revising. What a lot they had forgotten, Signora said, how much work there was to be done if they were all going to make the promised trip to Italy. Shamed, they struggled again with the phrases that had come so easily before the two-week break.

Lou tried to slip out when the class was over.

"Not helping me with the boxes tonight, Luigi?" Her look was unfaltering.

"*Scusi, Signora,* where are they? I forgot."

They lifted them into the now blameless store cupboard, an area that would never again house anything dangerous.

"Is um . . . Mr. Dunne coming to walk you home, Signora?"

"No, Luigi, but you on the other hand are walking out with Suzi, who is the daughter of the house where I stay." Her face looked cross.

"But you know that, Signora. We're engaged."

"Yes, that's what I wanted to discuss with you, the engagement, and the ring. *Un anello di fidanzamento,* that's what we call it in Italian."

"Yes, yes, a ring for the fiancée." Lou was eager.

"But not usually emeralds, Luigi. Not a real emerald. That is what is so strange."

"Aw, go on out of that, Signora, real emerald? You have to be joking. It's glass."

"It's an emerald, *uno smeraldo.* I know them. I love to touch them."

"They're making them better and better, Signora, no one can tell the real thing from the fakes now."

"It cost thousands, Luigi."

"Signora listen to me . . ."

"As that television set cost hundreds and hundreds . . . maybe over a thousand."

"What are you saying?"

"I don't know. What are *you* saying to me?"

No schoolteacher in the past had ever made Lou Lynch feel like this, humbled and ashamed. His mother and father had never been able to get him to conform. No priest or Christian Brother, and suddenly he was terrified of losing the respect and the silence of this strange woman.

"I'm saying . . ." he began. She waited with that curious stillness. "I suppose I'm saying it's over, whatever it was. There won't be any more of it."

"And are these things stolen, the beautiful emerald and the magnificent television set?"

"No, no they're not, as it happens," he said. "They were paid for, not exactly by me but by other people that I worked for."

"But that you don't work for anymore?"

"No, I don't, I swear it." He desperately wanted her to believe him. His soul was all in his face as he spoke.

"So, no more pornography."

"No more *what,* Signora?"

"Well of course I opened those boxes, Luigi. I was so worried with the drugs in the school, and young Jerry, Suzi's little brother . . . I was afraid that's what you had in the store cupboard."

"And it wasn't?" He tried to take the question out of his voice.

"You know it wasn't. It was ridiculous filthy stuff, judging by the pictures on the covers. Such a fuss getting them in and out, so silly and for young impressionable people probably very harmful."

"You looked at them, Signora?"

"I told you I didn't play them, I don't have a video, and even if I did . . ."

"And you said nothing?"

"For years I have lived silently saying nothing. It becomes a habit."

"And did you know about the key?"

"Not until tonight, then I remembered the nonsense about a key ring. Why did you need it?"

"There were some boxes accidentally left over Christmas," he said.

"Couldn't you have left them there, Luigi, rather than steal keys and get them back?"

"It was always a bit complicated," he said repentantly.

"And the television?"

"It's a long story."

"Tell me some of it."

"Well, it was given to me as a present for . . . er, storing the . . . er boxes of tapes. And I didn't want to give it to Suzi because . . . well, you know I couldn't have. She'd know, or guess or something."

"But there's nothing for her to find out now."

"No, Signora." He felt as if he were four years old with his head hanging down.

"*In bocca al lupo,* Luigi," said Signora, locking the door behind them firmly, leaning against it and testing to make quite sure it was closed.

CONNIE

When Constance O'Connor was fifteen, her mother stopped serving desserts at home. There were no cakes at tea, a low-fat spread was on the table instead of butter, and sweets and chocolate were forbidden from the house.

"You're getting a bit hippy, darling," her mother said when Constance protested.

"All the tennis lessons, all the smart places we go, will be no use at all if you have a big bum."

"No use for what?"

"To attract the right kind of husband." Her mother had laughed. And then before Connie could persist she said: "Believe me I know what I'm saying. I'm not saying it's fair, but it's the way things are, so if we know the rules why not play by them?"

"They might have been the rules in your day, Mother, back in the forties, but everything's changed since then."

"Believe me," her mother said. It was a great phrase of hers, she ordered people to believe her on this and on that. "Nothing has changed, 1940s, 1960s, they still want a slim, trim wife. It looks classy. The kind of men *we* want, want women who look the part. Just be glad you know that and lots of your friends at school don't."

Connie had asked her father. "Did you marry Mother because she was slim?"

"No, I married her because she was lovely and delightful and warm and because she looked after herself. I knew someone who looked after herself would look after me, and you when you came along, and the home. It's as simple as that."

Connie was at an expensive girls' school.

Her mother always insisted she invite her friends around to supper or for the weekend. "That way they'll invite you and you can meet their brothers and their friends," Mother said.

"Oh Mother, it's idiotic. It's not like some kind of society where we are all presented at court. I'll meet whoever I meet, that's the way it is."

"That's not the way it is," her mother said.

And when Connie was seventeen or eighteen, she found herself going out with exactly the people her mother would have chosen for her, doctors' sons, lawyers' sons, young people whose fathers were very successful in business. Some of them were great fun, some of them were very stupid, but Connie knew it would all be all right when she went to university. Then she could really meet the kinds of people she knew were out there. She could make her own friends, not just pick from the tiny circle that her mother had thought suitable.

She had registered to go to University College Dublin just before her nineteenth birthday. She had gone in and walked around the campus several times and attended a few public lectures there so that she wouldn't feel nervous when it all started in October.

But in September the unbelievable happened. Her father died. A dentist who spent a great deal of his time on the golf course, and whose successful practice had a lot to do with being a partner in his uncle's firm, should have lived forever. That's what everyone said. Didn't smoke, only the odd drink to be sociable, took plenty of exercise. No stress in his life.

But, of course, they hadn't known about the gambling. Nobody had known until later the debts that existed. That the house would have to be sold. That there would be no money for Connie or any of them to go to university.

Connie's mother had been ice-cold about it all. She behaved perfectly at the funeral, invited everyone around to the house for salads and wine. "Richard would have wanted it this way," she said.

Already the rumors were beginning to spread, but she kept her head up high. When she was alone with Connie, and only then, she let her public face fall. "If he weren't dead I would kill him," she said over and over. "With my own bare hands I would choke the life out of him for doing this to us."

"Poor Daddy." Connie had a softer heart. "He must have been very upset in his mind to throw money away on dogs and horses. He must have been looking for something."

"If he were still here to face me, he would have known what he was looking for," her mother said.

"But if he had lived, he would have explained, won it back maybe, told us." Connie wanted a good memory of her father, who had been kind and good-tempered. He hadn't fussed as much as Mother, and made so many rules and laid down so many laws.

"Don't be a fool, Connie. There's no time for that now. Our only hope is that you will marry well."

"Mother! Don't be *idiotic,* Mother. I'm not going to get married for years. I have all my college years to get through, then I want to travel. I'm going to wait until I'm nearly thirty before I settle down."

Her mother looked at her with a very hard face. "Let's get this understood here and now, there will be no university. Who will pay the fees, who will pay your upkeep?"

"What do you want me to do instead?"

"You'll do what you have to do. You'll live with your father's family, his uncles and brothers are very ashamed about this weakness of his. Some of them knew, some didn't. But they're going to keep you in Dublin for a year while you do a secretarial course, and possibly a couple of other things as well, then you'll get a job and marry somebody suitable as soon as possible."

"But Mother . . . I'm going to do a degree, it's all arranged, I've been accepted."

"It's all unarranged now."

"That's not fair, it can't be."

"Talk to your late Father about it, it's his doing, not mine."

"But couldn't I get a job and go to college at the same time?"

"It doesn't happen. And that crowd of his relatives aren't going to put you up in their house if you're working as a cleaner or a shop girl, which is all you can hope to get."

Maybe she should have fought harder, Connie told herself. But it was hard to remember how times were then. And how shocked and upset they all were.

And how frightened she was, going to live with her cousins whom she didn't know, while Mother and the twins went back to the country to live with Mother's family. Mother said that going back to the small town she had left in triumph long ago was the hardest thing a human should be asked to do.

"But they'll be sorry for you so they'll be nice to you," Connie had said.

"I don't want their pity, their niceness. I wanted my pride. He took that away. That's what I will never forgive him for, not until the day I die."

~~

AT HER SECRETARIAL course Connie met Vera, who had been at school with her.

"I'm desperately sorry about your father losing all his money," Vera said immediately, and Connie's eyes filled with tears.

"It was terrible," she said. "Because it's not like the awfulness of your father dying anyway, it's as if he were a different person all the time and none of us ever knew him."

"Oh, you *did* know him, it's just you didn't know him liking a flutter, and he'd never have done it if he thought you were all going to be upset," said Vera.

Connie was delighted to meet someone so kind and understanding. And even though she and Vera had never been close at school, they became very firm friends at that moment.

"I think you don't know how nice it is having someone being sympathetic," she wrote to her mother. "It's like a warm bath. I bet people would be like that to you around Grannie's home if you let them and told them how awful you felt."

The letter back from her mother was sharp and to the point. "Kindly don't go weeping for sympathy on all and sundry. Pity is no comfort to you, nor are fine soft words. Your dignity and your pride are the only things you need to see you into your middle age. I pray that you will not be deprived of them as I was."

Never a word about missing Father. About the kind husband he was, the good father. The photographs were taken out of the frames. The frames were sold in the auction. Connie didn't dare to ask whether the pictures of her childhood had been saved.

Connie and Vera got on very well at their secretarial college. They did the shorthand and typing classes, together with the bookkeeping and office routine that were all part of such a comprehensive type of training. The family of cousins that she stayed with were embarrassed by her plight and gave her more freedom than her mother would have done.

Connie enjoyed being young and in Dublin. She and Vera went to dances, where they met great people. A boy called Jacko fancied Connie, and his friend Kevin fancied Vera, so they often went out together as a foursome. But neither she nor Vera was serious, while both the boys were. There was a lot of pressure on both of them to have sex. Connie refused but Vera agreed.

"Why do you do it if you don't enjoy it, if you're afraid of getting pregnant?" Connie asked, bewildered.

"I didn't say I didn't enjoy it," Vera protested. "I said it's not as great as it's made out to be and I can't see what all the puffing and panting is about. And I'm not afraid of getting pregnant, I'm going to go on the Pill."

Even though birth control was still officially banned in Ireland in the early 1970s, the contraceptive pill could be prescribed for menstrual irregularity. Not surprisingly a large number of the female population were found to suffer from this. Connie thought it might be a good idea to go the same route. You never knew the day or the hour you might need to sleep with someone, and it would be a pity to have to hang around and wait until the Pill started to work.

Jacko had not been told that Connie was taking the contraceptive Pill. He remained hopeful that she would eventually realize that they were meant for each other, just like Kevin and Vera. He dreamed up more and more ideas that he thought would please her. They would travel to Italy together—they would learn Italian before they left at some night school or from records. When they got there they would be *scusi* and *grazie* with the best of them. He was good-looking, eager, and besotted with her. But Connie was firm. There would be no affair—no real involvement. Taking the Pill was just part of her own practicality.

Whatever version of the Pill Vera was taking did not agree with her, and in the time when she was changing over to another brand she became pregnant.

Kevin was delighted. "We always meant to get married anyway," he kept saying.

"I wanted to have a bit of a life first," Vera wept.

"You've *had* a bit of a life, now we'll have a real life, you and the baby and me." Kevin was overjoyed that they didn't need to live at home anymore. They could have their own place.

It didn't turn out to be a very comfortable place. Vera's family were not wealthy and were very annoyed indeed with their daughter's having, as they considered it, thrown away her expensive education and costly commercial course before she ever worked a day in her life.

They were also less than pleased with the family that Vera was about to marry into. While they considered Kevin's people extremely worthy, they were definitely not what they had hoped for their daughter.

Vera didn't need to explain this tension to Connie, Connie's own mother would have been fit to be tied. She could imagine her screaming: "His father a house painter. And he's going into the business! They call *that* a business to be going into." It was useless for Vera to point out that Kevin's father owned a small builders, providers, and decorators that in time might well become fairly important.

Kevin had earned a living every week of his life since he was seventeen. He was twenty-one now and extremely proud of being a father. He had painted the nursery of the two-up, two-down house with three coats. He wanted it to be perfect when the baby arrived.

At Vera's wedding, where Jacko was best man and Connie was the bridesmaid, Connie made a decision. "We can never go out with each other ever again after today," she said.

"You're not serious, what did I do?"

"You did nothing, Jacko, except be nice and terrific, but I don't want to get married, I want to work and go abroad."

His open, honest face was mystified. "I'd let you work, I'd take you away every year to Italy on a holiday."

"No Jacko. Dear Jacko, no."

"And I thought we might even make an announcement tonight," he said, his face drawn in lines of disappointment.

"We hardly know each other, you and I."

"We know each other just as much as the bride and groom here, and look how far down the road they are." Jacko spoke enviously.

Connie didn't say that she thought her friend Vera was very unwise to have signed on for life with Kevin. She felt Vera would tire of this life soon. Vera, with the laughing dark eyes and the dark fringe still in her eyes, as it had been at school, would soon be a mother. She was able to face down her stiff-faced mother and father, and force everyone to have a good time at her wedding party. Look at her now, with the small bump in her stomach obvious to all, leading the singing of "Hey Jude" at the piano. Soon the whole room was singing *la la la la la la Hey Jude*.

She swore to Connie that it was what she wanted.

And amazingly it turned out to be what she *did* want. She finished the rest of her course and went to work in Kevin's father's office. In no time she had organized their rather rudimentary system of accounts. There was a proper filing cabinet, not a series of spikes, there was an appointment book that everyone had to fill in. The arrival of the tax man was no longer a source of such dread. Slowly Vera moved them into a different league.

The baby was an angel, small and dark-eyed with loads of black hair like Vera and Kevin. At the christening Connie felt her first small twinge of envy. She and Jacko were the godparents. Jacko had another girl now, a pert little thing. Her skirt was too short, her outfit not right for a christening.

"I hope you're happy," Connie whispered to him at the font.

"I'd come back to you tomorrow. Tonight, Connie," he said to her.

"That's not only not on, it's not fair to think like that," she said.

"She's only to get me over you," he pleaded.

"Maybe she will."

"Or the next twenty-seven, but I doubt it."

The hostility that Vera's family had been showing to Kevin's had disappeared. As so often happened, a tiny innocent baby in a robe being handed from one to the other made all the difference . . . the looking for family noses and ears and eyes in the little bundle. There was no need for Vera to sing "Hey Jude" to cheer them up, they were happy already.

THE GIRLS HAD not lost touch. Vera had asked: "Do you want to know how much Jacko yearns over you or not?"

"Not, please. Not a word."

"And what should I say when he asks are you seeing anyone?"

"Tell him the truth, that I do from time to time but you think I'm not all that interested in fellows, and certainly not in settling down."

"All right," Vera promised. "But for me, tell me have you met anyone you fancied since him?"

"Ones I half fancy, yes."

"And have you gone all the way with them?"

"I can't talk to a respectable married woman and mother about such things."

"That means no," Vera said, and they giggled as they had when they learned typing.

Connie's good looks and cool manner were an asset at interviews. She never allowed herself to look too eager, and yet there was nothing supercilious about her either. She refused quite an attractive job in the bank since it was only a temporary one.

The man who interviewed her had been surprised and rather impressed. "But why did you apply if you didn't intend to take it?" he asked.

"If you see the wording of your advertisement there was nothing to suggest that my job would be in the nature of temporary relief," she said.

"But once with a foot in the bank, Miss O'Connor, surely that would be to your advantage."

Connie was unflustered. "If I were to go in for banking I would prefer to be part of the natural intake and be part of a system," she said.

He remembered her and spoke of her that night to two friends in the golf club. "Remember Richard O'Connor, the dentist who lost his shirt. His daughter came in to see me, real little Grace Kelly, cool as anything.

I wanted to give her a job, out of decency for poor old Richard, but she wouldn't take it. Bright as a button though."

One of the men owned a hotel. "Would she be good at a front desk?"

"Exactly what you're looking for, maybe even too classy for you."

So next day Connie was called for another interview.

"It's very simple work, Miss O'Connor," the man explained.

"Yes, but what could I learn then? I wouldn't like to do something that didn't stretch me, require me to grow with it."

"This job is in a new top-grade hotel, it can be what you make of it."

"Why do you think I would be suitable for it?"

"Three reasons, you look nice, you talk well, and I knew your dad."

"I didn't mention anything about my late father in this interview."

"No, but I know who he was. Don't be foolish, girl, take the job. Your father would like you to be looked after."

"Well, if he would have, he certainly didn't do much during his life-time to see that this would be the case."

"Don't talk like that, he loved you all very much."

"How do you know?"

"He was forever showing us pictures on the golf course of the three of you. Brightest children in the world, we were told."

She felt a stinging behind her eyes. "I don't want a job from pity, Mr. Hayes," she said.

"I would want my daughter to feel the same way, but also I wouldn't want her to make a big thing about pride. You know it's a deadly sin but that's not as important as knowing it's a very poor companion on a winter's evening."

This was one of the wealthiest men in Dublin sharing his views with her. "Thank you, Mr. Hayes, and I do appreciate it. Should I think about it?"

"I'd love you to take it now. There are a dozen other young women waiting for it. Take it and make it into a great job."

Connie rang her mother that night.

"I'm going to work for the Hayes Hotel starting on Monday. When the hotel opens I'll be introduced as their first hotel receptionist, chosen from hundreds of applicants. That's what the public relations people say. Imagine, I'm going to have my picture in the evening papers." Connie was very excited.

Her mother was not impressed. "They just want to make you into some kind of little dumb blonde, you know, simpering for the photographers."

Connie felt her heart harden. She'd followed her mother's instructions to the letter, done her secretarial course, stayed with her cousins, got herself a job. She was not going to be insulted and patronized in this way. "If you remember, Mother, what *I* wanted was to go to university and be a lawyer. That didn't happen, so I'm doing the best I can. I am sorry you think so poorly of it, I thought you'd be pleased."

Her mother was immediately contrite. "I'm sorry, I really am. If you knew how sharp-tongued I'm getting . . . They say here I'm like our great-aunt Katie, and you remember what a legend she was in the family."

"It's all right, Mother."

"No it's not, I'm ashamed. I'm very proud of you. I just say these hard things because I can't bear to have to be grateful to people like that Hayes man your father played golf with. He probably knows you're poor Richard's daughter and gave you the job out of charity."

"No, I don't think he would know that at all, Mother," Connie lied in a cool tone.

"You're right, why would he? It's nearly two years ago." Her mother sounded sad.

"I'll ring and tell you about it, Mother."

"Do that, Connie dear, and don't mind me. It's all I have left, you know, my pride. I won't apologize to any of them round here, my head is as high as ever."

"I'm glad you're pleased for me, give my love to the twins." Connie knew she would grow up a stranger now from the two fourteen-year-old boys who went to a Brothers school in a small town and not the private Jesuit college that had been planned.

Her father was gone, her mother was going to be no help. She was on her own. She would do what Mr. Hayes said. She would make a great job of this, her first serious position. She would be remembered in the Hayes Hotel as the first and best receptionist they ever had.

SHE WAS AN excellent appointment. Mr. Hayes congratulated himself over and over. And so like Grace Kelly. He wondered how long it would take before she met her prince.

⁓

IN FACT IT took two years. There were, of course, endless offers of all kinds of things. Businessmen staying regularly in the hotel longed to escort the elegant Miss O'Connor at the front desk to some of the smarter restaurants and, indeed, nightclubs that were starting up around the city. But she was very detached. She smiled and talked to them warmly and said she didn't mix business with pleasure.

"It doesn't have to be business," Teddy O'Hara cried in desperation. "Look, I'll stay in some other hotel if you just come out with me."

"That would hardly be a good way to repay Hayes Hotel for my good job here." Connie would smile at him. "Sending all the clients off to rival establishments."

She would tell Vera all about them. She called every week to see Vera, Kevin, and Deirdre, who was shortly to be joined by another baby.

"Teddy O'Hara asked you out?" Vera's eyes were round. "Oh please marry him, Connie, then we can get the contract for all the decorating on his shops. We'd be made for life. Go on, marry him for our sake."

Connie laughed, but she realized she had not been putting any business in her friends' way, which she could have been doing. Next day she said to Mr. Hayes that she knew a very good small firm of painters and decorators if they wanted to add them to their list of service suppliers. Mr. Hayes said that he left all that to the relevant manager, but he did need someone to do a job for him in his own house out in Foxrock.

Kevin and Vera never stopped talking about the size and splendor of the house, and the niceness of the Hayes family, who had a little girl themselves called Marianne, and Kevin and his father had done up the girl's bedroom for her with every luxury you could think of. Her own little pink bathroom off it, for a child!

Vera and Kevin never sounded jealous, and always grateful for the introduction. Mr. Hayes had been pleased with the work done and because of that recommended the small firm to others. Soon Kevin drove a smarter van. There was even talk of a bigger house when the new baby arrived.

They were still friendly with Jacko, who was in the electrical business. Could I put a bit of work *his* way? Connie had wondered. Vera said she'd test the water. What Jacko actually said was: "You can tell that stuck-up bitch to take her favors and stuff them." "He didn't seem keen" was the way Vera reported it, being someone who liked to keep the peace.

And just when Vera and Kevin's new baby, Charlie, was born Connie met Harry Kane. He was the handsomest man she had ever seen, tall with thick brown hair that curled on his shoulders, very unlike the business people she mixed with. He had an easy smile for everyone and a manner that seemed to expect he would get good attention everywhere. Doormen rushed to open doors for him, the girl in the boutique left other customers to get him his copy of the newspaper, and even Connie, who knew she was regarded as an ice maiden, looked up and smiled at him welcomingly.

She was particularly pleased that he saw her dealing with some difficult business travelers very efficiently. "Quite the diplomat, Miss O'Connor," he said admiringly.

"Always good to see you here, Mr. Kane. Everything's arranged in your meeting room."

Harry Kane with two older partners ran a new and very successful insurance firm. It was taking a lot of business from the more established companies. Some people looked on it with suspicion. Growing too big too fast, they said, bound to be in trouble. But it showed no signs of it. The partners worked in Galway and Cork, they met every Wednesday in Hayes Hotel. They worked from nine until twelve-thirty with a secretary in their conference room, then they entertained people to lunch.

Sometimes it was government ministers, or heads of industry or of big trade unions. Connie wondered why they didn't have their meeting in the Dublin office. Harry Kane had a big prestigious office in one of the Georgian squares, with almost a dozen people working there. It must be for privacy, she decided, that and lack of disturbance. The hotel had strict instructions that no calls whatsoever be put through to the conference room on a Wednesday. Obviously this secretary must know all their secrets and where the bodies were buried. Connie looked at her with interest as she went in and out with them each week. She would carry a briefcase of documents away with her and never joined the partners at lunch. Yet she must be a highly trusted confidante.

Connie would like to work like that for someone. Someone very like Harry Kane. She began to talk to the woman, using all her charm and every skill she could rustle up.

"Everything in the room to your satisfaction, Miss Casey?"

"Certainly, Miss O'Connor, otherwise Mr. Kane would have mentioned it to you."

"We have just stocked quite a new range of audiovisual equipment in case any of it would be of use for your meetings."

"Thank you, but no."

Miss Casey always seemed anxious to leave, as if her briefcase contained hot money. Maybe it did. Connie and Vera talked it over for hours.

"She's obviously a fetishist, I'd say," Vera suggested as they bounced baby Charlie on their knees and assured Deirdre that she was much more beautiful and much more loved than Charlie would ever be.

"*What?*" Connie had no idea what Vera was suggesting.

"Sadomasochism, whips them within an inch of their life every Wednesday. That's the only way they can function. That's what's in the case. Whips!"

"Oh, Vera, I wish you could see her."

Connie laughed till the tears came down her face at the thought of Miss Casey in that role. And, oddly, at the same time she felt a wave of jealousy in case the quiet, elegant Miss Casey did have an intimate relationship with Harry Kane. She had not felt that way about anyone before.

"You fancy him," Vera said sagely.

"Only because he doesn't look at me. You know that's the way of it."

"Why do you like him, do you think?"

"He reminds me a bit of my father," Connie said suddenly before she realized that this is what she had felt.

"All the more reason to keep a sharp eye on him then," said Vera, who was the only person allowed to mention the late Richard O'Connor's little gambling habit without getting a withering look from his daughter.

Without appearing to ask, Connie found out more and more about Harry Kane. He was almost thirty, single, his parents were from the country, small farmers. He was the first of his family to get into business in a big way. He lived in a bachelor apartment overlooking the sea, he went to first nights and to gallery openings, but always in a group.

His name had been mentioned in newspaper columns and always as part of a group, or sharing a box at the races with the highest of the land. When he married, it would be into a family like that of Mr. Hayes. Thank God that *his* daughter was only a young schoolgirl, otherwise she would have been ideal for him.

"MOTHER, WHY DON'T you come up to Dublin some Wednesday on the train and take a few of your friends for lunch in Hayes Hotel? I'll see they make the most enormous fuss of you."

"I don't have any friends left in Dublin."

"Yes, you do." She listed a few.

"I don't want their pity."

"What pity would there be if you invited them to a nice lunch? Come on, try it. Maybe *they'll* suggest it another time. You can take the day excursion ticket."

Grudgingly her mother agreed.

They were placed near Mr. Kane's party, which included a newspaper owner and two cabinet ministers. The ladies thoroughly enjoyed their lunch and the fact that they seemed to be even more feted than the amazingly important people nearby.

As Connie had hoped it would be, the lunch was pronounced a huge success, and one of the others said that next time it must be her treat. It would also be a Wednesday, in a month's time. And so it went on, her mother becoming more confident and cheerful since nobody mentioned her late husband apart from saying Poor Richard as they would to any widow about the deceased.

Connie always arranged to pass their table and offer them a glass of port with her compliments. Very publicly she would sign the bill for it so that everyone knew it was accountable for. She would flash a smile at the Kane table too.

After the fourth time she realized that he really *did* notice her. "You're very kind to those older women, Miss O'Connor," he said.

"That's my mother and some of her friends. They do enjoy their lunch here, and it's a pleasure to see her, she lives in the country, you see."

"Ah, and where do *you* live?" he asked, his eyes alert waiting for her reply.

It was her cue to say: "I have my own flat" or "by myself." But Connie was prepared. "Well, I live in Dublin, of course, Mr. Kane, but I do hope to travel sometime, I would love to see other cities." She was giving nothing away. She saw further interest in his face.

"And so you should, Miss O'Connor. Have you been to Paris?"

"Sadly not yet."

"I'm going next weekend, would you like to come with me?"

She laughed pleasantly, as if she was laughing with him not at him. "Wouldn't that be nice! But out of the question I'm afraid. I hope you have a good time."

"Perhaps I could take you to dinner when I come back and tell you about it?"

"I'd like that very much indeed."

And so it began, the courtship of Connie O'Connor and Harry Kane. And throughout it all she knew that Siobhan Casey, his faithful secretary, hated her. They kept the relationship as private as they could, but it wasn't easy. If he was invited to the opera, he wanted to take her, he didn't want to go with a crowd of singles handpicked for him. It wasn't long before their names were linked. She was described by one columnist as his blond companion.

"I don't like this," she said when she saw it in a Sunday paper. "It makes me look flashy, trash almost."

"To be my companion?" He raised his eyebrows.

"You know what I mean, the word 'companion' and all it suggests."

"Well, it's not my fault that they're not right about that." He had been urging her to bed and she had been refusing for some time now.

"I think we should stop seeing each other, Harry."

"You can't mean it."

"I don't want it but I think it's best. Look, I'm not just going to have a fling with you, and then be thrown aside. Seriously, Harry, I like you too much. I more than like you, I think of you all the time."

"And I of you." He sounded as if he meant it.

"So isn't it better if we stop now?"

"I don't know what the phrase is . . . ?"

" 'Get out in time.' " She smiled at him.

"I don't want to get out," he said.

"Neither do I, but it will be harder later."

"Will you marry me?" he asked.

"No, it's not that, I'm not putting a gun to your head. This isn't an ultimatum or anything, it's for our own good."

"I am putting a gun to *yours*. Marry me."

"Why?"

"I love you," he said.

THE WEDDING WAS to be in Hayes Hotel. Everyone insisted, Mr. Kane was like part of the family there, and Miss O'Connor had been the heartbeat of the place since it opened.

Connie's mother had nothing to pay for except her outfit. She was able to invite her friends, the ladies with whom she had regained contact. She even invited some of her old enemies. Her twin sons were ushers at the smartest wedding Dublin had seen in years, her daughter was a beauty, the groom was the most eligible man in Ireland. On that day Connie's mother almost forgave the late Richard. If he turned up alive now, she might not choke him to death after all. She had become reconciled to the hand that fate had dealt.

She and Connie slept in the same hotel room the night before the wedding. "I can't tell you how happy I am to see you so happy," she said to her daughter.

"Thank you, Mother, I know you've always wanted the best for me." Connie was very calm. She was having a hairdresser and beautician come to the room in the morning to look after her mother and Vera and herself. Vera was the matron of honor, and utterly overawed by the splendor of it all.

"You *are* happy?" her mother said suddenly.

"Oh, Mother, for goodness' sake." Connie tried to control her anger. Was there no occasion, no timing, no ceremony that her mother could not try to spoil? Yet she looked into the kind, concerned face. "I'm very, very happy. But just afraid I might not be enough for him, you know. He's a very successful man, I might not be able to keep up with him."

"You've kept up with him so far," her mother said shrewdly.

"But that's a matter of tactics, I didn't sleep with him like everyone else did from what I hear. I didn't give in easily, it might not be the same when *I'm* married."

Her mother lit another cigarette. "Just remember this one thing I said to you tonight and don't ever talk about it again, but remember it. Make sure he gives you money for yourself. Invest it, have it. Then in the end whatever happens won't be too bad."

"Oh Mother." Her eyes were soft and filled with pity for a mother who had been betrayed. A mother whose whole life had to be rewritten now that her husband had frittered away the future.

"Would money have made that much difference?"

"You'll never know how much, and my prayer for you tonight is that you will never have to know."

"I'll think about what you say," Connie said. It was a very useful phrase, she used it a lot at work when she had no intention whatsoever of thinking about what anyone said.

The wedding was a triumph. Harry's two partners and their wives said it was the best wedding they had ever been at, and this was like a seal of approval. Mr. Hayes from the hotel said that since the bride's father was sadly no longer with us, could he say that Richard would be so happy and proud to be here today and see his beautiful daughter so happy and radiant. It was the good fortune of the Hayes Hotel Group that Connie Kane, as she would now be known, had agreed to continue working until something might stop her doing so.

There was a titter of excitement at the thought of such a rich man's wife working as a hotel receptionist until she got pregnant. Which would be in the minimum time it took.

They had a honeymoon in the Bahamas, two weeks that Connie had thought would be the best in her life. She liked talking to Harry and laughing with him. She liked walking along the beach with him, making sand castles in the morning sunshine just by the water's edge, hand in hand at sunset before they went to dinner and dance.

She did not enjoy being in bed with him, not even a little bit. It was the last thing she would have expected. He was rough and impatient. He was terribly annoyed with her failure to respond. Even when she realized what he would like and tried to pretend an excitement she did not feel, he saw through it.

"Oh, come off it, Connie, stop all that ludicrous panting and groaning, you'd embarrass a cat."

She had never felt more hurt or more alone. To give him his due, he tried everything. He was gentle and wooing and flattering. He tried just holding her and stroking her. But as soon as penetration seemed likely she tensed up and seemed to resist it, no matter how much she told herself it was what they both wanted.

Sometimes she lay awake in the dark, warm night listening to the unfamiliar cicadas and the Caribbean sounds in the distance. She wondered did all women feel like this. Was it perhaps just a giant conspiracy for centuries, women pretending they enjoyed it when all they wanted was children and security? Was this what her mother had meant by telling her to demand that security? In today's world in the 1970s it didn't automatically exist for women. Men could leave home now without being considered villains, men could lose all their savings in gambling like her father and still be remembered as a good fellow.

In those long, warm, sleepless nights where she dare not stir for fear of wakening him and starting it all over again, Connie wondered too about the words of her friend Vera. "Go on, Connie, sleep with him now for God's sake. See do you like it. Suppose you don't—imagine a lifetime of it."

She had said no, it seemed cheating to hold back sex as if it was a prize, and then deliver it in consideration of an engagement ring. He had respected her wish to be a virgin when she married. There had been times in the last few months when she had felt aroused by him. Why had she not gone ahead then instead of waiting for this? A disaster. A disappointment that was going to scar both of them for life.

After eight days and nights of what should have been the best time for two young healthy people but which was actually becoming a nightmare of frustration and misunderstanding, Connie decided to become her old cool self, the woman who had attracted him so much. Wearing her best lemon and white dress, and sitting with the fruit basket and the china coffeepot on their balcony, she called to him: "Harry, get up and shower will you, you and I need to have a talk."

"That's all you ever want to do," he muttered into his pillow.

"Soon, Harry, the coffee won't stay hot forever."

To her surprise he obeyed her and came tousled and handsome in his white toweling robe to breakfast. It was a sin, she thought, that she could not please this man and make him please her. But more than that, it was something that had to be dealt with.

After the second cup of coffee she said: "At home in your work and indeed in my work, if a problem arose we would have a meeting and a discussion, do you agree?"

"What's this?" He didn't sound as if he was going to play along.

"You told me about your partner's wife who drank too much and would talk about your business. How you had to make sure she knew nothing important. It was a strategy . . . you all told her in deepest secrecy things that never mattered at all. And she was perfectly happy and is perfectly happy to this day. You worked that out by a strategy, all three of you. You sat down and said we don't want to hurt her, we can't talk to her, what do we do? And you solved it."

"Yes?" He didn't know where this was leading.

"And in my job, we had this problem with Mr. Hayes' nephew. Thick as two short planks . . . he was there, being groomed for a position of power. A vet with a curry comb couldn't groom him. How do we tell Mr. Hayes? We talked about it; three of us who cared sat down and had a meeting and said what do we do? We found out that the kid wanted to be a musician not a hotel manager. We employed him to play the piano in one of the lounges, he brought in all his rich friends, it worked like a dream."

"So what's all this about, Connie?"

"You and I have a problem. I can't understand it. You're gorgeous, you're an experienced lover, I love you. It must be my fault, I may need to see a doctor or a shrink or something. But I want to sort it out. Can we talk about it without fighting or sulking or getting upset?" She looked so lovely there, so eager, explaining things that were hard and distasteful to articulate. He struggled to reply. "Say *something*, Harry, say that after eight days and eight nights we will not give up. It's a happiness that's there waiting to happen for me, tell me that you know it will be all right." Still the silence. Not accusing, just bewildered. "Say anything," she begged. "Just tell me what you want."

"I want a honeymoon baby, Connie. I am thirty years of age, I want a son who can take over my business by the time I'm fifty-five. I want a family there over the next years; when I need them I come home to them. But you *know* all this. You and I have talked of aims and dreams for so long, night after night before I knew . . ." He stopped.

"No, go on," she said, her voice quiet.

"Well then, before I knew you were frigid," he said. There was a silence. "Now, you *made* me say it. I don't see the point of talking about these things." He looked upset.

She was still calm. "You're right, I did make you say it. And is that what I am, do you think?"

"Well, you said yourself you might need a shrink, a doctor, something. Maybe it's in your past. Jesus, I don't know. And I'm as sorry as hell because you're absolutely beautiful and I couldn't be more upset that it's no good for you."

She was determined not to cry, scream, run away, all the things she wanted to do. She had got on by being calm, she must continue like this.

"So in many ways we want the same thing, I too want a honeymoon baby," she said. "Come on, it's not that difficult. Lots of people do it, let's keep trying." And she gave him the most insincere smile she had ever given anyone and led him back to the bedroom.

WHEN THEY GOT back to Dublin, she assured him she would get it sorted out. Still smiling bravely, she said it made sense, she would consult the experts. First she made an appointment with a leading gynecologist. He was a very courteous and charming man, he showed her a diagram of the female reproductive area, pointing out where there might be blockages or obstructions. Connie studied the drawings with interest. They might have been plans for a new air-conditioning system in the hotel for all the relevance they had to what she felt in her own body. She nodded at his explanations, reassured by his easy manner and discreet way of implying that almost everyone in the world had similar problems.

But at the physical examination the problems began. She tensed so much that he could not examine her at all. He stood there despairing, his hand in its plastic glove, his face kind and impersonal at the same time. She did not feel that he was a threat to her, it would be such a relief to discover some membrane that could be easily removed, but every muscle in her body had seized up.

"I think we should do an examination under anesthetic," he said. "Much easier for everyone, and very probably a D and C, then you'll be as right as rain."

She made the appointment for the next week. Harry was loving and supportive. He came to the nursing home to settle her in. "You're all that matters to me, I never met anyone like you."

"I bet you didn't." She tried to joke about it. "Beating them off was your trouble, not like you have with me."

"Connie, it will be fine." He was so gentle and handsome and concerned. If she couldn't be loving to a man like this, there was no hope for her. Suppose she had given in to the persuasion of people like Jacko in the past, would it have been better or worse? She would never know now.

The examination showed that there was nothing physically wrong with Mrs. Constance Kane. At work Connie knew if you went down one avenue and came to a dead end, you had to go back to where you started from and go down another. She made an appointment with a psychiatrist. A very pleasant woman with a genuine smile and a matter-of-fact approach. She was easy to talk to, she seemed to ask shortish questions and expected longer answers. At work Connie was more accustomed to be in a listening mood, but gradually she responded to the interested questions of the psychiatrist, which never seemed intrusive.

She assured the older woman that there had not been any unpleasant sexual experiences in her past because there hadn't been any. No, she hadn't felt deprived, or curious or frustrated by not having had sex. No, she had never felt drawn to anyone of her own sex, nor had an emotional relationship that was so strong, it overshadowed anything heterosexual. She told the woman about her great friendship with Vera, but said that in all honesty there wasn't a hint of sexuality or emotional dependency in it, it was all laughter and confiding. And how it began because Vera was the only person to treat the whole business of her father as if it were a normal kind of thing that could happen to anyone.

The psychiatrist was very understanding and sympathetic and asked more and more about Connie's father, and her sense of disappointment after his death. "I think you're making too much of this whole business about my dad," Connie said at one point.

"It's quite possible. Tell me about when you came home from school each day. Did he get involved in your homework, for example?"

"I know what you're trying to say, that maybe he interfered with me or something, but it was not remotely like that."

"No, I'm not saying that at all. Why do you think I'm saying that?"

They went around in circles. At times Connie cried. "I feel so disloyal talking about my father like this."

"But you haven't said anything against him, just how kind and good and loving he was, and how he showed your picture to people at the golf course."

"But I feel he's accused of something else, like my not being able to be good in bed."

"You haven't accused him of that."

"I know, but I feel it's hanging there over me."

"And why is that do you think?"

"I don't know. I suppose it's because I felt so let down, I had to write my whole life story all over again. He didn't love us at all. How could he have if he was more interested in some horse or dog?"

"Is that the way it looks now?"

"He never laid a hand on me, I can't tell you that enough. It's not that I've suppressed it or anything."

"But he let you down, disappointed you."

"It couldn't be just that, could it? Because one man let us down as a family I'm afraid of all men?" Connie laughed at the notion.

"Is that so unlikely?"

"I deal with men all day, I work with men. I've never been afraid of them."

"But then you've never let any of them come close to you."

"I'll think about what you say," Connie said.

"Think about what *you* say," said the psychiatrist.

"DID SHE FIND anything?" His face was hopeful.

"A load of nonsense. Because my father was unreliable I think all men are unreliable." Connie laughed in scorn.

"It might be true," he said, to her surprise.

"But Harry, how could it be? We are so open with each other, you would never let me down."

"I hope I wouldn't," he said, so seriously that she felt a shiver go the whole way up and down her spine.

And the week went on. Nothing got any better, but Connie clung to him and begged. "Please don't give up on me, please, Harry. I love you, I want our child so much. Maybe when we have our child I'll relax and love it all like I should."

"Shush, shush," he would say, stroking the anxious lines away from her face, and it wasn't all repulsive or painful, it was just so very difficult. And they had surely had sex often enough now for her to have become pregnant. Look at all the people who got pregnant who were doing everything on earth to avoid it. In the wakeful night Connie wondered could fate have also decided that she be infertile on top of everything else. But no. She missed her period, and hardly daring to hope, she waited until she was sure. Then she told him the news.

His face lit up. "You couldn't have made me a happier man," he said. "I'll never let you down."

"I know," she said. But she didn't know, because she felt sure that there was a whole part of his life that she could never share and that sooner or later he would share that side at least with someone else. But in the meantime she must do all she could to shore up the parts of his life she could share.

Together they attended many public functions, and Connie insisted she be described as Mrs. Constance Kane of Hayes Hotel as well as just Harry's wife. She raised money for two charities with the wives of other successful men. She entertained in her own new and splendid home, where all the decorating had been done by Kevin's family.

She told her mother nothing about the situation between them. She told Vera everything. "When the baby's born," Vera advised, "go off and have a fling with someone else. You might get to like it and then come back and do it properly with Harry."

"I'll think about it," said Connie.

∽

THE BABY'S NURSERY was ready. Connie had given up her job. "No hope we could tempt you back, even part time, when the baby is old enough to leave with a nurse?" Mr. Hayes pleaded.

"We'll see." She was more calm and controlled than ever, Mr. Hayes thought. Marriage to a tough man like Harry Kane hadn't taken away any of her spirit.

Connie had made a point of keeping well in touch with Harry's family. She had driven to see them more often in one year than they had been visited by their son in the previous ten. She kept them informed about all the details of her pregnancy, their first grandchild, a very important milestone, she told them. They were quiet people, in awe of the hugely successful Harry. They were delighted and almost embarrassed to be so well included and to have their opinions sought about names.

Connie also made sure that she had the partners and their wives well within her own area. She took to giving light suppers in their house on a Wednesday night. The partners would all have wined and dined well at lunchtime after their weekly meeting, they would not want a huge meal. But each week there was something delicious for them to eat. Not too fattening, because one of them was always on a diet, and not too much alcohol served, since the other was inclined to hit the bottle.

Connie asked questions and listened to the answers. She assured the women that Harry thought so highly of their husbands that she was almost jealous of all his praise. She remembered every tiresome detail of their children's examinations and their home improvements and their holidays, the clothes they had bought. They were almost twenty years older than her. They had been resentful and suspicious at the outset. Six months after her marriage, they were her devoted slaves. They told their husbands that Harry Kane could not have found a more suitable wife, and wasn't it great that he hadn't married that hard-faced Siobhan Casey who had such high hopes of him.

The partners were unwilling to have a word said against the entirely admirable Siobhan. Because of discretion and male bonding they didn't see any need to explain that Miss Casey's high hopes might not have resulted in marriage, but there was distinct evidence that a romantic dalliance that had once existed between them had begun again. Neither of the partners could understand it. If you had a beautiful wife like Connie at home, why go out for it?

When Connie realized that her husband was sleeping with Siobhan Casey, she got a great shock. She hadn't expected anything like this so soon. It hadn't taken long before he let her down. He hadn't given the life they had together much of a chance. She was seven months married, three months pregnant, and she had kept her part of the bargain perfectly. No man ever had a better companion and a more comfortable lifestyle. Connie had brought all her considerable knowledge of the hotel industry to bear on their house. It was elegant and comfortable. It was filled with people and flowers and festivity when he wanted. It was quiet and restful when he wanted that. But he wanted more.

She could possibly have put up with it if it had been a one-night stand, at a conference or a visit abroad. But this woman who had obviously always wanted him! How humiliating that she should get him back. And so quickly.

His excuses were not even devious. "I'll be in Cork on Monday, think I'll stay," he had said, only the Cork partner had rung looking for him. So he wasn't in Cork after all.

Connie had played it down, and appeared to accept Harry's casual explanation. "That fellow couldn't remember his own name if it wasn't written on his briefcase. I must have told him three times I was overnighting in the hotel. That's age for you."

And then shortly afterward when he was going to Cheltenham, the travel agency sent the ticket around to the house and she saw there was a ticket for Siobhan Casey as well.

"I didn't realize she was going." Her voice was light.

Harry shrugged. "We go to make contacts, to see the races, to meet people. Someone has to stay sober and write it all down."

And after that he was away from home at least one night a week. And perhaps two nights a week so late that it was obvious he had been with somebody else. He suggested separate bedrooms so as not to disturb her, let her have all the sleep she needed in her condition. It was, Connie realized, as lonely as hell.

The weeks went on and their communication grew less. He was always courteous and praising. Particularly of her Wednesday suppers.

That had really helped to cement the partnership, he told her. It also meant that he spent Wednesday night at home, but she didn't tell him that was her aim. She arranged taxis to take the partners and their wives to Hayes Hotel, where they had suites at a special discount.

She would sit with Harry when they left and talk about his business, but often with only part of her mind. She wondered, did he sit in Siobhan Casey's flat and talk about his successes and failures like this? Or did he and Siobhan feel such a swelling of lust that they took the clothes off each other as soon as they got in the door and were at it on the hearth rug because they couldn't wait until they got to the bedroom?

One Wednesday evening he stroked the large bump of her stomach and there were tears in his eyes. "I'm so sorry," he said.

"What for?" Her face was blank. He paused as if considering whether to tell her something or not, so she spoke quickly. She wanted nothing admitted, acknowledged, or accepted. "What are you sorry about? We have everything, almost everything, and what we don't have, we may have in time."

"Yes, yes of course," he said, pulling himself together.

"And soon our baby will be born," she said soothingly.

"And we'll be fine," he said, unconvinced.

Their son was born after eighteen hours of labor. A perfect healthy child. He was baptised Richard. Connie explained that by chance this was Harry's father's name and her father's name, too, so it was the obvious choice. The fact that Mr. Kane senior had been called Sonny Kane all his life was never mentioned.

The christening party in their home was elegant and simple at the same time. Connie stood welcoming people, her figure apparently slim again a week after the birth, her mother overdressed and happy, her friend Vera's children, Deirdre and Charlie, honored guests.

The parish priest was a great friend of Connie's. He stood there proudly. Would that all his parishioners were as generous and charming as this young woman. A middle-aged lawyer friend of Connie's father was there too, a distinguished member of the Bar, with a very high reputation. He wasn't known for losing cases.

As Connie stood there in her elegant navy silk dress with its smart white trimmings, flanked by the priest and the lawyer and holding his baby son, Harry felt a frisson of alarm. He didn't know what it was and dismissed it. It might be the beginnings of flu. He hoped not, he had a lot of work in the weeks ahead. But he couldn't take his eyes off the tableau. It was as if they represented something. Something that threatened him.

Almost against his will he approached them. "This looks very nice," he said in his usual easy manner. "My son surrounded by the clergy and the law on his christening day, what more does he need as a start in life in Holy Ireland?"

They smiled and Connie spoke. "I was just telling Father O'Hara and Mr. Murphy here that you should be a happy man today. I was telling them what you said eight days after we were married."

"Oh yes, what was that?"

"You said you wanted a honeymoon baby that would be able to take over your business when you were fifty-five, and a family that would be there for you when you needed it." Her voice seemed pleasant and admiring enough to the others. He could hear the hardness of steel in it. They had never discussed that conversation again. He had not known she would recall the words, which, he remembered thinking at the time, were untempered. He had never believed it possible that she would repeat them to him in public. Was it a threat?

"I'm sure I said it more lovingly than that, Connie." He smiled. "It was the Bahamas, we were newlyweds."

"That's what you said and I was just pointing out to Father O'Hara and Mr. Murphy that I hope it doesn't seem like tempting fate, but it does seem to be more or less on course so far."

"Let's just hope that Richard likes the insurance business."

It was some sort of threat; he knew it but didn't realize where it was coming from.

❧

IT WAS MONTHS later that a solicitor asked him to come to a consultation in his office. "Are you arranging a corporate insurance plan?" Harry asked.

"No, it's entirely personal, it's a personal matter, and I will have a senior counsel there," the solicitor said.

In the office was T. P. Murphy, the friend of Connie's father. Smiling and charming. He sat silently as the solicitor explained that he had been

retained by Mrs. Kane to arrange a division of the joint property, under
the Married Women's Property Act.

"But she knows that half of mine is hers." Harry was more shocked
than he had ever been in his life. He had been in business deals where
people had surprised him, but never to this extent.

"Yes, but there are certain other factors to be taken into consideration," the solicitor said. The distinguished barrister said nothing, just
looked from one face to the other.

"Like what?"

"Like the element of risk in your business, Mr. Kane."

"There's an element of risk in every bloody business, including your
own," he snapped.

"You will have to admit that your company started very quickly, grew
very quickly, some of the assets might not be as sound as they appear on
paper."

God damn her, she had told these lawyers about the group that was
dodgy, the one area that he and the partners worried about. They
couldn't have known otherwise.

"If she has been saying anything against our company in order to get
her hands on something for herself she'll answer for it," he said, letting
his guard drop completely.

It was at this point that the barrister leaned forward and spoke in his
silky voice. "My dear Mr. Kane, you shock us with such a misunderstanding of your wife's concern for you. You may know a little of her
own background. Her father's own investments proved insufficient to
look after his family when . . ."

"That was totally different. He was a cracked old dentist who put
everything he got from filling teeth onto a horse or a dog." There was a
silence in the law office. Harry Kane realized he was doing himself no
good. The two lawyers looked at each other. "Decent man by all accounts, all the same," he said grudgingly.

"Yes, a very decent man as you say. One of my closest friends for
many years," said T. P. Murphy.

"Yes. Yes, of course."

"And we understand from Mrs. Kane that you and she are expecting
a second child in a few months time?" The solicitor spoke without looking up from his papers.

"That's true, yes. We're both very pleased."

"And Mrs. Kane of course has given up her successful career in Hayes Hotel to look after these children, and any more you and she may have."

"Listen, it's a goddamn receptionist's job, handing people their keys, saying have a nice stay with us. It's not a career. She's married to *me,* she can have anything she wants. Do I deny her anything? Does she say that in her list of complaints?"

"I'm really very glad that Mrs. Kane isn't here to listen to your words," said T. P. Murphy. "If you knew how much you have misrepresented the situation. There is no list of complaints, there is a huge concern on her part for you, your company, and the family you wanted so much to create. Her anxiety is all on your behalf. She fears that if anything were to happen to the company you would be left without the things you have worked so hard for, and continue to work so hard for, involving a lot of travel and being away from the family home so much."

"And what does she suggest?"

They were down to it now. Connie's lawyers wanted almost everything put in her name, the house and a certain high percentage of the annual pretax profit. She would form a company with its own directors. Papers were shuffled, obviously names were already in place.

"I can't do that." Harry Kane had got where he was by coming straight to the point.

"Why not, Mr. Kane?"

"What would it mean to my own two partners, the men who set this thing up with me? I have to tell them 'Listen lads, I'm a bit worried about the whole caboodle so I'm putting my share in the wife's name so that you won't be able to touch me if the shit hits the fan'? How would that look to them? Like a vote of confidence in what we do?"

Harry had never known a voice as soft and yet effective as T. P. Murphy's. He spoke at a barely audible level and yet every word was crystal clear. "I am sure you are perfectly happy for both of your partners to spend their profits as they wish, Mr. Kane. One might want to put all his into a stud farm in the West, one might want to buy works of art and entertain a lot of film and media people, for example. You don't question that. Why should they question that you invest in your wife's company?"

She had told them all that. How had she known anyway? The wives at the Wednesday evenings . . . well by God he'd put an end to this.

"And if I refuse?"

"I'm sure you won't do that. We may not have divorce on the statute book but we do have family law courts, and I can assure you that anyone who would represent Mrs. Kane would get a huge settlement. The trouble, of course, would be that there would be all that bad publicity, and the insurance business is so dependent on the good faith and trust of the public in general . . ." His voice trailed away.

Harry Kane signed the papers.

He drove straight back to his large, comfortable home. A gardener came every day, he was wheeling plants across toward a south-facing wall. He let himself in the front door and looked at the fresh flowers in the hall, the bright, clean look of the paintwork, the pictures they had chosen together on the walls. He glanced into the large sitting room, which would host forty easily for drinks without opening the double doors into the dining room. There were cabinets of Waterford glass. Only dried flowers in the dining room, they didn't eat there unless it was a dinner party. Out to the sunny kitchen where Connie sat feeding baby Richard little spoonfuls of strained apple and laughing at him, delighted. She wore a pretty flowered maternity dress with a white collar. Upstairs there was the sound of the vacuum cleaner. Soon the delivery van from the supermarket would arrive.

It was by any standards a superbly run home. Domestic arrangements never bothered him or intruded on his life. His clothes were taken and returned to his wardrobe and drawers. He never needed to buy new socks or underpants, but he chose his own suits and shirts and ties.

He stood and looked at his beautiful wife and handsome little son. Soon they would have another child. She had kept every part of her bargain. In a way she was right to protect her investment. She didn't see him standing there, and when he moved she gave a little jump.

But he noticed that her first reaction was one of pleasure. "Oh good, you were able to get home for a bit, will I put on some coffee?"

"I saw them," he said.

"Saw who?"

"Your legal team." He was crisp.

She was unmoved. "Much easier to let them do all the paperwork. You've always said that yourself, don't waste time, pay the experts."

"I'd say we'll be paying T. P. Murphy well to be an expert, judging by the cut of his suits and the watch he was wearing."

"I've known him a long time."

"Yes, so he said."

She tickled Richard under his chin. "Say hallo to your daddy, Richard. He doesn't often get home to see you in the daytime."

"Is it going to be like this all the time, barbed remarks, snide little references to the fact that I'm not home? Will he grow up like this and the next one, bad daddy, neglectful daddy . . . is that the way it's going to be?"

Her face was contrite. And inasmuch as he understood her at all, he thought she was sincere.

"Harry, I can't tell you how much I didn't mean that to be a barbed remark. I swear I didn't. I was pleased to see you, I was speaking stupid baby talk telling *him* to be pleased too. Believe me, it's not going to be full of barbed remarks. I hate it in other people, we won't have it."

For months she hadn't approached him, made a gesture of affection to him. But she saw him standing there desolate and her heart went out to him. She crossed to where he was standing. "Harry, please don't be like this, please. You are so good to me, we have such a nice life. Can't we get the best from it, get joy from it, instead of acting watchful and guarded the way we do?"

He didn't raise his hands to her even though her arms were around his neck. "You didn't ask me did I sign," he said.

She pulled away. "I know you did."

"Why do you know that? Did they call the moment I left the office?"

"No, of course they wouldn't." She looked scornful of such a thought.

"Why not, a job well done?"

"You signed because it was fair, and because you realize it was for your own good in the end," she said.

Then he pulled her toward him and felt the bump in her stomach resting against him. Another child, another Kane for the dynasty he wanted in this fine house. "I wish you loved me," he said.

"I do."

"Not in the way that matters," he said. And his voice was so sad.

"I try. I try, you know I'm there every night if you want me. I'd like you to sleep in the same bed in the same room, it's you who wants to be separate."

"I came home very, very angry, Connie. I wanted to tell you that you were a bitch going behind my back like that, taking me for every penny I have. I kept thinking you were well-named Connie, a real con woman all right . . . I wanted to tell you a lot of things." She stood there waiting. "But honestly I think you made just as big a mistake as I did. You are just as unhappy."

"I'm more lonely than unhappy," she said.

"Call it whatever you like." He shrugged. "Will you be less lonely now that you've got your money?"

"I imagine I'll be less frightened," she said.

"What were you frightened of? That I'd lose it all like your old man did, that you'd have to be poor again?"

"No, that's totally wrong." She spoke with great clearness. He knew she was telling the truth. "No, I never minded being poor. I could earn a living, something my mother couldn't do. But I was afraid of being bitter like she became, I was afraid I would hate you if I had to go back to a job that you made me leave, and go in at the bottom rung again. I couldn't bear the children to have grown up in expectation of one kind of life and end up in another. I know that from experience, so those were things I was frightened of. We had so much going for us, we were always so well suited, everywhere except in bed. I wanted that to go on until we died."

"I see."

"Can't you be my friend, Harry. I love you and want the best for you even if I don't seem to be able to show it."

"I don't know," he said, picking up his car keys to leave again. "I don't know. I'd like to be your friend, but I don't think I can trust you and you have to trust friends." He spoke to the gurgling Richard in his highchair. "Be good to your mummy, kid, she may look as if she has it nice and easy, but it's not all that great for her either." And when he had gone, Connie cried until she thought her heart would break.

〜

THE NEW BABY was a girl, she was called Veronica, and then a year later there were the twins. When the scan showed two embryos Connie was overjoyed. Twins had run in her family, how marvelous. She thought Harry, too, would be delighted. "I can see you're pleased," he said very coldly. "That makes four. Bargain completed. Curtains drawn on all that nasty, messy business. What a relief."

"You can be very, very cruel," she said.

〜

TO THE OUTSIDE world they were, of course, the perfect couple. Mr. Hayes, whose own daughter, Marianne, was growing up as a young beauty much sought after by the fortune-hunting young men of Dublin, was still a good friend of Connie's and often consulted her about the hotel business. If he suspected that her eyes were sometimes sad, he said nothing.

He heard rumors that Harry Kane was not an entirely faithful man. He had been spotted here and there with other women. He still had the pathetic devoted secretary in tow. But as the years went on the watchful Mr. Hayes decided the Kanes must have come to some accommodation.

The eldest boy, Richard, was doing well at school and even playing on the first fifteen in the schools rugby cup; the girl, Veronica, was determined to do medicine and had had no other aim since she was twelve; and the twins were fine boisterous boys.

The Kanes still hosted marvelous parties and were seen together in public a lot. Connie went through her thirties more elegantly than any other well-dressed woman of her generation. She never seemed to spend much time studying fashion, nor did she specialize in buying the designer outfits she could well afford, but she always looked perfectly groomed.

She wasn't happy. Of course she wasn't happy. But then Connie thought that a lot of people lived life like that, hoping that things would get better, and that lights would turn on, or the film turn into Technicolor.

Maybe that's the way most people lived, and all this talk about happiness was for the birds. Having worked in a hotel for so long, she knew how many people were lonely and inadequate. You saw that side of life among the guests. Then on the various charity committees she saw many members who were there only to banish the hours of emptiness, people who suggested more and more coffee-morning meetings because there was nothing else to fill their lives.

She read a lot of books, saw every play that she wanted to, and made little trips to London or down to Kerry.

Harry never had time for a family holiday, he said. She often wondered whether the children realized that his partners went on family holidays with their wives and children. But children could be very unobservant. Other women went abroad with their husbands, but Connie never did. Harry went abroad a lot. It was connected with work, he said. She wondered wryly what work there could be for his investment company in the south of Spain or on a newly developed resort in the Greek islands. But she said nothing.

Harry only went out for sex. He loved it. She had not been able to give it to him, it was unfair of her to deny it to him elsewhere. And she was not at all jealous of his sexual intimacy with Siobhan Casey and whoever else there might be. One of Connie's friends had once cried and cried over a husband's infidelity. She said that the very thought of him doing with another woman what he did with her made her sick to the point of madness. It didn't bother Connie at all.

What she would have liked was for him to get that side of things over with outside the home and be a loving friend within it. She would have been happy to share his bedroom and his plans and hopes and dreams. Was this utterly unreasonable? It seemed a hard punishment to be cut off from everything because she wasn't able to mate with him in a way that gave him pleasure. She had, after all, produced four fine children for him, and surely he could see that this rated some way in his evaluation of things.

Connie knew that some people thought she should leave Harry. Vera, for example. She didn't say it straight out, but she hinted at it. And so had Mr. Hayes in the hotel. They both assumed she stayed with him only for security. They didn't know how well her finances were organized and that she could have left that house a woman of independent means.

So why *did* she stay?

Because it was better for the family. Because the children needed both parents there. Because it required so much bloody effort to change everything and there was no guarantee that she would be any happier elsewhere. And it wasn't as if this was a *bad* life. Harry was courteous and pleasant when he was there. There was plenty to do, she had no trouble filling the hours that turned into weeks, months, and years.

She visited her own mother and Harry's parents. She still entertained the partners and their wives. She provided a home for her children's friends. The sound of tennis balls on the court, or music from their rooms, was always in the background. The Kane household was highly regarded by the next generation because Mrs. Kane didn't fuss and Mr. Kane was hardly ever there, two things people liked in their friends' parents.

◄∾◢

AND THEN WHEN Richard Kane was nineteen, the same age that Connie had been when her father died and left them bankrupt, Harry Kane came home and told them the dream was over. The company was closing the very next day with the maximum of scandal, and the minimum of resources. They would leave bad debts all over the country, people whose investments and life savings were lost. One of his partners had to be restrained from committing suicide; the other, from fleeing the country.

They sat in the dining room Connie, Richard, and Veronica. The twins were away on a school trip. They sat in silence while Harry Kane laid out how bad it would be. Across seven or eight columns in the newspapers. Reporters at the door, photographers struggling to capture images of the tennis court, the luxurious lifestyle of the man who swindled the country. There would be names of politicians who had favored them, details of trips abroad. Big names associated once, now denying any real relationship.

What had caused it? Cutting corners, taking risks, accepting people that others had thought unreliable. Not asking questions where they should have been asked. Not noticing things that should have been noticed by more established companies.

"Will we have to sell the house?" Richard asked. There was a silence.

"Will there be any money for university?" Veronica wanted to know. Another silence.

Then Harry spoke. "I should say to you both now at this point that your mother always warned me that this could happen. She warned me and I didn't listen. So when you look back on this day remember that."

"Oh Dad, it doesn't matter," Veronica said in exactly the same tone that Connie would have used had her own father been alive when *his* financial disasters emerged. She saw Harry's eyes fill with tears.

"It could happen to anyone," Richard said bravely. "That's business for you."

Connie's heart felt glad. They had brought up generous children, not little pups expecting the world as a right. Connie realized it was time to speak. "As soon as your father began to tell me this bad news I asked him to wait until you could be there, I wanted us all to hear it together and react to it as a family. In a way it's a blessing the twins aren't here, I'll sort them out later. What we are going to do now is leave this house, this evening. We are going to pack small suitcases, enough to do us for a week. I'll ask Vera and Kevin to send round vans to pick us up so that any journalists already outside won't see us leaving in our cars. We'll put a message on the machine saying that all telephone queries are to be addressed to Siobhan Casey. I presume that's right, Harry?"

He nodded, astounded. "Right."

"You will go to stay with my mother in the country. Nobody will know where she is or bother her. Use her phone to call your friends and tell them that it's all going to be fine in the end, but until it dies down you're going to be out of sight for a bit. Say you'll be back in ten days. No story lasts that long." They looked at her, openmouthed.

"And yes, of course you'll both go to university, and the twins. And we will probably sell this house but not immediately, not at the whim of any bank."

"But won't we have to pay what's owing?" Richard asked.

"This house doesn't belong to your father," Connie said simply.

"But even if it's yours wouldn't you have to . . . ?"

"No, it's not mine. It was long ago bought by another company of which I am a director."

"Oh, Dad, aren't you clever!" Richard said.

There was a moment. "Yes, your father is an extremely clever businessman, and when he makes a bargain he keeps it. He won't want people to be out-of-pocket, so I feel sure that we won't end up as villains out of all this. But for the moment it's going to be quite hard, so we're going to need all the courage and faith we can gather."

And then the evening became a blur of gathering things and making phone calls. They moved out of the house unseen in the back of decorators' vans.

A white-faced Vera and Kevin welcomed them both into their home. There was no small chat to be made, no sympathy to be offered or received, so they went straight to the room that had been prepared for them, the best guest room with its large double bed. A plate of cold supper and a flask of hot soup had been left out for them.

"See you tomorrow," Vera said.

"How do people know exactly what to say?" Harry asked.

"I suppose they wonder what they'd like themselves." Connie poured him a small mug of soup. He shook his head. "Take it, Harry. You may need it tomorrow."

"Does Kevin have all his insurance tied up with us?"

"No, none of it." Connie spoke calmly.

"How's that?"

"I asked them not to, just in case."

"What am I going to do, Connie?"

"You're going to face it. Say it failed, you didn't want it to happen, you're going to stay in the country and work at whatever you can."

"They'll tear me to pieces."

"Only for a while. Then it will be the next story."

"And you?"

"I'll go back to work."

"But what about the money all those lawyers salted away for you?"

"I'll keep as much as I need to get the children sorted then I'll put the rest back in to pay the people who lost their savings."

"God, you're not doing the Christian martyr bit on top of everything else?"

"What would you suggest I do with what is after all my money, Harry?" Her eyes were hard.

"Keep it. Thank your lucky stars that you saved it, don't plow it back in."

"You don't mean that. We'll talk about it tomorrow."

"I mean it. This is business, it's not a gentleman's cricket match. That's the whole point of having a limited company, they can only get what's in it. You took your bit out, what in God's name was the point if you're going to throw it back in again?"

"Tomorrow," she said.

"Take that prissy po-faced look off you, Connie, and be normal for once in your whole goddamned life. Stop acting for five minutes and let's have less of the pious crap about giving the poor investors back their money. They knew what they were doing, like anyone knows. Like your father knew what he was doing when he put your university fees on some horse that's still running."

Her face was white. She stood up and walked to the door. "Very high and mighty. Go on, leave rather than talk it out. Go down to your friend Vera and talk about the pure badness of men. Maybe it was Vera you should have moved in with in the first place. Could be that it was a woman you needed to get you going?"

She hadn't intended to do it, but she hit him right across the face. It was because he was shouting about Vera in her own house, when Vera and Kevin had rescued them, asked no questions. Harry didn't seem like a person anymore, he was like an animal that had turned wild.

Her rings drew blood from his cheek, a long smear of red. And to her surprise she felt no shock at the blood, no shame at what she had done.

She closed the door and went downstairs. At the kitchen table they had obviously heard the shouting from above, possibly even the words he had been saying. Connie, who had been so calm and in control during the previous hours, looked around the little group. There was Deirdre, Vera's handsome, dark-eyed daughter who worked in a fashion boutique, and Charlie, who had joined the family business of painting and decorating.

And between Kevin and Vera in front of a bottle of whiskey was Jacko. Jacko with a collar wide-open and red wild eyes. Jacko, who had been crying and drinking and hadn't finished doing either. She realized in seconds that he had lost every penny in her husband's investment company. Her first boyfriend, who had loved her simply and without complication, who had stood outside the church the day she was marrying Harry in the hope that she wouldn't go through with it, he sat now at his friends' kitchen table, bankrupt. How had all this happened, Connie wondered as she stood there with her hand at her throat for what seemed an age.

She couldn't stay in this room. She couldn't go back upstairs to where Harry waited like a raging lion with further abuse and self-disgust. She couldn't go outside into the real world, she would never be able to do that again and look people in the eye. Did people attract bad luck and encourage others to behave badly? She thought that the statistics against someone having both a father and a husband who lost everything must be enormous unless you decided that it was something in your own personality that drew you to exactly the same kind of weakness in the second as you had known in the first.

She remembered suddenly the open-faced, friendly psychiatrist asking all those questions about her father. Could there have been anything in it? She thought she had been there a long time, but they didn't seem to have moved, so perhaps it had only been a couple of seconds.

Then Jacko spoke. His voice was slurred. "I hope you're satisfied now," he said.

The others were silent.

In a voice that was clear and steady as always, Connie spoke. "No, Jacko, this is an odd thing to say, but I have never been satisfied, not in my whole life." Her eyes seemed far away. "I may have had twenty years of money, which should have made me happy. Truthfully it didn't. I've been lonely and acting a part for most of my adult life. Anyway, that's no help to you now."

"No, it's not." His face was mutinous. He was still handsome and eager. His marriage had failed, she knew from Vera, and his wife had taken the boy he cared about.

His business had been everything to him. And now that was gone. "You'll get it all back," she said.

"Oh yes?" His laugh sounded more like a bark.

"Yes, there *is* money there."

"I bet there is, in Jersey or the Cayman Islands or maybe in the wife's name," Jacko sneered.

"Quite a lot of it *is* in the wife's name as it happens," she said.

Vera and Kevin looked at her, openmouthed. Jacko couldn't take it in.

"So I got lucky by being an old boyfriend of the wife, is that what you're telling me?" He didn't know whether to believe it was a lifeline or throw it back in her face.

"I suppose I'm telling you that a lot of people got lucky because of the wife. If he's sane enough in the morning, I'll get him to the bank before his press conference."

"If it's yours why don't you keep it?" Jacko asked.

"Because I'm not, despite what you might think, a total shit. Vera, can I sleep somewhere else, like on the couch in the television room?"

Vera came in with her and handed her a rug. "You're the strongest woman I ever met," Vera said.

"You're the best friend anyone ever had," said Connie.

Would it have been good to have loved Vera? To have lived together for years with flower gardens and maybe a small crafts business to show for their commitment? She smiled wanly at the thought.

"What has you laughing in the middle of all this?" Vera asked.

"Remind me to tell you one day, you'll never believe it," said Connie as she kicked off her shoes and lay down on the couch.

❧

AMAZINGLY SHE SLEPT, and only woke to the sound of a cup and saucer rattling. It was Harry, pale-faced, with a long, dark red scar standing out from his cheek. She had forgotten that particular part of last night.

"I brought you coffee," he said.

"Thank you." She made no move to take it.

"I'm so desperately sorry."

"Yes."

"I am so sorry. Jesus, Connie, I just went mad last night. All I ever wanted was to be somebody and I nearly was and then I blew it." He had dressed carefully and shaved around the wound on his face. He was up and ready for the longest day he would ever have to live through. She looked at him as if she had never seen him before, as the people who saw him on television would see him, all the strangers who had lost their savings, and the people who had come across him in business deals or at social gatherings. A handsome, hungry man, all he wanted was to be somebody and he didn't care how he got there.

Then she saw he was crying.

"I need you desperately, Connie. You've been acting all your life with me, could you just act for a little bit longer and pretend you have forgiven me? Please, Connie, I need you. You're the only one who can help me." He laid his face, with the livid scar, on her knees, and he sobbed like a child.

SHE COULDN'T REALLY remember the day. It was like trying to put together the pieces of a horror movie that you have covered your eyes for, or a nightmare that won't go away. There was some of it set in the lawyer's office, where the terms of the trust she had set up for her children's education were explained to him. The money had been well invested. There was plenty. The rest had been equally well placed for her. Constance Kane was a very wealthy woman. She could see the scorn the solicitor had for her husband. He hardly bothered to disguise it. Her father's old friend T.P. Murphy was there, silent and more silver-haired than ever. His face was set in a grim line. There was an accountant and an investment manager. They spoke in front of the great Harry Kane as they would before a common swindler. In their eyes, this was what he was. This time yesterday morning, Connie reflected, those people would have treated her husband with respect. How quickly things changed in business.

Then they went to the bank. Never were bankers more surprised to see funds appear from nowhere. Connie and Harry sat silently while their advisers told the bank that not one penny of this *need* be recovered, and that it was being given only if the bank promised a package to rescue the investors.

By midday they had a deal. Harry's partners were summoned and ordered to remain silent during the press conference at Hayes Hotel. It was agreed that neither of the partners' wives would attend. They watched it together on a television set in one of the hotel bedrooms. Connie's name was not mentioned. It was just stated that emergency funds had been put aside against just such a contingency.

By the one o'clock news the morning papers' headlines were obsolete. One of the journalists asked Harry Kane about the wound on his face. Was it a creditor?

"It was someone who didn't understand what was happening, who didn't realize we would do everything under the sun to safeguard the people who had trust in us," Harry said, straight to the camera.

And Connie felt a little sick, a wave of nausea sweeping over her. If he could lie like that, what else could he not do? As part of the audience, Connie saw Siobhan Casey at the back of the big hotel room where the press conference was being held. She wondered how much Siobhan had known, and whether money would be taken from Connie's fund to provide for her. But she would never find out. She had assured the bank that since the whole thing would be administered by them, there would be no need for a policing operation from her side. She knew the money would be fairly and wisely distributed. It wasn't up to her to say that Siobhan Casey's shares should not be honored because she was sleeping with the boss.

They were able to go back to their house. In a week they were all beginning to breathe again. In three months things were almost back to normal.

Veronica asked him from time to time about his poor face. "Oh, that will always be there to remind your father what a foolish man he was," he would say, and Connie saw the look of affection pass between them.

Richard seemed to have nothing but admiration for his father as well. Both children thought he had grown from the whole experience.

"He spends much more time at home now, doesn't he, Mum?" Veronica said, as if asking for Connie's approval and blessing on something.

"Indeed he does," Connie said. Harry spent one night away each week and came home late to his bedroom two or three nights. This was going to be the pattern of their future.

Something in Connie wanted to change it, but she was tired. She was weary from the years of pretense, she knew no other life.

She telephoned Jacko one day at work.

"I suppose I'm meant to go down on my knees to thank her ladyship for the fact that I got my own money back."

"No, Jacko, I just thought you might want to meet or something."

"For what?" he asked.

"I don't know, to talk, go to the pictures. Did you ever learn Italian?"

"No, I was too busy earning a living." She was silent. She must have made him feel guilty. "Did you?" he asked.

"No, I was too busy not earning a living."

He laughed. "Jesus, Connie, there'd be no point in our meeting. I'd only fall for you all over again, and start pestering you to come to bed with me as I was doing all those years back."

"Not *still,* Jacko, are you still into all that sort of thing?"

"By God I am and why not? Aren't I only in my prime?"

"True, true."

"Connie?"

"Yes?"

"Just, you know. Thank you. You know."

"I know, Jacko."

THE MONTHS WENT by. Nothing had changed very much, but if you looked closely you would know that a lot of the life had gone out of Connie Kane.

Kevin and Vera talked about it. They were among the few who knew how she had rescued her husband. They felt strongly that Harry was not showing any serious gratitude. Everyone knew that he was seen publicly with his onetime personal assistant, the enigmatic Siobhan Casey, who was now a director of the company.

Connie's mother knew that her daughter had lost a lot of her spirit, and tried to cheer her up. "It wasn't permanent, the damage he did to you, not like in my case, and he did have that emergency fund ready. Your father never had that." Connie had said nothing. A sort of loyalty to Harry was one reason, but mainly she didn't want to admit that her mother had been right all those years ago about demanding her own money and getting independence from it.

Her children didn't notice. Connie was just Mother, marvelous and always here when you wanted her. She seemed happy in herself and meeting her friends.

Richard qualified as an accountant, and Mr. Hayes got him a splendid position with his son-in-law's firm. Mr. Hayes' beloved only daughter, Marianne, had married a handsome and very charming man called Paul Malone. The Hayes money and his own personality had helped him high up a ladder. Richard was happy there.

Veronica was racing through her medical studies. She was thinking of specializing in psychiatry, she said, most of people's troubles were in their heads and in their past.

The twins had finally separated in identity, one to go to art college one to join the civil service. Their big house was still in Connie's name. It had not been necessary to sell it when the money was being raised for the rescue package. Connie's solicitors kept pressuring her to draw up another formal document with similar provisions to the original arrangement, guaranteeing her part of the profits, but she was loath to do it.

"That was all years ago when I needed to assure the children's future," she said.

"Strictly speaking, it should be done again. If there was a problem a court would almost certainly decide for you within the spirit of the law, but . . ."

"What sort of problem could there be now?" Connie had asked.

The solicitor, who had often seen Mr. Kane dining in Quentin's with a woman who was not Mrs. Kane, was tight-lipped. "I would much prefer it done," he said.

"All right, but not with big dramas and humiliating him. The past is the past."

"It will be done with the minimum of drama, Mrs. Kane," the solicitor said.

And it was. Papers were sent to Harry's office to be signed. There were no confrontations. His face was hard the day he signed them. She knew him so well and could read his moods. He wouldn't tell her straight out, he would somehow try to punish her for it.

"I'll be away for a few days," he said that evening. No explanation, no pretense. She was preparing their supper, but she knew he wasn't going to stay and share it. Still, old habits die hard. Connie was used to pretending everything was fine even when it was not. She went on tossing the tomato-and-fennel salad carefully, as if it were something that required a huge amount of care and concentration.

"Will that be tiring?" she asked, careful not to ask where and why and with whom.

"Not really." His voice was brittle. "I decided to combine it with a few days rest as well."

"That will be good," she said.

"It's in the Bahamas," he said. The silence hung between them.

"Oh," she said.

"No objection? I mean you don't consider it our special place or anything?" She didn't answer but went to take the warm bacon flan from the oven. "Still, of course, you'll have all your investments, your handcuffs, your share of everything, your rights, to console you when I'm away." He was so angry he could hardly speak.

Only a few short years ago he had cried to her on his knees with gratitude, said that he didn't deserve her, sworn that she would never know another lonely hour. Now he was white-lipped with rage that she continued to protect her investment after it had been shown to be only too necessary.

"You know that's only a formality," she said.

His face had turned to a sneer. "As this business trip I'm going on is a formality," he said. He went upstairs to pack.

She realized he was going to Siobhan's flat tonight, they would leave tomorrow. She sat down and ate her supper. She was used to eating supper alone. It was a late summer evening, she could hear the birds in the garden, the muffled sound of cars out on the road beyond their high garden walls. There were a dozen places she could go this evening if she wanted to.

What she would like to do was meet Jacko and go to the pictures. Just stand in O'Connell Street looking at what was on and arguing with him over which film they would choose. But it was such a ludicrous notion. He had been right, there was nothing left to say now. It would be playing games going up to the working-class estate where he lived and hooting the horn of the BMW outside his house. Only fools thought they might have been happier if they had taken a different turning and wasted a lifetime regretting it. She might not have been at all happier if she had married Jacko, she would possibly have hated being in bed with him too. But somehow it might have been less lonely.

She was reading the evening paper when Harry came back downstairs with two suitcases. It was going to be a serious holiday in the Bahamas. He seemed to be both relieved and piqued at the same time that there was going to be no scene about his leaving.

She looked up and smiled at him over her glasses. "When will I say you'll be back?" she asked.

"Say? Who do you need to say it to?"

"Well, your children, for one thing, but I'm sure you'll tell them you're going, and friends or anyone from the office or the bank."

"The office will know," he said.

"That's fine, then I can refer them to Siobhan?" Her face was innocent.

"Siobhan's going to the Bahamas too, as you very well know."

"So, to someone else then?"

"I wouldn't have gone at all, Connie, if you'd behaved reasonably, not like some kind of tax inspector, hedging me here and confining me there."

"But if it's a business trip you have to go, don't you?" she said, and he went out slamming the door. She tried to go on reading the paper. There had been too many scenes like this, where he left and she cried. It was no way to live a life.

She read an interview with a schoolmaster who was setting up an evening class in Italian up in Mountainview school, a big community school or college in a tough area. It was Jacko's area. Mr. Aidan Dunne said he thought people from the neighborhood would be interested in learning about the life and culture of Italy as well as the language. Since the World Cup there had been a huge interest in Italy among ordinary Dubliners. They would offer a very varied program. Connie read the piece again. It was quite possible that Jacko might enroll. And if not, she would be in his part of the forest two nights a week. There was a telephone number, she would book now before she changed her mind.

❧

OF COURSE JACKO hadn't signed on for the class. That kind of thing only happened in fantasy. But Connie enjoyed it. This wonderful woman, Signora, not much older than she was, had all the gifts of a born teacher. She never raised her voice, yet she had everyone's attention. She never criticized, but she expected people to learn what she marked out for them.

"Constanza . . . I'm afraid you don't know the clock properly, you only know *sono le due, sono le tre* . . . that would be fine if it was always something o'clock but you have to learn half past and a quarter to."

"I'm sorry, Signora," Mrs. Constance Kane would say, abashed. "I was a bit busy, I didn't get it learned."

"Next week you will know it perfectly," Signora would cry, and Connie found herself with her fingers in her ears, saying *sono le sei e venti.* How had it come about that she was going up to this barrack of a school miles away and sitting in a classroom with thirty strangers chanting and singing and identifying great paintings and statues and buildings, tasting Italian food and listening to Italian operas? And what's more, loving it.

She tried to tell Harry about it when he returned tanned and less acerbic from the West Indies. But he didn't show much interest.

"What's taking you up to that bloody place, you want to watch your hubcaps up there," he said. His only comment on the whole undertaking.

Vera didn't like it either. "It's a tough place, you're tempting fate bringing your good car up there, and God, Connie, take off that gold watch."

"I'm not going to regard it as a ghetto, that would be patronizing."

"I don't know what has you there at all, aren't there plenty of places nearer to you where you could learn Italian if you want to?"

"I like this one, I'm always half hoping I'll meet Jacko at one of the classes." Connie smiled mischievously.

"God Almighty, haven't you had enough trouble in one lifetime without inviting more in?" Vera said, raising her eyes to heaven. Vera had her hands full, she was still running the office for Kevin and minding her grandson as well. Deirdre had produced an enormous and gorgeous baby but had said she didn't want to be shackled by outdated concepts of marriage and slavery.

Connie liked the other people in the class, the serious Bill Burke Guglielmo, and his dramatic girlfriend Elisabetta. He worked in the bank that had put together the rescue package for Harry and his partners, but he was too young to have known about it. And even if he had, how would he have recognized her as Constanza. The gutsy young couple of women Caterina and Francesca, hard to know if they were sisters or mother and daughter, they were good company.

There was the big, decent Lorenzo with hands the size of shovels playing the part of a guest in a restaurant, with Connie as the waitress.

Una tavola vicino alla finestra, Lorenzo would say, and Connie would move a cardboard box to where there was a drawing of a window and seat him there, waiting while Lorenzo thought up dishes he would like to order. Lorenzo learned all kinds of new dishes, like eels, goose liver, and sea urchins. Signora would remonstrate and tell him to learn only the list she had provided.

"You don't understand, Signora, these people I'll be meeting in Italy they'll be classy eaters, they wouldn't be your pizza merchants."

Then there was the terrifying Luigi with the dark scowl and particular way of murdering the Italian language. He was someone she would never have met in the ordinary run of things, yet sometimes he was her partner, such as the time they were playing doctors and nurses with pretend stethoscopes, telling each other to breathe deeply. *Respiri profondamente, per favore, Signora,* Luigi would shout, listening to one end of a rubber hose. *Non mi sento bene,* Connie would reply.

And gradually they were all getting less self-conscious and more united in this far-fetched dream of a holiday in Italy next summer. Connie, who could have paid for everyone in the class to take a scheduled flight, joined in the discussions of sponsorship and cost cutting and putting down early deposits for a group charter. If they got the trip together, she would certainly go.

Connie noticed that the school was improving week by week. It was getting a definite face-lift, a new coat of paint, trees planted, the school yard smartened up. The broken bicycle sheds were replaced.

"You're doing a real makeover here," she said approvingly to the shaggy, attractive-looking principal, Mr. O'Brien, who came in from time to time to give his general praise to the Italian class.

"Uphill work, Mrs. Kane, if you could put a word in for us to those financiers you and your husband meet we'd be grateful." He knew who she was all right, there was no calling her Constanza like all the others. But he was pleasantly incurious about what she was doing there.

"They are people without hearts, Mr. O'Brien. They don't understand about schools being a country's future."

"Tell me about it," he sighed. "Don't I spend half my life in bloody banks and filling in forms. I've forgotten how to teach."

"And do you have a wife and family, Mr. O'Brien?" Connie didn't know why she had asked him such a personal question. It was out of character for her to be intrusive. In the hotel business she had learned the wisdom of listening rather than inquiring.

"No, I don't as it happens," he said.

"Better, I suppose, if you're kind of wedded to a school. I think a lot of people should never marry. My own husband is a case in point," she said.

He raised an eyebrow. Connie realized she had gone too far for pleasant casual conversation. "Sorry." She laughed. "I'm not doing the lonely wife bit, I was just stating a fact."

"I would love to be married, that's a fact too," he said. It was polite of him to exchange a confidence. One had been given, it was courtesy to return one. "Problem was I never met anyone that I wanted to marry until I was too old."

"You're not too old now, surely?"

"I am, because it's the wrong person—she's a child. She's Mr. Dunne's child, actually," he said, nodding his head back at the school, where Aidan Dunne and Signora were saying good night to the members of the class.

"And does she love you?"

"I hope so, I think so, but I'm wrong for her, far too old. I'm *so* wrong for her. And there are other problems."

"What does Mr. Dunne think?"

"He doesn't know, Mrs. Kane."

She let out a deep breath. "I see what you mean about there being problems," she said. "I'll leave you to try and sort them out."

He grinned at her, grateful that she asked no more. "Your husband is a madman to be married to his business," he said.

"Thank you, Mr. O'Brien." She got into her car and drove home. Since joining this class she was learning the most extraordinary things about people.

That amazing girl with the curls, Elisabetta, had told her that Guglielmo was going to manage a bank in Italy next year when he had a command of the language, the glowering Luigi had asked her would an ordinary person know if someone was wearing a ring worth twelve grand. Aidan Dunne had asked her did she know where you could buy brightly colored secondhand carpets. Bartolomeo wanted to know if she had ever come across people who attempted suicide and did they always try it again. It was just for a friend, he had said several times. Caterina, who was either the sister or the daughter of Francesca, impossible to know, had said that she had lunch in Quentin's one day and the artichokes were terrific. Lorenzo kept telling her that the family he was going to stay with in Italy were so rich that he hoped he wouldn't disgrace himself. And now Mr. O'Brien said that he was having an affair with Mr. Dunne's daughter.

A couple of months back she had known none of these people or their lives.

When it rained, she would give people a lift home, but she didn't do it regularly in case she became an unofficial taxi service. But she had a soft spot for Lorenzo, who had to take two buses to get back to his nephew's hotel. This was where he lived and worked as an odd-job man and night porter. Everyone else went home to bed or television or to the pub or a cafe after class. But Lorenzo went back to work. He had said that the lift had made all the difference in the world, so Connie made sure she drove him.

His real name was Laddy, she learned. But they all called each other their Italian names, it made it easier in class. Laddy had been invited by some Italians to come and visit them in Rome. He was a big, simple, cheerful man of around sixty who found nothing odd about being driven back to his hotel porter's job by a woman in a top-of-the-range car.

Sometimes he talked of his nephew, Gus, his sister's boy, a lad who had worked every hour God sent, and now there was every possibility he would lose his hotel.

There had been a scare a while back, an insurance and investment company that had failed. But at the last moment hadn't it all come right and they were all to get their money after all. Lorenzo's sister was in the hospice at the time, and it nearly broke her heart. But God had been good, she lived long enough to know that her only son, Gus, would not be bankrupt. She died happy after that. Connie bit her lip as the story was being told. These were the people that Harry would have walked out on.

So what was the new problem? she wondered. Well, it was all part of the old problem. The company that had been in trouble and that had honored its debts in the end had made them all reinvest, a very large sum. It was as if to thank the company for having stood by them when it hadn't needed to. Lorenzo's understanding of it was vague, but his concern was enormous. Gus was at the end of his tether, he had been down every avenue. The hotel needed improvement, the health authorities had said that it could well be a fire hazard, there were no resources left. Everything that he could have called on was gone in this new investment, and there was no way he could cash it in. Apparently there was some law in the Bahamas that you needed an unholy amount of advance notice before you could get at it.

Connie pulled the car into the side of the road when she heard this.

"Could you tell me about it again please, Lorenzo." Her face was white.

"I'm no financial expert myself, Constanza."

"Can I talk to your nephew? Please."

"He mightn't like my telling his business . . ." Lorenzo was almost sorry he had confided in this kind woman.

"Please, Lorenzo."

During the conversation with the worried Gus, Connie had to ask for a brandy. The story was so squalid, so shabby. For the last five years since their investment had been saved, Gus and presumably many, many others like him had been persuaded to invest in two entirely separate companies based in Freeport and Nassau.

With tears in her eyes Connie read that the directors were Harold Kane and Siobhan Casey. Gus and Lorenzo looked at her, uncomprehending. First she took out her checkbook and wrote Gus a very substantial check, then she gave them the address of builders and decorators who were good friends of hers and would do an expert job. She wrote the name of an electrical firm as well, but suggested that they did not use her name in this context.

"But why are you doing all this, Constanza?" Gus was totally bewildered.

Connie pointed at the names on the stationery. "That man is my husband, that woman is his mistress. I have turned a blind eye to their affair for years. I don't *care* that he sleeps with her, but by God I do care that he has used my money to defraud decent people." She knew she must look mad and wild-eyed to them.

Gus spoke gently. "I can't take this money, Mrs. Kane, I can't. It's far too much."

"See you Tuesday, Lorenzo," she said, and she was gone.

❧

SO MANY THURSDAY nights when she had let herself into the house she had hoped he would be at home and he so rarely was. Tonight was no exception. It was late, but she telephoned her father's old friend the barrister T.P. Murphy. Then the solicitor. She fixed a meeting for the following morning. There were no apologies or recriminations. It was eleven o'clock at night when they had finished talking to her.

"What will you do now?" she asked the solicitor.

"Phone Harcourt Square," he said succinctly. That was where the Garda's fraud investigation unit was based.

He had not come home that night. She had not slept. She realized that it had been a ridiculous house to have kept for so long. The children all lived in their own apartments. Pale-faced, she drove herself into the city and parked her car. Taking a deep breath, she walked up the steps of her husband's office to a meeting that would end his life as he knew it.

They had told her that there would be a lot of publicity, most of it unfavorable, the mud would stick to her too. They suggested she find somewhere else to stay. Years ago she had bought a small apartment in case her mother had ever wanted to come and live in Dublin. It was on the ground floor and near the sea. It would be ideal. She could move her things in there in a matter of hours.

"Hours is what it will be," they told her.

She saw him on his own at her request.

He sat in his office watching as files and software were taken away. "All I wanted was to be somebody," he said.

"You told me that before."

"Well, I'm telling you again. Just because you say something twice doesn't mean it's not true."

"You were somebody, you were always somebody. That's not what you wanted, you wanted to have everything."

"You didn't have to do it you know, you were all right."

"I was always all right," she said.

"No you weren't, you were a tense frigid jealous bitch and still are."

"I was never jealous of what Siobhan Casey could give you, never." She spoke simply.

"So why did you do it?"

"Because it wasn't fair. You had your warning, you were rescued, wasn't that enough?"

"You know nothing of men. Nothing." He almost spat the words. "Not only do you not know how to please them, you actually think that a man could be a real man and accept your money and pats on the head."

"It would be a help if you were strong for the children's sake," she said.

"Get out of here, Connie."

"They loved you all through the last time, they really did. They have lives of their own but you are their father. You didn't care much about your father, but they do about theirs."

"You really hate me, don't you, you'll rejoice that I'm in jail."

"No, and you probably won't serve much time if any. You'll get away with things, you always do." She left the office.

She saw Siobhan Casey's name on a brass plate on her door. Inside that office, files and software were also being removed. Siobhan apparently had no family or friends to give her support. She was sitting with bankers, inspectors in the fraud squad, and lawyers.

Connie's steps never faltered as she walked out the door and pressed the remote switch that opened her car. Then she got in and drove to her new apartment on the sea.

LADDY

When Signora was choosing Italian names for people, she tried to make sure that they had the same initial rather than being too purist about the translation. There was a woman there called Gertie. Strictly speaking, that should have been Margaret, then Margeretta. But Gertie would never have recognized her own name in that form so she was called Gloria. In fact, she decided that she liked the name Gloria so much that she might keep it ever after.

The big man with the eager face said he was called Laddy. Signora paused. No future in trying to work out the origins. Give him something that he might like to roll around. "Lorenzo," she cried.

Laddy liked it. "Is that what all the people called Laddy in Italy call themselves?" he asked.

"That's it, Lorenzo," Signora rolled out the name again for him.

"Lorenzo, would you credit it?" Laddy was delighted with the name. He said it over and over. *"Mi chiamo Lorenzo."*

WHEN LADDY WAS christened in the 1930s the name they gave him at
the font was John Matthew Joseph Byrne, but he was never called anything except Laddy. The only boy after five girls, his arrival meant that
the small farm would be safe. There would be a man to run it.

But things don't always turn out the way people think.

Laddy was coming home from school, the mile and a half through
puddles and under dripping trees, when he saw his sisters coming out to
meet him and knew that something terrible had happened. He thought
first that something had happened to Tripper, the collie dog he loved so
much. Maybe it had hurt its paw or been bitten by a rat.

He tried to run past them, the crying girls, but they held him back and
told him that Mam and Dad had gone to heaven, and that from now on
they would look after him.

"They can't have both gone at the same time."

Laddy was eight, he knew things. People went to heaven one by one
and everyone wore black and cried.

But it had happened. They had been killed at a rail crossing, pulling a
cart that had got stuck in the rails and the train was on top of them
before they realized it. Laddy knew that God had wanted them, that it
was their time, but all through the years he wondered why God had
chosen that way.

It had caused such upset and hurt for everyone. The poor man who
had been driving the train was never the same again and went to a
mental home. The people who had found Mam and Dad never spoke of
it to anyone. Laddy once asked a priest why God couldn't have given his
mam and dad heavy winter colds if he had wanted them to die. And the
priest had scratched his head and said that it was a mystery, and that if
we understood all the things that happened on earth, we would be as
wise as God Himself, which of course couldn't happen.

Laddy's eldest sister, Rose, was a nurse in the local hospital. She gave
up her job and came back to look after the family. It was lonely for her,
and the boy who was courting her didn't continue the romance when it
meant a mile-and-a-half walk to see her and a family of children in the
house dependent on her.

But Rose made a good home for them. She supervised the homework
every night in the kitchen, she washed and mended their clothes, she

cooked and cleaned the house, she grew vegetables, kept hens, and employed Shay Neil as the farm man.

SHAY WORKED WITH the small herd of cattle, and kept the place ticking over. He went to fairs and markets, he did deals. He lived silently in a converted outbuilding separate from the farmhouse. It had to look right when people called. No one would like to think of a man, a working farmhand, living in the same house as all those girls and a child.

But the Byrne girls did not stay on the little farm. Rose made sure they got their exams, and with her encouragement one by one they left. One for nursing, another to be trained as a teacher, one to a job in a shop in Dublin, and one to a post in the civil service.

They had done well for the Byrne girls, the nuns and Rose. Everyone said that. And she was making a great fist of bringing up young Laddy. A big boy now sixteen years of age, Laddy had almost forgotten his parents. He could only remember life with Rose, patient and funny and never thinking he was thick.

She would sit for ages with him at his books, going over and over a thing until he could remember it, and she was never cross if he sometimes forgot it the next morning. From what he heard from other fellows at school, Rose was better than any mother.

There were two weddings the year that Laddy was sixteen, and Rose did all the cooking and entertaining for her younger sisters. They were great occasions and the photographs hung on the wall, pictures taken outside the house that had been newly painted by Shay for the festivities. Shay was there, of course, but in the background. He didn't really mix, he was the hired man.

And then Laddy's sister who was working in England said she was having a very quiet wedding, which meant that she was pregnant and it would be in a registry office. Rose wrote and said that she and Laddy would be happy to come over if it would help. But the letter back was full of gratitude and underlined words saying that it wouldn't be at all helpful.

And the sister who was nursing went out to Africa. So that was the Byrne family settled, people said, Rose running the farm until poor

Laddy grew up and was able to take over, God bless him if that were ever to happen. Everyone assumed that Laddy was slow. That was everyone except Rose and Laddy himself.

Now that he was sixteen, Laddy should have been right in the middle of all the fuss getting ready for his intermediate certificate, but there seemed to be no mention of it at all.

"Lord, but they take things very easily above in the Brothers," Rose said to him one day. "You'd think there'd be all sorts of revision and plans and studying going on, but not a squeak out of them."

"I don't think I'm doing it this year," Laddy said.

"Well of course you are, Fourth Year. When else would you do it?"

"Brother Gerald didn't say a word about it." He looked worried now.

"I'll sort it out, Laddy." Rose had always sorted everything out.

She was nearly thirty now, a handsome dark-haired woman, cheerful and good-natured. Over the years there had been a fair share of interest in her. But she never responded. She had to look after the family. When that was all sorted out, she would think of romance . . . she would say this with a happy laugh, never offending anyone because overtures were turned down at an early stage, before they had become serious and before anyone could be offended.

◦∾◦

ROSE WENT TO see Brother Gerald, a small kind man who had always been spoken well of by Laddy.

"Ah Rose, would you not open your eyes, girl," he said. "Laddy's the most decent boy that ever wore shoe leather into this school, but the poor divil hasn't two brains to rattle together."

Rose felt a flush of annoyance come to her face. "I don't think you understand, Brother," she began. "He's so eager and he wants to learn, maybe the class is too big for him."

"He can't read without putting his finger under the words, and only with difficulty then."

"That's a habit, we can get him out of it."

"I've been trying to get him out of it for ten years and I haven't got anywhere."

"Well, that's not the end of the world. He hasn't failed any exams. He hasn't had any tests that he did very badly in, he'll get the Inter, won't he?" Brother Gerald began to speak, and then paused as if changing his mind. "No, go on, Brother, please, we're not fighting over Laddy. We both want the best for him. Tell me what I should know."

"He's never failed a test, Rose, because he's never done a test. I wouldn't put a humiliation like that on Laddy. Why let the boy be last all the time?"

"And what do you do with Laddy when the others are doing a test?"

"I ask him to do messages for me, he's a good-natured reliable lad."

"What kind of messages, Brother?"

"Ah you know, carrying boxes of books and stoking up the fire in the teachers' room, and bringing something down to the post office."

"So I'm paying fees in this school for my brother to be a skivvy to the Brothers, is this what you're telling me?"

"Rose Byrne." The man's eyes were full of tears. "Will you stop getting the wrong end of things. And what fees are you talking about? A few pounds a year. Laddy's happy with us, you know that. Isn't that the best we can do for him. There isn't a notion of putting him in for the Inter or any exam, you must know that. The boy is slow, that's all I'm saying. I wish that was all I had to say about many a boy that went through the school."

"What will I do with him, Brother? I thought he might go to an agricultural college, you know, to learn about farming."

"It would be over his head, Rose, even if he were to get in, which he wouldn't."

"But how will he run the farm?"

"He won't run the farm. You'll run the farm. You've always known that."

She hadn't known. Not until that minute.

❧

SHE CAME HOME with a heavy heart.

Shay Neil was forking manure into a heap. He nodded his usual dour jerk of the head. Laddy's old dog, Tripper, barked a welcome-home. Laddy himself came to the door.

"Did Brother Gerald say anything against me?" he asked fearfully.

"He said you were the most helpful lad that ever came into the school." Without realizing it she had almost started to talk to him as if he were a toddler, speaking down to him in soothing baby talk. She fought to check it.

But Laddy hadn't noticed. His big face was one huge smile. "He did?"

"Yes, he said you were great to make up a fire and carry the books and do the messages." She tried to keep the bitterness out of her tone.

"Well, he doesn't trust a lot of them but he does trust me." Laddy was proud.

"I've a bit of a headache, Laddy. Do you know what would be great, could you make me a cup of tea and bring it up to me with a slice of soda bread, and then maybe make Shay's tea for him?"

"Will I cut him two bits of ham and a tomato?"

"That's right, Laddy, that would be great."

She went upstairs and lay on her bed. How had she not seen how backward he was? Did parents feel this about children, fiercely overprotective?

Well, she'd never know now. She wasn't going to marry anyone, was she? She was going to live here with her slow brother and the dour hired man. There *was* no future to look forward to. It would always be just more of the same. The light had gone out of a lot of what she did now.

Every week she wrote a letter to one of her sisters, so they all heard from her once a month. She had been telling the little titbit about the farm and about Laddy. She found the letters hard to write now. Did they realize that their brother was slow? Was all their praise and gratitude because she had given up her life to look after him?

She hadn't *known* this is what she was doing; she had thought she had taken time out of her youth, cut short her nursing career because of the accident. She felt bitter about her parents. Why were they pulling a bloody cart across, and why didn't they leave it and run to save themselves?

She had a birthday card for a niece with a ten-shilling note to send, and as she put it in the envelope she realized that the others must think she was well paid for her trouble. She had a farm of land. If they only knew how much she didn't want it, that she would have handed it to the first person who passed by if she thought they would give Laddy a happy home for the rest of his life.

THE CARNIVAL CAME to town every summer. Rose took Laddy and they went in the bumpers and the chair-o-planes. They went in the ghost train and he clung on to her with cries of terror, but then wanted another shilling so that they could do it again. She saw various people from the town, all of them saluting her warmly. Rose Byrne was someone who was admired. Now she saw why. They were praising her for having signed on for life.

Her brother was having a great day.

"Can we spend the egg money?" he asked.

"Some of it, not all of it."

"But what would be better to spend it on than a carnival?" he asked, and she watched him go to the three-ring stall and win her a statue of the Sacred Heart. He carried it back to her bursting with pride.

A voice beside her said, "I'll take that back to the farm, you won't want to be carrying it round all day," and there was Shay Neil. "I can put it in the bicycle bag," he said.

It was kind of him, because the big statue, hopelessly wrapped in newspaper, would have been a cumbersome weight to carry.

Rose smiled at him gratefully. "Well, Shay, aren't you the great fellow, always there when you're wanted?"

"Thank you, Rose," he said.

There was something about his voice, as if he had been drinking. She looked at him sharply. Well why not? It was his day off, he was allowed to drink if he wanted to. It couldn't have been a great life for him either, living in that outbuilding, forking dung, milking cows. He didn't have any friends, any family that she knew of. Weren't a few whiskies on a day out only a bit of comfort to him?

She moved away and directed Laddy toward the fortune-teller. "Will we give it a try?" she asked.

He was so pleased that she was staying at the carnival. He had feared she might want to go home. "I'd love my fortune told," he said. Gypsy Ella looked for a long time at his hand. She saw great successes at games and sport ahead for him, a long life, a job working with people. And travel. There would be travel over the water. Rose sighed. It had been fine so far, why had she mentioned travel? Laddy would never go abroad unless she were to take him. It didn't look like anything that would happen.

"Now you, Rose," he said.

Gypsy Ella looked up, pleased.

"Ah, but we know my future, Laddy."

"Do we?"

"My future is running the farm with you."

"But I'll be meeting people and going over the water traveling," he said.

"True, true," Rose agreed.

"So have your hand read, go on, Rose." He waited eagerly.

Gypsy Ella saw that Rose would marry within a year, that she would have one child, and that this would bring her great happiness.

"And will I be going over the water?" she asked, more from politeness than anything else.

No, Gypsy Ella saw no travel for Rose. She saw some poor health, but not for a long time. The two half crowns were paid and they got another ice cream before going home. The walk seemed long tonight, she was glad she didn't have to carry the statue.

Laddy talked on about the great day and how he wasn't really frightened by the ghost train. Rose looked into the fire and thought about Gypsy Ella, what a strange way to make a living, moving on from town to town with the same set of people. Maybe she was married to the man in the bumpers.

Laddy went to bed with the comics she had bought him, and Rose wondered what they were all doing in the carnival now. It would be closing soon. The colored light would be switched off, the people would go to their caravans. Tripper lay beside the fire snoring gently, upstairs Laddy would have fallen asleep. Outside it was dark. Rose thought of the marriage and the one child and the ill health late in life. They should really put a stop to these kinds of sideshows. Some people were foolish enough as to believe them.

SHE WOKE IN the dark thinking she was being suffocated. A great weight lay on top of her, she began to struggle and panic. Had the wardrobe fallen over? Had some of the roof fallen down? As she started to move and cry out a hand went across her mouth. She smelled alcohol. She realized in a moment of sick recognition that Shay Neil was in her bed, lying on top of her.

She struggled to free her head from his hand. "Please Shay," she whispered. "Please, Shay, don't do this."

"You've been begging for it," he said, still pushing at her, trying to get her legs apart.

"Shay, I haven't. I don't want you to do this. Shay, leave now we'll say no more about it."

"Why are you whispering then?" He spoke in a whisper too.

"So as not to wake Laddy, frighten him."

"No, so that we can do it, that's why, that's why you don't want him to wake."

"I'll give you anything."

"No, it's what I'm going to give you that we're talking about now." He was rough, he was heavy, he was too strong for her. She had two choices. One was to shout for Laddy to come and hit him. But did she want Laddy to see her like this, her nightdress torn, her body pinned down? The other choice was to let him get it over with. Rose made the second choice.

∽

NEXT MORNING SHE washed every item of bedclothes, burned her night-dress, and opened the windows of her room.

"Shay must have come upstairs in the night," Laddy said at breakfast.

"Why do you say that?"

"The statue I won for you is on the landing. He must have brought it up," Laddy said, pleased.

"That's right, he must have," Rose agreed.

She felt bruised and sore. She would ask Shay to leave. Laddy would ask endless questions, she must get a story together that would cover it, and cover it for the neighbors too. Then a wave of anger came over her. Why should *she,* Rose, who was blameless in all this, have to invent excuses, explanations, cover stories? It was the most unjust thing she had ever heard in her life.

The morning passed as so many mornings had passed for Rose. She made Laddy's sandwiches and he went to school, to do errands for the teachers as she now realized. She collected the eggs, fed the hens. All the time the sheets and pillowcases flapped on the line, the blanket lay spread on a hedge.

The custom had been that Shay ate bread and butter and boiled tea in his own quarters at breakfast time. After he heard the Angelus ring from the town, he washed his hands and face at the pump in the yard and came in for a meal. It wasn't meat every day, sometimes it was soup. But there was always a bowl of big floury potatoes, a jug of water on the table, and a pot of tea afterward. Shay would take his plate and cutlery to the sink and wash it.

It had been a fairly joyless business. Sometimes Rose had read through it; Shay had never been one for conversation. Today she prepared no lunch. When he came in, she would tell him that he must leave. But the bells of the Angelus rang and Shay did not come in. She knew he was working. She had heard the cows come in to be milked, she had seen the churns left out for the creamery to collect.

Now she began to get frightened. Maybe he was going to attack her again. Perhaps he took the fact that she had not ordered him out this morning as encouragement. Perhaps he took the whole of last night's passivity as encouragement, when all she was doing was trying to save Laddy from something he would not understand. That no normal sixteen-year-old would understand in relation to his own sister, but Laddy of all people.

By two o'clock she was very uneasy. There had never been a day when Shay had not come in for his midday meal. Was he waiting for her somewhere, would he grab her and hurt her again? Well, if he did, by God this time she would defend herself. Outside the kitchen door was a pole with some curved nails in it. They used it to rake twigs and branches off the thatched roof. It was the perfect thing to have to hand. She brought it inside and sat at the kitchen table trying to plan her next move.

He had opened the door and was in the kitchen before she realized it. She moved for the stick, but he kicked it out of her way. His face was pale and she could see his Adam's apple moving up and down in his throat. "What I did last night should not have been done," he said. She sat trembling. "I was very drunk. I'm not used to strong drink. It was the drink that made me do it."

She searched for the words that would make him leave their lives, the actual phrase of dismissal that would not goad him into attacking her again. But she found she still couldn't speak. They were used to silences. Hours, days, weeks of her life had been spent in this kitchen with Shay Neil and no words being said, but today was different. The fear and the memory of the grunts and obscenities of last night hung between them. "I would like it if last night had not happened," he said eventually.

"And so would I, by God so would I," she said. "But since it did . . ." Now she could say it, get him out from their place.

"But since it did," he said, "I don't think I should come in and eat dinner with you anymore in your house. I'll make my own food over beyond. That would be best from now on."

He seriously intended to stay on after what had happened between them. After the most intimate and frightening abuse of another human being, he thought that it could be put aside with just a minor readjustment of the meal schedule. The man must be truly mad.

She spoke gently and very deliberately. She must not allow the fear to be heard in her voice. "No, Shay, I don't think that would be enough, I really think you had better leave. It would not be easy for us to forget what happened. You should start somewhere else."

He looked at her in disbelief. "I can't go," he said.

"You'll find another place."

"I can't go, I love you," he said.

"Don't talk nonsense." She was angry and even more frightened now. "You don't love me or anyone. What you did had nothing to do with love."

"I've told you that was the drink, but I do love you."

"You'll have to go, Shay."

"I can't leave you. What is to happen to you and Laddy if I go?"

He turned and left the kitchen.

"WHY DIDN'T SHAY come in for his dinner?" Laddy asked on Saturday.

"He says he prefers to have it on his own, he's a very quiet sort of person," Rose said.

She had not spoken to Shay since. The work went on as it always did. A fence around the orchard had been mended. He had put a new bolt on the kitchen door, for her to fasten at night from the inside.

⟨∿⟩

TRIPPER, THE OLD collie dog, was dying.

Laddy was very upset. He sat stroking the dog's head and trying to administer him little sips of water on a spoon. Sometimes he would cry with his arms around the dog's neck. "Get better, Tripper. I can't bear to hear you breathing like this."

"Rose?" It was the first time that Shay had spoken to her in weeks. She jumped. "What?"

"I think I should take Tripper out to the field and shoot him through the head. What do you think?" Together they looked at the wheezing dog.

"We can't do it without telling Laddy." Laddy had gone to school that day with the promise that he was going to buy a small piece of steak for Tripper, it might build him up. He would call at the butcher's on his way home. The dog would never be able to eat steak or anything, but Laddy didn't want to believe this.

"So will I ask him then?"

"Do."

He turned away. That evening Laddy dug a grave for Tripper and they carried him out to the back field. Shay put the gun to the dog's head. It was over in a second. Laddy made a small wooden cross, and the three of them stood in silence around the little mound. Shay went back to his quarters.

"You're very quiet, Rose," Laddy said. "I think you loved Tripper as much as I did."

"Oh I did, definitely," she said.

But Rose was quiet because she had missed her period. Something that had never happened to her before.

⟨∽⟩

IN THE WEEK that followed, Laddy was anxious. There was something very wrong with Rose. It had to be more than just missing Tripper.

⟨∽⟩

THERE WERE THREE routes open to her in the Ireland of the fifties. She could have the child and live on in the farm, a disgraced woman, with the gossip of the parish ringing in her ears. She could sell the farm and move with Laddy to somewhere else, start a new life where nobody knew them. She could bring Shay Neil to the priest, and marry him.

There was something wrong with all these options. She could not bear to think of her changed status after all these years, if she were to be known as the unwed mother of a child for whom no father had ever been acknowledged. Her few pleasures, like a visit to the town, a coffee in the hotel, a chat after Mass, would end. She would be a matter of speculation and someone to be pitied. Heads would shake. Laddy would be confused. But could she sell the farm and leave under such circumstances? In a way the farm belonged to all of them, her four sisters as well. Suppose they were to hear that she had taken all the proceeds and gone to live with Laddy and an illegitimate child in some rooms in Dublin? What would they feel about it?

She married Shay Neil.

Laddy was delighted about it all. And overjoyed to think he would be an uncle. "Will the baby call me Uncle Laddy?" he wanted to know.

"Whatever you like," Rose said.

Nothing had changed much at home except that Shay slept up in Rose's bedroom now. Rose went less often to town than she used to. Perhaps it was because she felt tired now that she was expecting the baby, or maybe she had lost interest in seeing people there. Laddy wasn't sure. And she wrote less to her sisters, even though they wrote more to her. They had been very startled by the marriage. And the fact that there had been no big wedding breakfast as Rose had organized for them. They had come to visit and shaken Shay's hand awkwardly. They had

found no satisfactory explanations in the conversation of their normally
outgoing eldest sister.

꩜

AND THEN THE baby was born, a healthy child. Laddy was his godfa-
ther and Mrs. Nolan from the hotel his godmother. The child was baptised Augustus. They called him Gus. The smile came back to Rose's face
again as she held her son. Laddy loved the little boy and never tired of
trying to entertain him. Shay was silent and uncommunicative about the
baby as well as everything else. The strange household got on with their
lives. Laddy went to work for Mrs. Nolan in the hotel. The grandest
help she ever had, Mrs. Nolan said. Nothing was too much trouble for
him, they would be lost without Laddy.

And young Gus learned to walk and staggered around the farmyard
after the chickens, and Rose stood at the door admiring him. Shay Neil
was morose as ever. Sometimes at night Rose would look at him while
pretending not to. He lay for long times with his eyes open. What was he
thinking about? Was he happy in this marriage?

There had been very little sexual activity involved. First, because of
her pregnancy, she had been unwilling. But after the birth of Gus she
had said to him very directly: "We are man and wife and putting the past
behind us, we should have a normal married life."

"That's right," he had said, with no great enthusiasm at all.

Rose had found to her surprise that he did not revolt or frighten her.
It did not bring up memories of that night of violence. In fact it was the
only time they seemed to be in any way close. He was a complicated,
withdrawn man. Conversation would never be easy with him, on any
subject.

They never had alcohol at home, apart from the half bottle of whiskey
on the top shelf in the kitchen to be used in an emergency or for soaking
cotton wool if someone had a toothache. The drunkenness of that one
night was never mentioned between them. The events had such a strange
nightmarish quality that Rose had put them far from her mind as possible. She didn't even pause to rationalize that they had resulted in the
birth of her beloved Gus, the child that had brought her more happiness
than she would ever have believed possible.

So she was entirely unprepared to face a drunken, violent Shay when he came home from a fair almost incapable of speech. Slurred and maddened by her criticism of him, he took his belt from his trousers and beat her. The beating seemed to excite him and he forced himself on her in exactly the same way as the night she had managed to put out of her mind. Every memory came rushing back, the disgust and the terror. And even though she was familiar with his body now and had welcomed it to her own, this was something horrifying. She lay there bruised and with a cut lip.

"And you can't come the high-and-mighty lady tomorrow telling me to pack my bags and go. Not this time. Not now that I'm married in," he said. And turned over to fall asleep.

❧

"Whatever happened to you, Rose?" Laddy was concerned.

"I fell out of bed, half asleep, and I hit my head against the bedside table," she said.

"Will I ask the doctor to come out to you when I'm in town?" Laddy had never seen a bruise like it.

"No, Laddy, it's fine," she said, and joined the ranks of women who accept violence because it's easier than standing up to it.

❧

Rose had hoped for another child, a sister for little Gus, but it didn't happen. How strange that a pregnancy could result from one night of rape and not from months of what was called normal married life.

❧

Mrs. Nolan of the hotel said to Dr. Kenny that it was strange how often Rose seemed to fall and hurt herself.

"I know, I've seen her."

"She says she's got clumsy, but I don't know."

"I don't know either, Mrs. Nolan, but what can I do?" He had lived long enough to notice that a lot of women claimed they had got clumsy and had fallen over.

And the strange coincidence was that it often happened after the Fair Day or the market had been in town. If Dr. Kenny had his way, alcohol would be barred from fairs. But then who listened to an old country doctor who picked up the pieces and was rarely if ever told the truth about what had happened?

⁓

LADDY FANCIED GIRLS, but he was no good with them. He told Rose that he'd love to have slicked-down hair and wear pointed shoes, then the girls would love him. She bought him pointed shoes and tried to grease his hair. But it didn't work.

"Do you think I'll ever get married, Rose?" he asked her one evening. Shay was in another town buying stock. Gus was asleep, excited because tomorrow he would start school. It was just Rose and Laddy by the fire, as so often in the past.

"I don't know, Laddy, I really never expected to, but you remember that fortune-teller we went to years ago, she said I'd be married within the year and I was. I certainly didn't expect that, and that I'd have a child and love him, and I didn't think that would happen. She said to you that you'd be in a job meeting people and you are in the hotel. And that you'd travel across the water and be good at sport, so all that is ahead of you." She smiled at him brightly, reminding him of all the good things, glossing over what was left out, deliberately not mentioning that Gypsy Ella had forecast ill health for Rose, but not yet.

⁓

WHEN IT HAPPENED, it happened very unexpectedly. There was no fair, there would be no drinking, none of those large whiskies thrown back in the company of men who were more jovial and who were made merry by drink. She didn't fear his return that night, which was why it was such a shock to see him drunk, his eyes blurring, not focusing, his mouth drooping at one side.

"Don't look at me like that," he began.

"I'm not looking at you at all," she said.

"Yes you are, yes you bloody are."

"Did you get any heifers?"

"I'll give you heifers," he said taking off his belt.

"No Shay no. I'm having a conversation with you, I'm not saying a word against you. *No.*" Tonight she screamed rather than speaking in the demented pleading whisper to prevent her brother and her son knowing what was happening.

The scream seemed to excite him more. "You are a slut," he said. "A coarse slut. You can't get enough of it, that's always been your problem even before you were a married woman. You are disgusting." He raised the belt and brought it down first on her shoulders, then on her head.

At the same time his trousers fell to the floor and he ripped at her nightdress. She moved to get the bedroom chair to protect herself, but he got there first and, raising the chair, he broke it on the edge of the bed and came at her with it raised aloft.

"Don't Shay, in the name of God don't do this." She didn't care who heard. Behind him at the door she saw the small frightened figure of Gus, his hand in his mouth with terror, and behind him was Laddy. Wakened by the screams, both of them transfixed by the scene in front of them. Before she could stop herself, Rose cried, "Help, Laddy, help me." And then she saw Shay being pulled back, Laddy's huge arm around his neck restraining him.

Gus was screaming in terror. Rose gathered her torn nightdress and, uncaring about the blood flowing down her forehead, ran to pick her son up in her arms.

"He's not himself," she said to Laddy. "He doesn't know what he's doing, we'll have to lock him in somewhere."

"Daddy," screamed Gus.

Shay broke free and came at the mother and child. He still had the leg of the chair in his hand.

"Laddy, for God's sake," she implored.

Shay stopped to look at Laddy, the big boy with his face red and sweating, standing in his pajamas, uncertain, frightened.

"Well, Lady Rose, don't you have a fine protector here. The town simpleton in his pajamas, that's great to see, isn't it. The village idiot going to look after his big sister." He looked from one to the other, taunting Laddy. "Come on then, big boy, hit me now. Hit me, Laddy, you big fat queer. Come on." He had the chair leg with the spiky pointy bit where it had snapped, making it a dangerous weapon.

"Hit him, Laddy," Rose cried, and Laddy's big fist came out and hit Shay hard across the jaw. As Shay fell his head hit the marble washstand. There was a crunching sound and his eyes were open as he lay on the floor. Rose put Gus down on the floor gently, the child had stopped crying now. The silence lasted forever.

"I think he's dead," Laddy said.

"You did what you had to do, Laddy." Laddy looked at her in disbelief. He thought that he had done something terrible. He had hit Shay too hard, he had knocked the life out of him. Often Rose had said to him, You don't know your own strength, Laddy, go easy with this or that. But this time there wasn't a word said against him. He could hardly believe what had happened. He turned his face away from the staring eyes on the floor.

Rose spoke slowly. "Now Laddy, I want you to get dressed and cycle into town and tell Dr. Kenny that poor Shay had a fall and hit his head and he'll tell Father Maher and then they'll drive you back here."

"And will I say . . . ?"

"You'll say that you heard a lot of shouting and that Shay fell and that I asked you to go for the doctor."

"But isn't he . . . I mean will Dr. Kenny be able to . . . ?"

"Dr. Kenny will do what he can and then he'll close poor Shay's eyes for him. Will you get dressed and go now, Laddy, there's a good fellow?"

"Will you be all right, Rose?"

"I'll be fine, and Gus is fine."

"I'm fine," Gus said, his finger still in his mouth and holding on to Rose's hand.

Laddy cycled furiously through the night, the light on his bicycle bobbing up and down through the frightening shadows and shapes of the dark.

Dr. Kenny and Father Maher put his bicycle on the roof of the doctor's car. When they got home, Rose was very calm. She had dressed in a neat dark cardigan and skirt with a white blouse, she had combed her hair slightly over her forehead to hide the cut. The fire was burning brightly, she had built it up and burned the broken bedroom chair. It was in ashes now. No one would ever see that it had been used as a weapon.

Her face was pale. She had a kettle ready for tea, and candles for the last sacraments. The prayers were said, Laddy and Gus joining Rose in the responses. The death certificate was written, and it was obviously by misadventure and due to intoxication.

The women who would lay him out would be there in the morning. The sympathies that were offered and accepted were formal and perfunctory. Both the doctor and the priest knew that this was a loveless marriage of convenience, where the hired hand had made the woman of the house pregnant. Shay Neil couldn't hold his drink, that was known.

Dr. Kenny was not going to speculate about how Shay had fallen, nor was he going to discuss the fresh blood on her face. When the priest was busy elsewhere, the doctor took out his black bag and without waiting to be asked to do so, gave the wound a quick examination and dabbed antiseptic on it. "You'll be fine, Rose," he said. And she knew he wasn't just talking about the cut on her forehead. He meant about everything.

After the funeral Rose asked all her family back to the farm, and they sat around the table in the kitchen to a meal that she had prepared carefully. There had been only a few of Shay's relations at the funeral, and they had not been invited back to the farm.

Rose had a proposition to make. The place had no happy associations for her now, she and Gus and Laddy would like to sell it and live in Dublin. She had discussed it with an estate agent and had been given a realistic idea of what it would sell for. Did any of them have any objection to the place being sold? Would any of them like to live in it? No, none of them wanted to live there, and yes, they were all enthusiastic and happy for Rose to sell the farm.

"Good." She was brisk.

Were there any keepsakes or mementos they might like to take?

"Now?" They were surprised at the speed.

"Yes, today."

She was going to put the house on the market the next day.

❧

GUS SETTLED IN a Dublin school, and Laddy, armed with a glowing reference from Mrs. Nolan, got a job as a porter in a small hotel. He was soon regarded as part of the family and invited to live in. This suited everyone. And the years passed peacefully enough.

ROSE TOOK UP nursing again. Gus did well at school and went into a hotel management course. Rose was still a presentable woman in her forties, she could have her chances of marrying again in Dublin. The widower of a woman she had nursed seemed very interested in her, but Rose was firm. One loveless marriage behind her was enough. She wouldn't join again unless it was someone she really loved. She didn't mind missing out on love, because she didn't really think she had. Most people didn't have anything nearly as good as Gus and Laddy in their lives.

Gus loved his work, he was prepared to do the longest hours and the hardest jobs to learn the hotel business. Laddy had always taken the boy to football matches and boxing matches. He remembered the fortune-teller. "Maybe she meant I was going to be *interested* in sports," he told Gus. "Maybe she didn't mean good at it, more involved in it."

"Could be." Gus was very fond of the big, kind man who looked after him so well.

NONE OF THEM ever talked about the night of the accident. Sometimes Rose wondered how much Gus remembered. He had been six, old enough to have taken it all in. But he didn't appear to have nightmares as a child and later on he could listen to talk about his father without looking awkward. He did not, however, ask many questions about what his father had been like, which was significant. Most boys would surely have wanted to know. Possibly Gus knew enough.

THE HOTEL WHERE Laddy worked was owned by an elderly couple. They told Laddy that they would soon retire, and he became very agitated. This had been his home now for years. It coincided with Gus's meeting the girl of his dreams, a bright, sparky girl called Maggie, a trained chef with Northern Ireland wit and confidence. She was ideal for him in Rose's mind, she would give him all the support he needed.

"I always thought I'd be jealous when Gus found himself a proper girl, but it's not so, I'm delighted for him."

"And I always thought I'd have some wee bat out of hell as a mother-in-law and I got you," Maggie said.

All they needed now was a hotel job together. Even buy a small run-down place and build it up.

"Couldn't you buy my hotel?" Laddy suggested. It would be exactly what they wanted but, of course, they couldn't afford it.

"If you give me a room in it to live in, I'll give you the money," Rose said.

What better could she do with what she had saved and the proceeds of her Dublin flat when she sold it? It would be a home for Laddy and Gus, a start in business for the young couple. A place to rest her limbs when this ill health that had been foretold finally came. She knew it was sinful and even stupid to believe in fortune-tellers, but that whole day, the day of Gypsy Ella, was still very clear in her mind.

It had been, after all, the day that Shay had raped her.

❧

IT WAS NOT easy to get business at the start. They spent a lot of time studying the accounts. They were paying out more than was coming in.

Laddy understood that business was not good. "I can carry more coal upstairs," he said, anxious to help.

"Not much use, Laddy, when we've no one to light fires for." Maggie was very kind to her husband's uncle Laddy. She always made him feel important.

"Could we go out on the street, Rose, and I would wear a sandwich board with the name of the hotel and you could give people leaflets?" He was so eager to help.

"No, Laddy. This is Gus and Maggie's hotel. They'll come up with ideas, they'll get it going. Soon it will be very busy, as many guests as they can handle."

And eventually it was.

The young couple worked at it night and day. They built up a clientele of faithful visitors. They attracted people from the North, the word of mouth spread. And whenever they had a foreign visitor from the Continent, Maggie would give them a card saying *We have friends who speak French, German, Italian.*

It was true. They knew a German bookbinder, a French teacher in a boys' school, and an Italian who ran a chip shop. When they needed translation, these people were immediately found on the telephone to interpret for them.

Gus and Maggie had two children, angelic little girls, and Rose thought herself one of the happiest women in Ireland. She would take her little granddaughters to feed the ducks in Stephen's Green on a sunny morning.

&

ONE OF THE hotel guests asked Laddy was there a snooker hall nearby, and Laddy, eager to please, found one.

"Have a game with me," said the man, a lonely businessman from Birmingham.

"I'm afraid I don't play, sir." Laddy was apologetic.

"I'll show you," the man said.

And then it happened. The fortune-teller's forecast came true. Laddy had a natural eye for the game. The man from Birmingham didn't believe he had never played before. He learned the order: yellow, green, brown, blue, pink, black. He potted them all easily and stylishly. People gathered to watch.

Laddy was the sportsman that had been foretold for him.

&

HE NEVER WAGERED money on a game. Other people bet on him, but he worked too hard for his wages and they all needed them, Rose, Gus, Maggie, and the little girls. But he won competitions and he had his picture in the paper. And he was invited to join a club. He was a minor snooker celebrity.

Rose watched all this with delight. Her brother, a person of importance at last. She didn't even need to ask her son to look after Laddy when she was gone. She knew it wasn't necessary. Laddy would live with Gus and Maggie until the end. She made a scrapbook of his snooker triumphs, and together they would read it.

"Would Shay have been proud of all this, do you think?" Laddy asked one evening. He was a middle-aged man now, and he had hardly ever spoken of the dead Shay Neil. The man he had killed that night with a violent blow.

Rose was startled. She spoke slowly. "I think he might have been pleased. But you know, with him it was very hard to know what he thought. He said very little, who knows what he was thinking in his head."

"Why did you marry him, Rose?"

"To make a home for us all," she said simply.

As an explanation it seemed to satisfy Laddy. He had never given any more thought to marriage himself or women, as far as Rose knew. He must have had sexual desires and needs like any man, but they were never acknowledged in any way. And nowadays the snooker seemed a perfectly adequate substitute. So by the time Rose realized that the women's trouble she complained of meant hysterectomy and then that hysterectomy hadn't solved the problem, she was a woman with no worries about the future.

The doctor was not accustomed to people taking a diagnosis and sentence like this so calmly.

"We'll make sure that there's as little pain as possible," he said.

"Oh, I know you will. Now, what I'd really like is to go to a hospice, if that's possible."

"You have a very loving family who would want to nurse you," the doctor said.

"True, but they have a hotel to run. I'd much prefer not to be there just because they would give me too much time. Please, Doctor, I'll be no trouble up in the hospice, I'll help all I can."

"I don't doubt that," he said, blowing his nose hard.

Rose had her moments of rage and anger like anyone else. But they were not shared with her family or her fellow patients in the hospice. The hours that she spend brooding on the unfair hand that had been dealt to her were short compared to the time spent planning for the months that were left.

When the family came to visit, they got hardly any information about pain and nausea but a lot of detail about the place she was in and the work it was doing. The hospice was a happy place, open to ideas and receptive to anything new. This is what she wanted them to channel their energy into, not to bringing her sweets or bed jackets. Something practical, something that would help. That's what Rose wanted from her family.

So they set about organizing it.

Laddy got them a secondhand snooker table and gave lessons, and Gus came with Maggie to do cookery demonstrations. And the months passed easily and happily. Even though Rose was very thin now and her step was slower, she said she was in no pain and she wanted no sympathy, only company and enthusiasm. At least her mind was fine, she said.

It was too fine for Gus and Maggie, they couldn't hide from her the catastrophe that happened to them. They had insured and invested with a company that had gone bankrupt. They would lose the hotel, their hopes and dreams and future. Perhaps there was a hope that they could keep it from Rose. Maybe she could die without knowing what had happened to them. After all, she was so frail now that they could not take her back home to the hotel, as they had been able to do in the early months, for a Sunday lunch with her grandchildren. The only thing they could save from the disaster was the fact that Rose might not know how her investment in them had been lost.

But they could not hide it.

"You *have* to tell me what it is," she said to Gus and Maggie. "You cannot leave this room without telling me what's happening. I only have weeks left of my life, you won't let me spend them in torment, trying to work out what it is. Letting me imagine it even worse than it is."

"What would be the worst thing that you might think it is?" Maggie asked.

"That there's something wrong with one of the children?" They shook their heads "Or with either of you? Or Laddy? Some illness?" Again they said no. "Well, we can face anything else," she said, her thin face smiling and her eyes burning brightly out at them.

They told her the story. How it was in the papers that the assets were gone. There was nothing left in the funds to meet the calls that were being made. Then the plausible man Harry Kane had said on television that nobody would lose their investment, the banks would rescue them, but people still feared they would. Nothing was clear.

Tears poured down Rose's face. Gypsy Ella had never told her this. She cursed herself for believing the fortune-teller in the beginning. She cursed Harry Kane and all belonging to him for his greed and theft. They had never seen her so angry.

"I knew we shouldn't have told you," Gus said dismally.

"No, of course you had to tell me. And swear you'll tell me every single thing that happens from now on. If you tell me that it's fine and it isn't, I'll know, and I'll never forgive you."

"I'll show you every page of the paperwork, Mam," he said.

"And if he doesn't, I will," Maggie promised.

"And Mam, suppose it *does* go down you know, and we have to get another job, you know we'll take Laddy with us."

"Of course she knows that," said Maggie scornfully.

⌒᷄᷅⌒

AND AS THE days passed they brought her letters from the bank. And there did seem to be a rescue package. Their investment had been shaken but not lost. She read the small print carefully to make sure there was nothing she had missed.

"Does Laddy understand how near we came to losing everything?" she asked.

"He understands at a level of his own," said Maggie, and with a great rush of relief Rose realized that whatever happened when she was gone, Laddy would be in safe, understanding hands.

⌒᷄᷅⌒

SHE DIED PEACEFULLY.

⌒᷄᷅⌒

SHE NEVER KNEW that a woman called Siobhan Casey would call to the hotel and explain that a substantial reinvestment would now be called for, to make up for the hotel's having been rescued. Miss Casey pointed out that in similar circumstances when a limited company had failed, investors had not been recompensed, and that the money payable to the Neils for their hotel had come from the personal finances of Mr. Kane, who was now being supported in his new venture by all those whose businesses he had saved.

There was an element of secrecy about it, which was called confidentiality. The paperwork looked impressive, but it was requested that it should not be put through the books in the normal way. It was a gentleman's agreement, nothing for the accountants to be involved in.

At first the amount suggested was not a large amount, but then it increased. Gus and Maggie worried about it. But they *had* been pulled out of the fire when they assumed everything was gone. Perhaps in the swings and roundabouts of business this was accepted practice. Miss Casey spoke of her associates in a slightly respectful tone, as if these were people of immense power, people it might be foolish to cross.

Gus knew that if his mother were alive, she would be against it. This made him worry about why he was being so naive as to go ahead with it. They told Laddy nothing. They just made economies. They couldn't get a new boiler when they needed one, and they didn't replace the hall carpet, they bought a cheap rug instead to cover the worn bit. But Laddy realized that something was wrong and it worried him. It couldn't be that they didn't have enough business, the customers were coming in thick and fast. But the Hearty Irish Breakfasts weren't as hearty as they used to be, and Maggie said there was no need for Laddy to go to the market for fresh flowers anymore, they were too dear. And when one of the waitresses left, she wasn't replaced.

They were getting a fair few Italians now, and Paolo, who worked in the chip shop, was worn out coming to translate. "One of you should learn to speak the language," he said to Gus. "I mean we're all Europeans but none of you are even trying."

"I had hoped the girls might be interested in languages," Gus apologized. But it hadn't happened.

An Italian businessman, his wife, and two sons came to stay in the hotel. The man was holed up in offices with the Irish Trade Board all day, his wife was in the shops fingering soft Irish tweed and examining jewelry. Their two teenage sons were bored and discontented. Laddy offered to take them to play snooker. Not in a hall where there would be smoking and drinking and gambling, but in a Catholic boys' club where they would come to no harm. And he completely transformed their holiday.

From Paolo he got a written list . . . *tavola da biliardo, sala da biliardo, stecca da biliardo.* The boys responded by learning the words in English: billiard table, cue.

They were a wealthy family. They lived in Roma, that was all Laddy could get from them. When they were leaving, they had their photograph taken with him outside the hotel. Then they got into their taxi and went to the airport. On the footpath when the taxi pulled away Laddy saw the roll of notes. Irish banknotes tightly wrapped together with a rubber band. He looked up to see the taxi disappearing. They would never know where they dropped it. They might not notice it until they got home. They were wealthy people, they wouldn't miss it. The woman had spent a fortune in Grafton Street every time she got near the place.

They wouldn't need this money.

Not like Maggie and Gus, who badly needed some things. Nice new menu holders, for example. Theirs had become very stained and tattered. They needed a new sign over the door. He thought along these lines for about four minutes, then he sighed, and got the bus out to the airport to give them back the money they had lost.

He found them checking in all their lovely expensive soft leather luggage. For a moment he wavered again, but then he thrust out his big hand before he could change his mind.

The Italian family all hugged him. They shouted out to everyone around about the generosity and the marvelousness of the Irish. Never had they met such good people in their lives. Some notes were peeled off and put into Laddy's pocket. That wasn't important.

"Può venire alla casa. La casa a Roma," they begged him.

They're asking you to go to Rome to stay with them, translated people in the queue, pleased to hear such enthusiasm for one of their own.

"I know," said Laddy, his eyes shining. "And what's more I'll go. I had my fortune told years ago, and she said I'd go abroad across the

water." He beamed at everyone. The Italians all kissed him again and he
went back on the bus. He could hardly wait to tell them his good news.

Gus and Maggie talked about it that night.

"Maybe he'll forget it in a few days," Gus said.

"Why couldn't they just have given him the tip and left it?" Maggie
wondered. Because they knew in their hearts that Laddy would think he
was invited to stay with these people in Rome and that he would prepare
for it and then his heart would break.

◦∾⁹◦

"I'LL NEED TO get a passport you know," Laddy said next day.

"Won't you need to learn to speak Italian first?" Maggie said with a
stroke of genius.

If they could delay the whole expedition for some time, Laddy might
be persuaded that the trip to Rome was only a dream.

◦∾⁹◦

IN HIS SNOOKER club Laddy asked around about Italian lessons.

A van driver he knew called Jimmy Sullivan said there was a great
woman altogether called Signora who had come to live with them, and
she was starting Italian lessons up in Mountainview school.

Laddy went up to the school one evening and booked. "I'm not very
well educated, do you think I'd be able to keep up with the lessons?" he
asked the woman called Signora when he was paying his money.

"Oh there'll be no problem about that. If you love the whole idea of it
we'll have you speaking it in no time," she said.

"It'll only be two hours off on Tuesday and Thursday evening,"
Laddy said in a pleading tone to Gus and Maggie.

"Take all the time you like, for God's sake, Laddy. Don't you work a
hundred hours a week as it is?"

"You were quite right that I shouldn't go out there like a fool. Signora
says she'll have me speaking it in no time."

Maggie closed her eyes. *What* had made her open her mouth and get
him to go to Italian lessons. The notion of poor Laddy keeping up with
an evening class was ludicrous.

∾୨

HE WAS VERY nervous on the first evening, so Maggie went with him.

They looked a decent crowd going into the rather bleak-looking school yard. The classroom was all decorated with pictures and posters, and there even seemed to be plates of cheese and meat that they would eat later. The woman in charge was giving them big cardboard labels with their names on them, translating them into an Italian form as she went along.

"Laddy," she said. "Now that's a hard one. Do you have any other name?"

"I don't think so." Laddy sounded fearful and apologetic.

"No that's fine. Let's think of a nice Italian name that sounds a bit like it. Lorenzo! How about that?" Laddy looked doubtful, but Signora liked it. "Lorenzo," she said again and again, rolling the word. "I think that's the right name. We don't have any other Lorenzos in the class."

"Is that what all the people called Laddy in Italy call themselves?" he asked eagerly.

Maggie waited, biting her lip.

"That's it, Lorenzo," said the woman with the strange hair and the huge smile.

Maggie went back to the hotel. "She was a nice person," she told Gus. "There'd be no way she'd make poor Laddy feel a fool or anything. But I'd give it three lessons before he has to give it up."

Gus sighed. It was just one more thing to sigh about these days.

∾୨

THEY COULDN'T HAVE been more wrong about the class. Laddy loved it. He learned the phrases that they got as homework each week as if his very life depended on it. When any Italians came to the hotel, he greeted them warmly in Italian, adding *mi chiamo Lorenzo* with a sense of pride, as if they should have expected the porter at a small Irish hotel to be called something like that. The weeks went on, and often on nights when it rained they saw Laddy being driven home to the door in a sleek BMW.

"You should ask your lady friend in, Laddy." Maggie had peered out a few times and just seen the profile of a handsome woman driving the car.

"Ah no, Constanza has to get back. She has a long drive home," he said.

Constanza! How had this ridiculous teacher hypnotized the whole class into her game playing. She was like some pied piper. Laddy missed a snooker competition, which he would definitely have won, because he couldn't let down the Italian class. It was parts of the body that week, and he and Francesca would have to point out to the class things like their throats and elbows and ankles. He had them all learned: *la gola,* he had his hand on his neck; *i gomiti,* one hand on each elbow; and he bent down to touch *la caviglia* on each foot. Francesca would never forgive him if he didn't turn up. He'd miss the snooker competition, there'd be another. There wouldn't be another day with parts of the body. *He* would be furious if Francesca didn't turn up because she was in some sort of competition or other.

Gus and Maggie looked at each other, amazed. They decided that it was good for him. They had to believe that; other things were so grim at the moment. There were improvements that were now pressing, and they just couldn't afford to make them. They had told Laddy that things were difficult, but he didn't appear to have taken it on board. They were trying to live one day at a time. At least Laddy was happy for the moment. At least Rose had died thinking all was well.

─❧─

SOMETIMES LADDY FOUND it hard to remember all the vocabulary. He hadn't been used to it at school, where the Brothers hadn't seemed to need too much studying from him. But in this class he was expected to keep up.

Sometimes he sat, fingers in ears, on the wall of the school yard, learning the words. Trying to remember the emphasis. *Dov'è il dolore?* you must say that in a questioning way. It was the thing the doctor would say to you when you ended up in hospital. You wouldn't want to be an eejit and not know where you were hurting, so remember what he would ask. *Dov'è il dolore,* he said over and over.

Mr. O'Brien, who was the principal of the whole school, came and sat beside him. "How are you?" he asked.

"*Bene, benissimo.*" Signora had told them to answer every question in Italian.

"Great stuff . . . And do you like the classes? What's your name again?"

"*Mi chiamo Lorenzo.*"

"Of course you do. Well, Lorenzo, is it worth the money?"

"I'm not sure how much it costs, Signor. My nephew's wife pays it for me."

Tony O'Brien looked at the big simple man with the beginnings of a lump in his throat. Aidan Dunne had been right to fight for these classes. And they seemed to be going like a dream. All kinds of people coming there. Harry Kane's wife, of all people, and gangsters like the fellow with the low brow.

He had said as much to Grania, but she still thought that he was patronizing her, patting her father on the head for his efforts. Maybe he should learn something specific so he could prove to Grania that he was interested.

"What are you doing today, Lorenzo?"

"Well, all this week it's parts of the body for when we get heart attacks or have accidents in Italy. The first thing the doctor will say when you're wheeled in is *Dov'è il dolore?* Do you know what that means?"

"No, I don't. I'm not in the class. The doctor would say to you *Dov'è il dolore?*"

"Yes, it means Where is the pain? And you tell him."

"*Dov'è* is 'where is,' is that it?"

"Yes, it must be, because you have *Dov'è il banco; Dov'è il albergo.* So you're right, *Dov'è* must be 'where is?'" Laddy seemed pleased, as if he hadn't made the connection before.

"Are you married, Lorenzo?"

"No, Signor, I wouldn't be much good at it. My sister said I should concentrate on snooker."

"Well, it doesn't have to be one or the other, man. You could have had both."

"That's all right if you're very clever, and run a school like you do. But I wouldn't be able to do too many things at one time."

"I'm not either, Lorenzo." Mr. O'Brien looked sad.

"And are you not married, then? I'd have thought you'd have big grown-up children by now," Laddy said.

"No, I'm not married."

"Maybe teaching's a job where people don't get married," Laddy speculated. "Mr. Dunne he's not married either."

"Oh, is that so?" Tony O'Brien was alert to this piece of news.

"No, but I think he's having a romance with Signora!" Laddy looked around him as he spoke, in case he was overheard. It was so daring to say such a thing aloud.

"I'm not sure that's the situation." Tony O'Brien was astounded.

"*We* all think it is. Francesca and Guglielmo and Bartolomeo and I were talking about it. They laugh a lot together and go home along the road after class."

"Well, now," said Tony O'Brien.

"It would be nice for them, wouldn't it?" Laddy liked everyone pleased about things.

"It would be very interesting, yes," Tony O'Brien agreed. Whatever he had wanted to find out to tell Grania, he had never expected this. He wondered about the piece of information. It might be this poor fellow's oversimple interpretation, or it might in fact be true. If it was true, then things were looking up. Aidan Dunne could not be too critical if he himself was involved in something a little unusual, to put it mildly. There was no high moral ground he could claim and preach from. After all, Tony O'Brien was a straightforward single man wooing a single woman. Compared to the Aidan–Signora relationship, this was totally straight and uncomplicated.

But it wasn't something he would mention to Grania yet. They had met and the conversation had been stilted, both of them trying to be polite and forget the cruel timing that had upset them before.

"Are you going to stay the night?" he had asked.

"Yes, but I don't want to make love." She spoke without coyness or any element of game playing.

"And shall we sleep in the same bed or will I sleep on the sofa?"

She had looked very young and confused. He had wanted to take her in his arms, stroke her, and tell her that it would all work out in the end, it would be all right eventually. But he didn't dare.

"I should sleep on the sofa, it's your house."

"I don't know what to say to you, Grania. If I beg you to sleep in my bed with me it looks as if I am just being a beast and after your body. If I don't it looks as if I don't care. Do you see what a problem it is for me?"

"Please let me sleep on the sofa this time?" she had asked.

And he tucked her in and kissed her on the forehead. In the morning he had made her Costa Rican coffee and she looked tired with dark circles under her eyes.

"I couldn't sleep," she said. "I read some of your books. You have amazing things I've never heard of."

He saw *Catch-22* and *On the Road* beside her bed. Grania would not have read Heller or Kerouac. Possibly the gulf between them *was* too great. She had looked mystified at his collection of traditional jazz. She was a child.

"I would love to come back for supper again," she had said as she left.

"You tell me when and I'll cook it for you," he had said.

"Tonight? Would that be too soon?"

"No, tonight would be great," he had said. "But a little later because I like to look in on the Italian class. And before we fight again, I go because I want to, nothing to do with you or your father."

"Peace," she said. But her eyes had been troubled.

Now Tony O'Brien had gone home and got everything ready. The chicken breasts were marinating in ginger and honey, the table was set. There were clean sheets on the bed and a rug left on the sofa to cover every eventuality.

Tony had hoped to have something more appropriate to report from his visit to the class than the news that Grania's father was rumored to be having an affair with the very strange-looking Italian teacher. He had better go into the bloody classroom quick and find some damn thing to tell her about.

"*Dov'è il dolore?*" he said as a farewell to Lorenzo.

"*Il gomito,*" shouted Laddy, clutching his elbow.

"Right on," said Tony O'Brien.

The whole thing was getting madder by the minute.

THE PARTS-OF-THE-BODY class was great fun. Tony O'Brien had to keep his hand over his face to stop laughing as they poked at each other and shouted *eccolà*. But to his surprise they seemed to have learned a hell of a lot of vocabulary and to be quite unselfconscious about using it.

The woman was a good teacher; she would suddenly hark back to the days of the week or the ordering of a drink in a bar. "We won't spend all our time in hospital when we go on the *viaggio* to Roma."

These people really thought they were going on an excursion to Rome.

Tony O'Brien, who could cope with the Department of Education, the various teachers' unions, the wrath of priests and nuns, the demands of parents, the drug dealers and the vandals, and the most difficult and deprived of schoolchildren, was speechless. He felt slightly dizzy at the thought of the excursion.

He was about to tell Aidan Dunne that he was leaving, when he saw Aidan and Signora laughing over some boxes that were changing from being hospital beds into seats in a train. The way they stood was the way people who cared about each other might stand. Intimate without touching each other. Jesus God, suppose it was true!

He grabbed his coat and continued with his plans to wine, dine, and hopefully bed Aidan Dunne's daughter.

THINGS WERE SO bad in the hotel that Gus and Maggie found it very hard to cope with Laddy's learning problems. His mind was full of words, he told them, and some of them were getting jumbled.

"Never mind, Laddy. Learn what you can." Gus was soothing. Just like the Brothers years ago were soothing to Laddy, telling him not to push himself.

But Laddy would have none of it. "You don't understand. Signora says this is the stage we must be confident and no humming and hahing. We're having another lesson on parts of the body and I keep forgetting them. Please hear me, *please*."

Two guests had left today because they said that the rooms were not up to standard, one said she would write to the Tourist Board. They had barely enough to pay the wages this week, and there was Laddy, his big face working with anxiety, wanting his Italian homework to be heard.

"I'd be all right if I knew I were going to be with Constanza. She sort of helps me along, but we can't have the same partners. I could be with Francesca or Gloria. But very probably with Elisabetta, so can we go over them please?"

Maggie picked up the piece of paper. "Where do we begin?" she asked. There was an interruption. The butcher wanted to discuss when if ever his bill was going to be paid. "Let me deal with it, Gus," Maggie said.

Gus took the paper. "Right, Laddy. Will I be the doctor or the patient?"

"Could you be both, Gus, until I get the sound of it back. Could you say the words to me like you used to?"

"Sure. Now I have come in to the surgery and there's something wrong with me and you're the doctor, so what do you say?"

"I have to say: 'Where is the pain?' Elisabetta will be the patient, I'll be the doctor."

Gus never knew how he kept his patience. *Dov'è il dolore?* he said through clenched teeth. *Dov'è le fa male?* And Laddy repeated it all desperately over and over. "You see, Elisabetta used to be a bit silly when she came first and not learning properly, but Guglielmo has forced her to take it seriously and now she does all her homework too." These people sounded like the cast of a pantomime to Gus and Maggie. Grown people calling each other ridiculous names and pointing to their elbows and having pretend stethoscopes.

And that, of all nights, was the night he invited Constanza in. The most elegant woman that they had ever seen, with a troubled face. Of all the bloody nights of the year, Laddy would have to choose this one. When they had spent three hours in the back room going over and over the columns of figures trying not to face what was obvious, which was that they must sell the hotel. Now they would have to make small talk to some half-cracked.

But there was no small talk. This was the angriest person they had ever met. She told them that she was married to Harry Kane, the name

on the papers, the contracts, the documents. She told them that Siobhan
Casey was his mistress.

"I don't see how that could be, you're much better-looking," Maggie
said suddenly.

Constanza thanked her briefly, and took out her checkbook. She gave
them the name of friends whom she would like them to use in doing the
work. Never for a moment did they doubt that she was sincere. She said
that without them she might never have had the information and courage to do what she was about to do. Lives would change, and they must
believe that the money was theirs by right and would be recovered by
her when the wheels started to turn.

❧

"DID I DO right telling Constanza?" Laddy looked around fearfully at
the three of them. He had never spoken of their business outside before.
He had been afraid that they did not look welcoming when he had come
in with her beside him. But now, inasmuch as he could follow it all,
everything seemed to have sorted itself out marvelously. Far better than
he could have hoped.

"Yes, Laddy, you did right," Gus said. It was very quiet, but Laddy
knew that there was high praise hidden in there somehow.

Everyone seemed to be breathing more easily. Gus and Maggie had
been so tense when they were helping him with his Italian words a few
hours ago. Now it seemed to have gone away, whatever the problem
was.

He must tell them how well he had done in class. "It all went great
tonight. You know I was afraid I wouldn't remember the words but I
did, all of them." He beamed around.

Maggie nodded, not trusting herself to speak. Her eyes were very
bright.

Constanza decided to rescue the conversation. "Did you know Laddy
and I were partners tonight? We were very good," she said.

"The elbow and the ankle and the throat?" Gus said.

"Oh and much more, the knee and the beard," said Constanza.

"*Il ginocchio e la barba*," Laddy cried.

"Did *you* know Laddy has hopes of seeing this family in Rome?" Maggie began.

"Oh, we all know about it, yes. And next summer when we all go to Rome we'll certainly see them. Signora has it all under control."

Constanza left.

They sat together, the three of them who would always live together, as Rose had known they would.

FIONA

Fiona worked in the coffee shop of a big city hospital.

She often said it was as bad as being a nurse without any of the good bits, like making people better. She saw the pale, anxious faces of people waiting for their appointment, the visitors who had come to see someone who was not getting better, the children, troublesome and noisy, knowing that something was wrong but not sure what it was.

From time to time nice things happened, like the man who came out crying: "I don't have cancer, I don't have cancer." And he kissed Fiona and went round the room shaking people's hands. Which was, of course, fine for him and everyone smiled at him. But some of those who smiled *did* have cancer, and that was something he hadn't thought of. And some of those who did have cancer would get better, but when they saw him rejoicing over his sentence being lifted they forgot that they could get better and envied his reprieve.

People had to pay for tea, coffee, and biscuits, but Fiona knew that you never pressed for payment if someone was upset. In fact you pressed hot sweet tea into the hands of anyone suffering from shock. She wished they didn't have paper cups, but it would be impossible to wash cups and saucers for the numbers that passed through every day. A lot of them knew her by name and made conversation just to take their minds off whatever else they were thinking.

Fiona was always bright and cheerful, it was what they needed. She was a small, pixie-like girl with enormous glasses that made her eyes look even bigger than ever, and she wore her hair tied back with a big bow. It was warm in the large waiting room, so Fiona wore T-shirts and a short black skirt. She had bought shirts that had the day of the week on them, and she found people liked that. "I don't know what day it is unless I look at Fiona's chest," they would say. "Lucky you don't just have January, February, March" on them, others would say. It was always a talking point, Fiona and her days of the week.

Sometimes Fiona had happy fantasies that one of the handsome doctors would stop and look into her huge eyes and say that she was the girl he had been looking for all his life.

But this didn't happen. And Fiona realized that it was never likely to happen. These doctors had friends of their own, other doctors, doctors' daughters, smart people. They wouldn't look into the eyes of a girl wearing a T-shirt and handing out paper cups of coffee. Stop dreaming, she told herself.

⁓

FIONA WAS TWENTY and rather disillusioned about the whole business of meeting men. She just wasn't good at it. Look at her friends Grania and Brigid Dunne, now. They only had to go out the door and they met fellows, fellows they sometimes stayed the night with. Fiona knew this because she was often asked to be the alibi. "I'm staying with Fiona" was the great excuse.

Fiona's mother knew nothing of this. She would not have approved. Fiona's mother was very firmly in the nice-girls-wait-until-they-are-married school of thought. Fiona realized that she herself had no very firm views on the matter at all. In theory she felt that if you loved a fellow and he loved you, then you should have a proper relationship with him. But since the matter had never come up, she had never been able to put the theory to the test.

Sometimes she looked at herself in the mirror. She wasn't *bad*-looking. She was possibly a little too small, and maybe it didn't help to have to wear glasses, but people said they *liked* her glasses, they said she looked sweet in them. Were they patting her on the head? Did she look idiotic? It was so hard to know.

Grania Dunne told her not to be such a fool, she looked fine. But then Grania only had half a mind on anything these days. She was so infatuated with this man who was as old as her father! Fiona couldn't understand it. Grania had her pick of fellows, why did she go for this old, old man?

And Brigid said that Fiona looked terrific and she had a gorgeous figure, unlike Brigid, who put on weight as soon as she ate a sandwich. Why was it then that Brigid with the chubby hips was never without a date or a partner at everything? And it wasn't just people she met in the travel agency. Brigid said she never met a chap that you'd fancy in that line of work. There were just crowds of girls coming in booking sunshine holidays, and old women booking pilgrimages, and honeymoon couples that would make you throw up talking about somewhere Very Private. And it wasn't a question of Grania and Brigid's sleeping with *everyone* they met. That wasn't the explanation of their popularity with men. It was a great puzzle to Fiona.

The morning was very busy and she was rushed off her feet. There were so many tea bags and biscuit wrapping papers in her litter bin, she needed to move it. She struggled with the large plastic bag to the door. Once she got it out to the bin area, she would be fine. A young man stood up and took it from her.

"Let me carry that," he said. He was dark and quite handsome, apart from rather spiky hair. He had a motorcycle helmet under one arm, almost afraid to leave it out of his sight.

She held the door open to where the bins were lined up. "Any of those would be great," she said, and waited courteously for him to return.

"That was very nice of you," she said.

"It keeps my mind off other things," he said.

She hoped there wasn't something bad wrong with him, he looked so fit and young. But then Fiona had seen the fit and the well go through her waiting room to be told bad news.

"Well, it's a great hospital," she said. She didn't even know if it was.

She supposed it was all right as hospitals go, but she always said that to people to cheer them and give them hope.

"Is it?" He sounded eager. "I just brought her here because it was nearest."

"Oh, it's got a great reputation." Fiona didn't want to end the conversation.

He was pointing to her chest. *"Giovedì,"* he said eventually.

"I beg your pardon?"

"It's the Italian for Thursday," he explained.

"Oh is it? Do you speak Italian?"

"No, but I go to an evening class in Italian twice a week." He seemed very proud of this and eager and enthusiastic. She liked him and wanted to go on talking.

"Who did you say you brought in here?" she asked. Better clear the whole thing up at the start. If it were a wife or a girlfriend, no point in getting interested.

"My mother," he said, his face clouding. "She's in Emergency. I'm to wait here."

"Did she have an accident?"

"Sort of." He didn't want to talk about it.

Fiona went back to Italian classes. Was it hard work? Where were they held?

"In Mountainview, the big school there."

Fiona was amazed. "Isn't that a coincidence! My best friend's father is a teacher there." It seemed like a bond.

"It's a small world all right," the boy said.

She felt she was boring him, and there were people waiting at the counter for tea and coffee. "Thanks for helping me with the rubbish, that was very nice of you," she said.

"You're very welcome."

"I'm sure your mother will be fine, they're just terrific in Emergency."

"I'm sure she will," he said.

Fiona served the people and smiled at them all. Was she perhaps a very boring person? It wasn't something you would automatically know about yourself.

"Am I boring?" she asked Brigid that night.

"No, you're a scream. You should have your own television show."

Brigid was looking with no pleasure at a zip that had parted company with the skirt. "They just don't make them properly, you know, I couldn't be so fat that this actually burst. That's impossible."

"Of course it's impossible," Fiona lied. Then she realized that Brigid was probably lying to her, too. "I *am* boring," poor Fiona said, in a sudden moment of self-realization.

"Fiona, you're thin, isn't that all anybody in the whole bloody world wants to be. Will you shut up about being boring, you were never boring until you started yammering on that you were." Brigid had little patience with this complaint when faced with the incontrovertible evidence that she'd put on more weight.

"I met this fellow, and he started to yawn and go away from me two minutes after he met me." Fiona looked very upset.

Brigid relented. "Where did you meet him?"

"At work, his mother was in Emergency."

"Well, for God's sake his mother had been knocked down or whatever. What did you expect him to do, make party conversation with you? Cop yourself on Fiona, really and truly."

Fiona was only partly convinced. "He's learning Italian up in your father's school."

"Good. Thank God someone is, they were afraid they wouldn't get enough pupils for the class; he was like a weasel all the summer," Brigid said.

"I blame my parents, of course. I couldn't be anything else but boring, they don't talk about anything. There are no subjects of discussion at home. What would I have to say after years of that?"

"Oh will you shut up, Fiona, you're *not* boring, and nobody's parents have anything to say. Mine haven't had a conversation for years. Dad goes into his room after supper and stays there all night. I'm surprised he doesn't sleep there. Sits at his little desk, touches the books and the Italian plates and the pictures on the wall. In the sunny evenings he sits on the sofa in the window just looking ahead of him. How's that for dull?"

"What would I say if I ever saw him again?" Fiona asked.

"My father?"

"No, the fellow with the spiky hair."

"God, I suppose you could ask him how his mother was. Do I have to go in and sit beside you as if you were a puppet saying speak now, nod now?"

"It mightn't be a bad idea . . . Does your father have an Italian dictionary?"

"He must have about twenty, why?"

"I want to look up the days of the week," Fiona explained, as if it should have been obvious.

❧

"I WAS UP seeing the Dunne family tonight," Fiona said at home.

"That's nice," her mother said.

"Wouldn't want to see too much of them, not to appear to live in the house," her father warned.

Fiona wondered what he could mean. She hadn't been there in weeks. If only her parents knew how often the Dunne girls claimed to be staying overnight in *this* house! Now that would really cause them problems.

"Would you say Brigid Dunne is pretty?" she asked.

"I don't know, it's hard to say," her mother said.

Her father was reading his paper.

"But *is* it hard to say, suppose you saw her would you say that's a good-looking girl?"

"I'd have to think about it," said Fiona's mother.

❧

THAT NIGHT IN bed Fiona thought about it over and over.

How did Grania and Brigid Dunne get to be so confident and sure of things? They had the same kind of home, they went to the same school. Yet Grania was as brave as a lion. She had been having an affair with a man, an old, old man, for ages now. On off, on off, but it was the real thing. She was going to tell her father and mother about it, say that she was going to move in with him and even get married.

The really terrible thing was that he was Mr. Dunne's boss. And Mr. Dunne didn't like him. Grania didn't know whether she should pretend to begin the affair now so as to give her father time to get accustomed to it, or tell him the truth. The old man said people should be told the truth straight out, that they were often more courageous than you thought.

But Grania and Brigid had their doubts.

Brigid had her doubts anyway. He was so terribly old. "You'll be a widow in no time," she had said.

"I'll be a rich widow, that's why we're getting married. I'll have his pension." Grania had laughed.

"You'll want other fellows, you'll go off and be unfaithful to him and he'll come after you and find you in someone's bed and do a double slaying." Brigid looked almost enthusiastic at the prospect.

"No, I never really wanted anyone before. When it happens you'll all know." Grania looked unbearably smug about it.

Fiona and Brigid raised their eyes to heaven over it all. True love was a very exhausting and excluding thing to have to watch from the sidelines. But Brigid wasn't always on the sidelines. She had plenty of offers.

Fiona lay in the dark and thought of the nice boy with the spiky hair who had smiled so warmly at her. Wouldn't it be wonderful to be the kind of girl who could get a boy like that to fancy her.

IT WAS OVER a week before she saw him again.

"How's your mother?" Fiona asked him.

"How did you know about her?" He seemed annoyed, and worried that she had made the inquiry. So much for Brigid's great suggestion.

"When you were here last week you helped me carry out the rubbish bag and you told me your mother was in Emergency."

His face cleared. "Yes of course, I'm sorry. Well, she's not great actually, she did it again."

"Got knocked down?"

"No, took an overdose."

"Oh, I'm very, very sorry." She sounded very sincere.

"I know you are."

There was a silence. Then she pointed to her T-shirt. "Venerdì," she said proudly. "Is that how you pronounce it?"

"Yes it is." He said it in a more Italian way and she repeated it.

"Are you learning Italian too then?" he asked with interest.

Fiona spoke without thinking. "No, I just learned the days of the week in case I met you again," she said. Her face got red and she wanted to die that moment beside the coffee and tea machines.

"My name's Barry," he said. "Would you like to come to the pictures tonight?"

Barry and Fiona met in O'Connell Street and looked at the cinema queues.

"What would you like?" he asked.

"No, what would *you* like?"

"I don't mind, honestly."

"Neither do I." Did Fiona see a look of impatience crossing his face. "Perhaps the one with the shortest queue," she suggested.

"But that's martial arts," he protested.

"That's fine," she said foolishly.

"You *like* martial arts?" He was unbelieving.

"Do you like them?" she countered.

As a date it wasn't a great success so far. They went to a film that neither of them enjoyed. Then came the problem of what to do next.

"Would you like pizza?" he offered.

Fiona nodded eagerly. "That would be great."

"Or would you prefer to go to a pub?"

"Well, I'd like that, too."

"Let's have a pizza," he said, in the tone of a man who knew that if any decision was ever going to be made, it would have to be made by him.

They sat and looked at each other. The choosing of the pizza had been a nightmare. Fiona had said yes to both the *pizza margherita* and the *pizza napoletana,* so Barry had eventually ordered them a *quattro stagioni* each. This one had four different fillings, he said, one in each corner. You could eat them all, no further decisions would be called for.

He told her that at the Italian class Signora, the teacher, had brought in pizzas one evening. He said that she must spend all the money she earned on bringing them gifts. They all sat there eating and chanting the names of the various pizzas aloud, it had been wonderful. He looked boyish and so enthusiastic about it all. Fiona wished she could have that kind of life in her face and her heart. About anything.

IT WAS, OF course, all her mother and father's fault. They were nice, kind people but they had nothing to say to anyone. Her father said that "Least said soonest mended" should be tattooed onto everyone's arm at birth and then people wouldn't go round saying the wrong thing. It did mean that her father hardly said anything at all. Her mother had a different rule to live by. It had to do with not getting carried away over things. She had always told Fiona not to get carried away by the Irish dancing class, or the holiday in Spain, or anything at all that she got enthusiastic about. That's why she had no opinions, no views.

She had ended up as the kind of person who couldn't decide what film to see, what pizza to eat, and what to say next. Should she talk to him about his mother's suicide attempts, or was he just trying to have some time off to forget about it. Fiona frowned with the concentration of it all.

"I'm sorry, I suppose I'm a bit boring about the Italian classes."

"Oh no, heavens no, you're not," she cried. "I just love hearing you talk about them. You see, I wish I cared about things like you do. I was envying you and all the people who bothered to go to that class, I feel a bit dull." Very often, when she least expected it, she appeared to have said something that pleased people.

Barry smiled from ear to ear and patted her hand. "No you're not a bit dull, you're very nice and there's nothing to stop you going to any evening class yourself, is there?"

"No, I suppose not. Is your one full?" Again she wished she had not spoken. It looked too eager, chasing him, not being able to find an evening class of her own. She bit her lip as he shook his head.

"It wouldn't be any good joining ours now. It's too late, we're all too far ahead," he said proudly. "And anyway, everyone joined for some kind of reason, you know. They all had a *need* to learn Italian. Or that's the way it looks."

"What was your need to learn it?" she asked.

Barry looked a bit awkward. "Oh well, it has to do with being there for the World Cup," he said. "I went with a crowd but I met a lot of nice

Italian people and I felt as thick as a plank not being able to speak their language."

"But the World Cup won't be there again, will it?"

"No, but the Italians will still be there. I'd like to go back to the place I was in and talk to them," he said. There was a faraway look on his face.

Fiona wondered whether to ask him about his mother, but she decided against it. If he had wanted to tell her, he would have. It could be too personal and private. She thought he was very, very nice and would love to see him again. How did these girls who were great with fellows manage it? Was it by saying something witty? Or by not saying anything at all? She wished she knew. Fiona would love to have said something that would make this nice kind boy realize that she liked him and would love to be his friend. And even more in time. Why was there no way of sending out a signal?

"I suppose we should be thinking of going home," Barry said.

"Oh yes. Of course." He was tired of her, she could see.

"Will I walk you to the bus?"

"That would be nice, thank you."

"Or would you rather a lift home on my motorbike?"

"Oh, that would be terrific." She realized she had agreed to both things. What a fool he would think she was. Fiona decided to explain. "I mean when you offered to walk me to the bus, I didn't know that there was a chance of a lift on the bike. But I would prefer the bike actually." She was shocked at her own courage.

He seemed to be pleased. "Great," he said. "You'll hang on to me tight then. Is that a promise?"

"It's a promise," said Fiona, and smiled at him from behind her big glasses. She asked him to leave her at the end of the road, because it was a quiet place where motorbikes didn't often travel. She wondered would he ask to see her again.

"I'll see you," Barry said.

"Yes, that would be nice." She prayed that her face didn't look too hopeful, too beseeching.

"Well, you might run across me in the supermarket," he said.

"What? Oh sure. Yes. Easily."

"Or I might see you in the hospital?" he added as another possibility.

"Well, yes. Yes, of course, if you were passing by," she said sadly.

"I'll be passing by every day," Barry said. "They've kept my mother in. Thank you for not asking about her . . . I didn't want to talk about it."

"No, no of course not." Fiona held her breath with relief. She had been within a whisper of leaning on the table in the pizza place and asking him every detail.

"Good night, Fiona."

"Good night, Barry, and thank you," she said.

She lay awake in her bed for a long time. He did like her. And he admired her for not prying into his life. All right, she had made a few silly mistakes, but he *had* said he would see her again.

∿

BRIGID CALLED BY the hospital to see Fiona. "Could you do us a favor, come up to the house tonight?"

"Sure, why?"

"Tonight's the night. Grania's going to tell them about the Old Age Pensioner. There should be fur and feather flying."

"What good will I be?" Fiona asked anxiously.

"They might tone it down a bit if there's an outsider in the house. *Might.*" Brigid seemed doubtful.

"And will he be there, the old man?"

"He'll be parked in a car outside in case he's needed."

"Needed?" Fiona sounded fearful.

"Well, you know, needed to be welcomed in as a son-in-law, or to come in and rescue Grania if Dad beats her senseless."

"He wouldn't do that?" Fiona's mouth was an O of horror.

"No, Fiona, he wouldn't. You take everything so literally. Have you no imagination?"

"No, I don't think I have," Fiona said sadly.

∿

DURING THE DAY Fiona made inquiries about Mrs. Healy, Barry's mother. She knew Kitty, one of the nurses on the ward, who told her.

Heavy stomach-pumping job, second time. She seemed determined to do it. Kitty had no time for her, let them finish themselves off if they were intent on it. Why spend all that time and money telling them they were loved and needed? They probably weren't. If they only knew all the really sick people, decent people who didn't *bring* it on themselves, then they'd think again.

Kitty had no sympathy for would-be suicides. But she said Fiona wasn't to tell anyone that. She didn't want to get the reputation for being as hard as nails. And she did give this bloody woman her medication and was as nice to her as she was to all the patients.

"What's her first name?"

"Nessa, I think."

"What's she like?" Fiona asked.

"Oh, I don't know. Weak mainly, in shock a bit. Watches the door of the ward all the time waiting for the husband to come in."

"And does he?"

"Not so far, her son does but that's not what she's looking for, she wants to see the husband's face. That's why she did it."

"How do you know?"

"That's why they all do it," Kitty said sagely.

❧

IN THE DUNNES' kitchen they sat around the kitchen table. There was a macaroni cheese on it, but hardly anyone was eating. Mrs. Dunne had her paperback folded back on itself, as she so often had. She gave the impression of someone waiting in an airport rather than being in the center of her own home.

Brigid as usual was eating nothing officially but pulling little bits off the edge of the dish and taking bread and butter to mop up a bit of juice that spilled, and in the end eating more than if she had been able to take a sensible portion. Grania looked pale, and Mr. Dunne was about to head off to his room that he loved so much.

"Dad, wait a minute," Grania said. Her voice sounded strangulated. "I want to tell you something, all of you in fact."

Grania's mother looked up from her book. Brigid looked down at the table. Fiona felt herself go red and look guilty. Only Grania's father seemed unaware that anything of moment was to be said.

"Yes, of course." He sat down, almost pleased that there was to be general conversation.

"You'll all find this very hard to take, I know, so I'll try to explain it as simply as I can. I love somebody and I want to get married."

"Well, isn't that great," her father said.

"Married?" her mother said, as if it was the most unexpected thing that anyone who loved anyone might consider.

Brigid and Fiona said nothing, but gave little grunts and sounds of surprise and pleasure that anyone would have known were not a serious reaction to the news.

Before her father could ask whom she loved, Grania told him. "Now, you're not going to like this in the beginning, you're going to say he's too old for me, and a lot of other things, but it's Tony O'Brien."

The silence was worse than even Grania could have believed.

"Is this a joke?" her father said eventually.

"No, Dad."

"Tony O'Brien! The wife of the principal, no less." Her mother gave a snort of laughter.

Fiona couldn't bear the tension. "I hear he's very nice," she said pleadingly.

"And who do you hear that from, Fiona?" Mr. Dunne spoke like a typical schoolteacher.

"Well, just around," Fiona said feebly.

"He's not that bad, Dad. And she's got to marry someone," Brigid said, thinking this was helping somehow.

"Well, if you think Tony O'Brien will marry you, you have another think coming." Aidan Dunne's face was in a hard, bitter line.

"We wanted you to know about it first, and then we thought we might get married next month." Grania tried to keep the shake out of her voice.

"Grania, that man tells at least three girls a year that he's going to marry them. Then he takes them back to his bordello and he does what he likes with them. Well, you probably know that, you've been there often enough when you're telling us that you stay with Fiona."

Fiona cowered at the lie being unmasked.

"It's not like that. It's been going on for ages, well, it's been in the air for ages. I didn't see him anymore after he became principal because I thought he had sort of cheated us both, you and me, but he says he didn't and that things are fine now."

"Does he, by God?"

"Yes, he does. He cares about you and he has great admiration for you and the way the evening class is going."

"I know a boy who goes to it, he says it's just great," squeaked Fiona. She gathered from the looks she got that the interruption had not been hugely helpful.

"It took him a long time to persuade me, Dad. I was on your side and I didn't want to have anything to do with him. And he explained that there *were* no sides . . . you were all in it for the same reason . . ."

"I'm sure it took him a long time to persuade you. Usually about three days, he boasts. He boasts, you know, about how he gets young girls to bed with him. That's the kind of man we have running Mountainview."

"Not nowadays, Dad. Not now. I bet he hasn't. Think about it."

"Only because he's not in the staff room, because he's in his little God Almighty tin-pot throne room, the principal's office as he calls it."

"But Dad, wasn't it always the principal's office, even when Mr. Walsh was there?"

"That was different. He was a man worthy of the post."

"And hasn't Tony been worthy of it? Hasn't he painted the school, got it all smartened up? Started new things everywhere, given you money for your wild garden, set up the Italian class, got the parents to campaign for a better bus service . . . ?"

"Oh, he has you well indoctrinated."

"What do you think, Mam?" Grania turned to her mother.

"What do I think? What does it matter what I think. You're going to do whatever you want to anyway."

"I wish you would understand it's not easy for him either. He wanted to tell you a long time ago, he didn't like it being all secret, but I wasn't ready."

"Oh, yes." Her father was very scornful.

"Truly, Dad. He said he didn't feel good seeing you and knowing that sooner or later he would have to face you, knowing he had been keeping something from you."

"Oh dear me, the poor man, the poor worried soul." They had never seen their father as sarcastic and bitter as this. His face was literally twisted in a sneer.

Grania straightened her shoulders. "As Mam said, I am of course over twenty-one and I can and will do what I like, but I had hoped to do it with your . . . well, your encouragement."

"And where is he, the great Sir Galahad, who didn't dare to come and tell us himself?"

"He's outside, Dad, in his car. I told him that I'd ask him to come in if it were appropriate." Grania was biting her lip. She knew he would not be asked in.

"It's *not* appropriate. And no, Grania, I will *not* give you the blessing or encouragement you ask for. As your mother says, you'll go your own way and what can we do about it?" Angry and upset, he got up and left the table. They heard the door of his room bang behind him.

Grania looked at her mother. Nell Dunne shrugged. "What did you expect?" she said.

"Tony *does* love me," Grania protested.

"Oh he may or he may not. But do you think that matters to your father? It's just that you picked on the one person out of all the billions in the world that he will never get reconciled to. Never."

"But you, you understand?" Grania was dying for someone to support her.

"I understand that he's what you want at the moment. Sure. What else is there to understand?"

Grania's face was stony. "Thanks, that's a lot of help," she said. Then she looked at her sister and her friend. "And thank you, too, what a great support you were."

"God, what could we do, go down on our knees and say we always knew you were made for him?" Brigid was stung by the unfairness of the accusation.

"I did try to say he was well thought of," poor Fiona bleated.

"You did." Grania was grim. She stood up from the table with her face still hard.

"Where are you going? Don't go after Dad, he won't change," Brigid said.

"No, I'm going to pack some things and go to Tony's house."

"If he's so mad for you he'll still be there tomorrow," her mother said.

"I don't want to stay here anymore," Grania said. "I didn't realize it until five minutes ago, but I haven't ever been really happy here."

"What's happy?" Nell Dunne said.

And they were silent as they heard Grania's footsteps going upstairs and into her room to pack a case.

◦∾◦

OUTSIDE IN A car a man strained to see if he could get any indication of what was going on in the house, and wondered whether movement back and forth in the side bedroom was a good sign or a bad sign.

Then he saw Grania leaving the house with a case.

"I'll take you home, sweetheart," he said to her. And she cried on his shoulder and into his jacket, as she cried on her father not very long ago when she was a child.

◦∾◦

FIONA THOUGHT ABOUT it all for hours afterward. Grania was only a year older than she was. How had she been able to face up to her parents like that? Compared to the dramas in Grania's life, Fiona's were very small. What she must do now was something to get her locked into Barry and his life again.

She would think when she got into work next morning.

◦∾◦

IF YOU WORKED in the hospital, you could often get flowers cheap at the end of the day from the florist, blooms that had passed their best. She got a small bunch of freesias and wrote *Get well soon, Nessa Healy* on it. When nobody was looking, she left them at the nurses' station in the ward. Then she hurried back to her coffee shop.

She didn't see Barry for two days, but he looked cheerful when he came in. "She's much better, she'll be coming home at the end of the week," he said.

"Oh, I am glad . . . has she got over it, whatever it was?"

"Well, it's my father, you see. She thinks . . . well, she thought . . . anyway he wouldn't come and see her. He said he wasn't going to be blackmailed by these suicide attempts. And she was very depressed at first."

"But now?"

"Now it seems that he gave in. He sent her flowers. A bunch of freesias. So she knows he cares and she's going home."

Fiona felt herself go cold. "And he didn't come in himself . . . with the flowers?"

"No just left them in the ward and went away. Still, it did the trick."

"And what does he say about it all, your dad?" Fiona's voice was faint.

"Oh, he keeps saying he never sent her flowers, but that's part of the way they go on." He looked a bit worried about it.

"Everyone's parents are very odd, my friend was just saying that to me the other day. You couldn't understand what goes on in their minds at all." She looked eager and concerned.

"When she's settled in back at home will we go out again?" he asked.

"I'd love that," said Fiona. Please, please God, may no one ever find out about the flowers, may they decide to take the easy way out and go along with the notion that he had sent them.

❧

BARRY TOOK HER to a football match. Before they went, he told her which was the good team and which was the bad one. He explained the offside rule and said that the referee had been blind on some previous matches and it was hoped that his sight might have returned to him by now.

At the match Barry met a dark, thickset man. "Howaya, Luigi, I didn't know you followed this team."

Luigi couldn't have been more pleased to meet him. "Bartolomeo, me old skin, I've been with these lads since time began."

Then they both broke into Italian, *mi piace giocare a calcio*. They laughed immoderately at this, and Fiona laughed too.

"That means 'I like to play football,' " Luigi explained.

Fiona thought it must, but she sounded as if it was news to her. "You're all getting on great at the Italian then?"

"Oh sorry, Luigi, this is my friend Fiona," Barry said.

"Aren't you lucky your girlfriend will go to a match. Suzi says she'd prefer to stand and watch paint dry."

Fiona wondered should she explain to this odd man with the Dublin accent and the Italian name that she wasn't *really* Barry's girlfriend. But she decided to let it pass. And why was he calling Barry this strange name?

"If you're meeting Suzi later, maybe we'd all have a drink?" Barry suggested, and Luigi thought that was the greatest idea he'd ever heard and they named a pub.

All through the match Fiona struggled hard to understand it, and to cheer and be excited at the right time. In her heart she thought that this was great, it was what other girls did, went to matches with fellows and met other fellows and joined up with them and their girlfriends later.

She felt terrific.

She must just remember now the different circumstances which led to a goal kick or a corner, and which to a throw-in. And even more important, she must remember not to ask Barry about his mother and his father and the mysterious bunch of freesias.

Suzi was gorgeous, she had red hair and she was a waitress in one of those posh places in Temple Bar.

Fiona told her about serving coffee in the hospital. "It's not in the same league," she said apologetically.

"It's more important," said Suzi firmly. "You're serving people who need it, I'm just putting it in front of people who are there to be seen."

The men were happy to see the girls talking, so they left them to it and analyzed the match down to the bone. Then they started talking about the great trip to Italy.

"Does Bartolomeo talk night and day about this *viaggio*?" Suzi wanted to know.

"Why do you call him that?" Fiona whispered.

"It's his name, isn't it?" Suzi seemed genuinely surprised.

"Well, it's Barry actually."

"Oh. Well, it's this Signora, she's marvelous altogether. She lives as a lodger in my mother's house. She runs it all and she calls Lou Luigi. It's an improvement as it happens, I sometimes call him that myself. But are you going?"

"Going where?"

"To Roma?" Suzi said, rolling her eyes and the letter "r."

"I'm not sure. I don't really know Barry all that well yet. But if things go on well between us, I might be able to go. You never know."

"Start saving, it'll be great fun. Lou wants us to get married out there or at least have it as a honeymoon." Suzi waved her finger with a beautiful engagement ring on it.

"That's gorgeous," Fiona said.

"Yeah, it's not real but a friend of Lou's got some great deal on it."

"Imagine a honeymoon in Rome." Fiona was wistful.

"The only snag is that I'll be sharing a honeymoon with fifty or sixty people," said Suzi.

"Then you'll only have to entertain him at night, not in the day as well," said Fiona.

"Entertain *him*? What about *me*? I was expecting him to entertain me."

Fiona wished she hadn't spoken, as she so often wished. Of course someone like Suzi would think that way. She'd expect this Luigi to dance attendance on her. She wouldn't try to please him and fear she was annoying him all the time, as Fiona would. Wouldn't it be wonderful to be as confident as that. But then, if you looked like Suzi with all that gorgeous red hair, and if you worked in such a smart place, and probably had a history of fellows like Luigi giving you great rocks of rings . . . Fiona sighed deeply.

Suzi looked at her sympathetically. "Was the match very boring?" she inquired.

"No, it wasn't bad. I'd never been to one before. I'm not sure if I understand offside though, do you?"

"Jesus no. And I haven't a notion of understanding it. You'd find yourself stuck out in the freezing cold with people bursting your eardrums if you could understand that. Meet them afterwards, that's my motto." Suzi knew everything.

Fiona looked at her with undisguised admiration and envy. "How did you get to be . . . you know, the way you are, sure of things? Was it just because you were good-looking?"

Suzi looked at her. This girl with the eager face and the huge glasses wasn't having her on. She was quite sincere. "I have no idea what I look like," Suzi said truthfully. "My father told me I looked like a slut and a whore, my mother said I looked a bit fast, places I tried to get jobs in said I wore too much makeup, fellows who wanted to go to bed with me said I looked great. How would you know what you looked like?"

"Oh I know, I know," Fiona agreed. Her mother said she looked silly in the T-shirts, people in the hospital loved them. Some people said her glasses were an asset—they magnified her eyes; other people asked could she not afford contact lenses. And sometimes she thought her long hair was nice and sometimes she thought it was like an overgrown school-·girl's.

"So I suppose in the end I realized that I was a grown-up and that I was never going to please everyone," Suzi explained. "And I decided to please myself, and I have good legs so I wear short skirts, but not stupid ones, and I did tone down the makeup a bit. And now that I've stopped worrying about it nobody seems to be giving out to me at all."

"Do you think I should get my hair cut?" Fiona whispered to her trustingly.

"No I don't, and I don't think you should leave it long. It's your hair and your face and you should do what *you* think about it, don't take my advice or Bartolomeo's advice or your mother's advice, otherwise you'll always be a child. That's my view anyway."

Oh, it was so easy for the beautiful Suzi to talk like that. Fiona felt like a mouse in spectacles. A long-haired mouse. But if she got rid of the glasses and the long hair, she would just be a blinking short-haired mouse. What would make her grown up, and able to make decisions like ordinary people? Maybe something would happen, something that would make her strong.

Barry had enjoyed the evening, he drove Fiona home on his motor-bike, and as she clung to his jacket she wondered what she would say if he asked her to another match. Should she be courageous and, like Suzi, say she'd prefer to meet him afterward. Or should she figure out the offside rule with someone at work and go with him. Which was the better thing to do? If only she could choose which she wanted to do herself. But she hadn't grown up yet like Suzi, she was someone who had no opinions.

"It was nice to meet your friends," she said when she got off the bike at the end of her street.

"Next time we'll do something that you choose," he said. "I'll drop in and see you tomorrow. That's the day I'm taking my mother home."

"Oh, I thought she'd be home by now." Barry had said he would ask her out when his mother had settled in at home, obviously she had thought Mrs. Healy had been discharged. Fiona had not dared to go near the ward in case of being identified as the woman who had left the freesias.

"No. We thought she'd be well enough but she had a setback."

"Oh I'm sorry to hear that," Fiona said.

"She got it into her head that my dad had sent her flowers. And of course he hadn't, and when she realized that she had a relapse."

Fiona felt hot and cold at the same time. "How awful," she said. And then in a small voice: "Why did she think he had?"

Barry's face was sad. He shrugged his shoulders. "Who knows. There *was* a bunch of flowers with her name printed on it. But the doctors think she got them for herself."

"Why do they think that?"

"Because nobody else knew she was in there," Barry said simply.

ANOTHER NIGHT WITHOUT sleeping for Fiona. Too much had happened. The match, the rules, the meeting with Luigi and Suzi, the possibility of a trip to Italy, people thinking she was Barry's girlfriend. The whole idea that once you grow up you know what to do and think and decide for yourself. And then the horrible, awful realization that she had set Barry's mother back by her gift of the flowers. She had thought it would be something nice for the woman to wake up to. Instead it had made everything a thousand times worse.

Fiona was very pale and tired-looking when she went in to work. She had taken the wrong day from her pile of T-shirts. She created great confusion. People kept saying that they thought it was Friday and other people told her that she must have got dressed in the dark. One woman who saw Monday on Fiona's chest left before her appointment because she thought she had got the wrong day. Fiona went to the cloakroom and turned her shirt back to front. She just made sure that nobody saw her from the back.

Barry came in around lunchtime. "Miss Clarke the supervisor let me have a couple of hours off, she's really nice. She's in the Italian class too, I call her Francesca there and Miss Clarke at work, it's a scream," he said.

Fiona was beginning to think that half of Dublin was in this class masquerading under false names. But she had more on her mind than to feel envious of all these people who were playing childish games up in that tough school in Mountainview. She must find out about his mother without appearing to ask.

"Everything all right?"

"No it's not, as it happens. My mother doesn't want to come home and she's not bad enough for them to keep here, so they'll have to get her referred to a mental home." He looked very bleak and sad.

"That's bad, Barry," she said, her face tired with lack of sleep and anxiety.

"Yes, well, I'll have to cope somehow. I just wanted to say, that you know, I said we'd have another outing and you could choose what we did . . . ?"

Fiona began to panic, she hadn't dared to choose yet. God, he wasn't going to ask her now on top of everything else.

"I haven't exactly made up my mind what . . ."

"No, I mean, we may have to put it off a bit, but it's not that I'm going out with anyone else, or don't want to or anything . . ." He was stammering his eagerness.

Fiona realized that he *did* like her. About three quarters of the weight on her heart lifted. "Oh *no*, for heaven's sake I understand, whenever things have sorted themselves out, well I'll hear from you then." Her smile was enormous, the people waiting for their tea and coffee were ignored.

Barry smiled just as broadly and left.

FIONA LEARNED THE rules for offside in soccer, but she couldn't understand how you could make sure there were always two people between you and the goal. No one gave her a satisfactory answer.

〰️

SHE RANG HER friend Brigid Dunne.

Brigid's father answered the phone. "Oh yes. I'm glad to have an opportunity of talking to you, Fiona. I'm afraid I was rather discourteous to you when you were in our house last. Please forgive me."

"That's fine, Mr. Dunne. You were upset."

"Yes, I was very upset and still am. But it's no excuse for behaving badly to a guest. Please accept my apologies."

"No, maybe I shouldn't have been there."

"I'll get Brigid for you," he said.

Brigid was in great form. She had lost a kilo in weight, she had found a fantastic jacket that made you look positively angular, and she was going on a free trip to Prague. No awful nude beaches there showing people up for what they were.

"And how's Grania getting on?"

"I haven't an idea."

"You mean you haven't been to see her?" Fiona was shocked.

"Hey, that's a good idea. Let's go up to Adultery Mews and see her tonight. We might meet the geriatric as well."

"Shush, don't call it that. Your father might hear."

"That's what *he* calls it, it's his expression." Brigid was unrepentant.

They fixed a place to meet. It would be a laugh anyway, Brigid thought. Fiona wanted to know if Grania had survived.

Grania opened the door. She wore jeans and a long black sweater. She looked amazed to see them. "I don't believe it," she said, delighted. "Come in. Tony, the first sign of an olive branch has come to the door."

He came out smiling, good-looking, but very old. Fiona wondered how could Grania see her future with this man.

"My sister, Brigid, and our friend, Fiona."

"Come in, you couldn't have come at a better time. I wanted to open a bottle of wine. Grania said we were drinking too much, which meant that I was drinking too much . . . so now we have to." He led them into a room filled with books, tapes and CDs. There was some Greek music on the player.

"Is that the Zorba dance?" Fiona asked.

"No, but it's the same composer. Do you like Theodorakis?" His eyes lit up at the thought that he might have found someone who liked his era of music.

"Who?" said Fiona, and the smile fell sadly.

"It's very plush." Brigid looked around in grudging admiration.

"Isn't it? Tony got all these shelves made, same man who did the shelves for Dad. How is he?" Grania really wanted to know.

"Oh, you know, the same." Brigid was no help.

"Is he still ranting and raving?"

"No, more sighing and groaning."

"And Mam?"

"You know Mam, hardly notices you're gone."

"Thanks, you know how to make someone feel wanted."

"I'm only telling you the truth."

Fiona was trying to talk to the old man so that he wouldn't hear all this intimate detail about the Dunne family. But he probably knew it all already.

Tony poured them a glass of wine each. "I'm delighted to see you girls, but I have a bit of business up in the school to attend to, and you'll want a chat, so I'll leave you at it."

"You don't have to go, love." Grania called him "love" quite unself-consciously.

"I know I don't have to, but I will." He turned to Brigid. "And if you're talking to your father, tell him . . . well . . . tell him . . ." Brigid looked at him expectantly. But the words didn't come easily to Tony O'Brien. "Tell him . . . she's fine," he said gruffly, and left.

"Well," said Brigid. "What do you make of that?"

"He's desperately upset," said Grania. "You see, Dad doesn't speak to him at school, just walks out if he comes in, and it's hard for him there. And it's hard for me here not being able to go home."

"Can you not go home?" Fiona asked.

"Not really, there'd be a scene, and the no-daughter-of-mine speech all over again."

"I don't know, he's quietened down a bit," Brigid said. "Maybe he'd only moan and groan for the first few visits, after that he might be normal again."

"I hate him saying things about Tony." Grania looked doubtful.

"Bringing up his lurid past, do you mean?" Brigid asked.

"Yeah, but then I had a bit of a past too. If I was as old as he is I'd hope to have a very substantial past. It's just that I haven't been around long enough."

"Aren't you lucky to have a past?" Fiona was wistful.

"Oh shut up, Fiona. You're as thin as a rake, you must have a past to beat the band," said Brigid.

"I've never slept with anyone, made love, done it," Fiona blurted out.

The Dunne sisters looked at her with interest.

"You must have," Brigid said.

"Why must I have? I'd have remembered it if I did. I didn't, that's it."

"Why not?" Grania asked.

"I don't know. Either people were drunk or awful or it was the wrong place, or by the time I had decided I would it was too late. You know me." She sounded full of self-pity and regret. Grania and Brigid seemed at a loss for words. "But I'd like to now," Fiona said eagerly.

"Pity we let the stud of all time out, he could have obliged," Brigid said, jerking her head toward the door that Tony O'Brien had closed behind him.

"I want you to know that I don't find that even remotely funny," Grania said.

"Nor do I," said Fiona disapprovingly. "I wasn't thinking of doing it with just anybody, it's someone I'm in love with."

"Oh well, excuse *me*," Brigid said huffily.

Grania poured another glass of wine for them. "Let's not fight," she said.

"Who's fighting?" Brigid asked, stretching out her glass.

"Remember when we were at school we used to have truth or dare?"

"You always took dare," Fiona remembered.

"But tonight let's do truth."

"What should I do, the two of you tell me."

"You should go home and see Dad. He does miss you," Brigid said.

"You should talk about other things like the bank and politics and the evening class he runs, not things that would remind him of . . . er . . . Tony, until he gets more used to it," Fiona said.

"And Mam? Does she really not care?"

"No, I only said that to annoy you. But you know she's got something on her mind, maybe it's work or the menopause, you're not the big issue there like you are for Dad."

"That's fair enough," Grania said. "Now, let's do Brigid."

"I think Brigid should zip up her mouth about being fat," Fiona said.

"Because she's not fat, she's sexy. A huge bum and big boobs, isn't that what men just love?" said Grania.

"And a very small waist in between," Fiona added.

"But very, very boring about bloody calories and zip fasteners," Grania said with a laugh.

"Easy to say when you're like a brush handle."

"Boring and sexy, an unexpected combination," Grania said.

And Brigid was smiling a bit, she could see they meant it. "Right. Now Fiona," Brigid said, visibly cheered.

The sisters paused. It was easier to attack a member of your own family.

"Let me have another drink to prepare for it," Fiona said unexpectedly.

"Too humble."

"Too apologetic."

"No views on things."

"Not able to make up her mind on anything."

"Never really grew up and realized we all have to make up our own minds."

"Probably going to remain a child all her life."

"Say that again," Fiona interrupted.

Grania and Brigid wondered had they got too carried away.

"It's just that you're too nice to people and nobody really knows what *you* think," Grania said.

"Or *if* you think," Brigid added darkly.

"About being a child?" Fiona begged.

"Well, I suppose I meant that we have to make decisions, don't we. Otherwise other people make them for us and it's like being a child.

That's all I meant," Grania said, afraid that she had offended funny little Fiona.

"That's extraordinary. You're the second person who's said that to me. This girl, Suzi, she said it too when I asked her should I cut my hair. How amazing."

"So do you think you'll do it?" Brigid asked.

"Do what?"

"Make up your own mind in time about things, sleep with your man, get your hair cut, have views?"

"Will *you* stop bellyaching about calories?" Fiona said with spirit.

"Yeah, I will if it's that boring."

"Okay then," said Fiona.

Grania said she'd go out for a Chinese take-away if Fiona promised she wouldn't dither about what she wanted and if Brigid didn't say one word about things being deep-fried. They said that if Grania agreed to go and see her father next day, they would obey her rules.

They opened another bottle of wine and laughed until the old man came home and said that at his age he had to have regular sleep so he would chase them away.

But they knew by the way he was looking at Grania that he wasn't thinking about regular sleep.

❧

"WELL, THAT WAS a great idea to go and see them." Brigid thought it was her idea by the time they were on the bus home.

"She seems very happy," Fiona said.

"He's so old though, isn't he?"

"Well, he's what she wants," Fiona said firmly.

To her surprise Brigid agreed with her vehemently. "That's the point. It doesn't matter if he's from Mars with pointed ears if it's what she wants. If more people had the guts to go after what they want, the world would be a better place." She spoke very loudly, due perhaps to the wine.

A lot of people on the bus heard her and laughed, some of them even clapped. Brigid glared at them ferociously.

"Aw come on, sexy. Give us a smile," one of the fellows shouted.

"They called me sexy," Brigid whispered, delighted, to Fiona.

"What did we tell you?" Fiona said.

She resolved that she would be a different person when Barry Healy asked her out again. As he undoubtedly would.

∿

THE TIME SEEMED very long, even though it was only a week. Then Barry turned up again.

"Are things all right at home?" she asked.

"No, not really. My mother has no interest in anything, she won't even cook. And in the old days she'd have you demented baking this and that and wanting to force-feed you. Now I have to buy her instant meals in the supermarket or she'd eat nothing."

Fiona was sympathetic. "What do you think you'll do?" she asked.

"I've no idea, honestly I'm getting madder than she is herself. Listen, have you decided what you'd like to do when we go out?"

And suddenly there and then Fiona decided. "I'd like to come and have tea in your house."

"No, that wouldn't be a good idea," he said, startled.

"You did ask me what I'd like, that's what it is. Your mother would have to stir herself to get something for me if you said you were bringing a girl to supper, and I could be nice and cheerful and talk about things normally."

"No, Fiona, not yet."

"But isn't this the very time it would be a help. How's she going to think that things will ever be normal if you don't make it look as if they are."

"Well, I suppose you have a point," he began doubtfully.

"So what evening then?" With grave misgivings Barry fixed the date.

He expected Fiona to dither and say that she'd like anything at all, and really it didn't matter. But to his surprise she said that she'd be tired after a long day at work and she'd love something substantial like say spaghetti or maybe shepherd's pie, something nice and comforting. Barry was amazed. But he delivered the message.

"I wouldn't be able to do anything like that," Barry's mother said.

"Of course you would, Mam, aren't you a great cook?"

"Your father doesn't think so," she said. And Barry's heart turned to lead again. It was going to take much more than Fiona coming to supper to make his mother turn the corner. He wished that he weren't an only child, that he had six brothers and sisters to share this with. He wished that his father would just say the bloody things that his mother wanted to hear, that he loved her and that his heart was broken when she tried to take her own life. And that he would swear never to leave her for anyone else. After all his father was terribly old, nearly fifty for heaven's sake, of course he wasn't going to leave Mam for anyone else. Who would have him for a start? And why did he have to take this attitude that suicide attempts were blackmail and he wouldn't give in to blackmail. His father had no firm opinions on anything else. When there was an election or a referendum, his father would sigh and go back to his evening paper rather than express a view. Why did he have to feel so strongly about this of all things? Couldn't he say the words that would please her?

This bright idea of Fiona's wasn't going to work. He could see that.

"Well, all right, Mam, I suppose I could try to cook something myself. I'm not much good, but I'll try. And I'll pretend you made it. After all, I wouldn't want her to think you weren't welcoming her."

"I'll cook it," said his mother. "You couldn't make a meal for Cascarino." Cascarino was their big cat with only one eye. He had been called after Tony Cascarino, who played football for the Republic of Ireland, but was not as fleet of foot.

Fiona brought a small box of chocolates for Barry's mother.

"Oh you shouldn't have, they'll only make me put on weight," the woman said to her. She was pale-looking and had tired eyes. She wore a dull brown dress and her hair was flat and listless.

But Fiona looked at her with admiration. "Oh Mrs. Healy, you're not fat. You've got lovely cheekbones, that's how you know if a person's going to put on weight or not, the cheekbones," she said.

Barry saw his mother touch her face with some disbelief. "Is that right?" she said.

"Oh it's a fact, look at all the film stars who had good cheekbones . . ." Together they listed them happily. The Audrey Hepburns who never put on a pound, the Ava Gardners, the Meryl Streeps, then they examined the so-called pretty women whose cheekbones were not apparent.

Barry hadn't seen his mother so animated in weeks. Then he heard Fiona talk about Marilyn Monroe, who might not have stood the test of time if she had allowed herself to grow older. He wished she hadn't let the conversation get round to people who had committed suicide.

His mother naturally took up the theme. "But that's not why she killed herself, of course, not over her cheekbones."

Barry could see the color rising on Fiona's face, but she fought back. "No, I suppose she did it because she thought she wasn't loved enough. Lord it's just as well the rest of us don't do that, the world would be empty in no time." She spoke so casually and lightly about it that Barry held his breath.

But unexpectedly his mother answered in quite a normal voice. "Maybe she hoped she'd be found and whoever it was she loved would be sorry."

"I'd say he'd have been more pissed off with her than ever," Fiona said cheerfully.

Barry looked at Fiona with admiration. She had more spark about her today. It was hard to say what it was, but she didn't seem to be waiting to take her cue from him all the time. It had been a very good idea to insist on coming to supper. And imagine Fiona, of all people, telling his mother she had good cheekbones.

He felt it was a lot less disastrous than it might have been. He let himself relax a little and wondered what they would talk about next, now that they had been through the minefield of Marilyn Monroe's suicide.

Barry ran a list of conversational topics past himself, without success. He couldn't say Fiona worked in the hospital, that would remind everyone of the stomach pumping and the stay there, he couldn't suddenly start talking about the Italian class, the supermarket, or his motorbike because they would know he was trying to get on to other, less controversial subjects. He was going to tell his mother about Fiona's T-shirts but he didn't think she'd like that, and Fiona had dressed up in her good jacket and nice pink blouse for the meeting, so perhaps it would be letting her down.

At that moment the cat came in and fixed his one good eye on Fiona.

"I'd like to introduce you to Cascarino," Barry said, never having loved the big angry cat so much in his life. Please may Cascarino not claw at Fiona's new skirt, or pause to lick his nether regions in full view of everyone. But the cat laid his head on Fiona's lap and began a purr that sounded like a light aircraft revving up.

"Do you have a cat at home yourselves?" Barry's mother asked.

"No, I'd love one but my father says you never know what trouble they lead to."

"That's a pity. I find them a great consolation. Cascarino may not look much, but for a male he's very understanding."

"I know," Fiona agreed with her. "Isn't it funny the way men are so difficult. I honestly don't think they mean to be, it's just the way they're made."

"They're made without heart," Mrs. Healy said, her eyes dangerously bright. "Oh, they have something in there all right beating away and sending the blood out, but it's not a heart. Look at Barry's father, he's not even here this evening even though he knew Barry was having a friend to supper. He *knew* and he's still not here."

This was worse than Barry could have believed possible. He had no idea that his mother would go in at the deep end in the first half hour.

But to his amazement Fiona seemed to be able to cope with it quite easily.

"That's men for you. When I bring Barry home to my house to meet my family, my father will let me down too. Oh he'll be there all right, he's always there. But I bet you within five minutes he'll tell Barry it's dangerous to ride a motorbike, it's dangerous to drive a supermarket van, it's stupid to follow football. If he can think of anything wrong with learning Italian, he'll say that. He only sees all the things that are wrong with everything, not the things that are right. It's very depressing."

"And what does your mother say to all this?" Barry's mother was interested in the situation; her own attack on her husband seemed to be put aside for the moment.

"Well, I think over the years she started to agree with him. They're old, you see, Mrs. Healy, much older than you and Barry's father. I'm the youngest of a big family. They're set in their ways, you won't change them now." She looked so eager with her glasses glinting and a big pink bow tying back her nice shiny hair. Any mother would be glad to have a warm girl like this for her son.

Barry saw his mother beginning to relax.

"Barry, like a good lad will you go into the kitchen and put the pie into the oven, and do what has to be done out there."

He left them and clattered around, then he crept back to the door to hear what was going on in the sitting room. They were speaking in low voices and he couldn't make it out. Please God may Fiona not be saying anything stupid. And may his mother not be telling all the fantasies about Dad having another woman. He sighed and went back to the kitchen to set the table for the three of them. He felt annoyed with his father for not being there. It was after all an attempt at restoring the situation to normal. He *could* have made an effort. Did Dad not see he was only giving fuel to Mam's suspicions by all this?

Why couldn't he just come in and act the part for an evening? But still, his mother had made a chicken pie and had made an apple tart for afterward. This was an advance.

The supper went better than he dared hope. Fiona ate everything that was put in front of her and almost licked the plate. She said she'd love to know how to make pastry. She was no good at cooking, and then suddenly a thought struck her. "*That's* what I could do, go to a cookery class," she cried. "Barry was asking what I'd really like to learn, and now that I see this spread I know what I'd enjoy."

"That's a good idea," Barry said, delighted at the praise for his mother's cooking.

"You'd want to make sure that you got someone with a light hand to teach you pastry," his mother said.

Finding fault with the idea, of course. Barry fumed inside.

But Fiona didn't seem to mind. "Yes I know, and of course it would be the middle of the term and all. Listen . . . no, I couldn't ask . . . but maybe . . ." She looked at Barry's mother eagerly.

"Go on, what is it?"

"I don't suppose on Tuesday or Thursday when Barry's at his evening class, that *you* would show me, you know, give me a few hints?" The older woman was silent for a moment. Fiona rushed in. "I'm sorry, that's typical of me, open my big mouth before I think what I'm going to say."

"I'd be delighted to teach you to cook, Fiona," said Barry's mother. "We'll start next Tuesday, with bread and scones."

◦◦◦

BRIGID DUNNE WAS very impressed. "Getting his mother to teach you cooking, now that's a clever move," she said admiringly.

"Well it sort of came out naturally, I just said it." Fiona was amazed at her own daring.

"And you're the one who says she's no good with men. When are we going to meet this Barry?"

"Soon, I don't want to overpower him with all my friends, particularly sexy, overconfident ones like you."

"You have changed, Fiona," Brigid said.

◦◦◦

"GRANIA? IT'S FIONA."

"Oh great, I thought it was Head Office. How are you? Have you done it yet?"

"Done what?"

"You know," Grania said.

"No, not yet, but soon. It's all on course, I just rang to thank you."

"Whatever for?"

"For saying I was a bit dopey."

"I never said that, Fiona." Grania was stung.

"No, but you told me to get my act together and it worked a dream. He's mad about me, and his mother is. And it couldn't be better."

"Well, I'm glad." Grania sounded pleased.

"I just rang to ask did you do your bit, go back to see your father?"

"No. I tried, but I lost my nerve at the last moment."

"Grania!" Fiona sounded stern.

"Hey, you of all people lecturing me."

"I know, but we did promise to keep each other up to all the things we said that evening."

"I know."

"And Brigid hasn't talked about low-cal sweetener since then, and I've been as brave as a tiger about things. You wouldn't believe it."

"Oh bloody hell, Fiona. I'll go tonight," said Grania.

❧

GRANIA TOOK A deep breath and knocked on the door. Her father answered. She couldn't read his face.

"You still have your key, you don't have to have the door answered for you," he said.

"I didn't like to waltz in as if I still lived here," she said.

"Nobody said you couldn't live here."

"I know, Dad." They still stood in the hall, an awkward silence all around them. "And where's everybody else? Are they all at home?"

"I don't know," her father said.

"Come on, Dad. You must know."

"I don't. Your mother may be in the kitchen reading, and Brigid may be upstairs. I was in my room."

"How's it getting along?" she asked, to try to cover the loneliness. This wasn't a big house, not big enough for the man not to know whether his wife and daughter were at home or not. And not to care.

"It's fine," he said.

"Will you show it to me?" Grania wondered was it going to be like this forever, making conversation with her father like drawing teeth.

"Certainly."

He led her into the room, and she literally gasped in surprise. The evening sun came through the window, the yellow and gold colors all around the window seat picked up the light, and the curtains in purple and gold looked as if they were for a stage in a theater. His shelves were full of books and ornaments, and the little desk shone and glowed in the evening light.

"Dad, it's beautiful. I never knew you could make anything like this," Grania said.

"There's a lot we never knew about each other," he said.

"Please, Dad, let me admire your lovely, lovely room, and look at those frescoes, they're marvelous."

"Yes."

"And all those colors, Dad. It's like a dream."

Her enthusiasm was so genuine, he couldn't keep cold and stiff. "It is a bit of a dream, but then I've always been a stupid sort of dreamer, Grania."

"I inherited it from you then."

"No, I don't think you did."

"Not in this artistic way, I couldn't make a room like this in a million years. But I do have my dreams, yes."

"They're not proper dreams, Grania. Truly they're not."

"I tell you this, Dad, I never loved anyone before, apart from you and Mam, and to be honest, you more. No, I want to say this because you might not let me talk again. Now I know what love is about. It's wanting the best for someone else, it's wanting them to be happier than you are, isn't that it?"

"Yes." He spoke in a very dead voice.

"You felt that for Mam once, didn't you? I mean, you probably still do."

"I think it changes as you get older."

"But I won't have much time for it to get older. You and Mam have had nearly twenty-five years, Tony'll be dead and buried in twenty-five years time. He smokes and drinks and is hopeless. You know that. If I get a good ten years I'll be lucky."

"Grania, you could do so much better."

"You couldn't do better than to be loved by the person you love, Dad. I know that, you know that."

"He's not reliable."

"I rely on him absolutely, Dad. I would trust him with my life."

"Wait until he leaves you with a fatherless child. You'll remember these words then."

"More than anything else on earth I would love to have his child."

"Well, go ahead. Nothing's going to stop you."

Grania bent and examined the flowers on the little table. "You buy these for yourself, Dad?"

"Who else do you think would buy them for me?"

There were tears in her eyes. "I'd buy them for you if you'd let me, I'd come here and sit with you, and if I had your grandchild I would bring him or her here."

"You're telling me you're pregnant, is that it?"

"No, that's not it. I'm in control of whether I will be or not, and I won't until I know the child would be welcomed by everyone."

"That could be a long wait," he said. But she noticed that this time there were tears in his eyes too.

"Dad," she said, and it was hard to say which of them moved first toward the other until their arms were around each other and their tears were lost in each other's shoulders.

❧

BRIGID AND FIONA went to the pictures.

"Have you been to bed with him yet?"

"No, but there's no rush, it's all going according to plan," Fiona said.

"Longest plan since time began," Brigid grumbled.

"No, believe me, I know what I'm doing."

"I'm glad someone does," Brigid said. "Dad and Grania have gone all emotional on us. Grania's sitting in Dad's room talking to him as if a cross word had never been said between them."

"Isn't that good?"

"Yes, it's good, of course it's good, but it's a mystery," Brigid complained.

"And what does your mother say about it?"

"Nothing. That's another mystery. I used to think that we were the dullest, most ordinary family in the western world. Now I think I live in a madhouse. I used to think that you were the odd one, Fiona. But there you are, the little pet of the house, learning to be a gourmet chef from the mother and planning to bed the son. How did it all happen?"

Brigid hated mysteries and being confused by things. She sounded very disgruntled indeed.

❧

THE COOKERY CLASSES were a great success. Sometimes Barry's father was there. Tall and dark and watchful. He looked a lot younger than his wife, but then his mind was not so troubled. He worked in a big nurseries and vegetable farm delivering produce and flowers to restaurants and hotels around the city. He was perfectly pleasant to Fiona but not enthusiastic. He was not curious about her, and he gave the impression of someone passing through rather than someone who lived there.

Sometimes Barry came back from his own Italian class and ate the results of their cooking, but Fiona said he shouldn't hurry back specially. It was too late for eating anyway, and he liked talking to the people afterward. She would take the bus home herself. After all, they would meet on other nights.

Bit by bit she began to hear the story of the great Infidelity. She tried not to listen at first. "Don't tell me all this, Mrs. Healy, please, you'll wish you hadn't when you're all nice and friendly with Mr. Healy again and then you'll be sorry."

"No I won't, you're my friend. Chop those a lot finer, Fiona. You don't want great lumps in it. You have to hear. You have to know what Barry's father is like."

Everything had been fine until two years ago. Well, you know, fine in a manner of speaking. His hours had always been difficult, she had lived with that. Sometimes up for the four-thirty run in the morning, sometimes working late at night. But there had been time off. Grand time in the middle of the day sometimes. She could remember when they had gone to the cinema for the two o'clock show, and then had tea and buns afterward and she was the envy of every other woman around. None of them ever went to the pictures in the daylight with their husbands. And he had never wanted her to work in the old days. He had said that he brought in plenty for the two of them and the child. She should keep the home nice and cook for them and be there when he got time off. That way they could have a good life.

But two years ago it had all changed. He had met someone and started having an affair.

"You can't be sure, Mrs. Healy," Fiona said as she weighed out the raisins and sultanas for the fruitcake. "It could be anything, you know, like pressure at work, or the traffic getting worse, you know the way everyone's giving out about rush hour."

"There's no rush hour at four a.m. when he comes home." Her face was grim.

"But isn't it these awful hours?"

"I checked with the company, he works twenty-eight hours a week. He's out of here nearly twice that much."

"The traveling to and fro?" Fiona said desperately.

"He's about ten minutes from work," Barry's mother said.

"He might just want a bit of space."

"He has that all right, he sleeps in the spare room."

"Maybe not to wake you?"

"Maybe not to be near me."

"And if she exists who do you think she is?" Fiona spoke in a whisper.

"I don't know but I'll find out."

"Would it be someone at work, do you think?"

"No, I know all of them. There's no one likely there. But it's someone he met *through* work though, and that could be half of Dublin."

It was very distressing to listen to her. All that unhappiness, and according to Barry it was all in her mind.

"Does she talk to you at all about it?" Barry asked Fiona.

Fiona thought there was a sort of sacredness about the conversations over the floured boards and the bubbling casseroles, over cups of coffee after the cooking when Fiona would sit on the sofa and the huge, half-blind Cascarino would lie purring on her lap.

"A bit here and there, not much," she lied.

Nessa Healy thought that Fiona was her friend, it wasn't the action of a friend to repeat conversations back.

Barry and Fiona saw a lot of each other. They went to football matches and to the cinema, and as the weather got nicer they went on the motorbike out to Wicklow or Kildare and saw places that Fiona had never been.

He had not asked her to come on the trip to Rome, the *viaggio*, as they kept calling it. Fiona hoped that at some stage soon he would and so she had applied for a passport just in case.

Sometimes they went out in a foursome with Suzi and Luigi, who had invited them to their wedding in Dublin the middle of June. Suzi said that, mercifully, the idea of a Roman wedding had been abandoned. Her parents said no, Luigi's parents said no, and all their friends who weren't in the Italian class said they were off their skulls. So it would be a Roman honeymoon instead.

"Are you learning any Italian yourself?" Fiona inquired.

"No. If they want to talk to me they have to speak my language," said Suzi, the confident, handsome girl who would have expected Eskimos to learn her language if she were passing the North Pole.

Then there was the big fund-raising party. The Italian class, all thirty of them, were to provide the food. Drink was being sponsored by various liquor stores and the supermarket. Somebody knew a group that would play free in return for their picture in the local paper. Each pupil was expected to invite at least five people who would pay £5 a head for the party. That would raise £750 for the *viaggio* and then there would be a huge raffle. The prizes were enormous, and that might raise another £150 or even more. The travel agency was bringing the price down all the time. The accommodation had been booked in a *pensione* in Rome. There would be the trip to Florence, staying overnight at a hostel, and on to Siena before they went back to Rome.

Barry was drumming up his five for the party.

"I'd like you to come, Dad," he said. "It means a lot to me, and remember Mam and I always went to your work outings."

"I'm not sure I'll be free, Son. But if I am I'll be there, I can't say fairer than that."

And Barry would have Fiona, his mother, a fellow from work, and a next-door neighbor. Fiona was going to ask her friends Grania and Brigid, but they were going already because of their father. And Suzi was going with Luigi. It would be a great night.

The cookery lessons continued. Fiona and Barry's mother were going to make a very exotic dessert for the party, it was called cannoli. Full of fruit and nuts and ricotta cheese in pastry and deep-fried.

"Are you sure that's not one of the pastas?" Barry asked anxiously.

No, the women assured him, that was cannelloni. He knew nothing. They asked him to check with Signora. Signora said that *cannoli alla siciliana* was one of the most mouthwatering dishes in the world, she couldn't wait to taste it.

The confidences continued to be exchanged between Fiona and Nessa Healy as they cooked. Fiona said that she really did like Barry a lot, he was a generous, kind person, but she didn't want to rush him because she didn't think he was ready to settle down.

And Barry's mother told Fiona that she couldn't give up on her husband. There was a time she might have been able to say he didn't love her, and let him go to whoever it was that he did love. But not now.

"And why is that?" Fiona wanted to know.

"When I was in hospital that time, when I was a bit foolish you know, he brought me flowers. A man doesn't do that unless he cares. He brought a bunch of freesias in and left them for me. For all his blustering and all his saying that it wasn't him and that he's not going to be railroaded into things, he *does* care, Fiona. That's what I'm holding on to."

And Fiona sat, her eyes enormous behind her glasses and her hands floury. And cursed herself to the pit of hell and back for having been so stupid. She knew that if she spoke it would have to be at that very minute, and she did consider it.

But when she looked at Nessa Healy's face and saw all the life and hope in it, she realized what a problem she had. How could she tell this woman that she, the girl who worked selling coffee in the hospital waiting room, had delivered the bloody freesias? She, Fiona, who wasn't even meant to know about the suicide attempt. It had never been discussed. Whatever Fiona was going to attempt in order to try to undo the harm she had managed to create, it could not involve taking all this hope and life away. She would find some other way.

Some other way, Fiona said to herself desperately, as the days went by and the woman who might one day be her mother-in-law told how love could never be dead if someone sent a bunch of flowers.

Suzi would know what to do, but Fiona would not ask her, not in a million years. Suzi might well tell Luigi, and Luigi would tell his old pal Bartolomeo, as he insisted on calling Barry. And anyway, Suzi would despise her, and Fiona didn't want that.

Brigid and Grania Dunne would be of no use in a situation like this. They'd just say that Fiona was reverting to her old ways and getting into a tizz about nothing. There was an old teacher at school who used that word. Don't get in a tizz, girls, she would cry, and they would have to stuff their fists down their throats to stop laughing. But later on Brigid and Grania said that "tizz" was a good word for Fiona's temperament, sort of fussy and dizzy and troubled. She couldn't let them know how frightening and upsetting the tizz was this time because they would say it was all her own fault. And, of course, it undoubtedly was.

~~~

"YOU ARE FOND of me, Fiona?" Mrs. Healy asked after they had made a lemon meringue pie.

"Very fond," Fiona said eagerly.

"And you'd tell me the truth?"

"Oh, yes." Fiona's voice was a squeak at this stage. She waited for the blow to fall. Somehow the flowers had been traced back to her. Maybe it was all for the best.

"Do you think I should get my colors done?" Mrs. Healy asked.

"Your colors?"

"Yes. You go to a consultant and they tell you what shades suit you and what drain the color from your face. It's quite scientific apparently."

Fiona struggled for speech. "And how much does it cost?" she asked eventually.

"Oh, I have the money," Mrs. Healy said.

"Well, I'm not much good at these things but I have a very smart friend, I'll ask her. She'll know if it's a good idea or not."

"Thanks, Fiona," said Mrs. Healy, who must be about forty-five and who looked seventy-five and still thought her husband loved her, because of Fiona.

~~~

SUZI SAID THAT it was a brilliant idea. "When are you going?" she asked.

Fiona didn't have the courage to admit that she hadn't been talking about herself. She was also a little upset that Suzi felt she needed advice. But she was trying so hard to be grown up these days and not to dither that she said firmly yes, it had been something she was thinking of.

Nessa Healy was pleased with this news. "Do you know another thing I think we should do?" Mrs. Healy said confidingly. "I think we should go to an expensive hairstylist and have a whole new look."

Fiona felt faint. All the money she had been saving so painstakingly for the *viaggio*, if she ever went on it, would trickle away on these huge improvements that she and Barry's mother were about to embark on.

Fortunately, Suzi saved the day by knowing a hairdressing school.

And as the weeks went on Mrs. Healy stopped wearing brown and dug out all her pale-colored clothes and wore nice dark-colored scarves with them. Her hair was colored and cut short, and she looked fifty instead of seventy-five.

Fiona had her dark, shiny hair cut very short and thick, dead straight with a fringe, and everyone said she looked terrific. She wore bright reds and yellows, and one or two of the house surgeons said flirtatious things to her, which she just laughed at good-naturedly instead of thinking that they might be going to marry her, as she might have done in the old days.

And Barry's father stayed at home a little more, but not a lot more, and seemed perfectly pleasant anytime Fiona was in the house.

But it didn't look as if the colors or the new hairstyle were going to win him back to the way things had been before the Affair began two years ago.

~❧

"YOU'RE VERY GOOD to my mother, she looks terrific," Barry said.

"And what about me, don't I look terrific too?"

"You always looked terrific. But listen, never let her know that I told you about the suicide. She often asks me to swear that I never told you. She'd hate to lose your respect, that's what it is."

Fiona swallowed when he said this. She could never tell Barry either. There must be people who lived with a lie forever. It was quite possible. It wasn't even that important a lie, it was just that it had led to such false hopes.

Nothing prepared Fiona for the revelation that came as they were separating eggs and beating the whites for a meringue topping.

"I've discovered where she works."

"Who?"

"The woman. Dan's woman, the mistress." Mrs. Healy spoke with satisfaction, as if of a detection job well done.

"And where is it?" Did this all mean that Barry's poor mother would get another attack of nerves and try to kill herself again? Fiona's face was anxious.

"In one of the smartest restaurants in Dublin, it would seem. Quentin's no less. Have you heard of it?"

"Yes, you often see it in the papers," poor Fiona said.

"And you might see it in the papers again," said the older woman darkly.

She couldn't mean she was going to go there to Quentin's restaurant and make a scene. Could she?

"And are you sure that's where she is? I mean, how do you know exactly, Mrs. Healy?"

"I followed him," she said triumphantly.

"You followed him?"

"He went out in his van last night. He often does on a Wednesday. Stays in and watches television and then after twelve he says he has to go and do late-night work. I know it's a lie, I've always known that about Wednesday—there's no night work, and anyway he's all dressed up, brushing his teeth, clean shirt. The lot."

"But how did you follow him, Mrs. Healy? Didn't he go out in his van?"

"Indeed he did. But I had a taxi waiting, with its lights off, and away we went."

"A taxi waiting all that time? Until he was ready to go out?" The sheer, mad extravagance of it stunned Fiona more than the act itself.

"No, I knew it would be about midnight so I booked it for fifteen minutes earlier just in case. Then I got in and followed him."

"And merciful Lord, Mrs. Healy, what did the taxi driver think?"

"He thought about the nice sum clicking up on his meter, that's what he thought."

"And what happened?"

"Well, the van went off and turned into the lane behind Quentin's." She paused. She didn't *look* very upset. Fiona had often seen Mrs. Healy more strained, more stressed than this. What could she have seen on this extraordinary mission?

"And then?"

"Well, then we waited. I mean he waited, and the taxi driver and I waited. And a woman came out. I couldn't see her, it was so dark. And she got straight into the van as if she knew it was going to be there, and they took off so quickly that we lost them."

Fiona felt vastly relieved. But Mrs. Healy was practical. "We won't
lose them next Wednesday," she said determinedly.

Fiona had been very unsuccessful in trying to head off this second
excursion. "Would you look at the cost of it? You could get a lovely new
check skirt for what you pay the taxi driver."

"It's my housekeeping money, Fiona. I'll spend what I save on what
gives me pleasure."

"But suppose he sees you, suppose you're discovered."

"I'm not the one that's doing anything wrong, I'm just going out for a
drive in a taxi."

"But what if you do see her? What difference will it make?"

"I'll know what she's like, the woman he *thinks* he loves." And her
voice sounded so sure that Dan Healy only thought he loved another
that Fiona's blood ran chill.

❧

"DOESN'T YOUR MOTHER work in Quentin's?" Fiona asked Brigid.

"Yeah, she does. Why?"

"Would she know people who work there at night, like waitresses,
young ones?"

"I suppose she would, she's been there long enough. Why?"

"If I were to give you a name would you be able to ask her about
them, like without saying why you were asking?"

"I might, why?"

"You never stop asking why."

"I don't do anything without asking why," Brigid said.

"Okay, forget it then," said Fiona with spirit.

"No, I didn't say I wouldn't."

"Forget it. Forget it."

"All right, I'll check it out with her. Is it your Barry? Is that what it is?
Do you think he has someone else who works in Quentin's?" Brigid was
all interest now.

"Not exactly."

"Well, I could ask her of course."

"No, you ask too many questions. Let's leave it, you'd give everything
away."

"Oh come on, Fiona, we've all been friends forever. You cover for us, we cover for you. I'll find out, just give me the name and I'll ask dead casual like to my mum."

"Maybe."

"What is her name anyway?" Brigid asked.

"I don't know yet, but I will soon," said Fiona, and it was obvious to Brigid and anyone else who might have been listening that she was telling the truth.

᙮

"HOW COULD WE find out her name?" Fiona asked Mrs. Healy.

"I don't know. I think we just have to confront them."

"No, I mean knowing her name would give us an advantage. There might be no need to confront her."

"I don't see how that could be." Nessa Healy was confused. They sat in silence thinking about it.

"Suppose," said Fiona. "Suppose you were to say that someone from Quentin's rang and asked him to ring back, but whoever it was, she didn't leave a name, said he'd know who it was. Then we could listen who he asks for."

"Fiona, you're wasted in that hospital," Barry's mother said. "You should have been a private eye."

᙮

THEY DID IT that very evening, when Dan had been welcomed and given a little bit of peanut brittle to taste. Then, as if she had just remembered it, his wife told him about the message from Quentin's.

He went to the hall to phone, and Fiona kept the sounds of the electric mixer at high blast while Barry's mother crept to listen at the door.

They were both among the ingredients when Dan Healy came back into the kitchen. "Are you sure she said Quentin's?"

"That's what she said."

"It's just that I rang them now and they say that no one there was looking for me."

His wife shrugged. It implied that this was business for you. He seemed troubled and he left soon to go upstairs.

"Did you hear him ask for anyone?" said Fiona.

Mrs. Healy nodded, her eyes bright and feverish. "Yes, we have the name. He spoke to her."

"And who was it? What was her name?" Fiona could hardly breathe with the excitement and the danger of it all.

"Well, whoever it was answered the phone and he said, 'Jesus, Nell, why did you ring me at home?' That's what he said. Her name is Nell."

"*What?*"

"Nell. Little bitch, selfish, thoughtless little cow. Well, she needn't think he loves her, he sounded furious with her."

"Yes," said Fiona.

"So now we know her name, that gives us power," said Nessa Healy. Fiona said nothing.

Nell was the name of Brigid and Grania's mother. It was Nell Dunne who worked at the reception desk in Quentin's and answered the phone when it rang.

Barry's father was involved with her friends' mother. Not a silly little good-time girl as they had thought, a woman as old as Nessa Healy. A woman with a husband and grown-up daughters of her own. Fiona wondered were the complications of this ever going to end.

❧

"FIONA? IT'S BRIGID."

"Oh yes, listen, I'm not meant to get phone calls at work."

"If you'd done your leaving cert and got a proper job you'd have been able to have people phone you," Brigid complained.

"Yeah, well I didn't. What is it, Brigid? There's a crowd of people here waiting to be served." There was nobody, as it happened, but she felt ill at ease talking to her friend now that she knew such a terrible secret about the family.

"This bird, the one that you think Barry fancies, the one working in Quentin's . . . you were going to tell me her name and I was going to get the lowdown on her from my mam."

"No!" Fiona's voice was almost a screech.

"Hey, you were the one who asked me."

"I've changed my mind."

"Well, if he is having a bit on the side you should know. People should know, it's their right."

"Is it, Brigid? Is it?" Fiona knew she sounded very intense.

"Of course it is. If he says he loves you and if he tells her he loves her, then for God's sake . . ."

"But it's not exactly like that, you see."

"He doesn't say he loves you?"

"Yes he does. But well, what the hell!"

"Fiona?"

"Yes?"

"You are becoming quite seriously mad. I think you should know this."

"Sure, Brigid," said Fiona, grateful for once that she had always been considered a person in a permanent tizz.

❧

"WOULD YOU MIND more if she were young or old?" Fiona asked Barry's mother.

"Nell? She has to be young, why else would he have strayed?"

"There's no understanding men, everyone says that. She could be as old as a tree, you know."

Nessa Healy was very serene. "If he had a dalliance it was because some young one threw herself at him. Men go for flattery. But he loves me. That was always clear. When I was unavoidably in hospital that time I told you about, he came in when I was asleep and left me flowers. Whatever else there is to hold on to, there's that."

Barry came in full of excitement. The party on Thursday had been so well subscribed, you would never believe it. It was going to be fantastic. *Magnifico.* Mr. Dunne had said that he would be able to announce that with a success like this on their hands, a whole new program in adult education might start next year.

"Mr. Dunne?" Fiona said in a hollow voice.

"He was the one who set it up, he's a great pal of Signora's. You told me you knew his daughters."

"Yes, I do." Fiona spoke in a hollow voice.

"So he's delighted about the whole thing. It makes him look good too."

"And he'll be there?"

"Hey, Fiona, are you asleep or something? Didn't you tell me we couldn't sell tickets to his daughters because they're going with him?"

"Did I say that?" She must have, but it was long ago, before she knew all that she knew now.

"And do you *think* his wife is coming?" she asked.

"Oh I'd say so. Any of us who have a wife or a husband, a mother or a father, not to mention a loving girlfriend . . . well, we're making sure they're coming."

"And your father is coming?" Fiona said.

"As of today he says he is," said Bartolomeo, Italian speaker, pleased and happy that he was able to field a good team.

⁓

THE NIGHT OF the *festa* in Mountainview school was eagerly awaited.

Signora had been going to buy a new dress, but she decided at the last moment to spend the money on colored lights for the school hall.

"Aw, come on, Signora," said Suzi Sullivan. "I have a great dress picked out for you in the Good as New shop. Let them have whatever old lights are there, up in the school."

"I want them to remember this evening always. If there are nice colored lights it will add to the romance of it . . . what will anyone care if I spend forty pounds on a dress? Nobody will notice."

"If I can get you the lights will you get the dress?" Suzi asked.

"You're not going to suggest that Luigi . . ." Signora looked very doubtful about it indeed.

"No, I swear I won't let him get in touch with the underworld again. It took me long enough to get him out of it. No, I really do know someone in the electrical business, a fellow called Jacko. I needed someone to rewire the flat and Lou asked in the Italian class and Laddy knew this guy who did up the hotel where he works. He'd know what you want, will I send him up to you?"

"Well, Suzi . . ."

"And if he's cheap, as he will be, then you'll buy the dress?" She looked so eager.

"Of course, Suzi," Signora said, wondering why people set such a store by clothes.

❧

Jacko came up to look at the school hall. "Built like a bloody barn of course," he said.

"I know, but I thought if we had three or four rows of colored lights, you know, a bit like Christmas lights . . ."

"It would look pathetic," Jacko said.

"Well, we don't have enough money to buy anything else." Signora looked distressed now.

"Who said anything about buying? I'll light the place properly for you. Bring proper gear up, do it like a disco. Install it for the night, take it away after."

"But you can't do that. It would cost a fortune. There'd have to be someone to operate it."

"I'll come and see it doesn't blow up. And it's only for a night, I won't charge you."

"But we couldn't expect you to do all that."

"Just a nice big board advertising my electrical business," Jacko said, grinning from ear to ear.

"Could I give you a couple of tickets, in case you would like to bring a partner or anything?" Signora was desperate to return his kindness.

"No, I travel alone these days, Signora," he said with his crooked smile. "But you never know what I might pick up at the party. Minding the lights won't take up all my time."

❧

Bill Burke and Lizzie Duffy had to get ten people between them, and Bill found it hard to sell tickets at the bank because Grania Dunne had got in first. As it happened, Lizzie's mother was going to be in Dublin for the night.

"Do you think we dare?" Bill said. Mrs. Duffy was very much a loose cannon, the dangers might be greater than the rewards.

Lizzie thought about it seriously. "What's the very worst she could do?" she wondered.

Bill gave it serious thought. "She could get drunk and sing with the band?" he suggested.

"No, when she gets drunk she tells everyone what a bastard my father is."

"The music will be very loud, no one will hear her. Let's ask her," said Bill.

❧

CONSTANZA COULD HAVE bought every ticket and not noticed the dip in her bank balance, but that wasn't the point. She had to invite people, that's what it was about.

Veronica would come, of course, and bring a friend from work. Daughters were marvelous. More diffidently, she asked her son, Richard, would he like to take his girlfriend, and to her surprise he sounded eager. The children had been a huge support to her after the trial and sentence. Harry was serving a minimum prison sentence, as she had foretold. Every week in her small seaside apartment she got phone calls and visits from her four children. She must have done something right.

"You won't believe this." Richard rang her a couple of days later. "But you know your Italian *festa* thing up in Mountainview school. Mr. Malone, my boss, is going. He was just talking to me about it today."

"What a small world," said Connie. "Maybe I'll ask his father-in-law, then. Is Paul bringing his wife?"

"I imagine so," said Richard. "Older people always do." Connie wondered who on earth at their Italian class could have invited Paul Malone.

❧

GUS AND MAGGIE told Laddy that *of course* they would come to the *festa*. Nothing would keep them away. They would ask their friend who ran the chip shop to come too, to thank him for all his interpreting, and they would give prizes of free dinners in the hotel with wine for the raffle.

❧

JERRY SULLIVAN IN the house where Signora stayed wanted to know what was the lower age limit.

"Sixteen, Jerry. I keep telling you that," Signora said. She knew there was an inordinate interest in the school in a dance in their school hall, which would have disco lights and real liquor.

Mr. O'Brien, the principal, had discouraged even the older children from attending. "Don't you all spend enough time on these premises?" he had said. "Why don't you go to your horrible smoke-filled basements listening to ear-injuring music as usual?"

Tony O'Brien was like a devil these days. In order to please Grania Dunne, the love of his life, he had given up smoking and it didn't suit him. But Grania had worked a miracle for him, so in fairness he had to trade the smoking business. She had gone to visit her father and got him on their side.

He never knew how she had managed it, but the following day Aidan Dunne had strode into his office and offered his hand.

"I've been behaving like a father in a Victorian melodrama," he had said. "My daughter is old enough to know her own mind and if you make her happy then that's a good thing."

Tony had nearly fallen out of his chair with the shock. "I've lived a rackety old life, Aidan, and you know this. But honestly, Grania is the turning point for me. Your daughter makes me feel good and young and full of hope and happiness. I'll never let her down. If you believe anything, you must believe that."

And they had shaken hands with such vigor that both of their arms were sore for days.

It made everything much simpler both at school and at home. She had stopped taking her contraceptive pill. He knew it had taken a lot for Aidan to make that gesture. He was an odd man. . . . If he hadn't known him better, Tony O'Brien would have believed that the Latin master really did have a thing going with Signora.

But there wasn't a chance of that.

◦◦◦

SIGNORA'S FRIENDS BRENDA and Patrick Brennan were both coming to the party. What was the point of being successful, they said, if they could not delegate? There was an underchef, there was another greeter, the place could survive one evening without them or it wasn't run properly in the first place. And, of course, Nell Dunne from the cash desk would be there too, so Quentin's would be really running on the B team, they laughed to each other.

"I don't know why we're all going at all, we must be touched in the head," Nell Dunne said.

"For solidarity and support of course, what else?" Ms. Brennan said, looking at Nell oddly.

Nell felt, as she so often felt, that Ms. Brennan didn't really like her. It was, after all, a reasonable question. Smart people like the Brennans and yes, even herself, Nell Dunne, a person who mattered in Dublin in her black dress and yellow scarf sitting like a queen in Quentin's, and all of them traipsing up to that barracks of a school Mountainview, where Aidan had soldiered on so long and for nothing.

But she wished she hadn't spoken. The Brennans thought less of her for it somehow.

Still, she might well go. Dan wasn't free that night, he had to go to something with his son, he said, and her own children would be annoyed with her if she didn't make the effort.

It would be dreary, like everything always had been in that school. But at least it wasn't the kind of outing that you'd bother dressing up for. Five pounds for a bit of pizza and a band that would deafen you belting out Italian songs. God Almighty, what she did for her family!

Grania and Brigid were getting dressed for the *festa*.

"I hope it goes well for Dad's sake," Grania said.

"Dad can take anything if he accepts that you go to bed with his boss. Nothing's going to knock him off his perch now." Brigid was back-combing her hair in front of the sitting room mirror.

Grania was annoyed. "I wish you'd stop dwelling on the going-to-bed bit. There's a lot more to it than that."

"At his age would he not get exhausted?" Brigid giggled.

"If I were into talking about it I'd have you green with jealousy," Grania said, putting on her eyeshadow. Their mother came in. "Hey Mam, get a move on, we're going in a few minutes," Grania said.

"I'm ready."

They looked at their mother, hair barely combed, no makeup, an ordinary dress with a loose cardigan over her shoulders. There was no point in saying anything. The sisters exchanged a glance and made no comment.

"Right then," said Grania. "Off we go."

THIS WAS NESSA Healy's first outing since she had been in hospital. The woman who had done her colors had given her very good advice.

Barry thought he hadn't seen his mother looking so well in years. There was no doubt but that Fiona had been a wonderful influence on her. He wondered should he ask Fiona to go on the *viaggio* with him. It was implying a lot, like they would share a room, and that side of things had not progressed very far in the weeks they had been together. He wanted to, but there was never the opportunity or the place or the right occasion.

His father looked uneasy. "What kind of people will be there, Son?"

"All the people who go to the class, Dad, and whoever they could drag like I'm dragging you. It'll be great, honestly."

"Yes, I'm sure."

"And, Dad, Miss Clarke says I can drive the supermarket van even though it's a social outing. So I can take you home or Mam home if you get bored or tired or anything."

He looked so eager and grateful that his father felt ashamed. "When did Dan Healy ever leave a party while there was still drink on the table?" he asked.

"And Fiona's meeting us there?" Mrs. Healy would have liked the moral support of this lively young girl she had grown so fond of. Fiona had made her promise to hold off about confronting everyone with Nell. Just for a week. One week. And reluctantly Nessa Healy had agreed.

"Yes, she was very insistent. She wanted to go on her own," said Barry. "Right, are we off?"

They were off.

&

SIGNORA WAS THERE in the hall.

She had looked at herself in the long mirror before she left the Sullivans' house. Truly she hardly recognized herself as the woman who had come to Ireland a year ago. The widow, as she saw herself, weeping for her dead Mario, her long hair trailing behind her, her long skirt hanging unevenly. Timid, unable to ask for work or a place to live, frightened of her family.

Today she stood tall and elegant, her coffee and lilac dress somehow perfect with her odd-colored hair. Suzi had said that this dress might have cost £300. Imagine. She had let Suzi make up her face.

"Nobody will see me," she had protested.

"It's your night, Signora," Peggy Sullivan had insisted.

&

AND IT WAS. She stood there in a hall with flashing colored lights, with pictures and posters all over it, with the sound system playing a loop tape of Italian songs and music until the live band would arrive with a flourish. They had decided that "Nessun dorma," "Volare," and "Arrivederci Roma," should be played often on the tape. Nothing too unfamiliar.

Aidan Dunne came in. "I'll never be able to thank you," he said.

"It's I who have to thank you, Aidan." He was the only person around them who had not been given an Italianized form of his name. It made him more special.

"Are you nervous?" he asked.

"A little. But then, we are surrounded by friends, why should I be nervous? Everyone is for us, there's nobody against us." She smiled. She was putting out of her mind the fact that not one of her family, her own family, would come to support her tonight. She had asked them gently but had not begged. It would have been so nice, just once, to have said to people, this is my sister, this is my mother. But no.

"You look really terrific, Nora. Yourself, I mean, not just the whole place."

He had never called her Nora before. She hadn't time to take it in because people were arriving. At the door a friend of Constanza's, an extremely efficient woman called Vera, was taking the tickets.

In the cloakrooms, young Caterina from the Italian class and her friend, a bright girl called Harriet, were busy giving people cloakroom tickets and telling them not to lose them. Strangers were coming in and marveling over the place.

The principal, Tony O'Brien, was busy passing all compliments their way. "Nothing to do with me I'm afraid, all down to Mr. Dunne whose project this is, and to Signora."

They stood there like a bride and groom accepting compliments.

Fiona saw Grania and Brigid come in with their mother. She gasped. She had met Mrs. Dunne many times before, but tonight she hardly recognized her. The woman looked a complete wreck. She had barely bothered to wash her face.

Good, thought Fiona grimly. She felt a horrible sensation in her chest, as if she'd swallowed a lump of something that would not go up or down, like a piece of very hard potato or a piece of raw celery. She knew it was fear. Fiona, the mouse in spectacles, was going to interfere in everyone else's life. She was going to tell a whole lot of people a pack of lies and frighten them to death. Would she be up to it, or would she fall on the floor in a swoon and make everything worse?

Of course she would be up to it. Remember that night hanging around in the town house when the old man had gone out and Grania had bought the Chinese take-away. Fiona had changed her whole style then, and look how much good had come out of it. She had single-handedly persuaded Nessa Healy to dress up and come to this party. That wasn't the action of a mouse in spectacles. She had gone so far, she must get over this last fence. She must end the affair that was breaking everyone's heart. As soon as she had done this, then she could get on with her own life and begin her own affair properly.

Fiona looked around her, trying to fasten a confident smile on her face. She would just wait until it began to warm up a bit.

It took no time at all for it all to warm up. There was the roar of conversation, the clink of glasses, and then the band arrived. The dancing started to serious sixties music, which suited every age group.

Fiona went up to Nell Dunne, who was standing on her own looking very scornful. "Do you remember me, Mrs. Dunne?"

"Oh, Fiona?" She seemed to drag up the name with difficulty and not great interest.

"Yes, you were always nice to me when I was young, Mrs. Dunne, I remember that."

"Was I?"

"Yes, when I'd come to tea. I wouldn't want you to be made a fool of."

"Why would I be made a fool of?"

"Dan, the man over there."

"What?" Nell looked to where Fiona was pointing.

"You know he goes round telling everyone he has this frump of a wife, and that she's always committing suicide and he can't wait to leave her. But he has a string of women, and he tells them all the same story."

"I don't know what you're talking about."

"And you're probably, let me see, Wednesday's woman and one other day. That's the way he works it."

Nell Dunne looked at the smart woman with Dan Healy, laughing easily. This couldn't be the wife he had spoken of. "And what makes *you* think you know anything about him?" she asked Fiona.

"Simple," Fiona said. "He had my mother too. Used to come up in the van and collect her outside work and take her off. She was besotted over him. It was awful."

"Why are you telling me this?" Her eyes were wild, her voice was hushed. She was looking to the right and left of her.

Fiona realized that Mrs. Dunne was greatly rattled. "Well, he delivers vegetables and flowers to where I work, you see, and he's always talking about his women, even you, and how you're just made for it. 'Posh lady from Quentin's,' he calls you. And then I realized it was Brigid and Grania's mum he was talking about, just like it was once my mum . . . and I felt sick."

"I don't believe a word of this. You're a very dangerous and mad girl," Mrs. Dunne said through eyes narrow as slits.

LUIGI WAS DANCING up a storm with Caterina from the class. Caterina and her friend Harriet had been released from cloakroom duty now and were making up for lost time.

"Excuse me." Fiona dragged Luigi off the dance floor.

"What is it? Suzi doesn't mind, she *likes* me to dance." He looked indignant.

"Do me one big favor," Fiona begged. "One thing without asking any questions at all."

"That's me," Luigi said.

"Could you go over to that dark man over there near the door, and tell him that if he knows what's good for him, he'll leave his Wednesday-night lady alone."

"But . . . ?"

"You said you wouldn't ask why!"

"I'm not asking why, I'm only asking would he hit me?"

"No, he won't. And Luigi?"

"Yeah?"

"Two things. Could you not say anything at all about this to Suzi or Bartolomeo?"

"That's done."

"And could you try and look a bit ferocious when you're talking to him?"

"I'll try," said Luigi, who thought it was something he might have to work at.

NELL DUNNE WAS about to approach Dan. He was talking to a thickset, jowlish man with a very angry expression. She thought she would walk by and speak to him out of the corner of her mouth. Say she needed a word. Jerk her head to the corridor outside.

Why hadn't he told her he was coming to this anyway? So secretive. So hidden. There could be a lot more she didn't know. But just before she approached him he looked up and saw her, and a look of fear came into his eyes. He started to move away from her. She saw him grab his wife's arm and ask her to dance.

The band was playing "Ciao Ciao Bambino." *They* hated it, but a job was a job. They were going to appear in tomorrow's evening paper.

～

AND FIONA STOOD on a chair so that she could observe it all. And remember it forever. Barry had just asked her if she would come on the *viaggio* with him and she had said yes. Her future mother- and father-in-law were dancing with each other.

Grania and Brigid's mother was struggling to get out and look for her coat. She was demanding that Caterina and her friend Harriet open up the cloakroom for her. Only Fiona saw her go. Barry certainly didn't notice her. Maybe he might never have to know about her any more than anyone ever had to know about the freesias.

"Will you dance with me?" he said. It was "Three Coins in the Fountain." Sugary and sentimental.

Barry held her very tight. *"Ti amo, Fiona, carissima Fiona."*

"Anch'io," she said.

"What?" He could hardly believe it.

"Anch'io. It means me too. I love you too. *Ti amo da morire."*

"God, how did you learn that?" he asked, impressed as he never had been.

"I asked Signora. I practiced it. Just in case."

"In case?"

"In case you said it, so that I'd know what to say."

Around them people danced and sang the silly words of the song. Grania and Brigid's father hadn't gone hunting for his wife, he was talking to Signora. They looked like people who might dance at any moment if it occurred to one of them. Barry's father wasn't looking around anxiously, he was talking to his wife as if she were a real person again. Brigid wasn't laced into some tight skirt tugging at it, she wore a loose scarlet dress and had her arms around the neck of a man who would not escape. Grania was leaning on the arm of Tony, the old man.

They didn't dance, but they were getting married. Fiona had been invited to the wedding.

Fiona thought it was wonderful to be grown up at last. She hadn't made *all* this happen, but she had made a very important part of it happen.

VIAGGIO

"Why are we asking Mr. Dunne to our wedding?" Lou wanted to know.

"Because it would be nice for Signora, she won't have anyone."

"Won't she have everyone else? Doesn't she live with your family, for God's sake?"

"You know what I mean." Suzi was adamant.

"Do we have to have his wife as well? The list is getting longer every minute. You *do* know it's seventeen pounds a head and that's before a drink passes their lips?"

"Of course we're not asking his wife. Are you soft in the head?" Suzi said, and the look came over her face that Lou didn't like, the look that said she wondered was she marrying someone as thick as the wall.

"Certainly not his wife," Lou said hastily. "I must have been dreaming, that's all."

"Is there anyone else from your side that you'd like?" Suzi asked.

"No, no. In a way they're my side as well, and aren't they coming on the honeymoon with us?" Lou said, brightening up.

"Together with half of Dublin," said Suzi, rolling her eyes.

❧

"A REGISTRY OFFICE, I see," said Nell Dunne when Grania told her the date.

"Well, it would be hypocritical to get the job done in a church, neither of us ever going into one." Nell shrugged. "You will be there Mam, won't you?" Grania sounded concerned.

"Of course I will, why do you ask?"

"It's just . . . it's just . . ."

"What is it, Grania? I've said I'll be there."

"Well, you left that party up in the school before it even got going, and it was Dad's big night. And you're not going on his trip to Italy or anything."

"I wasn't asked on his trip to Italy," Nell Dunne said in a tight, hard voice.

❧

"CAN EVERYONE COME on this holiday to Rome and Florence?" Bernie Duffy asked her daughter Lizzie.

"No, Mother. I'm sorry, but it's restricted to the people in the class," Lizzie apologized.

"Wouldn't they want more people to swell the numbers?" Bernie had enjoyed herself boisterously at the *festa*. She thought the *viaggio* might be more of the same.

❧

"WHAT WILL WE do, she's at me all the time," Lizzie asked Bill later.

"We'll take her to Galway to see your father instead," Bill said suddenly.

"We can't do that, can we?"

"Wouldn't it sort a lot of things out? It would distract her, and one way or the other it would take up her time and she wouldn't feel she was being left out of any fun if she was in the thick of all that drama."

"That's a great idea." Lizzie was full of admiration.

"And anyway, I should meet him, shouldn't I?"

"Why? We're not getting married till we're twenty-five."

"I don't know. Luigi's getting married and Mr. Dunne's daughter is getting married . . . I think we should get married sooner, don't you?"

"*Perché non?*" said Lizzie, with a huge smile all over her face.

∾

"I'VE ASKED SIGNORA to write the letter to the Garaldis for me," Laddy said. "She said she'd explain everything."

Maggie and Gus exchanged glances. Surely Signora would realize how casual the invitation had been to Laddy, the exuberance and gratitude of a warmhearted family touched at the honesty of an Irish porter. They'd never expect him to take it so seriously, to go to Italian classes and to expect a huge welcome.

Signora was a mature woman who would understand the situation, wasn't she? Yet there was something childlike about the woman in the coffee and lilac dress, the woman at the *festa* that night who was so innocently thrilled with the success of the lessons and the support that had been given to her evening class. She was an unworldly sort of person, perhaps she would be like Laddy and think that these Garaldis were waiting with open arms for someone they must have well forgotten by now.

But nothing would let Gus and Maggie take from Laddy's excitement. He had his passport in the hotel safe, and he had changed money into lire already. This trip meant everything to him, not a shadow must be allowed to fall on it. It will all be fine, Gus and Maggie told each other, willing it to be so.

∾

"I'VE NEVER BEEN abroad in my life and imagine I'm going twice this summer," Fran told Connie.

"Twice?"

"Yes, as well as the *viaggio* Kathy won two tickets to America. You wouldn't believe it, she entered a competition in some business magazine

---

that her friend Harriet brought into the school, and she won two tickets to New York, so we're both going."

"Isn't that great. And have you anywhere to stay when you get there?"

"Yes. I have a friend, a fellow I used to go out with, he's going to drive to meet us. It's over four hundred miles, but they think nothing of that over there."

"He must like you still if he's going to drive that distance."

Fran smiled. "I hope so, I still like him," she said. "Wasn't it a miracle that Kathy won the tickets?"

"Yes."

"Do you know, when she told me I thought her father had given them to her. But no, when they came they were paid for by this magazine and all, so it's all aboveboard."

"Why would her father have given them and not told you?"

"Well, I don't see him now, and he's married to one of the richest women in Ireland, but I wouldn't take them from him as a pat on the head."

"No, of course not. And do you still have feelings for Kathy's father?"

"Not at all, it was all years and years ago. No, I wish him well, for all that he's married to Marianne Hayes and owns a quarter of Dublin."

"BARTOLOMEO, WILL YOU and Fiona be able to share a room do you think?" Signora asked.

"*Sì grazie,* Signora, that's all sorted out." Barry blushed a bit at the memory of how very pleasurably it had been sorted out.

"Good, that makes it all easier, single rooms are a big problem."

Signora was going to share with Constanza, and Aidan Dunne with Lorenzo. Everyone else had partners of some sort.

THE TRAVEL AGENCY had been marvelous, it was the place where Brigid Dunne worked. They had given the best price when it had all been analyzed down to the bone. Brigid Dunne said she almost wished she were going herself.

"Why don't you and the Old Man of the Sea go?" she asked Grania.

Grania just laughed at her now when she made these remarks. "Tony and I don't want to crowd Dad out on this, and anyway we're getting ready for the geriatric wedding of the century."

Brigid giggled. Grania was so happy that you couldn't offend her.

They were both thinking how odd it was that no mention at all of their mother had been made in the planning of this famous *viaggio*. But it was something they didn't speak of. It was somehow too trivial and too serious at the same time. Did it mean that Mam and Dad were over? Things like that didn't happen to families like theirs.

∽

FIONA BROUGHT BARRY home to supper in her house shortly before the *viaggio*.

"You practically live in my house," he complained, "and I'm never allowed into yours."

"I didn't want you to meet my parents until it was too late."

"What do you mean too late?"

"Too late for you to abandon me. I wanted you to be consumed with physical lust for me, as well as liking me and admiring me as a person."

She spoke so seriously and earnestly, Barry found it hard to keep a straight face. "It's just as well then that the physical lust bit has taken over so strongly," he said. "I'll be able to put up with them however awful they are."

And they were fairly awful. Fiona's mother said that Ireland was very nice for a holiday because you wouldn't get yourself sunburned and people wouldn't snatch your handbag.

"They do here just as much as anywhere else."

"But at least they speak English here," her father said.

Barry said he had been learning Italian in readiness, he would be able to order food and deal with police stations, hospitals, and breakdowns of the bus.

"See what I mean?" Fiona's father was triumphant. "Must be a very dangerous place if that is what they taught you."

"How much is the supplement for a single room?" her mother asked.

"Five pounds a night," Fiona said.

"Nine pounds a night," Barry said at exactly the same time. They looked at each other wildly. "It's . . . um . . . more for the men you see," poor Barry said in desperation.

"Why is that?" Fiona's father was suspicious.

"Something to do with the Italian character, really. They insist men have bigger rooms for all their clothes and things."

"Wouldn't you think women would have more clothes?" Fiona's mother was now suspicious. What kind of a peacock was her daughter involved with, needing a huge room for all his wardrobe?

"I know, that's what my mother was saying. . . . By the way, she's very much looking forward to meeting you, getting to know you."

"Why?" asked Fiona's mother.

Barry couldn't think why, so he said: "She's like that, she just loves people."

"Lucky for her," said Fiona's father.

❧

"WHAT'S THE ITALIAN for 'Good luck, Dad'?" Grania asked her father the night before the *viaggio*.

"In bocca al lupo." She repeated it. They sat in his study. He had all his maps and guidebook out. He would bring a small suitcase, which he would carry with him, containing all this. It didn't really matter, he said, if his clothes got lost, but this was what counted.

"Mam working tonight?" Grania said casually.

"I suppose so, love."

"And you'll have a suntan for the wedding?" She was determined to keep the mood cheerful.

"Yes, and you know we'd have it here for you, you know that."

"We'd prefer it in a pub really, Dad."

"I always thought you'd marry from here and I'd pay for it all."

"You're paying for a big cake and champagne, isn't that enough?"

"I hope so."

"It's plenty. And listen, are you nervous about this trip?"

"A little, in case it's not as good as we all promised, hoped, and

remembered even. The class went so well, I'd hate this to be an anticli-
max."

"It can't be, Dad, it will be great. I wish I were going in many ways."

"In many ways I wish you were too." And neither of them said a
word about the fact that Aidan's wife of twenty-five years was not going,
and according to herself had not been invited to go.

❧

JIMMY SULLIVAN HAD a driving job on the northside, so he drove Signora to the airport.

"You're miles too early," he said.

"I'm too excited. I couldn't stay at home, I want to be on my way."

"Will you go at all to see your husband's people in that village you
lived in?"

"No, no Jimmy, there won't be time."

"It's a pity to go all the way to Italy and not visit them though. The
class would let you off for a day or two."

"No, it's too far away, right at the far end of Italy on the island of
Sicily."

"So they won't hear you're there and take a poor view?"

"No, no they won't hear I'm there."

"Well, that's all right then, so long as there's no offense."

"No, nothing like that. And Suzi and I will tell you every detail when
we get back."

"God, the wedding was something else, wasn't it, Signora?"

"I did enjoy it, and I know everyone else did too."

"I'll be paying for it for the rest of my life."

"Nonsense, Jimmy, you loved it. You've only one daughter and it was
a real feast. People will talk about it for years."

"Well, they were days getting over their hangovers all right," he said,
brightening at the thought of his legendary hospitality. "I hope that Suzi
and Lou will get themselves out of that bed and make it to the airport."

"Oh, you know newlyweds," Signora said diplomatically.

"They were in that bed for many a month before they were newlyweds," Jimmy Sullivan said, brow darkening with disapproval. It always
annoyed him that Suzi was so utterly uncontrite about her bad behavior.

❧

WHEN SHE WAS alone at the airport, Signora found a seat and took out
the badges she had made. Each one had *Vista del Monte*—the Italian for
Mountainview—on it, and the person's name. Surely nobody could get
lost. Surely if there was a God, he would be delighted that all these
people were visiting the Holy City and he wouldn't let them get lost or
killed or into fights. Forty-two people including herself and Aidan
Dunne, just enough to fill the coach they had arranged to meet them. She
wondered who would be the first to arrive. Maybe Lorenzo? Could be
Aidan. He said he would help her distribute the badges.

But it was Constanza. "My roommate," Constanza said eagerly, and
pinned on her badge.

"You could easily have afforded the single room, Constanza," Signora
said, something that had not been mentioned before.

"Yes, but who would I have talked to . . . isn't that half the fun of a
holiday?"

Before she could answer, Signora saw the others arriving. A lot of
them had come on the airport bus. They came to collect their badges and
seemed pleased to see that they were from such an elegant-sounding
place.

"No one will know in Italy what kind of a dump Mountainview really
is," Lou said.

"Hey, Luigi, be fair, it's improved in leaps and bounds this year."
Aidan was referring to the rebuilding, the paint job, the new bicycle
sheds. Tony O'Brien had delivered all he had promised.

"Sorry, Aidan, I didn't realize you were in earshot." Lou grinned.
Aidan had been good company at the wedding. He had sung "La donna
è mobile" and knew all the words.

Brenda Brennan had come to the airport to wave them off. Signora
was very touched. "You're so good, everyone else has a normal family."

"No they don't." Brenda Brennan jerked her head toward where
Aidan was talking to Luigi. "He doesn't, for one thing. I asked his pill of
a wife why she wasn't going to Rome with the rest of you, and she
shrugged and said that she hadn't been asked, wouldn't push herself

where she wasn't wanted and wouldn't have enjoyed it anyway. So how's that for normal?"

"Poor Aidan." Signora was sympathetic.

Then the flight was called.

The sister of Guglielmo was waving like mad to everyone. For Olive, just going to the airport was a treat. "My brother is a bank manager, he's going to see the Pope," she said to strangers.

"Well, if he lays his hands on some of that money they'll be pleased with him," said a passerby. Bill just smiled, and he and Lizzie waved to Olive while they could still see her.

❧

"FORTY-TWO PEOPLE, we'll have to lose one of them," Aidan said as they counted the flock into the departure lounge.

"Aren't you optimistic! I keep thinking we'll lose all of them," Signora smiled.

"Still, the counting system should work." Aidan tried to sound more convinced than he felt. He had divided them into four groups of ten and appointed a leader of each. When they arrived anywhere or left anywhere, the leader had to report that all were present. It worked for children, but adults might resent it.

They didn't seem at all put out by it, in fact some of them positively welcomed it.

"Imagine, Lou is a leader," Suzi said in admiration to Signora.

"Well, a responsible married man like Luigi, who better?" Signora asked. The truth was, of course, that she and Aidan had chosen him because of his fierce scowl. Nobody in his team would be late if they were reporting to Luigi.

He marched them onto the plane as if he were taking them into war. "Can you raise your passports?" he asked them. Obediently they did. "Now, put them away very carefully. Zip them away, I won't want to see them unzipped until we get to Roma."

The announcements were made in Italian on the plane as well as in English. Signora had prepared all this with them, so it was familiar. When the air stewardess began to speak, the evening class all nodded at each other, pleased to hear familiar words and phrases. The girl pointed out the emergency doors on the right and the left, the class repeated them all happily, *destra, sinistra*. Even though they had heard it all in English already.

When it was over and she said *grazie*, all the evening class shouted *prego* and Aidan's eyes met Signora's. It was really happening. They were going to Rome.

Signora was seated beside Laddy. Everything was new and exciting to him, from the safety belt to the meal with its little portions of food.

"Will the Garaldis be at the airport?" he asked eagerly.

"No, Lorenzo. The first few days we get to know Roma . . . we do all the tours we talked about, remember?"

"Yes, but suppose they want me straight away?" His big face was worried.

"They know you're coming. I've written to them, they know we'll be in touch on Thursday."

"*Giovedì*," he said.

"*Bene, Lorenzo, giovedì.*"

"Aren't you going to eat your dessert, Signora?"

"No, Lorenzo. Please have it."

"It's just that I'd hate to waste it."

Signora said she would have a little sleep now. She closed her eyes. Please may it go well. May they all find magic there. May the Garaldis remember Lorenzo and be nice to him. She had put her heart into the letter and was distressed that there had been no reply.

THE BUS WAS there. "*Dov'è l'autobus?*" Bill asked, to show he remembered the phrase.

"It's here in front of us," Lizzie said.

"I know, but I wanted to talk about it," Bill explained.

"Don't the girls all have enormous bosoms and bums," Fiona whispered admiringly to Barry as she looked around her.

"I think it's rather nice actually," Barry said defensively. This was his Italy, he was the expert on the place since his visit for the World Cup, he didn't want any aspersions cast.

"No, I think it's great," Fiona explained. "It's just that I'd love Brigid

Dunne to see them . . . the way she's always bellyaching about herself."

"You could tell her father to tell her, I suppose." Barry was doubtful of the suitability of this.

"Of course I couldn't, she'd know I was talking about her. She says the hotel isn't going to be any great shakes. She says we're not to be disappointed."

"I won't be disappointed," Barry said, putting his arm around Fiona.

"Neither will I. I was only in a hotel once before, in Majorca. And it was so noisy that none of us could sleep at all, so we all got up and went back to the beach."

"I suppose they had to keep the prices down." Barry was terrified that there would be any criticism.

"I know it's dead cheap, and Brigid was telling me that some half-cracked one came in wanting to know where we were all staying, so the word must be out that we got good value."

"Did she want to join the group?"

"Brigid said she couldn't join, that we had been booked at this rate for ages. But she just insisted on knowing the name of the hotel."

"Well, now." Barry was pleased as they stepped out into the sunshine and the head counting began. *Uno, due, tre.* The team leaders were very serious about their roles for Signora.

"Did you ever stay in a hotel, Fran?" Kathy asked as the bus sped through the traffic, which seemed to be full of very impatient drivers.

"Twice, ages ago." Fran was vague.

But Kathy probed. "You never told me."

"It was in Cork, with Ken if you must know."

"Oho, when you said you were staying with a school friend?"

"Yes, I didn't want them thinking I was going to produce yet another child for them to look after." Fran nudged her good-naturedly.

"You'd be far too old for that sort of thing surely?"

"Listen here to me, if I get together with Ken again for a bit in America, now that you've won me a ticket there . . . I may well produce a little sister or brother for you to take home with us."

"Or maybe even stay there with?" Kathy said.

"It's a return ticket, remember?"

"They're not born overnight, remember," Kathy said.

The sisters laughed and pointed out sights to each other as the bus pulled in at a building in the Via Giolitti.

❧

SIGNORA WAS ON her feet and an excited conversation took place.

"She's telling him that we must be left at the hotel itself, not here at the terminus," Suzi explained.

"How do you know, you're not even in the evening class?" Lou was outraged.

"Oh if you work as a waitress you get to understand everything sooner or later." Suzi dismissed her skill. Then looking at Lou's face she added, "Anyway, you're always speaking bits of it at home so I pick up words here and there." That seemed entirely more suitable.

And Suzi was indeed right. The bus lurched off again and dropped them at the Albergo Francobollo.

"The Stamp Hotel," Bill translated for them. "Should be easy to remember." *"Vorrei un francobollo per l'Irlanda,"* they all chorused aloud, and Signora gave them a broad smile.

She had got them to Rome without any disaster, the hotel had their booking, and the class were all in high good spirits. Her anxiety was not necessary. Soon she would relax and enjoy being back in Italy again, its colors and sounds and excitement. She began to breathe more easily.

The Albergo Francobollo was not one of the smarter hotels in Rome, but its welcome was gigantic. Signor and Signora Buona Sera were full of admiration and praise over how well they all spoke Italian.

"Bene, bene benissimo," they cried as they ran up and down the stairs to the rooms.

"Are we really saying 'Good evening Mr. Good Evening'?" Fiona asked Barry.

"Yes, but look at the names at home like Ramsbottom, and we've even a customer in the supermarket called O'Looney."

"But we don't have people called Miss Goodmorning and Mr. Goodnight," Fiona insisted.

"We do have a place in Ireland called Effin, and they talk about the Effin football team and the Effin choir will sing at eleven o'clock Mass . . . what would outsiders make of that?" Barry asked.

"I love you, Barry," Fiona said suddenly. They had just arrived at their bedroom and Mrs. Good Evening heard the remark.

"Love. Very, very good," she said, and ran down the stairs to settle more people in their rooms.

❧

CONNIE HUNG HER clothes up carefully on her side of the small cupboard. Out the window she could see the roofs and windows of tall houses in the little streets that led off the Piazza dei Cinquecento. Connie washed at the small handbasin in the room. It had been years since she had stayed in a hotel without its own bathroom. But it had also been years since she had gone on a trip with such an easy heart. She did not feel superior to these people because she had more money. She wasn't even remotely tempted to hire a car, which she could have done easily, or to treat them to a meal in a five-star restaurant. She was eager to join in the plans that had been made in such detail by Signora and Aidan Dunne. Like every other member of the evening class, Connie sensed that their friendship was deeper than a merely professional one. Nobody had been surprised when Aidan's wife had not joined the group.

"*Signor Dunne, telefono,*" Signora Buona Sera called up the stairs.

Aidan had been advising Laddy not to suggest *immediately* that he should clean the brasses on the door, maybe they should wait until they had been there for a few days.

"Would that be your Italian friends?" Laddy asked eagerly.

"No, Lorenzo, I have no Italian friends."

"But you were here before."

"A quarter of a century ago, no one who would remember me."

"I have friends here," Laddy said proudly. "And Bartolomeo has people he met during the World Cup."

"That's great," Aidan said. "I'd better go and see who it is that *does* want me."

"Dad?"

"Brigid? Is everything all right?"

"Sure. You all got there then?"

"Absolutely, all in one piece. It's a gorgeous evening, we're going to walk down to the Piazza Navona and have a drink."

"Great, I'm sure it'll be terrific."

"Yes. Brigid, is anything . . . you know . . . ?"

"It's probably stupid, Dad, but a kind of loopy woman came in twice wanting to know what hotel you're all staying at. It might be nothing but I didn't like the feel of her, I thought she was off her rocker."

"Did she say why?"

"She said that it was a simple question and could I answer her and give her the name of the hotel or would she have to speak to my boss."

"And what did you do?"

"Well, Dad, I did think she was out of a funny farm, so I said no. I said my father was out there and if she wanted a message passed to anyone I'd get in touch."

"Well, that's it then."

"No, it's not. She went to the boss and said it was very urgent she contact a Mr. Dunne with the Mountainview party, and he gave the hotel name to her and gave me a ticking off."

"She must know me if she knew my name."

"No, I saw her reading my name Brigid Dunne from my badge. Look, I suppose I just wanted to say . . ."

"Say what, Brigid?"

"That she's sort of crazy and you should look out."

"Thank you very much my dear, dear Brigid," he said, and realized that it had been a long time since he had called her that.

❧

IT WAS A warm evening as they set out to walk through Rome.

They passed near Santa Maria Maggiore, but not near enough to stop and go in.

"Tonight is just a social night . . . we all have a drink in the beautiful square. Tomorrow we look at culture and religion for those who want to, and for those who want to sit and sip coffee they can do that too." Signora was anxious to remind them that they were not going to be herded, but she saw in their eyes that they wanted a little looking-after still. "What do you think we might say when we see the wonderful square with all the fountains and statues in the Piazza Navona?" she asked, looking around.

And there on the side of the street they all shouted out, *"In questa piazza ci sono molti belli edicifi!"*

"*Benissimo,*" said Signora. "*Avanti,* let's go and find them."

They sat at peace, forty-two of them, and watched the night fall on Rome.

Signora was beside Aidan. "No problems with the phone call?" she asked.

"No, no, just Brigid ringing to know if the hotel was all right for us. I told her it was wonderful."

"She was very helpful over it all, she really wanted it to be a success for you, for all of us."

"And it will." They sipped their coffees. Some of the group had a beer, others a *grappa*. Signora had said there were tourist prices here and she advised only one drink for the atmosphere. They had to keep *something* to spend when they got to Firenze and Siena. They smiled almost unbelieving when she mentioned the names. They were here in Italy to begin the *viaggio*. It wasn't just talk anymore in a classroom on a wet Tuesday and Thursday.

"Yes, it will be a success, Aidan," Signora said.

"Brigid said something else too. I didn't want to bother you with it, but some kind of madwoman came into the agency and wanted to know where we were all staying. Brigid thought she was someone who might cause trouble."

Signora shrugged. "We've got this lot here, we'll cope with whatever else turns up, don't you think?"

In small groups the evening class were posing each other by the Fountain of the Four Rivers.

He reached out his hand and took hers. "We can cope with anything," he said.

᷍᷍

"YOUR FRIEND ARRIVED, Signor Dunne," said Signora Buona Sera.

"Friend?"

"The lady from Irlanda. She just wanted to check the hotel and that all of you were staying here."

"Did she leave her name?" Aidan asked.

"No name, just interested to know if everyone was staying here. I said you were going on a tour tomorrow morning in the bus. That's right, yes?"

"That's right," Aidan said.

"Did she look like a madwoman?" he asked casually.

"Mad, Signor Dunne?"

"*Pazza?*" Signora explained.

"No, no, not at all *pazza.*" Signora Buona Sera seemed offended that a madwoman might be assumed to have called at the Hotel Francobollo.

"Well then," Aidan said.

"Well then." Signora smiled back at him.

The younger people would have smiled if they had known how much it had meant to them to sit there with their hands in each other's as the stars came out over the Piazza Navona.

❧

THE BUS TOUR was to give them the feel of Rome, Signora said, then they could all go back at their leisure to see particular places. Not everyone wanted to spend hours in the Vatican Museum.

Signora said that since they served cheese at breakfast, people often made themselves a little sandwich to eat later on in the day. And then there would be a big dinner tonight in the restaurant not far from the hotel. Somewhere they could all walk home from. Again nobody *had* to come, she said. But she knew that everyone would.

There was no mention of the woman who had called to look for them. Signora and Aidan Dunne were too busy discussing the bus route with the driver to give it any thought.

Would there be time to get out and throw a coin into the famous Trevi Fountain? Was there room for the bus to park near the Bocca della Verità? The party would enjoy putting their hands into the mouth of the great weatherbeaten face of stone that was meant to bite the fingers off liars. Would the driver leave them at the top of the Spanish Steps to walk down or at the bottom to walk up? They hadn't time to think of the woman who was looking for them. Whoever she might be.

❦

AND WHEN THEY came back exhausted from the tour, everyone had two hours rest before they assembled for dinner. Signora walked around to the restaurant, leaving Connie asleep in their bedroom. She wanted to check about the menu and to arrange that there would be no gray areas. Only a fixed menu was to be offered.

On the door she saw a notice draped in black crepe *CHIUSO: morte in famiglia.* Signora fumed with rage. Why couldn't the family member have died at some other time? Why did he or she have to die just as forty-two Irish people were coming to have supper? Now she had less than an hour to find somewhere else. Signora could feel no sympathy for the family tragedy, only fury. And why had they not telephoned the hotel as she had asked them to do if there was any hitch in arrangements?

She walked up and down the streets around Termini. Small hotels, cheap accommodation suitable for the people who got off trains at the huge station. But no jolly restaurant like the one she had planned. Biting her lip, she went toward a place with the name Catania. It must be Sicilian. Was this a good omen? Could she throw herself on their mercy and explain that in an hour and a half, forty-two Irish people were expecting a huge inexpensive meal? She could but try.

"Buona sera," she said.

The square young man with dark hair looked up. *"Signora?"* he said. Then he looked at her again in disbelief. *"Signora?"* he said again, his face working. *"Non è possibile, Signora,"* he said, coming toward her with hands stretched out. It was Alfredo, the eldest son of Mario and Gabriella. She had walked into his restaurant by accident. He kissed her on both cheeks. *"È un miracolo,"* he said, and pulled out a chair.

Signora sat down, she felt a great dizziness come over her, and she gripped the table in case she fell.

"Stock Ottanto Quatro," he said, and poured her a great glass of the strong sweet Italian brandy.

"No, grazie . . ." He held it to her mouth and she sipped. "Is this your restaurant, Alfredo?" she asked.

"No, no, Signora, I work here, I work here to make money . . ."

"But your own hotel. Your mother's hotel. Why do you not work there?"

"My mother is dead, Signora. She died six months ago. Her brothers, my uncles, they try to interfere, to make decisions . . . they know nothing. There is nothing for us to do. Enrico is there, but he is still a child, my brother in America will not come home. I came here to Rome to learn more."

"Your mother dead? Poor Gabriella. What happened to her?"

"It was cancer, very, very quick. She went to the doctor only a month after my father was killed."

"I am so sorry," Signora said. "I can't tell you how sorry I am." And suddenly it was all too much for her. Gabriella to die now instead of years ago, the hot brandy in her throat, no place for dinner tonight, Mario in his grave near Annunziata. She cried and cried while Mario's son stroked her head.

❧

IN HER BEDROOM Connie lay on her bed, each foot wrapped in a facecloth wrung through in cold water. Why had she not brought some foot balm with her or those soft leather walking shoes that were like gloves? She had not wanted to unpack a sponge bag full of luxury cosmetics in front of the unworldly Signora, that was probably it. But who would have known that her soft shoes would have cost what none of her companions would have been able to earn in three weeks? She should have taken them, she was paying the penalty now. Tomorrow she might slip away to the Via Veneto and buy herself some beautiful Italian shoes as a treat. Nobody would notice, and if they did, what the hell? These weren't people obsessed by wealth and differences in standards of living. Not everyone thought about the whole business of wealth. They weren't all like Harry Kane.

How strange to be able to think about him without emotion. He would be out of jail by the end of the year. She had heard from old Mr. Murphy that he intended to go to England. Some friends would look after him. Would Siobhan Casey go with him? She had inquired almost as you ask after strangers who have no meaning to you, or characters in a television series. Oh no, hadn't she heard, there had been a definite cooling of relationships there. He had refused to see Miss Casey when she went to see him in prison. He blamed her for everything that had happened, apparently.

It had given Connie Kane no huge pleasure to hear this. In a way it might have been easier to think of him in a new life with a woman he had been involved with forever. She wondered had they ever come here together, the two of them, Siobhan and Harry. And had they felt touched by this beautiful city the way everyone did, whether or not they were in love. It was something she would never know now, and it was of no importance really.

She heard a gentle knock at the door. Signora must be back already. But no, it was the small bustling Signora Buona Sera. "A letter for you," she said. And she handed her an envelope.

It was written on a plain postcard. It said: *You could easily die in the Roman traffic and you would not be missed.*

⁓

THE LEADERS WERE counting heads to go to dinner. Everyone was present and correct except for three. Connie and Laddy and Signora. They assumed Connie and Signora were together and they would be there any moment.

But where was Laddy? Aidan had not been in the room they shared, he had been busy getting his notes together for the tour the next day to the Forum and the Coliseum. Perhaps Laddy had fallen asleep. Aidan ran lightly up the stairs, but he was not to be found.

At that moment Signora arrived pale-faced and with the news that the venue had been changed but the price was the same. She had managed to secure a booking at the Catania. She looked stressed and worried. Aidan didn't want to tell her about the disappearances. At that moment Connie arrived down the stairs, full of apologies. She, too, looked pale and worried. Aidan wondered was it all too much for these women, the heat, the noise, the excitement. But then he realized he was being fanciful. It was his job to find Laddy. He would take the address of the restaurant and join them later. Signora gave him a card; her hand was shaking.

"All right, Nora?"

"Fine, Aidan," she lied to him.

THEY WERE GONE chattering down the street, and Aidan began the hunt
for Laddy. Signor Buona Sera knew Signor Lorenzo, he had offered to
clean windows with him. A very nice gentleman, he worked in a hotel in
Irlanda too. He had been pleased to hear that there was a visitor for him.

"A visitor?"

"Well, somebody had come and left a letter for one of the Irish party.
His wife had mentioned it. Signor Lorenzo had said this must be the
message he was waiting for and he was very happy."

"But was it for him? *Did* he get a message?"

"No, Signor Dunne, my wife she told him she had given the letter to
one of the ladies but Signor Laddy said it was a mistake, it was for him.
There was no problem, he said, he knew the address, he would go
there."

"God Almighty," Aidan Dunne said. "I left him for twenty bloody
minutes to do my notes and he thinks that bloody family have sent for
him. Oh Laddy, I'll swing for you yet, I really will."

First he had to go to the restaurant where they were all sitting down
and then standing up again to take pictures of the banner saying *Benve-
nuto agli Irlandesi.*

"I need the Garaldis' address," he hissed to Signora.

"No. He's never gone there?"

"So it would appear."

Signora looked up at him anxiously. "I'd better go."

"No, let me. You stay here and look after the dinner."

"I'll go, Aidan. I can speak the language, I've written to them."

"Let's both go," he suggested.

"Who will we put in charge? Constanza?"

"No, there's something upsetting her. Let's see. Francesca and Luigi
between them."

The word was out. Signora and Mr. Dunne had gone to hunt for
Lorenzo and two new people were in command, Francesca and Luigi.

"Why those?" someone muttered.

"Because we were the nearest," Fran said, a peacemaker.

"And the best," said Luigi, a man who liked to win.

❧

THEY GOT A taxi and they arrived at the house. "It's even smarter than I thought," Signora whispered.

"He never got into a place like this." Aidan looked amazed at the big marble entrance hall and the courtyard beyond.

"Vorrei parlare con la famiglia Garaldi?" Signora spoke with a confidence she didn't feel to the splendid-looking uniformed commissionaire. He asked her name and business and Aidan marveled as she told him and stressed the importance of it. The man in the gray and scarlet went to a phone and spoke into it urgently. It seemed to take forever.

"I hope they're managing back in the restaurant," Signora said.

"Of course they are. Weren't you great to find a place so quickly? They seem very welcoming."

"Yes, it was extraordinary." She seemed miles away.

"But everyone's been so nice everywhere, it's not really extraordinary," Aidan said.

"No. The waiter, I knew his father. Can you believe that?"

"Was that in Sicily?"

"Yes."

"And did you know him?"

"From the day he was born . . . I saw him going to the church to be baptized."

The commissionaire returned. "Signor Garaldi says he is very confused, he wants to speak to you personally."

"We must go in, I can't explain things on the telephone," Signora said. Aidan understood and marveled at her courage. He felt a little confused by this rediscovering of a Sicilian past.

Soon they were walking through a courtyard and up another wide staircase to a fountain and some large doors. These were seriously wealthy people. Had Laddy really penetrated in here?

They were shown into an entrance hall where a small, angry man in a brocade jacket seemed to hurtle out of a room and demand an explanation. Behind him came his wife trying to placate him, and inside, wretched and totally at a loss, was poor Laddy sitting on a piano stool.

His face lit up when he saw them. "Signora," he called. "Mr. Dunne.

Now you can tell them everything. You'll never believe it but I lost all my Italian. I could only tell them the days and the seasons and order the dish of the day. It's been terrible."

"*Sta calma, Lorenzo,*" Signora said.

"They want to know am I O'Donoghue, they keep writing it down for me." He had never looked so anxious and disturbed.

"Please Laddy, I am O'Donoghue, that's my name, that's why they thought it was you. That was what I put on my letter."

"You're not O'Donoghue," Laddy cried. "You're Signora."

Aidan put his arm around Laddy's shaking shoulders and let Signora begin. The explanation, and he could understand most of it, was clear and unflustered. She told of the man who had found their money in Ireland a year ago, a man who had worked hard as a hotel porter and had believed their kind words of gratitude to be an invitation to come to Italy. She described the efforts he had made to learn Italian. She introduced herself and Aidan as people who ran an evening class and how worried they had been that due to some misunderstanding their friend Lorenzo had believed there was a message for him to call. They would all go now, but perhaps out of the kindness of his heart Signor Garaldi and his family might make some affectionate gesture to show they remembered his kindness, and indeed spectacular honesty, in returning a wad of notes to them, money that many a man in many a city including Dublin might not have felt obligated to return.

Aidan stood there, feeling Laddy's shaking shoulder and wondering about the strange turnings life took. Suppose he had become principal of Mountainview? That's what he had wanted so much, not long ago. Now he realized how much he would have hated it, how far better a choice was Tony O'Brien, a man, not evil incarnate as he had once believed, but a genuine achiever, heartbroken in his battle against nicotine and shortly to become Aidan's son-in-law. Aidan would never have notes for a lecture in the Forum stuck in his pocket, he would never be standing here in this sumptuous Roman town house reassuring a nervous hotel porter and looking with pride and admiration at this strange woman who had taken up so much of his life. She had brought clarity and understanding to the face that had so recently been creased with anger and confusion.

"Lorenzo," Signor Garaldi said, and approached Laddy, who sat terrified at his approach. *"Lorenzo mio amico."* He kissed him on both cheeks.

Laddy didn't harbor a grudge long. "Signor Garaldi," he said and grabbed him by the shoulders. *"Mio amico."*

There were quick-fire explanations and the rest of the family realized what had happened. Wine was brought, and little Italian biscuits.

Laddy was beaming from ear to ear now. *"Giovedì,"* he kept saying happily.

"Why does he say that?" Signor Garaldi was raising his glass and toasting next Thursday as well, but he wanted to know why.

"I told him that we would be in touch with you then, I wanted to prevent him from coming here on his own. I put that in my letter, that we might call by the house for ten minutes on Thursday. Did you not get it?"

The little man looked ashamed. "I have to tell you I get so many begging letters I thought it was something like that, if he came some money would have been given. You have to forgive me but I didn't read it properly. Now I am so ashamed."

"No, please, but do you think he could come on Thursday? He is so eager, and maybe I could take his photograph with you and he could show it to people afterwards."

Signor Garaldi and his wife exchanged glances. "Why don't you all come here on Thursday, for a drink and a celebration."

"There are forty-two of us," Signora said.

"These houses were built for gatherings like that," he said with a little bow.

A car was called and they were soon crossing Rome to the Catania, in a street where a car like the Garaldis' had hardly ever driven before. Signora and Aidan looked at each other, as proud as parents who had rescued a child from an awkward situation.

"I wish my sister could see me now," Laddy said suddenly.

"Would she have been pleased?" Signora was gentle.

"Well, she knew it would happen. We went to a fortune-teller you see, and he said she would be married and have a child, and die young, and that I would be great at sport and I would travel across the sea. So it wouldn't have been a surprise or anything but it's a pity she didn't live to see it."

"It is indeed, but maybe she sees now." Aidan wanted to be reassuring.

"I'm not at all sure that there are people in heaven, you know, Mr. Dunne," said Laddy as they purred through Rome in the chauffeur-driven car.

"Aren't you Laddy? I'm getting more sure of it every day," said Aidan.

෨෨

AT THE CATANIA everyone was singing "Low Lie the Fields of Athenry." The waiters stood in an admiring group and clapped mightily when it was over. Any other guests brave enough to dine in the Catania that night had been absorbed into the group, and as the threesome came in there was a huge shout of welcome.

Alfredo ran to get the soup.

"*Brodo*," Laddy said.

"We'll go straight to the main course if you like," Aidan said.

"Excuse me, Mr. Dunne. I'm in charge until relieved of it, and I say that Lorenzo is to have his *brodo*." Luigi looked fiercer than he had ever looked. Aidan quailed and said, of course, it had been a mistake. "That's all right, then," Luigi had said generously.

Fran explained to Signora that one of the younger waiters kept asking young Kathy to go out with him later, and Fran was worried. Could Signora say that they all had to return together when the night was over.

"Certainly, Francesca," Signora said. Wasn't it amazing, none of them asked what had happened to Laddy, they had just assumed that she and Aidan would rescue him in Rome.

"Lorenzo has had us all invited to a party on Thursday," she said. "In a magnificent house."

"*Giovedì*," Laddy said, in case anyone should mistake the day. They seemed to take that for granted too. Signora finished her soup quickly. She looked around for Constanza and saw her, not animated as she normally was, but looking absently into the distance. Something had happened, but she was such a private person and would not say what it was. Signora was that kind of person herself, she would not make any inquiries.

Alfredo said that there was going to be a surprise for the Irlande. There was going to be a cake in the Irish colors, they had arranged it because all the people had been so happy and they wanted to make it a memory for them. They'd known the Irish colors since the World Cup.

"I can't thank you enough, Alfredo, for making the evening so special for us."

"You can, Signora, can you come and talk with me tomorrow? Please?"

"Not tomorrow, Alfredo, Signor Dunne is giving his talk about the Forum."

"You can hear Signor Dunne any time. I have only a few days to talk to you. Please, Signora, I am begging."

"Perhaps he'll understand." Signora looked over at Aidan. She hated letting him down, she knew how much he had put into this lecture. He was determined that everyone would see Rome as it was when chariots raced through it. But the boy did look very anxious, as if he had something to tell her. For the sake of the past and of everyone, she must listen.

❧

SIGNORA MANAGED TO get Caterina back to the hotel and out of the clutches of the waiter very easily, she just told Alfredo that the boy was to be called off immediately. So the soulful Roman eyes had beseeched Caterina for another evening, and he had given her a red rose and a kiss on the hand.

The mystery of the message had not been sorted out by Connie. Signora Buona Sera said she had delivered it to Signora Kane. Neither she nor her husband knew whether it was a man or a woman who had left it. It would always be a mystery, Signora Buona Sera said. But during the night Connie Kane lay awake and worried. She wondered why some things should always be mysterious. She longed to tell Signora but didn't want to intrude on the quiet woman who lived such a private life.

❧

"No, OF COURSE, if you have business of your own. Business to do with Sicily," Aidan said next day.

"I am so sorry, Aidan, I was looking forward to it."

"Yes." He turned away shortly so she wouldn't see the naked hurt and disappointment in his face, but it was too late. Signora had seen it.

"We don't have to go to this lecture," Lou said, pulling Suzi back to bed.

"I want to go." She struggled to get up.

"Latin, Roman gods and old temples . . . of course you don't."

"Mr. Dunne's been getting it ready for weeks, and anyway Signora'd like us to be there."

"She's not going to be there herself." Lou spoke knowledgeably.

"How on earth do you know that?"

"I heard her telling him last night," Lou said. "He was sour as a lemon."

"That's not like her."

"Well now we don't have to go," Lou said, snuggling back into the bed.

"No, now it's more important that we go to support him." Suzi was out of bed and into her dressing gown before he could protest. She was halfway down the corridor to the bathroom before he could reach out and catch her.

※

LIZZIE AND BILL were making their sandwiches carefully. "Isn't it a great idea?" Bill said eagerly, hoping that it was something that might be extended to their own life at home. The idea of saving money by any means at all was something that he prayed would catch on in Lizzie's mind. She had been very good on this visit and not even looked at a shoe shop. She had noted the cost of Italian ice cream in lire, translated it, and said it wasn't a good idea.

"Oh, Bill, don't be an idiot. If we were to buy ham and eggs and great chunks of bread like this to make sandwiches it would be dearer than having a bowl of soup in a pub like we do already."

"Maybe."

"But when you're an international banker out here, then we might consider it. Will we be living in a hotel do you think, or having our own villa?"

"A villa I imagine," Bill said glumly. It all seemed so unlikely and far from reality.

"Have you made any inquiries yet?"

"About villas?" Bill looked at her wildly.

"No, about opportunities in banking, remember that's why we are learning Italian." Lizzie was prim.

"It *was* in the first place," Bill admitted. "But now I'm only learning it because I enjoy it."

"Are you trying to tell me we'll never be rich?" Lizzie's huge, beautiful eyes were troubled.

"No, no, I'm not trying to tell you that. We *will* be rich. This very day I'll go into banks and ask relevant words. Believe me, I will."

"I believe you. Now I have all these done and wrapped, we can eat them in the Forum after the lecture, and we might send our postcards too."

"This time you'll be able to send one to your dad," Bill Burke said, always seeing the silver lining.

"You got on well with him, didn't you?"

They had a brief visit to Galway and a reasonably successful attempt to reunite Lizzie's parents. At least they were speaking to each other and on visiting terms now.

"Yes I liked him, he was very comical." Bill thought this was a masterly way to describe a man who had almost crushed Bill's whole hand in his, and who had borrowed a ten-pound note from him within minutes of their meeting.

"It's *such* a relief that you like my family," Lizzie said.

"And you mine," Bill agreed.

His own parents were warming more to Lizzie's ways. She wore longer skirts and higher necklines. She asked questions to his father about cutting bacon and the difference between smoked and green bacon. She played noughts and crosses endlessly with Olive, letting her win about half the time, which gave the games an air of frenzied excitement. The wedding wouldn't be nearly as fraught as Bill had once thought it would be.

"Let's go hear about Vestal Virgins," he said, smiling from ear to ear.

"What?"

"Lizzie! Didn't you read your notes? Mr. Dunne gave us one page, he said we'd all be able to remember that much."

"Give it to me quick," said Lizzie.

Aidan Dunne had drawn a little map highlighting the places they would visit and that he would describe. She read it speedily and returned it.

"Do you think he's in bed with Signora?" she asked, eyes shining.

"If so, Lorenzo and Constanza will be feeling a bit in the way," said Bill.

CONSTANZA AND SIGNORA had dressed and were about to come down to breakfast. There was an air that something was about to be said.

"Constanza?"

"*Sì, Signora?*"

"Could I ask you to take notes when Aidan is speaking today? I can't go, and I'm upset and, well, I think he's upset. He went to such trouble, such great trouble." Signora's face looked very sad.

"And you have to miss it?"

"Yes I do."

"I'm sure he'll understand but I will pay great attention, and yes of course I'll tell you everything." There was a pause, then Connie spoke again. "Oh, and Signora?"

"*Sì, Constanza?*"

"It's just that . . . well, did you ever hear anyone in our group saying anything bad about me, resentful, or possibly caught up in losing money to my husband or anything?"

"No, never. I never heard anyone saying anything about you. Why do you ask?"

"Someone left me a rather horrible note. It's probably a joke, but it upset me."

"What did it say? Please tell me."

Connie unfolded it and showed it to the other woman. Signora's eyes filled with tears. "When did this happen?"

"It was left at the desk yesterday evening before we went out. Nobody knows who left it. I have asked but the Buona Seras don't know."

"It can't be anyone in this group, Constanza, I tell you that."

"But who else knows we are in Rome?"

Signora remembered something. "Aidan said there was a madwoman back in Dublin inquiring what hotel we were all staying in. Could that be it? Someone who followed us here?"

"That's hard to believe, it's very far-fetched."

"But it's even harder to believe that it's any member of our group," Signora said.

"Why me? Now? And in Rome?"

"Is there anyone with a grievance, do you think?"

"Hundreds because of what Harry did, but he's locked up in jail."

"Not someone mad, disturbed possibly?"

"Not that I know." Connie shook herself deliberately. She must spend no time speculating and worrying Signora as well. "I'll just walk well away from the traffic side of things and be watchful. And, Signora, I'll take notes. I promise you, it will be just as good as being there."

◈

"ALFREDO, THIS HAD better be important. You have no idea how much I have upset somebody by missing a lecture."

"There are many lectures, Signora."

"This one was special. A great deal of trouble had been taken. Anyway?"

He made them coffee and he sat down beside her. "Signora, I have a very big favor to ask of you."

She looked at him, anguished. He was going to ask her for money. He could not know that she had nothing. Literally nothing. When she got back to Dublin, she would be penniless. She would have to ask the Sullivans to let her live free in their house until September, when payment would start again in the school. Every last coin she had, had been changed into lire so that she could pay her way on this *viaggio*. How could this boy from his simple village and working as a waiter in a shabby restaurant in Rome know this? He must see her as responsible for forty people, a person of importance. Power even.

"It may not be easy. There's a lot you do not know," she began.

"I know everything, Signora. I know my father loved you, and that you loved him. That you sat in that window sewing while we all grew up. I know that you behaved so well to my mother and that even though you didn't want to go, when she and my uncles said it was time to leave, you left."

"You know all this?" Her voice was a whisper.

"Yes, we all knew."

"For how long?"

"As long as I remember."

"It's so hard to believe. I thought . . . well it doesn't matter what I thought . . ."

"And we were all so sad when you went away."

She lifted her face and smiled at him. "You were? Truly?"

"Yes, all of us. You helped us all. We know."

"How do you know?"

"Because my father did things he would not have done otherwise, Maria's wedding, the shop in Annunziata, my brother going to America . . . everything. It was all you."

"No, not all. He loved you, he wanted the best. Sometimes we talked. That was all."

"We wanted to find you when Mama died. We wanted to write and tell you. But we didn't even know your name."

"That was good of you."

"And now, now God sends you into this restaurant. It was God who sent you, I really believe that." She was silent. "And now I can ask you the great, great favor." She held tightly onto the table. *Why* had she no money. Most women of her age had some money, even a little. She had been so uncaring about possessions. If there was anything she could sell for this boy, who must be very desperate to ask her . . .

"The favor, Signora . . ."

"Yes, Alfredo."

"You know what it is?"

"Ask me, Alfredo, and if I can I will."

"We want you to come back. We want you to come home, Signora. Home where you belong."

CONSTANZA DIDN'T EAT breakfast, she went off to the shops. She bought the soft shoes she yearned for, she got a long silk scarf for Signora and cut off the designer label in case Elisabetta would recognize the name and exclaim at how much it must have cost. And then she bought what she had set out to buy and went back to join the trip to the Forum.

THEY ALL LOVED the lecture. Luigi said you could nearly see the poor Christians being led into the Coliseum. Mr. Dunne said that he was only a crusty old Latin teacher and he promised he wouldn't keep them long, but when it was over they clapped and wanted more. His smile was surprised. He answered all their questions, and occasionally looked at Constanza, who seemed to be waving a camera near him all the time but never took a picture.

THEY SEPARATED FOR lunch to eat their sandwiches in little groups. Connie Kane watched Aidan Dunne. He had no sandwiches with him, he just walked to a wall and sat there looking absently out into the distance before him. He had told everyone the route back to the hotel. He made sure that Laddy was in the hands of Bartolomeo and his funny little girlfriend, Fiona. Then he just sat there, sad that the person he had prepared the lecture for had not turned up.

Connie wondered whether to join him or not. But she didn't think there was anything she could say that might help. So she walked to a restaurant and ordered herself grilled fish and wine. It was good to be able to do so easily. But she barely tasted the food as she wondered who could have come from Dublin to frighten her. Could Harry have sent someone? It was too alarming to think about. It would be preposterous to try to explain it to the Italian police, and difficult to get any detectives in Ireland to take her seriously either. An anonymous letter in a hotel in

Rome? It was impossible to take seriously. But she walked very close to the walls and shops as she returned to the hotel.

And she inquired nervously at the desk if there had been any more messages.

"No, Signora Kane, nothing at all."

❧

BARRY AND FIONA were going to the pub where Barry had met all the wonderful Italians during the World Cup. He had pictures taken that summer, flags and bunting and Jack Charlton hats.

"Have you written and told them we're coming?" Fiona asked.

"No, it's not that kind of scene, you just turn up and they're all there."

"Every night?"

"No, but you know . . . most nights."

"But suppose they came looking for you in Dublin, you mightn't be in the pub the night they came. Don't you have any names and addresses?"

"Names and addresses aren't important in something like this," Barry said.

Fiona hoped he was right. He had set so much store about meeting them all and living through those glory days again. He would be very disappointed if it turned out that nobody ever gathered there anymore. Or worse, if they had forgotten him.

❧

THAT WAS THE evening that everyone was at leisure. If things had been different, Connie might have gone window-shopping with Fran and Kathy and had coffee at an outdoor cafe. But Connie was afraid to go out at night in case somebody really was waiting to push her in front of the cars that sped up and down the Roman streets.

If things had been different, Signora and Aidan would have had supper together and planned the visit to the Vatican the next day. But he was hurt and lonely, and she had to be somewhere quiet until she could think over the turbulent proposal that had been made to her.

They wanted her to go back and help in the hotel, bring them English-speaking visitors, be part of the life she had looked on for so long as an outsider. It would make sense of all those years she had watched and waited. It would be a future for her now as well as a past. Alfredo had begged her to come back. Even for a visit first so that she could see how things were. She would realize all that she could contribute and know how much people had admired her. So Signora sat alone in a cafe thinking about what it would be like.

And a few streets away Aidan Dunne sat and tried to think about all the good things that had come out of this trip. He had managed to create a class that not only had stayed together for the year but had traveled in a block to Rome at the end of it. These people would never have done that without him. He had shared his love of Italy with them, nobody was bored at his lecture today. He had done all he had set out to do. It had, in fact, been a year of triumph. But of course he had to listen to the other voice, the voice that said it was all Nora's doing. It was she who had created the real enthusiasm, with her silly games and her boxes pretending to be hospitals and railway stations and restaurants. It was Nora who had called them these fancy names and believed that one day they would go on a *viaggio*. And now that she was back here in Italy, its magic had worked too strongly for her.

She had to talk business, she told him. What business could she have with a waiter from Sicily, even if she *had* known him as a child? He ordered a third beer without even noticing. He looked out at the crowds walking around on the hot Roman night. He had never felt so lonely in his life.

❧

KATHY AND FRAN said they were going for a walk, they had planned a route and it would end up in the Piazza Navona, where they went the first night. Would Laddy like to come?

Laddy looked at the route. It would pass the street where his friends the Garaldis lived. "We won't go in," Laddy said. "But I can point out the house to you."

When they saw the house, Fran and Kathy were dumbfounded.

"We can't possibly be going to a party in a place like that," Kathy said.

"*Giovedì,*" Laddy said proudly. "Thursday, you'll see. He wants all of us, the whole forty-two. I said to him *quaranta-due* but he said *sì, sì, benissimo.*"

It was only one more extraordinary thing about this holiday.

~~

CONNIE WAITED FOR a while in her room for Signora to return, she wanted to give her the information and the surprise. But it got dark and she never came back. From outside the window came the sounds of chatter and people calling to each other as they went along the street, the distant sound of traffic and of cutlery clinking in a nearby restaurant. Connie decided that she would not allow herself to feel imprisoned by this mean, cowardly letter writer. Whoever it was would not kill her in broad daylight, even if it was someone sent by Harry.

"To hell with him, if I stay in tonight he's won," she said aloud. She walked around the corner to a pizza parlor and sat down. She didn't notice someone following her from outside the door of the Hotel Francobollo.

~~

LOU AND SUZI were across the river in Trastevere. They had walked with Bill and Lizzie around the little piazza, but, as Signora had warned, the restaurants were a bit too pricey for them. Wasn't it wonderful that they had learned all that about the *piatto del giorno,* and how to think in lire rather than translating back into Irish money all the time.

"Maybe we should have kept our sandwiches from lunchtime," Lizzie said sadly.

"We can't go in the door of these places," Suzi said philosophically.

"It's not fair as a system you know," Lou said. "Most of those people are on the take somehow, they all have an angle, a scene for themselves. Believe me I know . . ."

"Sure Lou, but it doesn't matter." Suzi didn't want the murky past brought up. It was never discussed, but it was hinted at wistfully when Lou might sometimes tell her how the living could have been very easy had she not been so righteous.

"Do you mean like stolen credit cards?" Bill asked, interested.

"No, nothing like that, just doing favors, someone does a favor and they get a dinner, or a big favor and they get many dinners or a car. It's as simple as that."

"You'd have to do a lot of favors to get a car," Lizzie said.

"Yes and no. It's not doing a lot, it's just being reliable. I think that's what people want when favors are being exchanged."

They all nodded, mystified. Sometimes Suzi looked at her huge emerald engagement ring. So many people had claimed it was the real thing that she had begun to believe it might have been the result of a huge favor Lou had done for somebody. There was a way of finding out, like having it valued. But then she would know one way or the other. Far better to leave it as part of the unknown.

"I wish someone would ask us to do them a favor," Lizzie said, looking at the restaurant with the musicians going from table to table, and the flower sellers passing among the diners offering long-stemmed roses.

"You keep your eyes peeled, Elisabetta," said Lou with a laugh.

And at that moment a man and woman rose to their feet at a table near the road, the woman slapped the man across the face, the man snatched her handbag and leapt over the little hedge that formed the restaurant wall.

In two seconds Lou had caught him. He held one of the man's arms behind his back in a lock that was obviously extremely painful; he raised the other hand, the one holding the stolen handbag, high for all to see. Then he marched him through all the guests right up to the proprietor.

Huge explanations in Italian were exchanged, leading to the arrival of the *carabinieri* in a van and enormous excitement all around. They never got to know what had happened. Some Americans nearby said they thought the woman had picked up a gigolo. Some English people said that he was the woman's boyfriend who had been taking a cure for drug addiction. A French couple said that it was just a lovers' tiff but it was good that the man should be taken to a police station.

Lou and his friends were the heroes of the hour. The woman was offering him a reward. Lou was quick to translate it into a meal for four. This seemed entirely suitable to all parties.

"Con vino si è possibile?" Lou added. They drank themselves into a stupor and had to take a taxi home.

"It wash the besht time I ever had," Lizzie said as she fell twice before getting into the taxi.

"It's all a matter of looking for opportunities," said Lou.

CONNIE LOOKED AROUND the pizza place. They were mainly young people her children's age. They were animated and lively, interrupting each other laughing. Very alive and aware. Suppose this was to be the last place she was to see. Suppose it was really true and someone stalked after her, leaving frightening messages at the hotel. But she couldn't be killed in front of everyone here. It wasn't possible. And yet how else to explain the letter? It was still in her handbag. Maybe if she were to write a note to leave with it just in case, a note explaining how she feared it might be from Harry, or one of his associates, as he always called them. But was this madness? Or was he just trying to make her go mad? Connie had seen films where this happened. She must not let it happen to her.

A shadow fell over the table, and she looked up expecting the waiter or someone to ask for one of the spare chairs. But her eyes met those of Siobhan Casey, her husband's mistress of many years. The woman who had helped Harry salt away money not once but twice.

Her face was different now, older and much more tired. There were lines where they had never been before. Her eyes were bright and wild. Connie suddenly felt very afraid indeed. Her voice dried in her throat. No words would come out.

"You're still alone," Siobhan said, her face scornful. Connie still couldn't speak. "It doesn't matter what city or how many deadbeats you travel with, you still end up having to go out by yourself." She gave a little bark of a laugh with no humor in it.

Connie struggled to remain calm, she must not let the fear show in her face. Years of pretending that everything was normal stood her in good stead now. "I'm not by myself anymore," she said, pushing a chair toward Siobhan.

Siobhan's brow darkened further. "Always the grand lady with nothing to back it up. Nothing." Siobhan spoke loudly and angrily. People began to look at them, sensing a scene about to begin.

Connie spoke in a low voice. "This is hardly the setting for a grand lady," she said. She hoped her voice wasn't shaking.

"No, it's part of the slumming duchess routine. You have no real friends so you go and patronize a crowd of no-hopers, and you come on their cheapo trip with them and even then they don't want you. You'll always be alone, you should prepare for it."

Connie breathed a little more easily. Perhaps Siobhan Casey did not intend to launch a murderous attack on her after all. She wouldn't speak about an empty, lonely future if she were about to kill her. It gave Connie a little courage. "I am prepared for it. Haven't I been alone for years," she said simply.

Siobhan looked at her surprised. "You're very cool, aren't you?"

"No, not really."

"You knew the letter was from me?" Siobhan asked. Did she seem disappointed, or was she pleased she had instilled such fear? Her eyes still glinted madly. Connie was unsure which way to react. Would it be better to admit that she had no idea, or was it more clever to say that she had rumbled Siobhan from the start. It was a nightmare trying to guess which way would be the right one. "I thought it must be, I wasn't sure." She marveled at how steady her own voice was.

"Why me?"

"You're the only one who really cared enough about Harry to write it."

There was a silence. Siobhan stood leaning on the back of the chair. Around them the babble and laughter of the restaurant went on as before. The two foreign women did *not* appear to be about to have a fight, as had looked possible. There was nothing of interest there anymore. Connie would not ask her to sit down. She would not pretend that matters were so normal between them that they could sit together as ordinary people. Siobhan Casey had threatened to kill her, she was literally mad.

"You know he never loved you at all, you do know that?" Siobhan said.

"In truth possibly he did, in the very beginning, before he knew I didn't enjoy sex."

"Enjoy it!" Siobhan snorted at the word. "He said you were pathetic, lying there whimpering, tight and terrified. That was the word he used about you. Pathetic."

Connie's eyes narrowed. This was disloyalty of a spectacular sort. Harry knew how she had tried, how she had yearned for him. It was very cruel to tell Siobhan all the details. "I did try, you know, to get something done about it."

"Oh yes?"

"Yes. It was upsetting and distressing and painful, and in the end did no good at all."

"They told you that you were a dyke, was that it?" Siobhan stood swaying, mocking, her lank hair falling over her face. She was hardly recognizable as the efficient Miss Casey of former times.

"No, and I don't think that *was* it."

"So what *did* they say?" Siobhan seemed interested in spite of herself.

"They said that I couldn't trust men because my father had gambled away all our money."

"That is pure bullshit," Siobhan said.

"That's what I said too. A little more politely, but it's what I meant," Connie said with a weak attempt at a smile.

Unexpectedly Siobhan pulled out the chair and sat down. Now that Connie didn't have to look up at her anymore, she saw close up the ravages that the past months had worked on Siobhan Casey. Her blouse was stained, her skirt ill-fitting, her fingernails bitten and dirty. She wore no makeup, and her face was working and moving all the time. She must be two or three years younger than I am, Connie thought, she looks years older.

Was it true that Harry had told her that he was finished with her? This is what must have unhinged her. Connie noticed the way she picked up the knife and fork and fingered them, moving them from hand to hand. She was very disturbed. They were not out of the woods yet.

"It was all such a waste when you look back on it. He should have married you," Connie said.

"I don't have the style, I couldn't have been the kind of hostess he wanted."

"That was only a small and very superficial part of his life. He practically lived with you." Connie was hoping that these tactics would work.

Flatter her, tell Siobhan that she was central to Harry's life. Don't let her brood and realize it was all over now.

"He had no love at home, of course, he had to go somewhere," Siobhan said. She was drinking now, the Chianti from Connie's glass.

Connie, with a glance and an indication of her finger, managed to let the waiter know they needed more wine and a further glass. Something about her also communicated itself, so that instead of the usual friendly greetings and banter of a place like this, he just left the bottle and glass on the table and went away.

"I did love him for a long time."

"Fine way you showed it, shopping him and sending him to jail."

"I had stopped loving him by then."

"I never did."

"I know. And for all you may hate me, I didn't hate you."

"Oh yeah?"

"No, I knew he needed you and still does, I imagine."

"Not anymore, you put paid to that too. When he gets out he'll go to England. That's all your fault. You made it impossible for him to live in his own land." Siobhan's face was blotched and unhappy.

"I presume you'll go with him."

"You presume wrong." Again the sneer and the very, very mad look.

Connie had to get it right now. It was desperately important. "I was jealous of you but I didn't hate you. You gave him everything, a proper love life, loyalty, total understanding about work. He spent most of his time with you, for God's sake, why wouldn't I have been jealous?" She had Siobhan's interest now. So she continued. "But I didn't *hate* you, believe me."

Siobhan looked at her with interest. "I suppose you felt it was better that he should have just been with me than having lots of women, is that it?"

Connie knew she must be very careful here. Everything could depend on it. She looked at the ruined face of Siobhan Casey, who had loved Harry Kane forever and still loved him. Was it possible that Siobhan, who was so close to him, didn't know about the girl from the airline, the woman who owned the small hotel in Galway, the wife of one of the investors? She searched the other woman's face. Inasmuch as she could see, Siobhan Casey believed herself to have been the only woman in Harry Kane's life.

Connie spoke thoughtfully. "I suppose that's true, it would have been humiliating to think he was running around with everyone . . . but even though I didn't like it . . . I knew that what you and he had was something special. As I said, he should have been married to you from the start."

Siobhan listened to this. And thought it over. Her eyes were narrow and very mad when she finally spoke. "And when you realized that I had followed you here and written that note, why were you not afraid?"

Connie was very afraid still. "I suppose I thought you realized that whatever the difficulties were or maybe are, you were the only one who ever counted in Harry's life." Siobhan listened. Connie continued. "And of course I left a sort of insurance policy, so that you'd be punished if you did do me any harm."

"You what?"

"I wrote a letter to my solicitor to be opened in case I died suddenly in Rome, or indeed anywhere, enclosing a copy of your note, and I said I had reason to suspect that it might have come from you."

Siobhan nodded almost in admiration. It would have been marvelous to think that she saw reason. But the woman was still too distraught for that. It was not the time to give her a woman-to-woman talk about smartening herself, setting her appearance to rights, and providing a home for him in England to await his release. Connie was very sure there was still money that had escaped any detection. But she wasn't going to run Siobhan's life for her. In fact, her legs were still weak. She had managed to remain so normal and calm when faced with someone dangerous enough to follow her and make death threats, but Connie didn't know how much more she could take. She longed for the safety of the Hotel Francobollo.

"I won't do anything to you," Siobhan said in a small voice.

"Well, it would sure be a pity for you to have to go in one door of the jail as Harry is coming out another," Connie said, as casually as if they were talking about shopping for souvenirs.

"How did you get to be so cool?" Siobhan asked.

"Years and bloody years of loneliness," Connie said. She wiped an unexpected tear of self-pity from her eye and walked purposefully toward the waiter. She gave him lire that would cover the bill.

"*Grazie tante grazie, Signora,*" he said.

Signora! She would be back now surely, and Connie wanted to give her the surprise. It all seemed much more real to her than the sad woman sitting in this pizza house, the woman who had been her husband's mistress for most of her life, who had come to Rome to kill Connie. She glanced at Siobhan Casey briefly, but she didn't say good-bye. There was nothing more to say.

IT WAS VERY noisy in the bar where Barry and Fiona were looking for the friends from the World Cup.

"This is the corner we sat in," Barry said.

Great crowds of young people were gathered and the giant television set was being moved into a position of even greater prominence. There was a match, and everyone was against Juventus. It didn't matter who they were for, Juventus was the enemy. The game began and Barry got drawn into it in spite of his quest. Fiona too was interested and howled with rage at a decision that went against everyone's wishes.

"You like the football?" a man said to her.

Barry immediately put his arm around her shoulder. "She understands a little, but I was here, here in this very bar for the World Cup. Irlanda."

"Irlanda!" the man cried with delight. Barry produced the pictures, great happy shouting throngs then as now, but more bedecked. The man said his name was Gino, and he showed the pictures to other people and they came and clapped Barry on the back. Names were exchanged. Paul McGrath, Cascarino, Houghton, Charlton. A. C. Milan was mentioned tentatively and proved to have been a good way to go. These were good guys. More and more beer kept flowing.

Fiona lost all track of the conversation. And she was getting a headache. "If you love me, Barry, let me go back to the hotel. It's only a straight line along the Via Giovanni and I know where to turn left."

"I don't know."

"Please, Barry. I don't ask much."

"Barry, Barry," his friends were calling.

"Take great care," he said.

"I'll leave the key in the door," she said, and blew him a kiss.

It was as safe as the streets in her own part of Dublin. Fiona walked happily back to the hotel, rejoicing that Barry had found his friends. They seemed to be fairly casual in their great reunion, none of them remembering anyone's names at first. But still, maybe that's the way men were. Fiona looked at the window boxes with the geraniums and busy lizzies in them, clustered in little pots. They looked so much more colorful than at home. Of course, it was the weather. You could do anything if you had all this sunshine.

Then, passing a bar, she saw Mr. Dunne sitting on his own, a glass of beer in front of him, his face sad and a million miles away. On an impulse Fiona suddenly turned in the door to join him. "Well, Mr. Dunne . . . the two of us on our own."

"Fiona!" He seemed to drag himself back. "And where's Bartolomeo?"

"With his football friends. I got a headache so he let me go home."

"Oh, he found them. Isn't that marvelous!" Mr. Dunne had a kind, tired smile.

"Yes, and he's delighted with himself. Are you enjoying it all, Mr. Dunne?"

"Yes, very much." But his voice sounded a bit hollow.

"You shouldn't be out here on your own, you organized it with Signora. Where is she, by the way?"

"She met some friends from Sicily, that's where she used to live, you see." His voice sounded bitter and sad.

"Oh, that's nice."

"Nice for her, she's spending the evening with them."

"It's only one evening, Mr. Dunne."

"As far as we know." He was mutinous, like a twelve-year-old.

Fiona looked at him, wondering. She knew so much. She knew, for example, all about Mr. Dunne's wife, Nell, who had been having an affair with Barry's father. It was over now, but apparently there were still bewildered letters and phone calls from Mrs. Dunne, who had no idea that Fiona had been responsible for breaking everything up. Fiona knew from Grania and Brigid Dunne that their father was not happy, that he withdrew into his own little Italian sitting room all the time and hardly ever came out. She knew, as everyone on the *viaggio* knew, that he was in love with Signora. Fiona remembered that divorce was now possible in Ireland.

She recalled that the old Fiona, the timid Fiona, would have left things as they were, would not interfere. But the new Fiona, the happy version, went in there fighting. She took a deep breath. "Signora was telling me the other day that you had made the dream of her life come true. She said she never felt of any importance until you gave her this job."

Mr. Dunne didn't respond, not as she would have liked. "That was before she met all these Sicilians."

"She said it again today at lunchtime," Fiona lied.

"She did?" He was like a child.

"Mr. Dunne, could I speak to you frankly and in total secrecy?"

"Of course you can, Fiona."

"And will you never tell anyone what I said, particularly not Grania or Brigid?"

"Sure."

Fiona felt weak. "Maybe I need a drink," she said.

"A coffee, a glass of water?"

"A brandy I think."

"If it's as bad as that I'll have a brandy myself," Aidan Dunne said, and they ordered it flawlessly from the waiter.

"Mr. Dunne, you know that Mrs. Dunne isn't here with you."

"I had noticed," Aidan said.

"Well, there's been a bit of unfortunate behavior. You see she's friendly, rather overfriendly actually, with Barry's father. And Barry's mother, she took it badly. Well, very badly. She tried to kill herself over it all."

"*What?*" Aidan Dunne looked utterly shocked.

"Anyway it's all over now, it was over on the night of the *festa* up in Mountainview. If you remember, Mrs. Dunne went home in a bit of a hurry, and now Barry's mother is all cheered up and his father isn't, well, unsuitably friendly, with Mrs. Dunne anymore."

"Fiona, none of this is true."

"It is, actually, Mr. Dunne, but you swore and promised you'd tell nobody."

"This is nonsense, Fiona."

"No it's not, it's utterly true. You can ask your wife when you get home. She's the only person you can tell about it. But maybe better not bring it up at all. Barry doesn't know, and Grania or Brigid don't, no point in getting everyone upset about it." She looked so straightforward, with her huge glasses reflecting all the lights in the bar, that Aidan believed her utterly.

"So why are you telling me if no one is to know and no one is to get upset about it."

"Because . . . because I want you and Signora to be happy, I suppose, Mr. Dunne. I don't want you to think that you were the one to make the first move cheating on your wife. I suppose I wanted to say that the cheating had started and it was open season." Fiona stopped abruptly.

"You're an amazing child," he said. He paid the bill and they walked back to the Hotel Francobollo in total silence. In the hall he shook her hand formally. "Amazing," he said again.

And he went upstairs to the bedroom where Laddy had arranged all the items that would be blessed by the Pope tomorrow. The papal audience in St. Peter's. Aidan put his head in his hands. He had forgotten all about it. Laddy had six pairs of rosary beads to be blessed by the Pope. He was sitting in the little anteroom sorting them out. He had already polished the shoes for the Buona Seras, who didn't know what to make of him. *"Domani mercoledì noi vedremo Il Papa,"* he said happily.

∾

UPSTAIRS, LOU HAD to admit to Suzi that he was full of desire for her but didn't think that the performance would live up to it. "A bit too much drink," he explained, as if this were an insight.

"Never mind, we need our energy to see the Pope tomorrow," Suzi said.

"Oh God, I'd forgotten the damn Pope," said Lou, and fell asleep suddenly.

∾

BILL BURKE AND Lizzie had fallen asleep with their clothes on, lying on the bed. They woke frozen at five o'clock in the morning.

"Is today a quiet day by any chance?" Bill asked.

"After the papal audience I think it is." Lizzie had an inexplicable headache.

❧

BARRY FELL OVER the chair and Fiona woke in alarm. "I forgot where we were living," he said.

"Oh Barry, it was a straight line from the pub and then you turn left."

"No, I meant in the hotel. I kept opening the wrong people's doors."

"You're so drunk," Fiona said sympathetically. "Was it a nice night?"

"Yesh, but there's a myshtery," Barry said.

"I'm sure there is. Drink some water."

"I'll be going to the loo all night."

"Well go, you will anyway after all the beer."

"How did *you* get home?" he asked suddenly.

"As I told you, it was only a straight line. Drink up."

"Did you have a convershashun with anyone?"

"Only Mr. Dunne, I met him along the way."

"He's in bed with Signora," Barry reported proudly.

"He never is! How do you know?"

"I could hear them talking when I passed the door," Barry explained.

"What was he saying?"

"It was about the temple of Mars the Avenger."

"Like the lecture?"

"Just like that. I think he was giving her the lecture again."

"God," said Fiona. "Isn't that weird?"

"I'll tell you something even more weird," Barry said. "All those fellows in the pub, they're not from here at all, they're from somewhere else . . ."

"What do you mean?"

"They're from a place called Messagne way down at the bottom of Italy, near Brindisi where you get the boat from. Full of figs and olives, they say." He sounded very troubled.

"What's wrong with that? We all have to be from somewhere." Fiona gave him more water.

"This is their first time in Rome they say, I couldn't have met them when I was here before."

"But you were such friends." Fiona was sad.

"I *know*."

"Could it have been a different pub, honestly?"

"I don't know." He was very glum.

"Maybe they forgot they'd been to Rome," she said brightly.

"Yes, it's not the kind of thing you'd forget though, is it?"

"But they remembered you."

"And *I* thought I remembered them."

"Come on, go to bed. We have to be bright-eyed for the Pope," Fiona said.

"Oh God, the Pope," said Barry.

❦

IN THEIR BEDROOM Connie had given her surprise to Signora. It was a full tape-recording of Aidan's speech. She had bought the tape recorder and got every word of it for her.

Signora was touched to the heart. "I'll listen to it under my pillow here so that it won't disturb you," she said, after they had tried some of it out.

"No, I'm happy to hear it again," Connie said.

Signora looked at the other woman. Her eyes were bright and she seemed flushed. "Is everything all right, Constanza?"

"What? Oh yes, absolutely, Signora."

And they sat there, each of them having had an evening that might change their lives. Was Connie Kane in any real danger from the mentally disturbed Siobhan? And would Nora O'Donoghue go back to the small town in Sicily that had been the center of her life for twenty-six years? Even though they had confided in each other a little, they both had a strong tradition of keeping troubles to themselves. Connie wondered what had kept Signora from Aidan's lecture and, indeed, out so late on her own tonight. Signora longed to ask if Constanza had heard anything more from the person who had written the unpleasant letter.

They got into bed and discussed the time for the alarm.

"Tomorrow is the papal audience," Signora said suddenly.

"Oh God, I'd forgotten," Connie admitted.

"So had I, aren't we a disgrace?" said Signora with a giggle.

❧

THEY LOVED SEEING the Pope. He looked a little frail but in good spirits. They all thought he was looking directly at them. There were hundreds and hundreds of people in St. Peter's, and yet it seemed very personal.

"I'm glad it wasn't a private audience," Laddy said, as if such a thing could ever have been possible. "This big one is better somehow. It shows you religion isn't dead, and what's more you wouldn't have to think of anything to say to him, yourself like."

Lou and Bill Burke had three cold beers each before they went, and when Barry saw them he joined in quickly. Suzi and Lizzie had two very cold ice creams each. They all took photographs. There was an optional lunch, which everyone took. Most of them had been too hungover or upset to have thought of making sandwiches at breakfast time.

❧

"I HOPE THEY'LL all be in better shape for the party at Signor Garaldi's tomorrow," Laddy said disapprovingly to Kathy and Fran.

Lou was passing by when he said it. "God Almighty, the party," he said, holding his head.

❧

"SIGNORA?" AIDAN SPOKE to her after lunch.

"That's a bit formal, Aidan, you used to call me Nora," she said.

"Ah well."

"Ah well what?"

"How was your meeting yesterday, Nora?"

She paused for a moment. "It was interesting, and despite the fact that it was in a restaurant, I managed to stay sober, unlike almost everyone else in the group. I'm surprised the Holy Father wasn't lifted out of his chair with the fumes of alcohol from our group."

He smiled. "I went to a bar and drowned my sorrows."

"What are these sorrows now?"

He tried to keep it light. "Well, the main one was that you weren't there for my talk."

Her face lit up and she reached into her big handbag. "But I *was*. Look what Constanza did for me. I've heard the whole thing. It was wonderful, Aidan, and they clapped so much at the end and they loved it. It was so clear, I could see it all. In fact, when we have a little free time I'm going back there and I'll play the tape just for myself. It will be as if I got a special tour all for myself."

"I'd give you a repeat, you know that." His eyes were full of warmth, he was reaching out for her hand, but she pulled away.

"No, Aidan don't, please don't it's not fair. To make me think things I shouldn't think, like that you . . . that you care about me and my future."

"But God, Nora, you know I do."

"Yes, but we've been fond of each other in this way for over a year and it's impossible. You live with your wife and family."

"Not for much longer," he said.

"Ah well, Grania's getting married but nothing else has changed."

"Yes it has. A lot has changed."

"I can't listen to you, Aidan. I have to make up my mind about something huge."

"They want you to go back to Sicily, don't they?" he said, his heart heavy and his face rigid.

"Yes they do."

"I never asked you why you left."

"No."

"Nor why you stayed so long there either."

"So doesn't that show something?"

"I don't ask about you either. I don't ask questions I might like to know the answers to."

"I'd answer them, I promise you, and I'd hold nothing back."

"Let's wait. It's too hothouse to ask each other questions and answer them here in Rome."

"But if we don't, then you may go away and live in Sicily, and then . . ."

"And then what?" Her voice was gentle.

"And then the whole point of my life will have gone away," he said, and his eyes filled with tears.

◦◦◦

THE FORTY-TWO GUESTS arrived at the Garaldi residence at five o'clock on Thursday. They had dressed in their best finery, and they all carried cameras. Word had got around that this was the kind of house that you might see in *Hello!* magazine. They wanted it recorded.

"Will we be able to take photos, do you think, Lorenzo?" Kathy Clarke asked.

Laddy was the authority on all aspects of the visit. He thought about it for a while. "There should be an official group photograph certainly, to record the occasion, and as many shots of the outside as we like. But I somehow feel that we shouldn't take pictures of their possessions you know, in case they were to be seen and stolen later."

They nodded their agreement. Laddy had certainly worked it all out. When they saw the building they all stopped, amazed. Even Connie Kane, who was used to visiting splendid places, was knocked backward.

"We can't be allowed in here," Lou whispered to Suzi, loosening his tie, which had begun to choke him.

"Shut up, Lou, how are we going to go up in the world if you panic in front of a bit of money and class," Suzi hissed back at him.

"This is the kind of life I was born to," Lizzie Duffy said, bowing graciously at the staff who conducted them in, and up the steps.

"Don't be ridiculous, Lizzie." Bill Burke was anxious. He hadn't learned any really good phrases about international banking that would advance his career. He knew she would be disappointed in him.

◦◦◦

THE GARALDI FAMILY were there, and they had invited a photographer of their own. Would anyone mind if they took pictures? Then these could be developed and given to the guests as they departed. Mind? They were thrilled. First there was Lorenzo with Signor Garaldi. Then one of Lorenzo and the whole Garaldi family. Then that group plus Signora and Aidan, and after that, everyone ranked on the stairs. This was a house that had seen the need for group photography before.

The two sullen sons of the family, whom Laddy had entertained in the snooker halls of Dublin, had cheered up mightily, and they bore him away to show him their own games room. There were trays of wine and soft drinks. There was beer in tall, elegant glasses, plates of *crostini* and little cakes and tartlets.

"May I take a picture of the food?" Fiona asked.

"Please, please." Signor Garaldi's wife seemed touched.

"It's my future mother-in-law, she's teaching me to cook, I'd like her to see something elegant like this."

"Is she a kind person, *la suocera* . . . the mother-in-law?" Signora Garaldi was interested.

"Yes, very kind. She was a bit unstable, she tried to commit suicide you see, because her husband was having an affair with that man's wife. But it's all over now. Actually I ended it. Myself personally!" Fiona's eyes were bright with excitement and marsala wine.

"Dio mio." Signora Garaldi had her hand to her throat. All this in Holy Catholic Ireland!

"I met her through the suicide," Fiona continued. "She was brought to my hospital. In many ways I pulled her around, and she's very grateful to me, so she's teaching me high-class cooking."

"High class," Signora Garaldi murmured.

Lizzie passed by her eyes wide with admiration. *"Che bella casa,"* she said.

"Parla bene italiano," Signora Garaldi said warmly.

"Yes, well I'll need it when Guglielmo is appointed to an international banking post, quite possibly Rome."

"Really, he might be sent to Rome?"

"We *could* choose Rome, or anywhere he wants really, but this is such a beautiful city." Lizzie was gracious in her praise.

There was going to be a speech, people were gathered together, Laddy from the games room, Connie from the picture gallery, Barry from the car and motorbikes down in the underground garage.

While they assembled, Signora took Aidan's arm. "You won't believe what the Garaldis have made of this. I heard the wife explaining that someone in the group is an international surgeon who saves lives, and Elisabetta has said that Guglielmo is a famous banker contemplating settling in Rome."

Aidan smiled. "And do they believe any of it?" he asked.

"I doubt it. For one thing Guglielmo has asked three times can he cash a check and what is today's rate of exchange. It wouldn't inspire huge confidence." She smiled back at him too. Anything either of them said seemed warm or funny or full of insights.

"Nora?" he said.

"Not yet . . . let's try and get the show on the road."

The speech was warm in the extreme. Never had the Garaldis been made so welcome as in Ireland, never had they met such honesty and friendship. Today was just one more example of it. People had come to their house as strangers and would leave as friends. *"Amici,"* a lot of them said when he said "friends."

"Amici sempre," said Signor Garaldi.

Laddy's hand was raised high in the air. He would come to this house forever. They would visit his nephew's hotel again.

"We could have a party for *you* when you come to Dublin," Connie Kane said, and at this they all nodded eagerly, promising to take part. The pictures arrived. Marvelous big pictures on elegant steps in the courtyard. Among the thousands of shots taken on this *viaggio,* snaps of people squinting into the sun, these would have pride of place in all the different homes over Dublin.

There were a lot of *ciao*s and *arrivederci*s and *grazie*s, and the evening class from Mountainview were out again on the streets of Rome. It was after eleven o'clock, the crowds were beginning to have their little *passeggiata,* the evening stroll. Nobody felt like going home, they had been having too exciting a time.

"I'm going back to the hotel. Will I take everyone's pictures?" Aidan said suddenly. He looked across the group, waiting for her to speak.

Signora spoke slowly. "So am I, we can carry them back for you and so if you all get drunk again you won't lose them."

They smiled at each other knowingly. What they had all suspected over the past year was about to happen.

They walked hand in hand until they found an open-air restaurant with strolling players. "You warned us against these," Aidan said. "I only said they were expensive, I didn't say they weren't wonderful," said Nora O'Donoghue. They sat and talked. She told him about Mario and Gabriella, and how she had lived happily in their shadow for so long.

He told her about Nell and how he could never see when and why the good times had gone from their marriage. But gone they had. They lived now like strangers under the same roof.

She told him how Mario had died first and then Gabriella, how their children wanted her to go back and help with the hotel. Alfredo had said the words she had ached to hear, that they had always thought of her as a kind of mother anyway.

He told her that he knew now Nell had been having an affair. That he had neither been shocked nor hurt by this, but just surprised. It did seem a very male response, he thought, a little arrogant and very insensitive, but that's the way it was.

She said that she would have to meet Alfredo again and talk to him. She didn't know yet what she was going to say.

He told her that when they got home, he would tell Nell that they would sell their house and give her half the proceeds. He didn't know yet where he was going to live.

They went slowly back to the Hotel Francobollo. They were too old to have the where-do-we-go problem of youngsters. Yet that was exactly what they had. They couldn't lock Laddy out of his room for the night. Nor Constanza. They looked at each other.

"*Buona sera,* Signor Buona Sera," began Nora O'Donoghue. "*C'è un piccolo problema . . .*"

It wasn't a problem for long. Signor Buona Sera was a man of the world. He found them a room with no delays and no questions asked.

❧

THE DAYS FLEW by in Rome, and then it was just a short walk across to Termini and the train to Florence.

"*Firenze,*" they all chorused when they saw the name come up on the notice board at the station. They didn't mind leaving because they knew they were coming back. Hadn't they all put their coins in the Trevi Fountain? And there would be so much more to see and do once they had mastered intermediate or improvers' Italian. They hadn't decided what to call it, but everyone was signing on.

∿

THEY SETTLED IN the train, their picnics packed. The Buona Seras had left out plenty of supplies. This group had been no trouble. And imagine the unexpected romance between the two leaders. Far too old for it, of course, and it would never last when they went back to their own spouses, but still, part of the madness of a holiday.

∿

NEXT YEAR'S *viaggio* they would go south from Rome not north. Signora said they must see Naples, and then they would go to Sicily to a hotel she had known when she lived there. She and Aidan Dunne had promised Alfredo. They had also agreed to tell him that Aidan's daughter Brigid or one of her colleagues would come out and see if they could set up package holidays to his hotel.

At Signora's insistence Aidan had telephoned his home. The conversation with Nell had been easier and shorter than he ever could have believed.

"You had to know sometime," Nell said curtly.

"So we'll put the house on the market when I get home and split it down the middle."

"Right," she said.

"Don't you care, Nell? Doesn't it mean anything to you, all these years?"

"They're over, isn't this what you're saying?"

"I was saying we should discuss the fact that they will be over."

"What's there to discuss, Aidan?"

"It's just that I didn't want you to be getting ready for my coming home and preparing for it . . . and then this being a bombshell." He was always too courteous and possibly too self-centered, he realized.

"I don't want to upset you, but truly I don't even know what day you *are* coming back," Nell said.

∽

THEY SAT APART from the others on the train, Aidan Dunne and Signora in a world of their own with a future to plan.

"We won't have much money," he said.

"I never had any money at all to speak of, it won't bother me." Signora spoke from the heart.

"I'll take all the things from the Italian room. You know, the desk, the books, and the curtains and sofa."

"Yes, better to put back a dining room table in there, for the sale, even just borrow one." Signora was practical.

"We could get a small flat, I'm sure, as soon as we get back." He was anxious to show her that she wasn't going to lose out by refusing to go back to Sicily, her only real home.

"A room would do," Signora said.

"No, no, we must have more than a room," he protested.

"I love you, Aidan," she said.

And for some reason, the others were all quiet and the train wasn't making any of its noises, so everyone heard. For a second they exchanged glances. But the decision was made. To hell with discretion. Celebration was more important. And the other passengers on the train would never know why forty people wearing badges saying *Vista del Monte* cheered and cheered and sang a variety of songs in English including "This Is Our Lovely Day," and eventually ended up in a tuneless version of "Arrivederci Roma."

And they would never understand why so many of them were wiping tears quickly away from their eyes.